Lizzie

Also by Lena Kennedy

MAGGIE
AUTUMN ALLEY
NELLY KELLY
LILY, MY LOVELY

Lizzie

LENA KENNEDY

Macdonald

TO ·
MY LOVING AND CARING FAMILY

A Macdonald Book

First published in Great Britain in 1982
by Macdonald & Co (Publishers) Ltd
London and Sydney

Reprinted 1985

ISBN 0 356 07874 4

Printed in Great Britain by
Redwood Burn Limited, Trowbridge, Wiltshire
Bound at the Dorstel Press

Macdonald & Co
London & Sydney
Maxwell House
74 Worship Street
London EC2A 2EN

A BPCC plc company

CHAPTER ONE

Grass Roots

To overseas tourists our city of London is a grand sight. They see the Houses of Parliament and the splendour of Westminster Abbey. They pass down Whitehall and emerge onto Trafalgar Square to view the statue of the great Lord Nelson, looking down the Mall from on high, as if reviewing his fleet. They may even admire the setting sun as it shines down the Embankment, gilding the shadowy dome of St Paul's and lighting up the gold flash on top of the Monument.

But if those travellers had come before the Second World War they would have stumbled with some surprise upon a maze of small slum streets which twisted and turned through houses built so close together that they seemed to fall over one another. Here there were houses with shiny slate roofs and smoky chimneys, for this was before the age of demolition and before the Blitz, as the Londoners called the hail of bombs that tore the heart out of our great city.

It was in this area of back-to-back houses and long narrow market streets hemmed in by the river that Lizzie grew up. Here, amid the city office blocks, the shopping crowds and the market stalls which sold commodities to the working class folks who inhabited this noisy and colourful district. The buying and selling went on from early morning till as late as ten at night, when huge paraffin flares would light up the stalls and the ragged-arsed kids still scavenged under them. Lizzie was a Coster, a true cockney, born within the sound of Bow bells in a little house just off the market street, address number four, Brady Street, The Nile, N1.

Her mother was the local flower seller. On weekdays she sat in the market with her big basket of blooms, and on Sundays outside the hospital in the main road she would cry out in her hoarse voice, ' 'Ere yer are, lidy, luverly blooms. Nice flowers very cheap.' Her drooping shoulders were wound very tight in a black shawl, a flat battered old hat hid her wispy hair, and her face was florid and weather-beaten, for she plied her trade in all weathers.

From her ears swung little gypsy earrings made of tiny turquoise stones framed in gold that matched her hard, shrewd, blue eyes. Lizzie would sit beside her mum and carefully wrap tissue around the flowers she had sold. She had nice curly blonde hair and deep brown eyes, but even in her teens Lizzie was very small, frail-looking and rather timid, and she never strayed very far away from her mum.

'Lizzie's the last of me litter,' Mum would often jokingly remark. She had brought up a big family, but Lizzie was different from the rest of Mum's husky brood and was kept firmly under her heavy wing.

When she was fourteen Lizzie had started as a junior at the local Black Cat cigarette factory in the immediate locality. Now, at seventeen, she had adjusted to her working class way of life, trudging back and forth every day to the factory and helping Mum at weekends. On her way to work each day she would pass the spot where Bobby Erlock lounged. Hands in trouser pockets, cap on the back of his head, he nonchalantly whistled a popular tune as he kept a watchful eye out for the law to come prowling down the narrow street. For Bobby was a bookie's runner, recruited from the out-of-work population of the Depression. Betting was strictly illegal, but most of the street corner bookies made a very profitable business.

'Up and dahn, double stakes, any back glad of it,' was a favourite cockney expression, meaning that you could back a horse both ways but would be lucky to see any of your money back. On the day of a big race like the Derby or the Grand National the excitement would be intense as all the threepenny and sixpenny bets were placed and the population waited expectantly for the results. Then suddenly the coppers would come out from the Police Station in the main road in all sorts of disguises: trilby hats, dark glasses, raincoats, even overalls, anything to confuse the runner and catch the bookie with the pay slips in his possession. The alarm would go out and the runner would tear off down the street with the coppers chasing him, while the bookie sneaked into the greengrocer's and hedged the bets — that is phoned them off to a big up-town bookie so that all the money was not lost.

In most cases the runner was caught, fined or did twenty-eight days. The bookie would compensate him when he came out and usually looked after his family while he was away. And because of this system Bobby Erlock had spent most of his youth in and out of the nick, as the cockneys called prison. He had grown very big and was as tough and hard as nails. But so tall and good-looking, that Lizzie held her breath with excitement every time she passed by, always hoping that he would notice her as he hung about that corner every day, chatting up the factory girls. Then one day he said:

'Howdy, blondie,' and she was too thrilled to reply.

'Wanna come up the flicks on Saturday?' he asked the next day. She gave a coy little smile that lit up her pale face and nodded assent. Bobby was no stranger to her. He had always lived in a funny little house at the end of her street which backed onto a yard full of old lumber. His father was well-known locally as 'Old Tom the Totter' who pushed a coster barrow around the streets crying out, 'Any old iron, any old rags, any old lumber'. Lizzie remembered Bobby as a long-legged barefoot lad, who raced along beside the barrow knocking at the street doors to collect the lumber, then sat outside the local pub when his day's work was over while his father got drunk.

Now this tall young man with the charming smile and a mop of brown wavy hair had actually asked her out on Saturday night. He had been Lizzie's dream lover for a long time. She could not believe her luck. Saturday night did not come around soon enough. Lizzie put on her best outfit, a navy blue dress and a tammy hat, and was there on time. They went to the cinema in the City Road. He put a rough arm around her shoulders in the darkness and planted a wet kiss on her cheek.

Then, having done what he considered was expected of him, he concentrated on the cowboy film.

While they were walking home, he suddenly picked her up in his arms and exclaimed, 'Why, you're like a little old dolly! So small.'

Lizzie's Mum, spying through her window, confronted Lizzie as she went in.

'Lizzie,' she declared loudly, 'don't you go out with that lad any more. Why, he is twice your size!'

Yet in spite of Mum's warning Lizzie still continued to meet her Bobby. Then one Saturday night he called for her. He smelt of brown ale and his cap was set very jauntily on the back of his head. It was a cool, dark evening and they walked to Bunhill Fields – part of an ancient cemetery where lovers could be found sheltering under the huge grave stones most nights.

When they got there, Bobby said, 'Now Liz, if you really want to be my regular girl you must let me love you.'

So they sat down on the grass and she allowed him to fondle her, to touch her breasts and to put his hand up her skirt. She had never allowed liberties and was so totally unprepared for the shock and the pain of losing her virginity that she fainted away in fright.

Afterwards Bobby held her close and whispered, 'I'm sorry if I hurt you, Lizzie, but now you are really my very own girl.'

The next week Bobby went off to do another stretch in the nick, and this time, because he had clobbered the copper, it was six months' hard labour. Every day on her way to work Lizzie passed the corner that Bobby had occupied, and wept. But it was not for several weeks that she began to worry about the queasiness which now attacked her every morning.

It was only a matter of time before Mum heard her vomiting and waylaid her as she came out of the outside toilet. Peering into her eyes, she dragged her into the bedroom and felt her stomach with her hard hands.

'Oh my gawd,' cried Mum, 'not our Lizzie!'

That there was such a thing as cockney pride might really astound some of us, but there is no doubt that a kind of built-in stiff pride did exist in that small slum area. Troubles were shared, but only within the family circle, and so the coster family crisis was handled under a veil of strict secrecy. Once it was known that young Lizzie had got herself in the family way the heavy mob descended on one of its infrequent visits to Mum's. The mob consisted of three brothers, one of whom owned a shop, the other a transport depot; and the third brother who lived locally.

They all gathered in Mum's front parlour to discuss the crisis and eventually agreed to chip in and give Mum the money to get Lizzie's baby aborted. They were true born costers and owed no allegiance to any church or religion, but even so the decision was a hard one. In those days abortion was considered a terrible disgrace. Normally when a young girl got into trouble she would have the baby and it would be raised in the family — often with grandma taking charge.

But Lizzie's mum was too old and the father was missing, so finally the brothers decided to get young Lizzie out of trouble and settle with Bobby when he came out of the nick. Without a murmur of protest, Lizzie went with Mum a few weeks later to visit the local back street abortionist: a woman known as Crochet Hook Kate.

Lizzie always recalled the morning when she went cold and trembling to Crochet Hook Kate's smelly house. Kate was middle-aged, a kind, cheerful, chatty woman, always smiling, whose front teeth stuck out and were very discoloured. She had a strange, upturned nose clogged with brown powder, for Kate was addicted to snuff, and on her head she wore a grubby grey turban. 'Come on in, gel,' she said cheerfully.

Lizzie sat nervously on the edge of a wooden chair in the slovenly kitchen while Kate and Mum disappeared to the next room and talked in loud voices, just as if she were not there.

'She'll be all right, it won't hurt her.'

'I don't like the idea,' said Mum tearfully. 'But what else can I do?'

'You can't watch them all the time.'

'He's a rogue, never have been any good to her.'

'Bloody shame . . . in the nick of time . . .'

A period of whispering.

Then Kate said loudly, 'Well better get on with it. Cost yer a tenner, but I knows me stuff. She won't come to no harm with me.'

All this time Lizzie sat listening and shivering with fear. In a moment Kate came bustling in, cleared the dirty dishes from the draining board and produced an enamel bowl. She began to slice huge chunks of red soap into it with a big carving knife, poured in some bright yellow liquid from a bottle, then a kettle full of boiling water. Lizzie sat watching. She was absolutely terrified. Mum hovered in the background in a very nervous manner. Kate busily rinsed her hands under the cold water tap, then stirred up the contents of the bowl with her hands. Lizzie felt sure she would vomit, but sat perfectly still, too afraid even to move.

'Yer wanna pee?' asked Kate.

'No thank you,' whispered Lizzie.

'Yer'd better go and empty yerself out,' said Kate, holding open the back door for Lizzie to use the outside toilet.

So Lizzie got up and did as she was told. When she returned to the room a stool had been placed in the middle of the room, and on it was a white china chamber pot. Kate rolled up her sleeves.

'Come on, luv,' she said, 'cock yer leg over that. Now take orf yer drawers, silly cow.' Mum stepped forward to help Lizzie off with her knickers. Lizzie cried out in alarm.

'Now keep still, there's a good girl,' said Kate. 'It won't take a minute.'

Lizzie felt a sudden sharp pain and fainted right away. When she came round she was sitting on a chair, Mum was passing smelling salts under her nose, and Kate was busy clearing up the scene of her crime.

'Now get her home quick before she starts,' she instructed Mum.

As soon as Lizzie stepped out into the air, a dreadful, searing hot pain shot through her. She hung desperately onto Mum. Behind them Kate closed her front door with a definite slam, her job over.

All that day Lizzie lay in bed, rolling and screaming in pain. Poor old harassed Mum sat weeping beside her, awaiting the abortion of her grandchild. Mum heaved a sigh of relief it was over, but for Lizzie the suffering was just beginning. Many a young woman in that district had died at the hands of Crochet Hook Kate. But such was the code of the cockney that it was *stumm*. Finger to the nose and no one dared tell. Our Lizzie survived, but only a pale shadow of her former self. She was more retiring than ever, and absolutely terrified lest anyone learn about her misdemeanour.

When Bobby finished his sentence, her brothers gathered to beat him up, as was the custom. But Bobby, being Bobby, compromised and offered to marry Lizzie. So they were wed one Saturday morning just before the war at Shoreditch Register Office; big, tough, rather uncouth Bobby, and tiny, pale, nervous Lizzie.

Mum wept very loudly, crying repeatedly, 'You will rue the day you wed that oaf, Lizzie.'

But Lizzie was very happy. They moved into Mum's back room upstairs and Bobby went back to his spot on the corner to keep a weather eye out for the law. He brought in very little money. What he did earn went back on the gee gees, so Lizzie kept her job at the Black Cat. In this way, they got by. The only cloud was Lizzie's fear of sex. Ever since the abortion she had had an absolute terror of lovemaking. But even that didn't really matter because Bobby seemed temporarily to have lost interest.

'It's the stuff they put in the tea at the nick,' he would complain.

But Lizzie was pleased and did all she could to avoid close contact.

Then one day Mum came in, and putting her basket of flowers in the sink for the last time, she sat down in that rickety chair and went into her last deep sleep. Lizzie was devastated, but consoled herself with the thought that now she had her big husband to cling to. She and Bobby became the tenants of Mum's little house in The Nile and settled down. Lizzie went out to work and Bobby tried to keep out of trouble.

CHAPTER TWO

Gambling Man

Six and a half years later Lizzie still worked at the Black Cat cigarette factory. But now she held the important position of checker and charge hand. Living with Bobby had developed her personality. Her hair was now a brassy blonde shade. Kept very bright with peroxide rinses, it contrasted oddly with her deep brown eyes and lily white skin. Lizzie liked to dress up to her position as charge hand, and wore very dressy black lace gowns with chiffon sleeves, usually rather long, full and flowing. The factory girls called her flash, for to dress up to work was rather overdoing it. In that depressed area one wore a blouse and skirt. Anything did under an overall. Best dresses were kept for Sunday. But small Lizzie ignored convention and paraded the factory in her smart gowns, with little golden medallions swinging from her ears, and nice diamond rings on her fingers.

In her gentle voice she would explain, 'Mum left me the earrings. They were all she had to give me, poor old Mum.'

Then one day Lizzie's nice jewellery began to disappear.

'Gone to uncle,' she said frankly. 'Gone to keep me squirrel coat company.' Uncle was the cockney term for the pawnbroker, the most essential trader in that poor district. At once the catty little claws of her workmates would come sliding out.

'Ain't your Bobby working then?' one would inquire.

'Oh yes,' Lizzie replied haughtily, 'but he's working away from home.'

A kind of gloomy silence would descend while the girls exchanged meaningful glances.

'Told yer so, he's been nicked again,' one would say.

'Spends more time in than out he does,' was another's bitchy comment.

'I think it's a pity, she's so sweet and so gentle,' said a third.

'She's a bloody fool if yer ask me. Been married six years, no kids, and him still a bookie's runner.'

'What a shame, gets picked up regular. Silly sod,' was the final verdict.

Lizzie would trot by, her gown flowing out gracefully, as the white-coated women slaved and gossiped amid the thud and drone of the huge machines, while the endless supplies of fags rolled off them and many nimble fingers pushed them into packets. Lizzie sorted out their problems, checked their bonuses, working through the long day that began at eight in the morning and went on till six at night.

Regularly at ten past six Lizzie would return to her own home in the small slum street behind the market. This was the house that she had been born in. The rest of the family had gone out into the world when Mum died, but Lizzie, the last of the litter had stayed on amid the gloom and squalor of number four, Brady Street, The Nile.

As she inserted her latch key into the battered old street door, a kind of black melancholy seemed to possess her. It seemed so cold and lonely in there. Oh how she wished she had moved on when her Mum had died. She went into that untidy back kitchen and lit the gas mantle, which flickered and flared into action, disclosing grimy walls and shabby surroundings. She put her supper, a paper full of fish and chips, down onto the littered table and still with her outdoor clothes on sat down to eat, finding it difficult to swallow the food, even though she was very hungry. Gloomily she surveyed the muddle. Oh dear, she wished she had the energy to tidy up, but with Bobby away it was no longer home for her. She made herself a cup of tea, and with big tears pouring down her cheeks, went wearily up to bed.

The bedroom seemed cold and damp. She lay awake a long time, thinking over the days when the house rang with noise from that host of big brothers and sisters. She recalled the scrub-down in that old tin bath in front of the fire on Friday nights; she remembered perspiring, hard-handed Mum, the strong smell of lifebuoy soap, and the apple and glass of lemonade with which she was sent to bed. Oh yes, they were great times. She could still smell them faintly: the cut flowers reposing in the kitchen sink, ready for Mum to put in her basket in the morning. She began to recall those early morning trips with Mum to the flower market. They would walk through the City all the way to Covent Garden where the flower market was. The early morning air was so cold that it would nip her fingers and make her nose red. Mum would talk about the rest of the family and of her own youth during the First World War. Usually a very glum silent woman was Mum. But on those early morning market trips, she chatted quite light-heartedly. Lizzie had a clear picture in her mind of her Mum with her black shawl flying out in the wind as she briskly strode along, and knew that the memory would stay with her for the rest of her life.

She fingered the blue earrings that Mum had left her. She would never let them go to uncle, however hard up she became. Mum's voice as she said, 'You will rue the day if you marry that oaf Bobby Erlock', echoed in her mind. Yet she had no regrets. Bobby was her man, even though he spent so much time in prison, and she loved him with all her heart.

'Ow, 'e's 'ome then,' was the cockney girls' first remark when Lizzie arrived at work on that important day. She had prepared for her entrance with meticulous care, and wore a new black satin dress with a silver trim. Her hair, freshly washed and bleached, formed a halo of curls around her head, and her sensitive brown eyes glowed with a kind of inner love light.

'Oh yes,' she said in a friendly manner, 'my Bobby came home on Friday.' She was quite oblivious of any hidden spite.

'He got me rings out of pawn,' she informed them. 'Get me coat out next week.'

'Oh good for you,' they giggled.

'Like my new dress?' She was anxious to be admired.

'Oh it's lovely,' murmured the kinder girls.

'Let's hope he stops out,' muttered the catty ones.

None of them meant to hurt Lizzie. On the whole they

allowed her to live undisturbed in her dreamworld. Happy with her fantasies, Lizzie knew only that Bobby was at home once more. She did not mind the poverty, the depressed area where she lived, or the fact that she trotted around for eight hours each day for very little wages. The square block of slum streets, squashed in between the big city office blocks, was her town, as was the long busy market street, and the slum dwellings. She had no desire for any other place.

A trip down to the market to rummage over the stalls was the highlight of her weekend. When she was able to afford it she would buy cream for her skin and the cheap perfume of which she was so fond. She was well-known in the little community with her neat figure and her bright blonde head, and she would walk very sedately, smiling serenely, occasionally stopping to talk to people. Bobby had nicknamed her his duchess and liked nothing more than to see her all dressed up.

'All right, duchess,' he would say when he was in the money. 'Just tell Bobby and it's yours.'

So Lizzie had furs and jewels. They were not always honestly come by, but Bobby did not let small things like that bother him. There was always someone who wanted to flog something that had fallen off a lorry.

Bobby would say, 'You and I, Liz, were deprived as kids, so there's no need for us to do without anything we want now. Let's spend it while we're still healthy enough to enjoy it. We take the rough with the smooth because that's the way I've been raised.'

Bobby was a compulsive gambler. He made a precarious living, but spent most of it on his duchess. They survived mainly on the money that Lizzie earned and because she was very thrifty they managed quite well. When he returned from his last spell of twenty-eight days hard labour he put a bundle of notes on the table and Lizzie smiled at him in her sweet, slow way. He was far from happy.

'Went to see old Simon first to dig my stake out of him. The old bastard's getting meaner than ever. Someone's going to take up a razor and chiv him one day. And it might even be me.'

Lizzie's lower lip trembled, and tears came to her eyes.

'Oh Bobby,' she pleaded, 'don't talk that way.'

'Oh well, I get mad when I think of us lads doing his time for him, and him rolling in money.'

Lizzie had already begged him not to go back with the bookie. 'Now,' she said, 'couldn't you get a job on the trams, or something regular?'

He stared at her in amazement, and then, in a very loud voice, roared, 'Oh my gawd, duchess, you must be joking. I'm just about to set myself up in business. Why, I could end up a bleeding millionaire.'

He stood up and proceeded to wave his arms about like a maniac, now and again touching his nose and his cheek, then frantically waving his arms in the air again.

She stared dolefully at his antics, 'It's no time for jokes, Bobby.'

'Yer don't get it, do yer, duchess?'

She shook her head.

'It's tic tac,' he yelled gleefully. 'Some old lad in the nick taught me. Now I'm an expert. I picked it up very quickly, now I'm going to try my luck on the racetrack.'

'Horse racing,' muttered Lizzie, very dismayed.

'Yes, me darlin', it's a code known only to the bookie. It will make us a fortune. Now don't get upset, duchess, put your titva on and we'll go and have a booze-up.'

Lizzie put on her new black velvet hat with a brim and a nice long, curled feather.

Bobby held out his arm, 'Come on, duchess, we're on our way.'

Like a royal couple they stepped out to the pub in City Road which belonged to Pat O'Keefe. He was an old chum of Bobby's, and a one time champion all-in wrestler. There was nothing spectacular about Pat's pub, it was just a dreary old tavern where everything was painted a dull emerald green. There was sawdust on the floor, there were spittoons and long wooden benches for the customers to sit on, although most of them hung around the bar with its old-fashioned brass beer pumps. On the shelf behind the bar stood rows of trophies and silver cups, souvenirs of Pat's wrestling days. Prints of famous racing horses decorated the walls and everyone talked wrestling, gee gees or football. There were huge notices proclaiming that the writing of bets or the taking of them was illegal. But Pat had a few shares invested in some very good racehorses, and spent his leisure at racetracks all over the country, so the writing and making of bets did not worry him unduly. All day little wizened old men would sit in there to keep warm and to study the racing page, or even get a tip straight from the horse's mouth. Whenever Pat came back from some big event his tavern was the regular rendezvous for Lizzie and Bobby. There was just one wooden seat with arms on the corner and that was Lizzie's spot. There she would sit, all dressed up in her finery, quietly sipping her white port, while her Bobby stood up at the bar arguing and talking sport. The duchess, as they called her, was well taken care of. The small table in front of her was covered with glasses of port, her favourite drink.

Occasionally Bobby would call out, 'All right over there, duchess?' And she would reply quietly, 'Yes Bobby, I'm fine.'

Pat's wife was an Irish woman, who brought up their five lovely daughters very strictly and seldom entered the bar herself. So it was serviced by a grizzled old gel called Gladys, the barmaid and general maid of all work. Gladys was a strange character. She was exceedingly short, her tousled head barely showed above the counter as she served at the bar, grabbing at the beer pumps as if they were old enemies. Not even a grimace or a smile, not one hint of a friendly gesture did anyone get from Gladys. Pat called her 'ole poker face'.

'She will only hear if she wants to, and that's for sure.' Gladys was impervious to insults and praise alike, worked continuously, and seldom took a day off. Everyone was quite used to her. She was part of the surroundings.

'She will only go with the foundations,' some wag said.

On this special Saturday night after Bobby had come out of prison, a strange thing happened. Gladys broke down and became very angry, and it was all Lizzie's fault. Bobby joined his cronies at the counter as usual, while Lizzie sat demurely in her corner, her pale face contrasting with the enormous black hat and its raven feather.

Bobby, in a peculiarly hilarious mood, shouted, 'Have something different, duchess, something nice and expensive.'

She thought for a moment and then replied in a whisper, 'I'll have a Pimms Number One.' Not that Lizzie had ever drunk a Pimms No 1, but she had heard the girls at work talk about drinking them when they went up the West End.

A kind of uneasy silence descended on the bar. Gladys stood still and stared evilly in Lizzie's direction with her little dark eyes.

'Come on, Gladys, old gel,' yelled Bobby, 'get your finger out. If the duchess wants a posh drink she will have it.'

Gladys began to stomp about the bar with a very aggressive expression on her face, then disappeared up the stairs and rattled down again to the cellar. The regulars banged their pint pots on the counter, shouting, 'Fill 'em up Gladys', but she marched back and forth, totally ignoring everyone, in her quest for the ingredients that went into a Pimms No 1. At last she emerged triumphantly with a tall frothy glass of liquid on a tray. On top of it floated a slice of lemon, a slice of orange, cucumber and watercress and sticking out of it were three straws. Flushed and excited she banged it down on the counter in front of Bobby.

'That will cost you five bob,' she snarled nastily.

'Christ,' roared Bobby, gazing down at it. 'Where you been to get it? Spitalfields's Market?' and the bar rang with coarse laughter.

Gladys almost exploded, blew out her cheeks and showed her teeth like an enraged puppy, then rampaged round the bar, banging down the bottles and glasses. Lizzie stayed silent, feeling very embarrassed.

'I never liked it,' she said. 'I'll stick to port in future.' But the joke of Pimms No 1 for the duchess was never to die down in Pat's sporting tavern.

Once Bobby had drunk his fill that night he decided to give an impromptu display of his new found art, tic tac. He stood on a chair amid his admiring audience and, with Pat's aid, put on a show. With flailing arms, fingers and elbows, Bobby flashed the message, while Pat decoded it and wrote it on the slate beside the dartboard.

'Two to one the field,' signalled Bobby.

'What price Wise Child?' returned Pat.

'Ten to one.'

'Whose bastard?'

'Don't know,' returned Bobby. 'It's a favourite, should win if he don't stop to shit.'

Amid the applause Bobby held his hands high, clenched together in a sign of victory, and all agreed that he was the best of the tic tac men. Meanwhile Lizzie sat yawning in her corner, waiting for Bobby to take her home.

After this Lizzie's Bobby became a professional tic tac man, going with Pat several times a week to different racetracks up and down the country, gambling away most of the money he earned. But whenever he got a good run of luck, he brought the money home to Lizzie. She would stare at the notes in a bewildered way, then march straight to the Post Office and put them in her savings book. Life began to get more comfortable. Bobby had discarded his old cloth cap and wore a soft felt hat, and a nice suit with well-padded shoulders. He was tough, husky and as happy-go-lucky as ever. He walked with a swagger and wore a wide grin most of the time. Sometimes he would lose his temper with Lizzie.

'Why don't you clear up this bloody dump?' he would yell when the muddle of washing up and dust got especially chaotic.

'I don't get the time, Bobby,' she replied mildly. 'I do go out to work all day, you know.'

'Well give that bleeding job up. I give you enough money,' he complained. 'Can't ever find me best ties. Got to have a clean shirt; can't travel with old Pat looking scruffy, can I?'

Lizzie had no intention of giving up her job in order to clean the house. She hated housework, and never liked to spoil her lily-white hands and long manicured nails. They were her chief vanity. She would take care of her own nice things and Bobby's white shirts. She would wash, starch and iron them, taking lots of time to get them in good condition, but it was the general donkey work, the dusting and the cleaning that she hated. After a bit of squabbling Bobby would roll up his sleeves, clean the floors, scrub the outside lavatory and clean the windows.

'You *are* a good boy,' she would say sweetly.

'Someone's got to do it. Might as well be me, poor sod.' Between them was a deep and unique understanding of each other's faults.

When he came back with Pat O'Keefe after a trip to some northern racetrack, Lizzie would cuddle up to Bobby's broad back, and she would not have minded his tough arms around her, or his big body on top of her. But Bobby would mutter, 'Go to sleep, I'm tired, I've been travelling.' Their marriage was still not a passionate one. In fact their sex life was almost non-existent, for he was big and robust and Lizzie, being small and rather frail, found lovemaking painful. She often wondered if he found that part of their married life irksome.

She had no idea that once out of sight and at large Bobby enjoyed everything that life offered. Many was the time that he went on a binge with Pat and ended up in a strange bed. He was constantly off to Ally Pally, as they called Alexandra Palace, the London racetrack, or away down south at Brighton with Pat. Of late a new love had come into his life; he had gone to White City and won money on the great racing greyhound, Mick the Miller, and couldn't stop talking about him. Lizzie was not very interested but she would listen quietly as she carefully ironed the white shirts he was so fond of.

'Might take a trip over to Ireland with old Pat,' he informed her on one such evening. 'Going to take a look at a dog over there.'

'Why all that way?'

'Because, duchess, that happens to be the best place to buy a dog.'

'Why can't he go down the Lane and get one?'

Bobby went off into cascades of laughter. 'Because we are going to buy a racing dog that runs around a track.'

'Well I never did,' replied Lizzie, really amazed.

Bobby was almost a week in Ireland and came back looking as if he had been swimming in booze, and completely broke.

'Got to ask you for a loan, duchess,' he said, 'but guess what I bought you?' She stared at him in concern. 'Half a bloody dog, that's what,' roared Bobby. 'I bought you half a greyhound.'

'I don't think I want a dog,' complained Lizzie. 'They tiddle around the place.'

'Not this one,' grinned Bobby. 'He's a champion, going to make us a fortune.'

She sighed. 'How much do you want?'

'Twenty quid,' said Bobby. 'Just enough to get a few bets going.'

Reluctantly she unlocked her cash box and handed him the notes. 'Don't be late tonight.'

'I'll come straight home once the racing's over,' he promised. But like the proverbial pie crust, his promises were made to be broken.

Later that week he said cheerfully, 'How'd yer like to come out for a trip Sunday morning?'

'Hampstead?' she said eagerly. They often used to go over the heath to the fair when they were first married.

'Nope,' he shook his head. 'I'm going to take you to see our dog make a trial run over Hackney Marshes.'

She sighed. 'Well, if you want, but I'm not really keen.'

'Get ready, I'll call for you in an hour.'

So Lizzie put on her best silk suit and her large hat. She made up her face, put gloves on her dainty hands, nice high-heeled shoes on her feet, and waited until Bobby returned with an old lorry. Fat Pat sat in the driving seat and in the back were three greyhounds.

'Squeeze in,' said Bobby, 'you can sit on my knee!'

She held onto her best hat as they sped off over to the place where the river crossed the flat windy marshes. There were no women out there, only men and young boys who drank out of bottles while they yelled and argued about dogs. While Bobby and Pat took wager on the dogs, Lizzie sat on a damp park seat holding down her flowing skirts, looking nervously at the greyhounds, and wishing she were back at home beside the fire. The dog of which Bobby owned half was called Marzipan. It looked so thin that Lizzie thought it must be underfed and felt sorry for it. After a lot of excitement the dogs, which had been held by their owners, were let loose to chase a rabbit skin that went past on a rope. Pat and Bobby stood haggling with men they had taken bets with, for this was an unlicensed track.

At length Bobby brought his greyhound over to Lizzie. 'Cop hold of this dog, Lizzie,' he said. 'Might be some trouble with the lads.'

She gazed down at the skinny dog in surprise. For a second his long moist nose twitched as if he sensed he was in alien hands, then he shot away. Lizzie held valiantly onto the lead, her feet slipping and sliding, her skirt billowing high as Marzipan gathered speed, towing her after him. Bobby came tearing back, roaring with laughter. 'Ten to one on the duchess!' he yelled.

Lizzie fell headlong onto the muddy field and the dog sat on his haunches, looking just as if he was sneering at her. She wept with mortification.

Bobby cuddled her. 'Sorry, duchess, but you looked so funny.'

'It's no joke, Bobby,' she said seriously. 'I've ruined my best dress.' He retrieved her hat with its now crumpled feather, and put it on her head.

'I'll buy you a new one. Come on, we'll go home in a cab. Pat can take care of the dogs.'

Lizzie said, 'Bobby, don't you ever ask me to go racing with you again, because I will not go, and I mean it.'

So that was the beginning and the end of Lizzie's sporting career.

CHAPTER THREE

On the Run

There were times during those pre-War years when Lizzie would very much have liked to give up going out to work each day, when she played with the idea of staying at home, and of having a baby. Often when the young married girls left to have their first baby Lizzie would be the one to go around with a subscription list collecting money from the rest of her workmates. Sometimes she made the lucky mum-to-be a present of the money, but often they preferred her to go down Nile Street to buy baby clothes. How tenderly she would examine those white ribbon-trimmed bonnets, those tiny woolly pram suits, and she would wish they were hers to put on her own darling newborn baby.

She could not help worrying about her childless state, and she thought frequently about the confused pattern of her sex life. She was puzzled by what had happened to her in the past. She and Bobby had been very young when they had lain down on the wet grass in Bunhill Fields. She had not been afraid, just anxious to make him happy. He had been gentle and very persuasive, and perhaps that was why she had immediately got pregnant. But why was Bobby so different now? It had all begun the first time he had come out of prison. At first he had shown no interest in sex, and she had been grateful. But then, on the very rare occasions that he wanted to make love, he was rough and uncaring, as if he did not realize that only gentleness would make Lizzie enjoy sex again.

'For Christ's sake, Lizzie, relax,' he would holler at her. But she screwed up inside with a kind of hidden terror. Often she thought it was to do with the abortion, and she wondered if Crochet Hook Kate had permanently injured her. She remembered the terrible pains, and the fever through which Mum had nursed her for weeks afterwards. She wished she had the courage to discuss it all with someone, as the other girls at work did. Bedroom secrets were part of the daily conversation. But Lizzie could not even bring herself to talk to her Bobby about it.

'Blimey, Lizzie,' Bobby would say, with his usual dry humour, 'I'll have to go up the Dilly if you won't let me in.'

Yet lately he had stopped pestering her, would fuss and fondle her, put her hands on the stiffened part of him and whisper, 'Go on Lizzie, you do it for me.' So she would gently massage him until he was relieved. They settled for this peculiar kind of lovemaking and Lizzie had begun not to care. He was good and kind to her. But it would have been nice to have a baby of her own, and she knew that would not happen until she conquered her fear of the sexual act. She loved her big, rough rogue Bobby with all her heart, but there was a deep coldness inside her which she could not overcome. Sometimes she thought she might summon up enough courage to consult a doctor, but she always seemed to be too busy at work, or coping with Bobby's problems.

Every weekend during that Spring of 1939, Bobby raced Marzipan the greyhound over at the White City dogtrack, and at last he began to get lucky. Lizzie did not mind. She was caught up with her domestic chores and had to rest to be fresh for work on Monday. He would come home bringing fruit and flowers for her, wanting to talk about his racing dog. But Lizzie seldom heard him. She would get ready for bed with her meticulous care, cold-creaming her face, putting thirty or forty big curlers in her hair, neatly rolled up and covered in a lace nightcap. She was happy just to have Bobby home, and didn't really want to hear details of the life he led when he was away from her.

One night, after a big win, be brought her home a gold bracelet, but her face was white and doleful.

'Crikey, don't you like it?' he asked. 'That's cheap. Some bloke wanted a quick sale, having done all his money in.'

'I've been listening to the wireless,' said Lizzie, 'and they say we might have a war with Germany.'

'Never in our life,' announced Bobby. 'Besides, what's it to do with us? They'll never get me in the bleeding army. Had enough of being institutionalized when I was in the nick.'

'But Bobby, they say we will be bombed. Isn't it terrible?'

'Give over, duchess,' cried Bobby. 'Don't get bleeding melancholy, because I don't intend to let it worry me, and if it does happen I'll go on the run.'

'Oh Bobby, don't say that.'

'What? No dogs, no gee gees? Life won't be worth bloody well living.'

'Oh Bobby,' wailed Lizzie, 'I do wish you would take something seriously, just once. The girls at work have all been up the town hall to get their ration and identity cards.'

'Good luck to them,' said Bobby, 'I'll stay as I am.' Then with a little show of temper he added, 'Are you coming up to bed, or are you going to sit there all night worrying about something that might never happen.'

But Lizzie had developed a kind of cold fear inside her and couldn't dismiss it from her mind.

The factory was very busy turning out specially packed cigarettes for the forces. Jokes about Hitler and Mr Chamberlain's umbrella had now died down, and there was a quite realistic atmosphere, as if they knew their fate. But the machines thumped on, young boys left and joined the forces, and the territorial soldiers marched around the streets on Sunday mornings – pimply-faced boys in free uniforms, feeling very smart. Tall Bobby and small Lizzie stood in the doorway of their tiny house, waving them past.

'Look,' sneered Bobby, 'stupid gits. For just two bob a day those silly sods will be first at the front when the war comes.'

Lizzie looked up at him with her steady brown eyes. She did not even reach his top waistcoat button.

'So you do think a war is coming and you won't admit it?'

'Well, Liz, it looks pretty bad I will admit. Come on, let's go,' he grinned. ' 'Fore old Hitler gets us.'

From the little front parlour the wireless announced that the

Prime Minister was coming on the air to make a special announcement. They stood listening as he told them that with deep regret they were now at war with Germany. Before they had time to take it in, the first war siren screeched out its warning of an air raid. Lizzie ran to her big man and he held her tight.

'Don't worry so much, Liz, he can't kill us all,' he jested.

And indeed it was a false alarm. As soon as everyone had calmed down, Lizzie went down to the market and watched all the little kids being evacuated: a long line, queueing outside the school with gas masks, suitcases and tickets of identification round their necks. A crowd of weeping mums and dads stood with her, but the kids seemed to be having a great time. Lizzie wished she were a little girl again and could run away from the cold fear that gripped her. It was just as well that she didn't have a child. How awful it would have been to part with it, never knowing when you would all meet again. She was so depressed.

'Oh Bobby,' she wept, 'why can't all the people say that they don't want a war.'

'It's out of our hands, duchess,' replied Bobby. 'It's the blokes with the lolly that's running this event. But I'm bloody sure they won't get me. I'll go on the run.'

'Oh Bobby, don't say such things. It'll get you into trouble.'

'I've been in plenty of bloody trouble before,' Bobby retorted, 'so a bit more won't hurt me.'

They temporarily closed race tracks and dog tracks, much to Bobby's chagrin. The greyhounds were kennelled in Pat O'Keefe's back yard and Pat O'Keefe and Bobby hung around there nearly all day, looking after them.

'Might as well let Marzi have a litter. War can't last that long,' he announced.

Lizzie bottled up her sick fear inside and still went off to work each day. Money began to get short, with Bobby not working the tracks. Gradually the husbands and boyfriends of her workmates got called up. There were farewell parties and unhappy scenes as they were drafted abroad.

Bobby only jeered. 'Soppy sods. A few shiny buttons and two bob a day. I ain't that kind of fool.'

Then the Blitz began in earnest and Pat sent his family to Ireland. Lizzie took up residence in Old Street tube station and went down regularly every night, whether there was an air raid or not. As soon as dusk fell she put a blanket over her arm, packed her treasures in a suitcase and went underground to the small space which had been allotted to her on the platform. She found herself between a well-built, quarrelsome Jewish couple on one side and a mum with two nervous little girls whom she had refused to have evacuated, on the other. Once down there Lizzie felt safe. The sick feeling in her stomach disappeared.

Bobby would jest, 'I do believe that you've got a fancy man to sleep with down there, duchess.'

'Bobby,' she said severely, 'there's no reason why you should not come down with me. Other men sleep with their wives.'

'Get away,' cried Bobby, 'and have the law pick me up? No thanks, I'll take my chance up here.'

So he hung around all day with Marzipan and her puppies, then got drunk and slept through the Blitz down in Pat's cellar. Meanwhile Lizzie lay awake listening to the crump of the falling bombs and worrying about where he was. Early in the mornings she came up to see the devastation, the piles of burning rubble, the fire and the ambulances tearing around. She would go home in a daze, and be astonished to find her own house still standing, then make herself a cup of tea and go to work.

During the first winter of the Blitz this was the pattern of her life. But in spite of the separation and the dangers, Lizzie and Bobby still remained very close. When he was in the right sort of mood and needed to borrow some money from her, Bobby would walk as far as the entrance to the tube and carry her suitcase.

'Why don't you come down with me, Bobby?' she pleaded.

'Sorry, duchess, you ain't never going to get me down there. I've got plenty to do up here. See you in the morning.'

Lizzie, with a deep sigh, would find her regular spot and

carefully prepare for the night. She would rub cold cream on her face and hands, put in her hair curlers, and cover them with a lace cap. Then she would take off her rings and put them into separate little boxes, before stowing them away in the suitcase.

'Gawd blimey, Lizzie,' the cockneys yelled, 'are you expecting visitors?'

'I like to keep my hair and my skin nice,' she replied gently, then grasping the handle of her suitcase, she would cover herself with a blanket and try to sleep through the long night. Lizzie provided immense entertainment for the surrounding inhabitants.

'Who's she?'

'Duchess of Nile Street, didn't yer know?'

'What's in the case?'

'All the bloody family heirlooms, of course.'

Undeterred by their laughter Lizzie would hold firmly on to her suitcase and settle under the ground while the bombs rained down on London. That autumn it became much worse. The London docklands caught fire and more and more families were bereaved.

All the boys in Lizzie's family had gone out into the world, but she had one sister four years older than herself, who had married a docker. Sallie lived in the East End and had four children of whom Lizzie was very fond. They often visited her in the school holidays but she had had no news of them since the Blitz. It was with some amazement, therefore, that she returned from the shelter and found Sallie on the doorstep with her four bedraggled children. Sallie was plump, and as extrovert as Lizzie was introvert.

As soon as she saw her sister, Sallie opened her mouth wide and howled, 'Ow Lizzie, I've been bombed out.'

'Poor cow,' cried Lizzie, holding out her arms to the children.

'Oh Lizzie, we ain't got nowhere else to go.'

Sallie and her brood moved in with Lizzie. That night they all went together down to the shelter: long-legged Charlie who was ten years old, skinny, slow-moving Rene who had turned twelve, short plump Maisie who was nine, and two-year-old baby Robin, sitting in a pram piled high with covers.

'Blimey, you got a house full tonight, Lizzie,' said the warden when she arrived.

'It's my sister, she's been bombed out down the docks.'

'Tell you what, they have started to put in wooden bunks further down the line. I'll see if I can get you some.'

So Lizzie got new premises, an alcove with two wooden bunks on each side and nice new, striped mattresses.

'Crikey,' cried Sallie, 'it's bleeding home from home.'

So the kids were packed down and Sallie and Lizzie sat gossiping about the good old days before the war. Sallie's man was out in France.

'Why ain't your Bobby been called up?'

Lizzie lowered her voice. 'He's gone on the run, he didn't want to go in the army.'

'He would,' replied Sallie in disgust. 'It's a good job they ain't all like him. Bloody old Hitler would be here tomorrow.'

Lizzie fell silent, feeling for the first time truly ashamed of Bobby.

When Bobby came home in the morning he found the house full of kids.

'Where's all the bloody kids come from?' he yelled.

'They're all Sallie's children, and they are staying with me while the Blitz is on,' Lizzie told him firmly.

'Well I'm orf,' retorted Bobby, 'because I ain't going to get no bloody sleep with that lot rampaging about.'

Lizzie was quite calm about it. 'He won't go far,' she told Sallie, 'just down old Pat O'Keefe's pub.'

But even Lizzie was surprised when Bobby turned up again a few days later bringing oranges and tins of spam — real luxuries which were very hard to come by.

'Just a bit of grub to feed all those kids,' he said.

'Now Bobby, where did you get all that stuff?' Lizzie inquired.

He put his finger to his nose, '*Stumm*,' he said, 'got a little fiddle going. See if you can get me some fags to flog, will you, Liz?'

Lizzie did not have to be told twice. Bobby was now very profitably employed in the black market. She was not sure if she cared; at least he was not out in France being shot at. So, without a twinge of conscience, she scrounged fags from the factory for him to sell at a profit. Sallie did the housework and the shopping, and that meant Lizzie could keep her job. Each night they went to sleep down in the deep shelter. By this time they had made it fairly comfortable; they had coloured curtains for privacy and always took a flask of tea and food down with them. A canteen had even been installed, along with a first aid post. When the kids were in bed, the parents took it in turns to pop out for a drink. If it was a quiet night with no air raids, it often became chaotic down there what with family parties, family squabbles and even the odd amateur concert. Lizzie was quite content; she played games with the children, and loved and fussed them. What happened in the outside world did not worry her; she felt safe underground.

She used to let Sallie go out for a drink while she took care of the children. Sallie would paint her face, put on her beads and earrings and go out through the Blitz to the local pub. She would always come back sloshed, and swore loudly throughout the night.

'Lizzie's a mug,' said the gossips.

'Her ol' man is a real villain, and on the run from the army.'

'Oh yes, I know him. Tall, good-looking. Don't arf like the women.'

'He ain't got a lot of competition, what with all the men being in the forces.'

'Do you think she knows?'

'Too naive. Spends all her time with those kids of her sister's.'

'She's a right one, that Sallie.'

'Likes the men and the booze.'

So the tongues wagged as the knitting needles clicked. If Lizzie had heard this conversation she would have been extremely hurt, but luckily no one wanted to upset her. And at length Sallie became a bit sheepish.

After one particularly long week of raids she said to Lizzie,

'I think I'll get the kids evacuated. It's not much of a life for you, stuck down here looking after them.'

'Don't be silly, Sallie,' returned Lizzie. 'I love it. Why, I've never been so happy. I always wanted children. You know that.'

Sallie shrugged. 'Wish I could say the same. But if you want children, you should spend more time with your Bobby. I know men, more's the pity, and I assure you that it don't take long for them to start looking around for someone else.'

Lizzie looked up at her in concern. Gossip never bothered her; it went in one ear and out the other. But this was Sallie, her own sister, trying to warn her. Sallie lowered her gaze and went on counting the stitches in the sock she was knitting.

'All right, Sallie, if you promise to stop down here with the kids, I might go back up on Saturday night. I hope it will be a quiet night; I think I'd drop dead with fright if I was caught out in an air raid.'

Sallie brightened up. 'I'll certainly do that, Liz. It's a hard world we live in. Don't hurt us to help each other.'

At ten o'clock that Saturday night Lizzie gave her treasures into Sallie's keeping, put a headscarf over her bright hair and went timidly into the blackout. It was the first time she had done so since the war began. She shone her little torch on the ground until she reached home. The house was in darkness. Of course Bobby was up at the pub. He would be home soon, and so pleased to see her. She was glad she had found the courage to come up out of the tube. She wouldn't put on the light because the blackout curtains were not all that good. She did not want the warden knocking. So Lizzie sat calmly in her kitchen and waited.

She did not have long to sit there. Pretty soon she heard the ring of familiar footsteps. Bobby was tipsily strolling down the street. She perched anxiously on the edge of the chair, then started as a high-pitched giggle rent the silent air. Someone was with him. She could hear a lot of whispering outside the front door.

Bobby's boozy voice came through quickly, 'It's all right,

the old gel's down the shelter.' There were more giggles as he pushed his companion inside.

Lizzie sat almost paralysed with shock as they crept up the stairs. She trembled violently, unable to move. A strong voice within her said, 'Get up, Lizzie. Go and stop them. He is your man.' Her knees were so weak that she could not rise – or even call out. She heard the footsteps overhead and the laughter and the creak of the bed as they fell into it. 'That's your bed, Lizzie,' the voice went on, 'a wedding present from Mum.' She stirred, then looked wildly about the room for some sort of weapon. The broom stood in the corner; she grasped it and slowly got up, then crept up the stairs to the bedroom.

They were completely naked on the bed. Lizzie brought the broom down on Bobby's bare back. He yelled out in terror, rolled off onto the floor, and stared up at Lizzie as if she were the devil in disguise. Then he grabbed his pile of clothes, dashed madly down the stairs and out of the front door.

But Lizzie was not finished yet. She proceeded to lash the naked terror-stricken girl, then beat her as she crawled from the room and hurled herself down the stairs. At length the wretched girl fell out into the street, bruised and battered, without a stitch on. Lizzie's eyes were merciless, they burned like live coals. She dragged off the bedclothes and the girl's dress and underwear from the chair, then jumped on them. Thick and fast came the tears. She sobbed hysterically, before sinking down weakly to the floor, once her passion had cooled. Finally she got up, dried her eyes, locked the door and went back to the shelter just as the siren blew an air raid warning.

'Just made it back in time,' said Sallie looking at her very curiously.

'Had a good time, Lizzie?' asked one nosy old lady.

'Not too bad,' replied Lizzie with her gentle smile.

At work the next day the air buzzed with gossip of how Margie Coombs, a very young girl who worked in the office, had been discovered out in the blitz, all naked and bruised and battered. The rumour was that she had been raped. Lizzie's lips twitched slightly but she made no comment.

The next evening, before they left for the shelter, Lizzie

locked all the doors and windows and closed the front door. Then, with young Charlie's help, she stripped and dismantled the big double bed. She muttered to herself, 'She won't get in there again.' Sallie suppressed a giggle, knowing that Bobby was indeed in the dog house.

He had been missing for a few days, when one lunchtime Lizzie found him waiting outside her place of work, looking very grubby and unshaven, and wearing an old grey jersey several sizes too big, which he had borrowed from Pat. He walked along very dejectedly beside her.

'I can't get in, Liz,' he said. 'I didn't want to break the lock. I only want me best whistle and flute for Saturday night.'

She stared up at him shrewdly. 'No one is stopping you going into your home, Bobby, but it was locked to keep them whores out of my bed. I happen to be very fussy.'

He gave a subdued grin. 'Sorry, Liz. It won't happen again.'

'I don't care what you do, Bobby, but not in my bed,' she said firmly. 'Here's the key, go in and put the kettle on. I'll see if I can rustle up something from the butcher.' She looked at him very severely. 'Sallie and the kids will be in soon, so tidy yourself up.'

He gazed down at her affectionately, touching the sticking plaster on his forehead. 'Blimey,' he said, 'who would have thought that you'd be so vicious? Jesus Christ, what you did to young Margie!'

'Well let's hope it taught you both a lesson,' she said.

That night they had steak and kidney pudding. Lizzie had got her meat ration, as well as a bit of extra kidney, and she cooked a particularly nice meal. Bobby, clean and spruce, was very pleasant to Sallie and the kids, but Lizzie did not seem to have a lot of appetite. She gazed solemnly at her Bobby from across the table.

'Sometimes, Bobby,' she said, 'I wish you were in the nick or in the army. At least I'd know where you are.'

'Oh blimey, duchess, don't put the mockers on me,' pleaded Bobby. 'Come on, give us a kiss.'

'No, Bobby,' she said firmly, 'I might forgive, but it will take me along time to forget.'

'Please yourself. Come on I'll walk with you to the shelter.'

They stood at the entrance. 'Don't ask me to go down there, Liz,' he pleaded. 'I'd feel trapped. Why, it would be worse than being in the Scrubs.'

She sighed. 'All right, but for goodness' sake, behave yourself.'

Yes, she knew that he was weak but she would never ever stop loving him.

Not long after this incident, Bobby changed his pattern of existence. Lizzie locked up the house meticulously and securely every night.

Bobby said, 'I'm not worried, I'll kip down old Pat's cellar with the dog.' But he would arrive early every morning, bringing with him two or three pals. 'Rustle up some grub for me mates before you go to work, will you, duchess?' Out would come his pack of cards and they would sit there playing solo all day.

Sallie's children now went to a kind of temporary school which had been started up in the church because so many children had returned from evacuation. Sallie took on a part-time domestic job and took the baby with her, so the house was empty for the best part of the day. That was until the spivs, as Bobby's companions were called, took over. They wore big black felt hats and striped suits with padded shoulders, and idled about Lizzie's living-room all day, casting dog ends into the fireplace, drinking tea and playing cards. When Liz came home in the evening they'd get up, and without so much as a greeting, one would say, 'Come on lads, piss off, pub's open.'

Lizzie always stared at them with the utmost suspicion. 'Bobby,' she demanded after a week of two of this, 'who are those horrible men?'

'Just a few lads like myself, on the run,' replied Bobby amiably.

'Well, I don't want them in here gobbling up all the tea and sugar rations. I need it for the children.'

'Oh don't be like that, duchess. The boys have got to have some place to hang out during the day.'

'Well let them go to work or into the army. They aren't coming here.' She got very angry, her face was flushed and her lips quivered, but Bobby stood his ground.

'Now Lizzie, I ain't pulling the birds, I'm just having a harmless game of cards with me mates.'

'Well it's got to stop. I will not have my home made a doss house for a lot of shifty crooks.'

'Right then,' said Bobby slamming on his big hat, 'seeing as you're the boss and bringing in the lolly, we'll find another hideout. Don't expect me to keep running back here every day, will yer.' And in a great huff he dashed out and slammed the front door.

The kids were all playing out in the street. 'Hallo, Uncle Bobby,' they cried, running towards him.

'Get out of me bleeding way,' yelled Bobby as he dashed past.

'What's up with him?' demanded the forthright Sallie.

'Oh well, you know Bobby,' said Lizzie mildly, 'he'll be back.'

CHAPTER FOUR

The Deep Shelter

Bobby did not come back, and Lizzie tried very hard not to miss him. But miss him she did, and she was growing very anxious about his prolonged absence when suddenly, one night, she saw the big shape of Pat O'Keefe ambling slowly down the platform. He was looking around him as if in search of someone.

'Hallo, Liz,' he said, as soon as he saw her. 'Well, to be sure, 'tiz home from home down here.'

She gave him a slow smile of welcome; there was only one reason for Pat to come down here and that was to bring news of Bobby.

'Seen Bobby around?' she asked.

'Well now, my love, that's just what I came to tell you. It's not good news. He got nicked a week ago; I warned him not to hang around with those spivs.'

Lizzie heaved a deep sigh. 'How long has he got this time?'

'Eighteen months hard, I'm afraid, Liz. Caught unloading a lorry full of black market food.'

'Oh well, at least I know where he is,' she said forlornly.

'I got rid of the dogs, all except Marzipan. Going to keep her. Here is one fifty; that's Bobby's share from the sale of the dogs. He told me to give it to you.'

With a wry grin Lizzie took the notes. 'Oh well, that will be handy,' she said. 'Have a cup of tea, Pat.'

'Well that would be nice. And I'll say this, you're a brave little body. Never one to make a fuss.'

So Pat got out his flask, spiced the tea with whiskey, and when Sallie came back, a good time was had by all.

'Why don't you go off to the country, Lizzie?' Pat asked as he left.

'No. I feel safe here, and I know everyone. I wouldn't like to be with strangers.'

When Pat had gone, Sallie said pathetically, 'Never mind, Liz, you won't miss Bobby so much, now you have got me and the kids.'

Lizzie looked sad. 'I will.'

'Crikey,' said Sallie. 'How much else can he do to you?'

Lizzie smiled, 'I'll miss him,' she said, 'because he always made me laugh.'

'Crikey,' Sallie retorted, 'a man's got to do a bit more than make me laugh.'

A month later Sallie received a telegram. It was short and quite impersonal. 'Your husband missing. Believed killed.' Sallie, who had always had a happy-go-lucky attitude to life, wallowed in her grief. To drown her sorrows she got drunk every night, leaving Lizzie more and more often alone with the kids.

Sometimes she would say, 'Sorry, Liz, I can't stand that shelter tonight. I'm going up the West End dancing. Don't mind, do you?'

Lizzie would gaze at her solemnly, trying not to condemn, but in her heart she disapproved; for she knew that Sallie could not live without a man.

Then one night Sallie did not come home, and Lizzie became really worried. She was sure that her sister had been killed in the Blitz, so in one way she was relieved when at last a letter arrived. 'Am sorry, Lizzie,' it read, 'but I cannot stand being shut up in that tube night after night. I have met a bloke and I am going back to camp with him. I might try to get a job down here. If you like you can get the kids evacuated, but I hope you will keep young Robin with you as he loves you and he will miss me. Sorry, Liz, love Sallie.'

'Why, the bloody cow!' exclaimed Lizzie out loud, after she had read the letter.

'Who is, who is?' asked Irene, the eldest girl.

'Your mum,' replied Lizzie angrily. 'She says you're to be evacuated.'

'I won't go,' cried Rene.

'Nor will I,' said Charlie defiantly.

Maisie climbed onto Lizzie's lap. 'I love you, Auntie Liz,' she said, 'don't send me away.'

They all stood before her looking very forlorn, and little Robin woke up demanding his tea.

'No, darlings,' said Lizzie, embracing them, 'we will all stay together. Oh Sallie, that bloody Sallie,' she muttered to herself as she prepared a bottle for Robin. Then when Robin was made comfortable she said, 'Come on, kids, help me get ready for the tube.'

The blankets were piled into the pram and Lizzie pushed it with Robin perched on top, while Maisie held on tight to her coat and long-legged Charlie rushed on ahead to get a place in the queue. To Lizzie the deep shelter was a haven, a place to hide from the terrible desolation, the distress and the ruined buildings which she could see all around her as she plodded along, herding the children and fiercely clutching her suitcase.

The problem for her now was how to care for little Robin and keep her job at the same time. When she realized that it would be impossible to do both, Lizzie had no hesitation. She gave up her work at the factory and concentrated all her efforts on her new-found family. Her determination was well rewarded, for the children all insisted that, come what may, they would stay with Aunt Lizzie always. Each day they came home from the deep air raid shelter at eight o'clock and had their breakfast. There was no school, so they all played about the house while Lizzie did a few chores; then at three o'clock they had a meal, and went back to the shelter. It was a monotonous kind of existence but no one seemed to mind. Aunt Lizzie was sweet and kind; she bought them comics to read, sweets to suck and never told them off. Even Robin was placid, now that he was clean and well-fed.

In this way they all got through the next six months of the war without even missing Sallie. Maisie made a very close friend of the girl in the next set of bunks; Rene hung around with the teenagers at the other end of the tunnel, putting on lipstick and the high-heeled shoes which Sallie had left behind.

Charlie became a real scavenger. He would hang about outside the tube entrance when there was not a raid on, and chase after the passers-by. 'Got a ha'penny, guv'nor?' he would cry, or 'give us a fag.' With his short patched breeches and long thin legs, he chased about everywhere.

Then Hitler produced a new weapon known as a land mine: a kind of a string of bombs which landed all in one place. One morning Lizzie went home and found that her house was just a pile of smoking ruins. Not only her house but the whole street had been swept away by the blast.

Lizzie stood looking dolefully at what had once been home, and Charlie said, 'Blimey, Aunt Lizzie! If we ain't been bombed out again.'

So Lizzie, with the kids all walking sadly behind her, pushed the pram, full of blankets and Robin, along to the next road. There were all the girls standing outside the factory, which had also been blitzed.

'I've been bombed out,' Lizzie said.

'We know, Lizzie,' they said sympathetically, 'we've lost our jobs too.'

'I don't know where to go.'

'Better go to the Town Hall. Everyone else has. I expect they will evacuate you all.'

'No,' said Lizzie, firmly walking into City Road, 'I'm not going there.'

Old Pat's pub was in City Road, but it was a gutted ruin. Pat himself stood forlornly outside it, trying to rescue a few valuables.

'Oh,' said Lizzie hesitantly, 'so you copped it too, Pat.'

He gazed at her in melancholy reflection, 'Yes, love, the whole darned district, it's terrible.' He looked down at the big hole that had once been his bar. Smoke and dust still poured out of it. 'Poor old Gladys is down there,' he said. 'It's funny how we all used to joke about her going down with the foundations . . .'

Lizzie's eyes filled with tears. 'Bobby was lucky. I know he used to kip down there.'

'Oh well,' sighed Pat, 'it's the luck of the draw. I'm pleased that I sent the family back home to Ireland.'

'I'd better get the kids something to eat. Is the cafe still there?'

'No, but the Italian's is, up the main road. Why don't you get these kids out of town?'

'No!' said Lizzie. 'We're all right down the tube. So long, Pat.'

So began a new phase in her life: Lizzie became a homeless wanderer. She spent each day walking along the streets with the kids, visiting various parks and sitting in the cafes that remained open. The city workers would see her wearily trailing along, dressed in her old fur coat. Her shoes had begun to wear out, and all the children looked unkempt. Lizzie washed their hair and their socks down in the toilets; all they had was what they stood up in, but every day she allotted enough money for them to have a hot meal.

'We will have one good meal a day,' she told them.

Her little store of money soon dwindled. Off came that nice solitaire which Bobby had bought her and into Uncle's, the pawnshop. But Lizzie kept going, quiet and undismayed. The kids, of course, were extremely happy, because there was no school, only larking about in the park all day, scoffing the cakes and sweets that Lizzie managed to scrounge for them.

Old neighbours would stop her and say, 'Go to the Welfare, Lizzie. You'll get another house in a new district.'

'No.' She shook her head. 'I don't want to get too far away from the tube. I feel safe down there.' Lizzie was really afraid of the authorities, having avoided them all her life.

All through the autumn, when the cold winds blew over the park, Lizzie and those four very ragged children could be seen roaming London. But before long the Blitz got very bad again, and they spent nearly all of their time underground, clinging for dear life to their comfortable position, knowing that if they were delayed outside, someone else might pinch it. Indeed, Lizzie stayed there even at Christmas and joined in the community celebrations under the ground. She had finally fallen into a sort of decline. She did not bleach her hair, and now it hung down straight, showing a distinct brown line at the roots. She was minus all her rings, her money was running out, and she could no longer conceal her worries. So when a tall figure came into view one evening, as she sat dolefully watching Robin play, she hardly bothered to look up.

A rough voice said, 'Oh blimey, duchess! Is that you? I'd never have recognized you.'

There stood Bobby with a very short haircut, and wearing his best suit, which seemed to have got too big for him.

Lizzie looked dolefully at him, too stunned to say a word, until he yelled, 'Christ, duchess, what the hell have you done to yourself?'

'Oh Bobby!' she cried. 'Is it really you?' and the tears began to flow.

He put a rough arm about her. 'Oh now, don't cry, Liz. Ain't you pleased to see me?'

All the kids came running up. 'What's the matter, Aunt Lizzie?'

'Oh!' exclaimed Rene, 'It's only Uncle Bobby come home,' and they dashed off again to their own pursuits.

Bobby sat on the bunk and looked around. 'Why! I was more comfortable in the nick,' he said.

Lizzie just smiled.

'What are those kids still doing here? Why weren't they evacuated?'

'They want to stay with me,' said Lizzie softly.

'Where's Sallie?'

'Oh that cow Sallie,' said Lizzie, 'she run off and left them.'

'An' you have been taking care of them all this time? Why, Lizzie, you are a bigger mug than I thought you were.'

'Oh don't scold me, Bobby.'

'No, it's all right, mate,' said Bobby. 'I'm only on parole. Got to go and register for the army. Should have done two years ago. Come on, let's find our house. It's a bleeding wilderness up there.'

'But Bobby, we've been bombed out,' said Lizzie anxiously.

'Well, where do we eat?'

'In the Italian cafe.'

'Well, come on then, let's go. This place gives me the creeps.'

So they all went out to the cafe. 'Sit up that end,' Bobby ordered the kids, 'so that I can talk to Auntie Lizzie.'

They were all quite happy with a whole meat pie and spuds each. Bobby had under-the-counter house special, eggs and bacon, while Lizzie just drank a cup of tea.

'How you been managing for money?' Bobby asked.

'I pawned my rings, and Pat give me one fifty for you, but I spent it.'

'Now yer tells me,' cried Bobby with a touch of his old humour, and Lizzie gave a little giggle.

'Well, seeing as I got a ready-made family, I'd better find you a house,' he said. 'I'm due back next Friday, and bet yer life the bleeding army will whip me up when I get out next month.'

That night Bobby, for the first time, slept down in the deep shelter. He even tried to cuddle Lizzie in the confines of her narrow bunk, but it was hopeless, what with Charlie's grinning face peeping out from the other side, and little Robin kicking up a dreadful row because he usually slept with Lizzie.

So Bobby got up and sat around smoking and complaining, and in the morning he went to the council to get some accommodation for his new-found family. But he was not very successful.

'You can go out of London to a rest centre, or we might get you a compulsory house in Loughton or Woodford, just as temporary accommodation.'

'Oh no,' cried Lizzie, 'I'll not move away from the tube, I feel safe down there.'

'All right, I'll see what else I can rout up,' the council man promised. 'Got a fancy man down there? A shelter dweller down there?'

'No I have not!' returned Lizzie indignantly. 'That's Bobby, my husband, and he's waiting to go into the forces.'

Meanwhile Bobby prowled his old haunts, and managed to

get them a flat. 'A mate of mine just called up to say his wife has hopped it.'

'How far away is it?' asked Lizzie anxiously.

'Only round the corner,' he said, 'one of the few left standing. You know Chatham Dwellings?'

'Oh,' said Lizzie, remembering that it had always been a very dreary slum, a pre-First-War block of flats with dismal stone steps, and dark, poky rooms. Still, it was near the tube, and at least she would be able to cook a decent meal for the kids there, and do the washing.

Bobby paraded them all inside. 'Not a bad place, but it needs a clean up, so you kids get cracking.'

The walls were grimy, but there was some scant furniture left by the last tenant, and a greasy gas stove. With broom and bucket Bobby set to organizing the kids, until the small living room was as clean as a barracks.

After tea Bobby said, 'I know where I can scrounge some sheets off a bloke I know.'

But Lizzie was adamant. 'I'll not sleep here tonight, Bobby. We're all going back to the tube.'

'Just what the hell have we been slaving away all day for? Blimey, Lizzie, I thought you would have had enough of that shelter. Especially now the raids have died down.'

'No,' said Lizzie firmly, picking up Robin. 'Get ready, kids. We're off to the tube.'

'I'll be gone in the morning,' said Bobby.

'Oh don't go.' She looked sad.

'Sorry, duchess. The law wants me, and God knows when I'll be back once the army gets me.'

She reached up and kissed his cheek. 'Take care, Bobby. I'm sorry.'

'Don't worry, love,' he smiled ruefully. 'I'll get by.'

So Lizzie pushed her pramful back to Old Street tube station. In the morning he had gone, and she found the cold flat cheerless and depressing. Nevertheless, she set about making it a bit more comfortable. At least it was a home for them to come back to. For the kids things didn't change much. Charlie chased about outside the tube, scrounging off this person and that, and Rene disappeared as usual, down into the dark tunnel to lark about with the boys.

Then one day Rene was a bit off colour. Unusually quiet, she stayed in and played cards with Maisie. Lizzie looked at Rene, at her high breasts and podgy stomach and noticed that she was putting on a lot of weight. No doubt it was because she was getting better food now that Lizzie had an army pay book, a regular income, and an allowance for the children. All benefits of Bobby being in the army with the R.E.M.E., somewhere up north.

One evening soon after that, Charlie and Rene had a row during which both of them got very agitated. At length Charlie said, 'I'm going to tell about you.'

'You shut up. You're a thief, you are,' Rene shouted.

'Tell me what?' asked Lizzie.

'She's in the pudding club,' cried Charlie. 'Someone told me.'

Rene started to weep.

Lizzie looked amazed, 'What are you two talking about?'

'Some soldier done it,' cried Rene.

'I told her not to lark about down that dark tunnel,' said Charlie, grave-faced and belligerent.

'Charlie,' said Lizzie, 'hop it, go out and play.'

'Now Rene, come over here, dear, and tell Auntie.'

Rene sat beside her and wept bitterly. 'I am sorry, Aunt Liz. Oh where's me Mum?'

'Now darling what has happened? Tell me,' repeated Lizzie patiently.

'It was six weeks ago this fellow, a soldier, came down the tunnel and grabbed hold of me. I was afraid to tell you, and now I think I am pregnant. Kept feeling sick.'

'Oh dear,' sighed Lizzie. 'Come on, let's go and see the First Aid Sister.'

The Nursing Sister confirmed their fears. 'Into the second month,' she said. 'What will you do, Lizzie?'

'I am not sure yet.'

'Well dear, you come to me if you need help.'

That night Lizzie lay awake worrying over this latest

catastrophe. The lady in the next door cubicle came to see her, she had heard about Rene. She said, 'What can you expect with the kind we get down here. Poor little kid. I know someone who might help her out; cost a tenner, Lizzie.'

Lizzie was very restless that night. How could she put young Rene through what she had endured in her own youth? She thought about Crochet Hook Kate and the pain, about her sexual confusion, and about her childlessness. No, she could never subject Rene to that.

CHAPTER FIVE

It's Over

The tall, white-haired lady, known to the shelter-dwellers as the Red Cross Sister, had for many years been a hospital matron but had come out of retirement to take charge of the underground shelter. She attended to minor ailments such as earache or grit in the eye, and sat rolling bandages, or making hot nourishing drinks for those suffering from shock. One and all depended on the Red Cross Sister, so it was to her that Lizzie poured out all her troubles.

'Don't worry, Lizzie,' Sister told her, 'I don't believe in destroying life either. Rene must take the consequences, and she will be a better woman for it. I'll negotiate to get her into the Salvation Army Home just before the baby is due; in the meantime we will look after her down here.'

Charlie had got himself a job as a messenger in a city newspaper office. He drew his ten bob wages on Friday and shared it with the family; he supplied the younger kids with sweets and pop, but he was also very independent and liked to go his own way. He was very ashamed of Rene's predicament; his face flushed scarlet whenever he caught sight of her.

'What she wanna go and do that for?' he complained. 'I warned her not to lark about down that dark tunnel.'

'Well, Charlie boy,' said Lizzie placidly, 'what's done is done. We'll get by as long as we survive the Blitz. Nothing else matters.'

'You know what, Auntie Lizzie?' returned Charlie. 'I think you are a champion, you don't make no fuss about anything. When I get me wages I'm going to treat you to something nice.'

Lizzie giggled. 'Now Charlie,' she said, 'be a good boy up

there in the city, and if the warning goes you make sure you take cover.'

'Oh I will, Aunt Lizzie.'

Charlie boy had suddenly grown up; he wore long trousers which he placed religiously under his mattress every night in order to keep a good crease in them. He had also purchased a nice handkerchief which he kept in the top pocket of his jacket, together with a comb and mirror, and he would repeatedly take out the comb and pull it through his fair wavy hair.

'Poof!' Rene would sneer at him, sitting on the lower bunk, sullenly knitting little woolly vests.

On Saturday night when there were boozy family fights going on down the shelter and family parties, Charlie liked to roam around, what Lizzie called, 'poking his nose in'. Despite his previous wild behaviour Charlie was turning into a very nice boy. He would sit beside Lizzie and chat to her.

'The boss likes me,' he boasted. 'Says he is going to send me to night school. You see, Aunt Liz, he is always a bit drunk, and when he hollers for a boy all the others duck out, but I always turn up. 'Ere 'e ain't 'arf a lad,' Charlie added humorously, ' "Spell this big word," he hollers at me. "Gor blimey!" says I, "I can't." "Bugger off," he hollers again, "and don't come back till you can." So off I goes to the library room, finds it in the dictionary and writes it down. Then when he calls out, "Boy! boy!" I dashes in and before he starts on me I spells it out-loud to him. You know, he don't 'arf laugh and I think he likes me.'

Not long after this Rene was taken to the Salvation Army maternity home for wanton girls by the Red Cross Sister, and almost at the same time the buzz bombs started.

The buzz bombs really flummoxed Lizzie because they came in daylight. Their high-pitched droning sound came out of the sky even before the siren could begin its warning. Then there would be an eerie silence as the engine cut out and the bomb started its death dive to the ground. Lizzie was terrified of those bombs and was more loath than ever to leave the shelter. She hated the gloomy flat that Bobby had found for them and spent as little time as possible in it.

Rene's baby daughter was born in December, and because it was so close to Christmas, she called her Carol.

'Rene must stay in the home until the baby is at least twelve weeks old,' the Red Cross sister informed Lizzie. 'Then we will put the child up for adoption, so there's no need for you to worry, Lizzie.'

But Lizzie did worry. She thought nightly of that little one whom no one really wanted.

One morning, when she came home from the shelter, Rene was sitting on the cold gloomy landing with a tiny white bundle in her arms.

'Oh Aunt Lizzie,' she wailed, 'I've run away, I can't stand it in that place.'

'You naughty girl,' cried Lizzie, relieving the distressed girl of the child.

'Open up and put the kettle on, Maisie,' she said, looking down with loving gentleness at the tiny baby with its small puckered mouth and black hair.

'Ow Aunt Lizzie! Don't make me go back,' howled Rene. 'They made me scrub the floors and wash the other babies' dirty nappies.'

'All right,' said Lizzie, 'have some tea and something to eat — and for Gawd's sake calm down. You'll wake up the baby.'

So Rene came home, and baby Carol was washed and fed by Lizzie, then popped into the old pram, well wrapped up.

They all went on the usual trek to the shelter. 'Can't stand them bloody buzz bombs,' said Lizzie. 'Like to get back to the shelter as soon as I can.'

'Whose baby, Lizzie?' asked the other shelter dwellers.

'It's mine,' replied Lizzie. 'Had it in the change.'

'Oh Lizzie, don't tell us you are the Virgin Mary,' they jested.

But Lizzie did not care, she had taken the babe under her wing and no one could dislodge it from her.

'Oh dear!' cried the Red Cross Sister, when she came to investigate. 'Are you sure you will be able to manage?'

'Why not?' said Lizzie. 'What's one more baby? I don't mind how many children I look after. But it's her that worries me.'

She glared at Rene's sulky face. 'How do I know she won't go off down that tunnel and do the same thing all over again?'

Sister's stern face relaxed into a smile. 'Rene can come down to the post and help me every night, then I will try to get her a position somewhere. Come on, love.' Rene brightened up immediately. 'Send for me if you need any help, Lizzie.'

Maisie became a great help with the baby. Short and plump with two long brown plaits of hair hanging down her back, she was a real busybody and a born mother. She wheeled the baby about in her pram, chatting with one and all. Rene, on the other hand, was too shy to take much notice of her child, despite the fact that Carol was everybody's sweetheart, a beautiful four-month-old baby with wide blue eyes, curly black hair and rosy cheeks.

Lizzie went out one Saturday to the market to shop for food, which was getting very scarce. 'I'll take Robin and Maisie,' she said, 'so Rene, you stay with the baby, and go under the stairs if the buzz bombs start to come over.'

When Lizzie reached the shops, there was a long queue for vegetables because they were giving out two bananas to each customer. Robin liked bananas and Lizzie decided that it might be a nice change for the baby to have one as well. But no sooner had she joined the end of the queue, than she heard a droning sound in the sky. Everyone looked up uneasily, then quickly began to scatter as silence fell — a silence that meant the deadly weapon had started its dive to earth. Lizzie crouched in a doorway with the children close to her. There was a great blast, and the ground shuddered beneath her. On looking up she saw a cloud of smoke rising up from the direction of the buildings. Lizzie started to run, dragging the children with her.

'Oh the bastards, the bloody German bastards,' cried Lizzie as she ran home. Only there was no home, just a smoking ruin and the air raid wardens digging in the rubble.

'Oh, my Rene's in there,' cried Lizzie.

But the men kindly held her back.

'If she is alive we will bring her out, so stand back please.'

They brought out a grubby little bundle all covered in dust, and placed it in Lizzie's arms.

'Got the baby. Ain't found the girl yet.'

Lizzie looked down at the little face all covered in dirt. The mouth opened wide, let out a yell and tiny fists rubbed the eyes.

'Thank God!' cried Lizzie, took her hankie and wiped the babe's face.

A sympathetic silence fell around her as the wardens re-emerged from the house, carrying a stretcher.

'Sorry love,' one of them said, 'she's had it.'

Lizzie stood silent and bewildered, unable to believe that her lovely young Rene, who had been on the threshold of life, was dead.

'Is the baby all right?' asked the ambulance man. 'Shall I take you to the hospital?'

'No.' Lizzie clutched the baby tight. 'Come on, kids. We'll go back to the tube, and we won't come out till this bloody war is over.'

The last of her treasures had gone. The suitcase and the old pram were now flattened out of existence, and lovely Rene . . . What would she say to Sallie?

The Red Cross Sister washed the baby and fed her. Lizzie was too distraught to do anything but weep.

'Lizzie dear, you have been through too much, let me send you all away for a little holiday. You can come back when you feel better.'

'I'll not leave the baby,' said Lizzie. 'And I feel safe down here.' ·

'Lizzie, it's not good for the children. They have seen too much. Please dear, be sensible.'

Lizzie looked at her little family, remembered the poor flattened body of Rene, and gave in. 'All right, just till they get over the shock.'

Charlie boy said, 'Don't you worry about me, Aunt Lizzie. I'll stay with me mate.'

A very reluctant Lizzie went with the children to a rest

centre in the country where there were many other mums and kids, all of them homeless and waiting to be rehoused.

They were given new attire and a room of their own. The rest of the house was nice, and the grounds had swings and a see-saw which Maisie and Robin liked immensely. Poor little Robin, almost all his life had been spent in the shelter, or traipsing the blitzed streets. The wide open space and all the fresh green grass so excited him that he rolled over and over on the grass like a frisky young pony. Maisie was a little down-hearted, because she missed her friend, Christine, but she soon settled down to bossing the other small kids around. All the mums and kids got together in the afternoons and went on long walks or played with the children in the house if the weather was bad. All except Lizzie, who was terribly homesick, and sat hunched up on the garden seat, depressed by the nice, quiet, peaceful countryside.

'I'm not used to all this fresh air,' she complained, 'I can't seem to keep warm.'

All responsibility had been taken away from her. The baby was taken care of in the nursery, the children played with the others, and the young mums looked after them. So Lizzie would sit huddled up, thinking of Bobby and Rene. No bombs, no air raid warnings; it seemed an endless day. In the old-fashioned, ill-fitting cotton dress that they had supplied her with, Lizzie toddled into her meals and out again without saying much. She did not even have the heart to curl her hair which was so long now that all the blonde had grown out and she wore it tied back with a bootlace.

'Poor Lizzie,' the staff would say, 'still suffering from shock I expect.'

'Wait your turn,' they scolded whenever she asked to be sent home. 'We are going to rehouse you soon, but if you insist that it's got to be in London it will take a long time.'

One Saturday morning bright and breezy Charlie-boy came to see Lizzie. He was much taller than she remembered, wore a nice neat blue serge suit, and had slicked back his blonde hair with Brylcream.

'I am so miserable here, I want to go back home and go down the tube,' were her first words to him.

'They've shut the bloody tube, Aunt Lizzie!' yelled Charlie. 'The bloody war is over.'

'Don't joke about such things, Charlie.' Lizzie never read a paper or even listened to the wireless.

'Yes! It's over! Today! That's why I'm here!' he cried.

Lizzie looked up, bewildered. She was so wrapped up in her own miseries that it had never occurred to her the war could end.

'And guess what?' said Charlie. 'We have got a nice new house in Highbury and Uncle Bobby is coming home.'

'How do you know?' Lizzie was suspicious.

'Because you've got a letter from him. Came to the paper, it did. I opened it. Shall I read it to you?'

'Oh no you won't,' said Lizzie, suddenly coming to life.

She snatched at the precious letter, and in Bobby's large illiterate hand she read:

'Not to worry, duchess, come home, bring the kids, army welfare got us a nice house, meet you at the station on Monday morning, Love Bobby.'

Lizzie smiled her gentle smile for the first time in weeks and put the letter in her coat pocket.

'Come on, Charlie boy,' she said, 'let's go and tell the kids.'

CHAPTER SIX

The Family

Lizzie was still quite unable to believe that the war was over at last. Nothing had seemed normal since Rene died — it was as if her life were happening to someone else. Now she was leaving a kind of twilight home where the staff spoke in hushed whispers behind her back.

'Yes, that poor woman's still suffering some shock. Been in London all through the Blitz,' she overheard them say.

Stung at last into action, Lizzie began to prepare for her return to London. She curled and bleached her hair, put on her favourite perfume and her one remaining ring.

'I am so very glad that I never had to part with his nice cluster ring,' she said to herself, admiring it as she manicured her nails.

Maisie had come to join her. 'We *are* going then, Aunt Lizzie?' she asked in her dark brown voice.

'Yes darling, isn't it great?'

'I dunno,' returned Maisie, sombrely.

Lizzie cuddled her. 'Why, what is the matter?'

'My friend Christine is going to live in Beacontree, so I won't see her again, never.'

'Oh never mind.' Lizzie cuddled her close. 'Never is a long time. I'll help you write a letter to her.'

Robin arrived and stated definitely that he was not going home. 'They've got a nice swing here.'

But in spite of the protests they were all bundled into a station wagon on Saturday morning and then put on the train for London. Lizzie carried baby Carol in her arms.

The matron had offered to keep the baby until Lizzie was settled.

But Lizzie held on tight. 'Carol stays with me,' she told them.

Charlie and Bobby were at the station to meet them. Bobby very spruce in his army uniform, his teeth white, his skin tanned. Army life had obviously suited him. He gave Lizzie a peck on the cheek. 'Hullo, me old mate,' he said. 'Long time no see.' Then he looked down at Lizzie's solemn face. 'Cheer up, duchess!' he roared. 'The war is over!'

They all got on the bus and Bobby said, 'We got a nice house. My officer got it for me.'

'Where is it?' Lizzie asked.

'It's in Highbury. Still north London, but very posh.'

'I'd sooner have gone back to The Nile,' said Lizzie mournfully.

'Gawd blimey! What are you beefing about? Some poor sods ain't got no place to go, I was very lucky to get this place.' Bobby was angry.

Lizzie remained silent. The new house was a tall, rambling Victorian dwelling, one in a line of bombed-out houses with broken window panes and untidy front gardens. It was three stories high with stone steps going down to the basement and more stone steps going up to the front door. In the last century these places had housed the gentry, now they stood blitzed and derelict, awaiting new owners from every walk of life

'Oh dear,' said Lizzie, looking very dismayed. 'It's much too big.'

'Now turn it up, Lizzie,' Bobby warned. 'We got a big family, ain't we?'

They went down the steps into the big kitchen which was below the level of the road but which opened out into an untidy garden at the back.

'I've scrounged some crocks and groceries. Now, Lizzie, get your finger out and make a cup of tea.' Bobby marshalled them all as if he were still in the army. 'Charlie, take Robin with you and get all the wood you can find. We'll light a big fire. That's a nice old range. And anything else you find in them other houses that's usable, bring it back, lads. Maisie, take the baby, and Lizzie you get the supper going. I'll have this place shipshape in no time.'

Lizzie pottered nervously about the strange, empty house. The high ceilings and large rooms really frightened her. Meanwhile Bobby cleaned the big wooden table and lit the fire. Charlie and Robin found several chairs, saucepans and other useful household things.

'Well,' said Bobby, as they all sat around having hot tinned soup and making toast, 'not a bad camp, is it, kids?'

Lizzie sat in a rickety old chair which Charlie had acquired, and her brown eyes grew misty as a warm feeling suffused her. At last Bobby had accepted all the kids; he no longer opposed her, absence had done wonders for him.

Early in the morning, the kids ran out into the big untidy garden. 'Uncle Bobby!' Robin's shrill voice came from the wilderness. 'There's a big tree, can we make a swing?'

So a swing made of thick rope was installed in the big sycamore tree, and Robin was as happy as the day was long, swinging and twisting about.

Maisie in her busybody way took charge of the baby. Robin wanted to know what relation they were to her.

'I am her aunt and you are her uncle,' replied Maisie very seriously.

Robin rolled about the floor, creased with laughter. 'Me, an uncle, that's funny.'

Bobby stood beside the fire, his elbow on that old-fashioned mantlepiece. 'Lizzie,' he said, 'has it occurred to you that now it's over, Sallie will come looking for these kids?'

'And I shall tell that cow where to go,' cried Lizzie, unusually angry.

'Well, Lizzie, don't say I didn't warn you; she'll have the law on her side. It's all right by me, you can keep them. I don't care, I've got used to them, but I don't want you to be hurt.'

But Lizzie was not even listening. She had begun to take an interest in her big rambling house. All her thoughts were on how best to improve it.

'We'll paint the stairs and passage,' she said. 'That will brighten it up.'

So Bobby just grinned and said, 'I'm still in the army, Lizzie. I'll get demobbed soon, but I'm only over at Woolwich, so I'll be home every night. Come on, give us a kiss.'

Lizzie's small shape melted into his big arms. She had found peace once more, and number fourteen, Mortimer Road, as it was known, became a home for her and her kids. Bobby scrounged and pilfered from the army, bringing home tins of spam and corned beef, and army blankets. He would sit playing cards in camp and with his winnings he got Lizzie's rings out of pawn, and bought clothes for the children. Slowly but surely the house began to take shape.

'Lizzie,' said Bobby, when he saw the battered old coat that she still wore, 'that looks like a dead cat.' And he went out and bought her a tweed utility coat. 'I like you to look nice.'

'Pity I lost all my nice dresses and my fox furs in the Blitz.'

'No, duchess, never look back,' said Bobby. 'You was always my duchess, now I will make you a queen. You can have all the furs and sparklers that you can wear.'

'I hope so, Bobby,' she said, with little confidence.

'That's one thing I learned in the army, Lizzie. It's the survival of the fittest and the most dodgy, and it's the most dodgy ones that survive. That's how I intend to go on. In our days the big bloke with the money got it all. We was nothing, but the war's changed all that.'

'Well let's hope so,' said Lizzie once more.

As Lizzie went about her chores she would often worry about what would happen if Sallie turned up. Lizzie knew she could not part with the kids. After all this time, how would she ever live without them?

Bobby got demobbed from the army that summer with a nice little stake in his pocket. He took it to the races and somehow managed to double it.

'Told you so Lizzie. Can't do wrong. Lady Luck is with me.'

'But Bobby, I had hoped you would settle down to a regular job,' said Lizzie quietly.

'Give over, duchess. Had enough discipline in the army. Can do without it in civvy street.'

Charlie became Bobby's special pal. They went over the Arsenal together and down to the dog track.

Lizzie would nag continually, 'Don't take Charlie to the dogs. He's a good boy; I don't want him getting into bad ways.'

'Lizzie, old gel, leave the boy alone. He goes to work, brings home all his wages. What he does in his leisure is a working man's own privilege.'

Lizzie retired defeated.

That autumn night the White City dog track was full to over-flowing. The stand was packed tight and the huge white arc lights flooded the arena. At one end stood the cigar-smoking, pot-bellied businessmen, the spivs with their wide hats and padded shoulders, and quite a sprinkling of women. At the other end were the flat-capped, working class punters, who squandered their hard-earned money on the long thin dogs which tore around after the hare every Saturday night. The touts and the pickpockets moved in among the crowd; the bookies yelled the odds, and the excitement was intense. Bobby was back in action as a tic-tac man; he stood on a kind of bench signalling around the track. Charlie boy, with a bright choker about his neck and his hair slicked back, prowled around picking up tips and putting on bets.

Soon he sidled up close to Bobby. 'Got a good tip, Uncle Bobby?'

'Dead cert called Poor Gladys. First time on this track; put us a tenner on it, Charlie-boy.' Bobby looked at his list again. ' 'Arf a mo',' he said, 'why didn't I see that before? Poor Gladys, out of Marzipan. Owner Pat O'Keefe. Well if it ain't old Pat! We'll find him later; he's a good old pal of mine.'

Poor Gladys romped home at twenty to one, so it was with their pockets full and in a very jovial mood that they went to find Pat. They discovered him in the lounge bar, bigger and more robust than ever.

'Bobby, me boyo!' Pat pumped his hand up and down. 'Who's this then; your son?'

'No, Pat, it's me nephew. It's great to see you. Cor blimey!'

cried Bobby, pushing his cap to the back of his head, 'I can't believe it.'

'Poor Gladys, the barmaid,' Pat said. 'I hope you backed the dog.'

'Of course I did.' Bobby grinned. 'Now we're here to celebrate.'

Pat's head was as shiny as a billiard ball and his tummy twice its normal size, but he was still the great sportsman, full of Irish humour and generosity.

'I've got a bar in Commercial Road now, Bobby, down there near the docks. Bridie's home and the girls; they have really grown up. Eileen got married, Kate and Dinaper are a right couple of flappers, and the two young ones are away at school. Got any family, Bobby?'

'Yes,' said Bobby with a grin. 'I've got four.'

'You're joking.' Pat knew perfectly well that Bobby had spent a fair time in the nick.

'Well it's a long story, but all the same, I got a big family.'

The whiskey was chased down with beer, then, after many rounds had been bought, they went in a taxi to Pat's new pub and had a party. Charlie got drunk for the first time in his life and fell passionately in love with Pat's very pretty daughter, Dinaper.

Meanwhile Lizzie had contentedly spent the evening with the kids, playing dominoes with Robin and Maisie, rocking to and fro to get Carol to sleep on her comfortable lap. There was a big fire in the kitchen range and the room was strung with lines of washing. Lizzie liked this nice big, warm kitchen. In fact now that it was fairly comfortably furnished and the rooms had all been redecorated, she liked the house better than any she had lived in before.

The two youngest children had recently started school and Maisie became obsessed with the big church at the end of the road. She went regularly to Sunday School and was very friendly with the vicar. Lately she had taken to reading the small text book he had given her.

'Don't you believe in Jesus, Aunt Lizzie?' she asked one night as Lizzie tucked her up in bed, after she had knelt beside her bed and prayed, 'God bless Aunt Lizzie, Uncle Bobby, Robin and baby Carol.'

Lizzie, very amused, said, 'You missed out Charlie-boy.'

'Yes, because he is a naughty boy,' said Maisie solemnly, then repeated her question. 'Why don't you like Jesus, Aunt Lizzie?'

Lizzie looked embarrassed. 'Well, I never had a lot to do with him.'

'Oh well, that's all right,' said Maisie, 'because you can easily be perverted, I heard the vicar say so.'

Lizzie suppressed a giggle. 'I think, he meant converted. But who am I to argue with your nice vicar?'

In her calm gentle way Lizzie loved and protected the children. When Robin said, 'All the boys at school got farvers, why haven't I?' Lizzie explained, 'You got an uncle. Your Daddy got killed in the war, so we are taking care of you.'

'And our Muvver went out in the Blitz and never came back,' piped Maisie.

'Well it don't matter, because I love you and Uncle Bobby all the world,' said Robin, making a big circle with his arms to portray the amount of his love.

That Saturday night Lizzie watched anxiously as usual for Bobby and Charlie to get off the last bus, but they did not arrive. She sat at the kitchen table with her head on her hands, and wondered what had happened to her boys. Memories of the war days were going through her mind, when she heard a taxi draw up and saw Bobby stagger up the path with Charlie on his back. Lizzie was horrified. 'Oh Bobby,' she cried, 'Charlie's drunk! You should be thoroughly ashamed of yourself.'

Bobby laid Charlie down in front of the fire, then flopped into his armchair and passed out. Lizzie covered them up.

'You're both going to get a piece of my mind in the morning,' she threatened.

On Sunday morning Bobby was a mass of apologies and Charlie hid in his room, then went out to the pictures to escape Lizzie's wrath.

Bobby was full of beans. 'Cor blimey! Liz, it was such a treat to meet old Pat once more.' He handed her a bundle of notes. 'Look! I won on Poor Gladys. You remember the old barmaid he had in the City Road pub. He named his dog after her.'

'I remember when she was killed,' said Lizzie solemnly. 'She was still under the debris when I was there.'

'Oh come on, Liz, cheer up,' said Bobby. 'Don't be so gloomy, I'll take you down the East End to Pat's new pub.'

'Won't go!'

'All right, please your bloody self,' said Bobby huffily.

'You got Charlie drunk. I won't have him getting into your bad habits.'

'Bad habits!' yelled Bobby, losing his temper. 'Who brings in all the lolly to feed them bleeding kids? Honestly, there is no pleasing you these days. You're getting to be a miserable old cow. Come on, kids! Let's go over the fields for a game of football.'

Maisie and Robin dashed off with their Uncle Bobby. But Lizzie sat down and wept. He was right; that was just what she was, a miserable old cow, but she couldn't help herself. She was so afraid Bobby would go back to his old gambling ways.

The next weekend Charlie and Bobby went off to the dogs, then to Pat's pub. Lizzie anxiously watched them go, knowing that they would not be back till early morning and only then in a very poor condition.

In the bar they talked of old times, of dogs and gee-gees. Then Bobby said to Charlie-boy, 'No booze for you tonight, son. Lizzie never stopped nagging.'

But Charlie was not interested in the booze this time – only in Pat's lovely blonde daughter, whose eyes were sky-blue and whose skin was milk-white. She spoke with a kind of a lilt in her voice and Charlie was transfixed. He stared at her all night, but no matter how he gazed, Dinaper remained cold and aloof.

Bobby could see that Charlie was getting the brush-off, and on the bus going home decided to give Charlie a bit of old-fashioned advice.

'Listen, son, if you want to pull the birds, there's plenty down the racetrack. You can see them, beehive hairdos, big bristols, the lot.'

Charlie smiled. 'Not me, Uncle Bobby. I'll never be interested in a tart.'

'Don't get too set on that gel of Pat's, Charlie-boy. She looks a bitch, young as she is.'

'That's not very nice, Uncle Bobby.'

'Look, lad, take a bit of good advice. I've had plenty in my time and I can read them birds like a book. She fancies herself. Anyway she's probably all booked up with some Catholic bloke and he won't let her look at you.'

Charlie flushed scarlet. 'What's wrong with me?'

'Nothing, son, you are fine, but I know Pat's family. They're very careful with those girls, and I don't want you to get hurt.'

'I can take care of myself,' said Charlie sullenly.

On the following Saturday, Charlie refused to go to the dogs, said he was going to the pictures, and came back early with a box of chocolates and a fish and chip supper for them all.

Lizzie instinctively knew that he had been stood up and made an extra fuss of him.

Charlie sat beside her when the kids were in bed. 'Don't you mind Uncle Bobby always being out?' he asked her.

'I can't do much about it, Charlie-boy. That's my Bobby. I just put up with it.'

'If ever I find someone to like me I'll never go out and leave her,' said Charlie. 'Tell me, Aunt Lizzie, my mother wasn't much good, was she?'

'I wouldn't say that, Charlie. Your Dad got killed in the war and she found it hard to live without a man. Some women do.'

'Do you think she'll turn up one day?'

A look of anxiety crossed Lizzie's face, but she did not reply.

Then Charlie said, 'I'll tell you what, Aunt Lizzie, if she does, I'll have nothing to do with her, nor will the other kids.'

'Oh, you mustn't be bitter,' she said. 'It takes all kinds to make this lousy world.'

'There aren't many like you, Aunt Lizzie. That much I have discovered. I intend to work hard and get promotion at my job. I'll not let anyone look down on me again, and I am through with girls and drink.'

'Charlie,' she said, 'you're a funny boy, but I love you and I want you to get all the best out of life.'

Bobby stopped out all night, left a little packet with his winnings on the dresser for her, and stayed in bed all day Sunday. Lizzie did not bother to count the notes but put them in a little jug on the dresser and with a deep sigh, murmured to herself, 'Oh dear, here we go again.'

CHAPTER SEVEN

A Haven

Lizzie was often amazed at how easily she had settled into this rather selective district. The slum dwelling of The Nile, the stalls and the cockney traders seemed to have vanished far away into the distant haze of time. She spent her hours escorting the children back and forth to school. The young mums would look curiously at the artificial shade of her blonde hair, at the outlandish, long out-of-date dresses that she wore, and they would try to guess her age.

'In spite of those golden curls I bet she's getting on a bit,' they would remark. 'They say those kids aren't hers. Apparently she adopted them after the war. She's very fond of them and they seem to love her. Look at her rings and those lovely turquoise earrings. I've never seen her old man, but they don't seem to be short of anything.'

Lizzie gave those nosy parkers no satisfaction, just a sweet smile as she passed on her way home to her comfortable kitchen.

The population all around her was changing as more families were rehoused and some of the larger houses were converted into flats. Many of the families who occupied these flats were Jamaicans who had come to England after the war.

Robin was the first to make a coloured friend, and he brought him home to tea. 'This is my friend Marty,' he said.

The little boy, all black and shiny, with a wide grin, stood in the doorway.

'Come in,' said Lizzie. 'Take a cake. I'll pour out some pop for you.'

The child sat down nervously, his big eyes rolling.

'Don't you think he's nice, Aunt Lizzie?' asked Robin.

'Yes,' said Lizzie still staring. 'He's very nice.'

During the school holidays, kids of all description congregated in Lizzie's garden. They were Robin's friends and they played cowboys and Indians and fought over the swing, while Lizzie stood placidly at the kitchen door with Carol, watching over them all. Maisie sat on the front steps with the girls, playing some strange games. The din was terrible but Lizzie never seemed to mind, nor to lose her temper with the children.

Bobby now went racing several days a week with Pat O'Keefe, who ran a book with Bobby as his tic-tac man. Lately Bobby had lost more money than he earned and was always borrowing from Lizzie.

'It's only a loan till me luck picks up,' he would say.

Lizzie would take some notes from the little jug on the dresser. 'I know it won't come back, Bobby. I can't see why you don't get a regular job.'

'Don't be a bloody fool, Liz. What with the tax man and the low wages, we would never make ends meet.'

Lizzie spent her lonely evenings, when the children were in bed, doing her ironing on the kitchen table. She found it relaxing. There were Charlie's nice white shirts with stiff collars, for he was now installed in the office of the local newspaper and studying to pass his exams. There were Bobby's flashy striped shirts and all the children's school wear; she liked to see them going to school spick and span. Then there were those lovely frilly little dresses which Carol wore. Lizzie would take special pains with them.

Then Bobby's luck ran out altogether. When Lizzie looked at the store of money in the little jug, she saw that it had dwindled to practically nothing. That Saturday night Bobby staggered in with his head in bandages and his right arm encased in a plaster cast.

Maisie looked over the banisters and said, 'Oh, it's Uncle Bobby come home, and he's been duffed up.'

Lizzie came out from the kitchen, complete in her curlers and lopsided cap, and looked at him as he leaned, ashen-faced, against the wall.

'Oh Bobby,' she said, 'you are a bleeding nuisance.'

'That's nice. Those bastards might have killed me and that's all you can say.'

Bobby hung about the house all morning with a mournful expression on his face. 'Can't go to the track, Lizzie,' he said. 'I owe the bookies and that's only a starter.'

Lizzie folded the washing with meticulous care and sighed. 'How much do you owe them?'

'Fifty quid.'

'All right,' she said, 'I'll put on my coat and go up the road and pawn me rings.'

'It's only to get me out of this spot, duchess,' pleaded Bobby. 'I'll soon get them back for you.'

Lizzie looked at him steadily. 'You know, Bobby, I'm getting a bit fed up with your gambling ways.'

'I know, duchess, but one day I'll strike it rich and I'll see you have everything you want.'

'That'll be the day.'

Once Lizzie had cleared up Bobby's debts, things settled down for a while. He went back to the racetrack and brought home his wages, rather than gambling them away.

One day, as Lizzie sat watching the children play, there was a knock on the front door. Outside stood a dumpy figure in a tight, short skirt. She stood looking at Lizzie, who in turn squinted back at her.

'Oh my Gawd!' cried Lizzie. 'It's Sallie.'

'Well don't stand there gawping,' said Sallie. 'Ask me in. Where are the kids? Had such a bloody job to find you.' She bustled past Lizzie, making her way downstairs to the kitchen.

'You got a bleeding cheek turning up after all this time and asking for your kids.' Lizzie glared at Sallie.

Sallie started to grizzle. 'Don't be like that, Lizzie; you don't know what a rotten time I've had. The only way I found you was through the school. I've been looking everywhere. Thought you'd all gone down with the house.'

Lizzie sat tight-lipped.

'Whose kid?' Sallie looked at Carol.

'She's your Rene's baby; she was killed in the blitz,' Lizzie said harshly.

'Oh my God,' yelled Sallie. 'Oh no! Not my lovely Rene. Why wasn't she evacuated? Oh Lizzie, what kind of aunt are you to let her get into trouble?' Sallie's tears fell fast.

'You're one to talk!' yelled Lizzie back at her. 'Went off with your fancy man! Now you're back asking for your kids. They're mine; I've taken care of them all this time.'

The little girl started crying, but both women's tempers were up and they took no notice, just stood glaring at each other while the kids peered nervously round the door.

'You was always a simpleton, Lizzie. Mother used to say that.'

'Not too silly to look after your family.'

'All right, don't let's quarrel,' said Sallie. 'I've not had it so good. I got married again and he left me with two boys to bring up all alone. It's not been easy.'

'Well, you won't need Maisie and Robin,' said Lizzie spitefully. 'And as for the baby, I'll sooner die than let you have her.'

'Now Lizzie, give over. I've got the law on my side. They're still my children.'

'No they're not,' said Lizzie, getting up, and giving Sallie a punch. 'Get out of my house!'

'It's all your fault young Rene died,' sobbed Sallie. 'I'll get the police.'

But Lizzie gave her another push towards the door. 'Hop it,' she yelled, and slammed the door shut.

The kids rushed in. 'Who was that?' they cried.

'It was your mother. She has come to take you away from me,' wept Lizzie, her tears falling fast.

'We won't go, Aunt Lizzie,' they cried, hanging onto her, as she sank exhausted into a chair.

Sallie, on the other hand, stood on the doorstep for a while before going on her way.

When Charlie came in from work, little busybody Maisie rushed up to him. 'Our muvver's been,' she cried. 'Wants to take us away from Aunt Lizzie.'

Charlie kissed Lizzie's cheek. 'Now don't you upset yourself,

Aunt Lizzie. It can probably be worked out. We're all happy with you, and the kids have forgotten her.'

'But Charlie-boy, she can do it. She's going to the law.'

'Stop worrying. I'll talk to my boss about it. He'll know all the legal angles.'

'You are a good boy,' said Lizzie, but both of them knew that the only solution was to settle the problem amicably.

Bobby arrived home a day later from a northern racetrack. He dashed in, jubilantly dragging behind him a long, thin greyhound.

'Look what I bought yer,' he yelled. 'She's called The Duchess, a real thoroughbred. I'm going to train her for the White City Derby.'

Lizzie, very depressed, gazed at the forlorn-looking dog with its ribs showing through its skin, shivering with fright as the kids milled around it.

'Take that bloody mongrel out of here,' she cried. 'It might bite Carol.'

'Blimey, Lizzie! Is that nice? That racing dog cost two hundred quid, she did, and half of it is mine. She's a great granddaughter of Mick the Miller.'

'I don't care if King George fathered her. Take her outside.'

'She ain't 'arf got the 'ump,' said Bobby. 'Come on, kids, we'll put the dog in the shed for tonight.'

Robin, Maisie and their horde of friends all went with Bobby to bed down The Duchess for the night. But over supper, the subject of Sallie took precedence over that of the new greyhound.

'Why, the cow! Turning up after all this time,' said Bobby. 'Hope she didn't upset you, Lizzie.'

'Well, as a matter of fact she did. Wants to take the children away.'

Charlie said, 'I've been studying the subject. She can't touch me because I'm seventeen, and she can't demand Carol because she is only her granddaughter, but Robin and Maisie are still liable to be returned to her.'

'Oh dear,' said Bobby, 'Lizzie, perhaps you'd better give in. I don't like you having a lot of bother with the law.'

'Never!' cried Lizzie. 'Not while there's breath in my body.

All you care about is that bleeding greyhound. I'll not part with my kids.'

In the morning Charlie said, 'Here's my phone number at work. If Sallie turns up I'll come home and talk to her. I reckon you could blackmail her.'

'Do what!' cried Lizzie, aghast.

'Well it's pretty obvious she's no good. If you can prove she's an unfit person to look after her own children, you might win the case.'

'Oh no, I couldn't do that, not to my own sister,' cried Lizzie.

'Well it's up to you. Remember, Aunt Lizzie, I'm with you all the way.'

After the children had left for school Lizzie walked to the park with Carol thinking to herself, 'That's it, I'll move, then Sallie'll never be able to find me. I'll send the children to school under another name.'

'Bobby,' she said quietly that evening. 'We're going to move.'

'What for? I thought you liked it here?'

'I'll not part with my kids,' she said. 'I'll move. Might even go back to The Nile.'

'Don't be a bloody fool. The Nile's gone, swept away. There's only sky-scraper flats there now.'

Lizzie's bottom lip trembled, she was about to cry.

'Look here, duchess, I'm fond of those kids too, but you can still see them even if they go home. Don't knock yourself out over it. You say Sallie lives in Shepherds Bush. That ain't the end of the world.'

'No,' Lizzie cried, 'I won't let them go.'

So Bobby got up, grabbed his hat and went down to drink in Pat's bar.

Sallie was as good as her word. On Monday an elderly, pleasant woman from Child Welfare called on Lizzie.

'I can see you have taken excellent care of this family, Mrs Erlock, but your sister has her rights. Let Robin and Maisie go and as long as your husband agrees we'll negotiate for you to adopt the little girl legally. It seems a pity to drag this little family through the courts and if you can't agree, you know the children might easily end up in care.'

'In care!' gasped Lizzie. 'What's that?'

'Well, the Council for Child Welfare will step in and send them away to school until they are old enough to earn their own living.'

'A home like an orphans' home! Oh no,' cried Lizzie, 'not that!'

'Well, be sensible, dear.'

The thought of Maisie and Robin in a school far away from her was a knife in Lizzie's heart, but although the health visitor sympathized with her, she could not show it. Lizzie was clearly a born foster-mother, but the law was on Sallie's side.

On Saturday morning when Bobby was down at Southend, racing his greyhound, the welfare visitor came to take Robin and Maisie back to their mother.

Lizzie had explained gently to them that they were going to share a house with Sallie, and they would go for a little holiday to see if they liked it.

'I don't know her, so I ain't going to live in her house,' said Robin. 'And what about me mates?'

'You have two nice brothers to play with,' said Lizzie, her voice choked with emotion.

'I'll go,' said Maisie, 'to look after Robin, but if I don't like it we're coming back.'

'We're waiting for your mother now,' said the welfare visitor. 'I'm sure you will be pleased to see her.'

Sallie came rigged up very smartly in a blue suit, a red beret and long dangling earrings. She gave sweets to Robin and put him on her lap.

'Oh darling, my own little baby,' she cried emotionally.

Lizzie sat like a statue. Maisie put her arms around her neck, 'I'll look after Robin,' she said, 'and I'm not stopping. I love you, Aunt Lizzie.' But Lizzie didn't move except to cover her face with her hands so as not to see them go.

Maisie said, 'I want to go in and say goodbye to Mr Blew the vicar.'

Carol put a little finger to Lizzie's eyes. 'Mummy crying,'

she said, and Lizzie held her tight. 'Oh thank God I've still got you, darling!' she cried.

When Charlie came home he was very angry and said, 'There's no justice in this lousy world. I'm sure you would win if you went to court because it's obvious she's a tart.'

'Oh Charlie-boy, don't say things like that about your own mother,' begged Lizzie.

'She's no mother of mine,' said Charlie bitterly.

When Bobby bounced in at midnight all bright and breezy, Lizzie was still sitting in a depression, elbows on the kitchen table.

Bobby produced a wad of notes, 'Lady Luck is mine again. Count that. All for you, duchess, two hundred smackers. The Duchess romped home.'

But Lizzie just looked up mournfully, 'They took the kids,' she said.

'Oh blimey!' he cried, picking her up in his arms like a baby. 'Oh duchess, I'm so sorry, how can I make it up to you?'

Lizzie just cried broken-heartedly on his shoulder and he carried her up to bed. For the first time since the war she let him make love to her, and because he was gentle, she felt no pain — only warmth and happiness at being so close to her Bobby. Later, cuddling close in his arms, she began to talk about the children again.

'I've still got Carol,' she told him. 'They want us to adopt her legally.'

'And that we will do, love, so no need to cry any more.'

Bobby bought her a gold watch, and got her rings out of pawn. 'Lizzie,' he said, 'I believe I have hit the jackpot at last; me and old Pat is going into business together. Between us we got four good dogs and this new track at Clapton is very popular.'

So he kept bringing home the lolly; it overflowed the Toby jug and Lizzie started another horde in an old teapot. But she got very little pleasure out of it. The house was still and quiet; no children played in the garden and she missed walking with them to school. She just sat idly in her kitchen while Carol played with her dolls. After a couple of weeks she had a letter from Maisie.

'Dear Aunt Liz, Me and Robin want to come home, we don't like it here, love to Mr Blew, Maisie. Come and get us.'

Lizzie wept a hail of tears.

Charlie said, 'I'll go over at the weekend and find out how they are, Aunt Lizzie.'

'Thank you, darling.'

But in the morning two dusty dishevelled children arrived on the doorstep, and looked forlornly at Lizzie.

Maisie said, 'We've run away, Aunt Lizzie, it was terrible.'

Lizzie swept them into her arms, and once they had eaten and had a good wash, she asked them how they had got home to her.

'We came on the tram. We used the money that Uncle gave us.'

'She's got a lot of uncles,' said Robin.

'And we used to have to mind those horrible boys when she went out with our uncles,' said Maisie.

Lizzie looked very grim. 'That cow Sallie,' she cried. 'I won't let you go back, even if they kill me.'

So Maisie and Robin jubilantly went to bed that night in their own old room. 'Shall we have cream buns tomorrow, Aunt Lizzie?'

'You certainly will, my darlings,' said Lizzie with fervour.

In the morning over breakfast she listened to Maisie's chatter about the Scottish uncle whose breath smelled funny, and how he tried to rub his whiskers on Maisie's face. Robin recounted how Sallie had slapped him and said he was a naughty boy.

'It's all over now, darlings,' said Lizzie. 'You're back home.'

Lizzie had burned her boats and when the big policeman came knocking, she said, 'Quick kids, into the cupboard, and don't make a sound.'

'I am looking for two children missing from South London. Their mother thinks they might be here.'

'No children here,' said Lizzie, 'only my baby.'

'Well if they turn up, get in touch with the local station, will you?'

'Oh yes, I will,' said Lizzie.

The kids giggled and thought it was great fun, but Bobby was worried.

'They won't let you get away with it, Lizzie,' he told her. Then suddenly he banged his fist on the table. 'Why that effing cow Sallie,' he cried, 'if she comes here, you turn her over to me. I'll settle her.'

'Now watch your language, Bobby,' said Lizzie.

'Sorry, duchess,' he said and dashed off. 'I've the dogs to be with.'

After that, every time there was a knock at the door the kids dashed into the cupboard and had lots of fun. By mid-week a letter arrived from Sallie stating that she knew the children were with Lizzie, and that she was about to take out a case against Lizzie for abduction of her family.

'I told you what to do, Aunt Lizzie. You have got to blackmail her,' said Charlie.

Lizzie looked terrified.

'Nothing to worry about,' he assured her. 'Just send her a letter stating that you know all about her goings on and that you are going to tell the court she is morally unfit to have charge of minors.'

It all sounded very grand, and Lizzie dismissed it as typical Charlie talk until Bobby spoke up from behind *The Sporting Life*, 'He's right, you know, duchess.'

So Lizzie overcame her inner fears and allowed Charlie to write Sallie a long letter reminding her of her past misdemeanours, and telling her that Lizzie intended to fight for the kids.

'Tell her, if she wants to negotiate, to come Sunday afternoon when I am around and I'll settle that bitch once and for all,' Bobby muttered threateningly.

So Lizzie, having regained her courage, allowed Charlie to pop out and post the letter.

Bobby had come home early that Sunday morning in a good mood after winning a packet at the dogs and had gone straight up to bed, while Lizzie, all on edge, sent the children to church, saying that if their mother was here when they came back to make themselves scarce.

'I'll go back and help Mr Blew,' said Maisie. 'He likes me to get ready for the Sunday school class.'

It was punctually after midday that Sallie arrived, attired in a stunning black velvet suit and a frilly white blouse, her hair freshly waved and wearing lots of makeup.

'In battle dress, so to speak,' said Charlie.

'Now, go and wake Bobby,' said Lizzie. 'I'll let her in.'

But as she opened the door Lizzie found herself feeling sorry for Sallie, who flounced in saying, 'What's all this, Lizzie? They're my kids; you can't get away with it.'

Charlie stood in the doorway, looking superciliously at his mother.

'Hullo, Charlie,' she said. 'You've grown into a very tall boy, just like your Dad.'

But Charlie sneered and sauntered away in a lordly manner.

Sallie was looking very sorry for herself when Bobby staggered in, his shirt sleeves rolled up and his feet bare from having jumped straight out of bed.

'Now, me gel!' he hollered. 'What's all this bloody business, upsetting your own sister who has taken such good care of them kids when you hopped it?'

Sallie began to look crestfallen. 'I don't want to upset anyone, Bobby,' she said, 'but after all, they are my own flesh and blood. I want them back.'

'Nuts!' shouted Bobby. 'That ain't the reason. The kids told me about your fancy men; you can't look after those two poor little sods you got. You're always out on the prowl, leaving them alone.'

Sallie got very red-faced, stuttered, and looked at Lizzie for help. But Lizzie looked in the other direction.

'Well?' hollered Bobby. 'What you got to say for yourself?'

'It's all right for you, you get paid by the state for those kids and by right I'm entitled to that money.'

A wide grin crossed Bobby's face. 'Ah! Now we are getting nearer the truth; it's the lolly you want, not the kids.'

Sallie broke down and started weeping.

Lizzie trotted forward and put the kettle on for a cup of tea.

'Right!' said Bobby. 'You can have the bloody allowance if you leave Lizzie alone. I'll double it, so that'll be about six quid. You'll be better off; you can blow it on fags, booze and bingo, but you leave them kids alone.'

Sallie wiped her eyes and looked more cheerful. Lizzie handed her a cup of tea just as Charlie stormed out of the front door banging it hard shut to show his feelings. Bobby found his slippers and walked into the garden.

Lizzie said in her gentle voice, 'It does seem a pity for you and me to quarrel over the children. After all, Sallie, my Bobby will keep his word and he has supported them kids without one complaint ever since the war was over.'

'Oh I suppose so,' said Sallie. 'But sometimes I am at my wits' end to make ends meet. I am all alone and it's not easy. I'd get a little job if I had Maisie to give eye to the boys.'

'Well now you have to look after them yourself. It's not good to give Maisie all that responsibility; our Mum wouldn't have liked it.'

'Oh well,' said Sallie, 'you've always been able to get round me, Lizzie. You're not as daft as you look.'

'Thank you for the compliment, Sallie,' giggled Lizzie, happy now that it had all been settled amicably. 'I'll send you the money every week or every month, whichever you want.'

'Who cares, as long as I get it,' said Sallie. 'I've got a lot on me plate at the moment, so it's just as well. I've got the worry of those two buggers, very saucy they are.'

'I know,' smiled Lizzie sipping her tea. 'Want another cup of tea, Sallie?'

'No thanks, I'd better go. Left the kids on their own.'

Lizzie handed her a five pound note. 'Just a bit to go on with. I'll see that Bobby keeps his word.'

Just then Bobby went past them back to bed, muttering, 'See you keep *your* word, Sallie, or I'll get one of the boys to chiv yer.'

Sallie grinned cheekily; she had pretty features and two very nice dimples on her cheeks. 'Same old Bobby,' she said, 'you haven't changed a bit.'

When Sallie had gone, the kids dashed in. 'Is it all right, Auntie? We haven't got to go back, have we?' cried Maisie.

Lizzie put her arms about them. 'No, my darlings, it's all right now.'

CHAPTER EIGHT

Temptation

Those were a good couple of years, after the war and before the fifties. Bobby joined a syndicate and raced dogs up and down the country. On Sunday mornings he would hand Lizzie a bundle of notes.

'Quick, grab these, before the bookies get 'em,' he would say.

Lizzie started a Post Office account and bought saving certificates, always thinking that a rainy day might yet come.

Every week Sallie came personally to collect her money, bringing with her two small, undernourished-looking boys aged about four and five who were a real couple of terrors. Sallie would sit and complain about her hard luck and the trouble the boys caused.

'Can't leave them a moment. A real couple of sods.'

Lizzie would smile gently at them, give them money for sweets and feed them with cream cakes. There was no doubt that she was very happy. She kept herself looking nice, still bleached her hair, wore her rings, her earrings and the gold bracelet which Bobby had bought, no longer fearing that they might disappear into the pawn shop at any moment.

Charlie was now eighteen and had to register for his two years' National Service.

'It seems a pity,' said Lizzie. 'You're doing so well at your job.'

'My boss said he's going to keep my job open for me,' Charlie told her proudly. 'Also, Aunt Lizzie, I am still going to get half of my wages, I've made it over to you.'

'Oh Charlie-boy,' she said, 'that's great. I'll save it up for you.'

'No, it's for you, Aunt Lizzie. I haven't forgotten the hard times. I want to show my gratitude.'

They had a farewell party for Charlie. He looked grand in his uniform, and Lizzie wept a hail of tears.

Bobby said, 'Stop worrying, he's got it made. What's the peacetime army? Nothing to do, only eat and booze.'

But Lizzie missed Charlie-boy very much, especially now that Bobby spent less and less time at home. He had endless fine, tailored suits in his wardrobe, silk shirts, flashy ties and went off to racetracks all over the country, a punter of horses as well as dogs.

That winter Pat caught a bad dose of flu' and often stayed at home. Bobby kept his place in the various bookies' pitches, but usually they met at Clapton on Saturday nights and celebrated until Sunday morning. Sometimes he was accompanied by one or two of his daughters. They were very smart, pretty young women: tall dark Eileen, who had married an Italian and owned a restaurant, Kate who lived in the East End, and Dinaper, the youngest sister who had married out in Ireland but was often home on a visit.

Bobby often drank with Kate and Eileen, but one night Dinaper arrived when he was there. She was a cool blonde with platinum-coloured hair and icy blue eyes. Small and slim, she straightened out her silk-clad legs in a very suggestive manner as she perched on the bar stool in the saloon bar at the Clapton dogtrack.

Bobby was immediately attracted to her. He could hardly believe that this was the young girl Charlie had fancied, and against whom he had warned Charlie.

'Dad's not well, so we are here to represent him tonight,' said Kate. 'This is my sister Dinaper, home from Ireland.'

Bobby looked at her open-mouthed, remembering that she had quite recently married a rich trainer of horses.

'Got any hot tips?' asked Dinaper in that cool, lilting tone.

'I might have,' said Bobby moving closer to her.

She smelled of Chanel perfume as he bent over her to inspect the racecard she held. For the first time since the war, Bobby really fancied another woman. It was a very pleasant evening and they all went home to Pat's to supper. In the taxi Dinaper's smooth leg slid close to his. Before the evening ended Bobby asked her if she were staying long.

'Long enough,' she replied with a coy smile.

'See you next week then,' said Bobby, getting the message.

That week Bobby decided to buy a secondhand Morris car, and arrived home with it. The kids were very excited.

But Lizzie said, 'You'll have to keep sober, Bobby, if you're going to drive that thing.'

'Now don't be like that, duchess,' he cried. 'Hop in. I'll take you for a ride.'

'No thanks. I like to keep my feet on the ground.'

Bobby rode the kids around in the car until it broke down and he lost interest in it. Ever afterwards it was parked outside, while Bobby went on the bus and got as boozed as he wanted to.

One Saturday he spent an unusual amount of time getting spruced up. Lizzie, looking at him, thought how nice he looked. He was tall, fresh-complexioned and still had that disarmingly wide and cheeky grin. Yes, she thought, her Bobby was wearing very well. Being in the money certainly suited him.

Because he was busy on the track Bobby did not see Dinaper until late in the evening, when she turned up with her sister Kate. Kate was dark, but Dinaper's hair was like a silver cap. She wore a silky grey dress and her pale face was cool and composed. When she saw Bobby the small mouth broke into a smile of welcome.

'What about you and I having a bit of supper together?' he whispered.

She nodded assent. 'Kate's husband is picking her up.'

In the taxi going up west, they melted into each other's arms without a word.

'Oh Bobby, I really fancy you,' she said.

'You can say that again,' said Bobby. 'Where shall we eat?'

'Who wants to eat?' she said, running her hands over his thigh.

'Oh dear,' cried Bobby, 'you really have got me going. Who

would have thought that young Dinny would grow up into such a smasher?'

Her face clouded. 'You will be careful of papa?'

'Sure I will. Don't I know how old Pat worships you. What's wrong, Dinny? Are you unhappily married?'

'He's a lot older than I am,' she said. 'And I didn't get a lot of choice. It was a case of out of convent school into the marriage bed, and that was a washout.' Her voice was hard and bitter.

'Well, I'm a lot older than you, and I'm married too.'

'Sure, but you're a man after my own heart, Bobby,' she said, smothering his face with kisses.

Bobby was defeated; any hopes he had of resisting her were gone completely.

'Stop at the Wilton,' she told the taxi driver, once the West End came in sight.

'What's that?' Bobby asked. 'A restaurant?'

'It's a hotel.'

Bobby looked worried.

'Don't worry, it's near Euston Station. I often stay there on my way home and luckily they've never seen my husband.'

'Well, you certainly know what you want and how to get it. I've got to admire you, Dinny.'

'I'll need more than that,' she smiled.

So Bobby spent the night of his life at the Wilton Hotel. They took a bottle of brandy up to bed with them and Dinaper made love to Bobby as he had never been made love to before. Lizzie, the kids, even the greyhounds, were forgotten.

For the next few weeks Bobby went around with his head in the clouds. Lizzie would speak to him, but he did not seem to hear her.

'I honestly think you're going deaf, Bobby. Twice I asked you a question and you didn't answer me.'

'Sorry, duchess, got a lot on my mind.'

Lizzie began to look at him askance. When she washed his shirts she noticed that they smelled of heavy perfume, something like Chanel. Lizzie herself never indulged in expensive perfume, but stuck to April Violet.

'It's me aftershave,' said Bobby, when she asked him about it.

'Aftershave!' she was incredulous. In Lizzie's day the men smelled of tobacco and perspiration and no one worried.

'I must say it's coming to something when men wear scent,' she said.

'Lizzie, it's a different world out there. After all, I am an up and coming businessman.'

'Oh well, I suppose you're right.'

But she was not convinced. Last week he had been away for four nights out of five and had not come home till noon the next day. He was beginning to look a bit careworn, was short-tempered with the kids, and never even gave Lizzie a kiss. She tried to dismiss from her mind the possibility that she might have a rival. She realized that some woman might have got a hold on him. Lizzie recalled the girl in the Blitz, and how upset she had been. This time she would just be patient and not do anything; time would tell.

At the end of the month Charlie got his first leave. He arrived, looking very fit and smart in his battle dress and forage cap; the outdoor life seemed to suit him. There were candies for the kids and a little broach with a Devon scene on it for Aunt Lizzie.

Charlie talked of the army and the pals he had made. 'Me outfit's off to Germany next week. Always wanted to travel abroad. I'm really looking forward to it.'

After a good tea, Charlie said, 'I think I'll pop up to Clapton dogs and rout out Uncle Bobby. Only got a weekend pass. Don't want to waste it.'

'Don't let him get you drunk, Charlie,' warned Lizzie.

But Charlie just laughed, put on his forage cap and said, 'So long. See you later.'

When Charlie arrived, Bobby was already installed in the bar and with him was a lovely blonde girl. Charlie came shyly up to them and Bobby said, 'Why, if it ain't Charlie-boy! Come and have a drink.'

Bobby was slightly drunk and in a very festive mood. Charlie looked appraisingly at the young blonde with her silvery hair and smart, expensive suit. He recognized her after a few moments, but she eyed Charlie coldly and did not speak.

Bobby came back with the drinks. 'You've met Dinny before; Pat O'Keefe's daughter,' he said casually.

Charlie shook hands, trying to hide his surprise. He could not understand Uncle Bobby's attentiveness. It wasn't like him. Charlie had heard him talk endlessly of dogs and horses but never about women. What was this smart, icy young woman to big, blustery Bobby Erlock? Hadn't Bobby once called her a bitch?

After a few drinks Charlie became acutely aware that an atmosphere was building up. As soon as the bar started closing Bobby held out some notes to Charlie: 'Get a cab home, boy. I've got a bit of business to settle.'

Charlie was very disappointed. He had looked forward to a night out on the town. He instantly refused the money. 'I'll manage to get that last bus,' he said as he walked away.

As he was standing at the bus stop a taxi passed him travelling up west, and it carried two passengers: Uncle Bobby and the young blonde — locked in a close embrace. Charlie stiffened, it was as if someone had dealt him a physical blow.

Lizzie had waited up for him and sat with her elbows on the kitchen table, a big pile of freshly ironed clothes beside her.

'Hullo. See Bobby?' she asked.

'Yes, Aunt Lizzie, he'll be along later,' Charlie said in a muffled voice, and went on up to bed.

That's not like him, he's always one for a chat, thought Lizzie, but perhaps he's tired. She immediately put out the light and went up to bed. As she passed Charlie's bedroom she could hear him tossing restlessly, then she heard a strange sound like a sob.

She crept in softly to his room to investigate, put her hand on his head and asked, 'What is it, love? Tell Aunt Lizzie. Is it a girl that's upset you?'

'No. I am crying because of you. That bastard Bobby, why didn't you warn me?'

'Warn you about what?'

'Him and that Dinaper O'Keefe. Bloody little bitch.'

Lizzie sighed.

'Oh, Aunt Lizzie, I'm sorry if you didn't know. What have I said?'

'It's all right, Charlie, I did know, but I wasn't sure who.'

'When I see him again I'll kill him. I had such great respect for him, and I shan't ever forgive him for doing that to you.' His voice broke with sorrow.

Lizzie cuddled him. 'No Charlie-boy, it takes all kinds to make this lousy world, and we just got to live in it the best way we can.'

'What will you do, Aunt Lizzie? I'm going abroad. There'll be no one to look after you and the kids.'

'It's not that serious. Bobby's done it before. Bobby's like a big kid, that's why I feel so responsible for him. So Charlie-boy, don't worry, I'll handle it.' She smiled her gentle smile in the darkness. 'The last time it happened and I found out, I beat his bird with broom. But such a lot of water has flowed under the bridge since then that I'll not interfere this time.'

'You are a real champion, Aunt Lizzie.'

'Now go to sleep.' Lizzie kissed him on the forehead.

Later Lizzie would recall the careworn expression on young Charlie's face, as he stood in the doorway with his kitbag and all the other odds and ends of army equipment.

'Oh Aunt Lizzie, I don't like to leave you!' he cried.

The errant Bobby had still not arrived home, although it was six o'clock on Sunday evening. Charlie was due back at camp at ten o'clock, and he still had to travel to Aldershot.

Lizzie looked with great concern at Charlie's troubled face. 'Now Charlie, be a good boy and go back to camp. I can handle Uncle Bobby. There's no need for you to worry over me. I've got the kids for company and I'm quite capable of handling my own affairs, so don't spoil your own life.' She stood on tiptoe to kiss his cheek and he clasped her in his arms with great affection.

'OK, Aunt Lizzie. But let me know how it goes with you. So long, kids.'

'Have your supper and go to bed, there's good kids,' Lizzie said, after he had gone.

Once they were all asleep she sat in her usual position beside the kitchen table, which was littered with children's debris, paint books, pencils and empty cups. With her chin cupped in her hands, she sat dreaming. After a while she got up, fetched a small hand mirror and looked contemplatively into it. Her small face was white and rather drawn. Yes, it was true, she was really beginning to look her age; her hair was still a nice bright colour but constant home bleaching had made it dry and brittle, and it was long and untidy. They wore their hair much shorter these days. She examined her skin critically; that was still nice and soft without many wrinkles, for she had always taken good care of it. She had also spent a lot of time on her hands which sparkled with lovely rings.

Thoughtfully she fingered the earrings that her Mum had given her. In spite of all the hard times Lizzie had never taken them out of her ears and she never would. Tears came into her brown eyes. She could still see her Mum sitting outside the hospital with a basket of blooms to sell. But crying over the past wouldn't bring Bobby back. Lizzie wiped her eyes. How could she compete with Dinaper O'Keefe, who had been a beauty even as a child, with her milk-white skin and soft, light hair? She was not much of a bargain herself at thirty-two, just a faded old hag. Bobby, still looked young, all six foot two of him. Now that he had put on weight Lizzie thought him really magnificent. Such a man was bound to attract younger women.

She thought about confronting Dinaper and realized that she couldn't do it. Usually she could cope with problems, but this one really perplexed her. She simply could not bear to think of them in bed together, although she realized that sex was probably at the bottom of it all. Lizzie was still deeply prudish, and the trouble was that when she and Bobby did not make love, she didn't really miss it. For the first time Lizzie began to think that she might be a genuinely cold person and to realize that Bobby had probably always wanted a lot more than she could give – even though he needed her to look after him.

If that was true how could she blame him? After all, he had forged a living and looked after the kids. Most important of all he had defended her from Sallie. Why should she risk losing him? No, he was kind and cheerful, and she would make no fuss. Having made up her mind, Lizzie returned the mirror to the dresser drawer, got up and busied about, saying to herself, 'Must get the kids' things ready for school in the morning.'

At one thirty in the morning, when Bobby came in, she was still ironing.

'Still working, Liz? Why ain't you in bed?' he asked.

'I wasn't tired,' she said amiably. 'Had a good weekend?'

'Not bad. There's some lolly on the shelf for you. I'm going up to bed.

Lizzie followed him upstairs later. She smiled to herself as she crept in beside him. He lay on his back, snoring like an old badger. He was obviously feeling the effects of his randy way of life. Even Bobby wasn't getting any younger.

CHAPTER NINE

The Irish Journey

Not long after this Mr Blew, the vicar, called on Lizzie for an afternoon cup of tea. He was a small, fair man with a pair of steel-rimmed specs perched on the end of a little turned-up nose.

'I was wondering if you would like to join our women's guild,' he said. 'We have recently gathered some very nice young women — the aftermath of the war, you know — and the parish needs a little resettling.'

Lizzie looked at him very curiously. She had never seen a vicar so close up before. Her Mum had never trusted church-goers and always steered clear of them. But this one was very good to Maisie and Robin, and they were exceedingly fond of him. He kept them occupied and stopped them running about the streets. Lizzie was very grateful for that, but her grass roots were too strong to let her unbend.

'Sorry,' she said, 'I don't mix very well. I like to keep myself to myself.'

'That's a pity,' he replied. 'By the way, Maisie tells me that you are her aunt, not her mother. I was rather surprised.'

'Oh that's a long story,' replied Lizzie, closing up like an oyster. She had no intention of putting him in the picture, so Mr Blew was forced to go away unrewarded and did not call any more.

Lizzie had adapted herself fairly well to this still very middle class district with its Victorian houses and big church, even though it was rapidly changing as the blitzed houses were reconditioned and turned over to the homeless. Some had been pulled down completely and huge blocks of flats erected in their place. She spent her time going back and forth to the school to meet the children. She had Carol for company all day, who played happily with her dolls, making up names and chattering to them. At four and a half years old she was a lovely child, and Lizzie worshipped her. She kept trying to persuade Bobby to adopt her legally but Bobby would not be pinned down to such a tedious thing. Although he loved Carol and was very proud of her, he kept putting off the moment of going to see the Child Welfare. He had an inner dread of authority that was his birthright, and it held him back. Of course he was still a gambling man and lately he had taken to a new kind of punting called the football pools. Uncle Bobby's new enthusiasm was a source of amusement to one and all. On Monday nights he sat studying form, as he called putting little crosses down on the coupon, then he left instructions for Lizzie to post them before Wednesday. 'Don't forget, Lizzie. If we get a good pools win we are made for life.'

On Saturday evening the kids had to sit very quiet while he listened to the pools forecast, then, with a big sigh of disappointment, he would say, 'Never mind, better luck next week.'

Religiously every Monday morning, Lizzie took the coupon to the Post Office, got a postal order and sent it off, then put the cheque which Charlie's boss had sent into a separate Post Office account.

Bobby would inform his pals, 'Can always trust Lizzie to do things regularly. When she has something to do she never forgets.'

He would say brightly on Tuesday, 'Posted me pools, Liz?'

'You know I have,' she grumbled.

Sometimes he would say to her, 'Come on, Lizzie, have a flutter. Give us a couple of bob and put a couple of crosses down here. You could end up in the big money.'

'I don't like gambling.'

'Come on, get yer lolly out, don't keep hoarding it.'

So eventually she gave in and invested two bob a week in the new venture.

Charlie was still out in Germany and wrote long letters to Lizzie which never even mentioned Uncle Bobby.

Bobby said, 'He's getting a bumptious sod. It's all that army bullshit doing it to him.'

But Lizzie, who was very proud of Charlie and had a photo of him in uniform stuck up on the mantelpiece, knew it was to hide his hurt feelings, for Bobby and Charlie had been real pals.

Lately Bobby had come home fairly early at weekends and often spent evenings at home with the family, when he larked with the kids and baked chestnuts on the open fire. Lizzie looked at him and wondered if the affair with Dinaper was over. Bobby was kind, but still strangely remote, so she wasn't really surprised when in the spring he suddenly announced that he was going away to Ireland. 'Going with Pat to see a greyhound. It's a good dog but I'll be gone a couple of weeks. Will you be OK?'

She looked at him closely. Dinaper had obviously gone home; that was why Bobby had been spending more time with them. But now he was going out to Ireland to be with her, and it hurt like a knife sticking in her heart.

For a week Lizzie was very depressed, Bobby bought brand new suitcases and insisted that she iron his socks flat. Before he could not have cared less if his socks were rolled into a ball. Lizzie was overwhelmed with grief; that one demand had told her that Bobby was a changed man. He bought silk underwear, pyjamas and fancy shirts. He stowed them away tidily in the suitcases with such bland indifference that she wanted to scream out at him, 'I know what you are up to, Bobby,' but she never did. Suppose he never came back, what would she do? She carried her wounded heart silently and listened to his lies about the famous dog kennel he was going to visit. She knew that Pat O'Keefe's health was failing and very much doubted if he was going.

At last Bobby gave her a good peck on the cheek and breezed off in a taxi, dressed in his brand new tweed suit and carrying his smart luggage. Lizzie closed the door then sat down and wept the tears she had held back so long.

'Where's he gone?' demanded the kids.

'Only on a holiday.'

'Why ain't we going on holiday?' asked Robin.

'Aunt Lizzie likes to stay home. She don't like to go on holidays. It's all right, we'll stay with you,' said Maisie. 'Mr Blew is taking us all to the zoo tomorrow.'

'I'll make some nice cakes you can take with you,' said Lizzie, getting up and wiping the tears from her eyes.

The next day the house seemed very lonely. Carol was a little off colour and slept most of the day. Then in the afternoon there was a loud knock at the front door. Lizzie opened it timidly, to see Sallie, standing on the doorstep, loaded with bags and bundles. Beside her were the two pale-faced little boys who stared up at Lizzie wide-eyed from beneath their tousled locks.

'Oh Lizzie,' wailed Sallie. 'I've been chucked out.'

'Oh dear,' cried Lizzie. 'Come in, Sal.'

'Got nowhere else to go,' grizzled Sallie. 'You are my only sister, who else can I go to?'

Lizzie placidly washed the little boys' hands, then gave each of them a cake and said, 'Now go and play with Carol. She's upstairs.'

'Now, Sal, tell me what happened. I've got the kettle on.'

Sallie said, 'Thanks, Liz, but you know I never married that bloke, and it was his house. Now his wife has claimed half, so he sold it and they evicted me. Oh dear,' she started to cry again.

Lizzie handed her a hot cup of tea. 'Well I suppose you'll have to stay here till you get something. Can't see those little boys without a place to sleep.'

'But Bobby! What will Bobby say?' gasped Sallie.

'Never mind him. You're my own flesh and blood; our Mum wouldn't have turned you out. Make do tonight, and tomorrow we'll send for your bits and pieces and see if we can't make it a bit homely for you on the top floor.'

Sallie threw her arms about Lizzie. 'I'll not forget, Lizzie. You're a great person, with a heart of gold.' Lizzie felt a warm glow. Here was someone who needed her, not to mention those poor little boys, who looked as if they could do with a good feed.

So for the time being Bobby was forgotten. The next day a van brought the remains of Sallie's home and the day was spent making the two rooms at the top of the house habitable, and the children played happily together.

Lizzie said, 'You can get a job if you like, Sallie. The boys will be all right with me. It'll get you on your feet.'

'That's a great idea, Lizzie. But what about Bobby. What will he do when he comes home?'

Lizzie sat with her elbows on the table, chin in her hands, 'I don't know if Bobby is coming home,' she said.

Bobby was suffering. The rough Irish sea crossing was more than he had bargained for. He had eaten and drunk his fill before boarding the SS *Innisfallen*, which was packed tight with patriots going home on leave. Many were big Irishmen who worked on the roads. Quarrels and fights broke out, of course, but many were so sick that they lay in their own vomit. Bobby stowed himself away in a second class cabin until dawn, when the green shores of Ireland came into view; never had he been so glad to be on land again.

Dinaper had written a letter to remind him, 'You promised to come over in the spring, Bobby, and I am looking forward to seeing you. I've got everything laid on, so don't worry.' A call from Dinaper was like a royal command, for Bobby was still totally obsessed with her.

She was there to greet him in a smart tweed suit and jaunty felt hat. She held out her dainty grey-gloved hand to him, with the air of a queen.

'How delightful. You did come.' So cold, calm and cool.

Bobby wanted to kiss and hug her but knew he was being warned to restrain himself.

She drove out into the country in her small red sports car, and they booked into a cosy hotel.

'Never know who's getting off the boat, Bobby,' she said. 'This isn't like England. But now, my lover, I'm all yours.' Gracefully she took off her smart jacket, while Bobby's eyes admired the high moulded breasts under her white embroidered blouse.

She held out her arms and Bobby went to her.

'Oh!' he cried, 'how I've longed for this moment.'

They spent most of that evening making love, then they went down to dinner and ate huge slices of salmon, which Bobby had never tasted before. Then back upstairs to a world of silk, perfume and more passionate lovemaking.

On Sunday morning she said, 'We had better book out this morning and I'll take you into Cork to a commercial hotel. It'll be cheaper for you and you will feel more comfortable.'

'Why? Where are you going?' he asked a trifle dejectedly, feeling that he was being organized.

'I have to show up at home you know. Edward, my husband, is in Ireland. I'd like you to meet him, so I'll try and arrange something.'

'Hey! Turn it up, Dinny,' shouted Bobby in his old tone. 'You ain't getting me mixed up with your old man. What sort of ponce do you take me for?'

Dinny looked angry. 'No need for such coarseness, Bobby. I'm doing what is best for both of us.'

'No thanks, I'll go home. I ain't sticking my neck out.'

But she kissed, fondled and sweet-talked him into staying.

'Edward is a gentleman and can be very useful to you, Bobby. I've told him you are my father's agent and that you have come over to see some dogs and horses in training. He knows father isn't well.'

'And Pat comes every year for the racing in Kerry,' Bobby retorted.

'Now, Bobby, don't be foolish.'

'I feel sorry for your old man. Poor sod.'

'You're not in the East End now, so do try to behave yourself,' she implored.

Dinaper took Bobby with his luggage to a hotel in the city, then drove off and left him. Bobby was not very happy but at least there was a nice big bar in the hotel which was filled with men who talked of racing, and farmers up for some kind of convention. Once he settled into his room, Bobby changed, washed and went down to join the drinkers. The men were civil and the service was good, so Bobby never knew the evening was over till he staggered up to bed. At midday, he was just coming round when the phone rang. It was Dinaper.

'Make yourself look nice this evening, Bobby, I'm taking you out to dinner. I'll meet you outside the hotel at seven o'clock.'

She wore a low-cut evening gown of silvery blue and a fur jacket, and her hair was set in a new style.

'You certainly look smart,' he told her.

'Well one has to keep up appearances out here. Whatever you may think of the Irish, they have a fairly respectable society.'

'I'm not sure I can stand it,' complained Bobby. 'Sorry I ain't got a monkey suit. I've never wore one yet.'

She looked at him curiously. 'Oh, evening dress; the men don't bother, and that's a good suit you have on.' She gave a slow smile. 'You'll pass, Bobby. In fact I might find it a bit difficult to hang on to you. You will behave yourself, dear, just for my sake?'

On the way they picked up another couple. This time Dinaper was driving a long gleaming saloon that Bobby liked very much. 'What is it?' he inquired.

'Oh, this is Edward's car. I usually drive him.'

The couple they picked up were a couple of goofy gigglers, a young woman and a man who talked so fast that Bobby didn't understand him.

'This is Jack and Dodi, she is an old school pal of mine,' said Dinaper.

They drove out of town up a high hill to where a big white stone house stood overlooking the harbour.

'This is where we live when in town,' she said. 'It's a swish part of Cork called Montenotte.'

It was a big house and they entered it through a lovely garden. The scent of flowers was everywhere and there were long high-ceilinged rooms. It was a clear starlit night and you could see the river and the lights of the boats as they sailed out to sea. Bobby was impressed most by the room lined with books and prints of famous horses. While he was admiring it, a small very spruce man entered and held out a firm hand in welcome.

'This is my husband, Edward O'Leary,' Dinaper said coolly. 'This is Daddy's agent from England, Mr Bobby Erlock. He's come over for the racing. Poor Daddy wasn't well enough this year.'

'Pleased to meet you. Have a drink.'

And from that moment onward Edward took to Bobby and Bobby liked him back. Over a well served dinner they talked of dogs and horses. Dinaper was very quiet and took little notice of Bobby, but entertained her other guests. There was a priest, an old couple who were related to Edward, Dinaper's schoolfriends and the fast-talking fellow who got drunk very easily.

Bobby really enjoyed himself. Over and over in his mind went the words: 'Well, this is real living. Wait till I've made a packet. This is the kind of house I'd like.'

Bobby addressed Edward repeatedly as the guv'nor, which amused Edward.

'I've got some good stock out in my training stables. As a matter of fact I've got a cert for Aintree; belongs to the actor Tom Walls.'

Bobby was home and dry; he had always yearned to be one of the racing elite and now he was being handed the opportunity on a plate.

'Have to drive out there tomorrow to pick up a young jockey. Will you come with us, Bobby?'

'I certainly will,' said Bobby. Then full of good Irish whiskey and excellent food he told humorous tales of the London dog track.

Edward laughed heartily and said, 'See if you can arrange for Bobby to stay overnight, Dinny, then we can all make an early start in the morning.'

'I'll see what I can do,' said Dinny rather icily, and that was the last Bobby saw of her.

At two o'clock a manservant tried to get both Edward and

Bobby upstairs to bed but they were loudly singing, 'Cheer up my lads, bless 'em all, the long, the short and the tall.'

In the morning Bobby woke up in strange surroundings and felt extremely guilty, convinced that he had really let himself down. He rose and took a shower, then he went downstairs. No one was about, the house seemed very silent and he stood out on the patio looking down over the river. The gulls were swooping down over the river and there was a splendid view of the bay. It was so high up that the air almost took his breath away. He stood very still and held on to the silence; how lucky some folk were. His mind went back to the slum streets, to the crammed dwellings and the crowded streets. It was obvious that money made all this luxury possible; money the one essential of life.

Bobby's reverie was interrupted by the sight of Edward striding briskly towards him, clad in a smart riding habit.

'Morning, Bobby. How do you feel? Just had my morning constitutional; always ride every morning. Can't get through the day without it. What about some breakfast? We'll eat out here. Dinny has gone to church, I expect; she often does first thing.'

Bobby was again very surprised but made no comment.

Breakfast was a jolly meal, eggs and bacon, with lots of coffee laced with whiskey, and once more the conversation was of dogs and horses.

Bobby felt a bit gloomy. He tried to imagine what Edward would say if he knew about himself and Dinny. It did not bear thinking of; Edward was such a charming, good-hearted gentleman. Bobby's conscience was playing hell with him. Well, he had better head for home tomorrow. Dinny seemed to have cooled off, might as well let sleeping dogs lie.

Dinny arrived about mid-morning carrying a picnic basket. 'Are we well this morning, Bobby?' she asked brightly.

Bobby looked at her like a sick dog.

'Our friend has got a big hangover,' jested Edward. 'We rather overdid it last night.'

'Oh well, get ready. The drive will do you good,' she said briskly.

So they climbed once more into the long cream-coloured Sunbeam. In town they picked up a very small fellow with a wide grin and a very red face.

'This is Tim, my top jockey,' said Edward. 'We are starting a few trials later this week.'

They sped through the lovely Irish countryside, cool misty and very green with its high hills and deep valleys, Bobby had never seen such rural beauty before. As a matter of fact he never noticed the countryside at all when he travelled through England on trains with Pat. He was usually involved in a card game and never even looked out of the windows while the countryside rushed past. But this was different, purring along in an expensive car steered by the slim hands of sweet-smelling Dinny along the white winding roads, over the dark hills patched with blues and greens. The smooth, rolling, emerald meadowland shrouded by the low, hanging misty clouds, excited him. This was real living.

'You're very quiet, Bobby. Like a drink?' asked Edward who sat with the cocktail cabinet opened in front of him.

'I'm OK,' replied Bobby. 'Just thinking that as a kid, the highlight of the year was one trip to lousy Loughton with the Sunday School treat.'

'It must have been very hard in London during the depression. One cannot really visualize it. I went to Sandhurst after Eton and then to the war, so I knew very little about that sort of thing. But I can assure you, Bobby, it has always had my sympathy and I feel sure that the life of the poor will vastly improve. What did you think of the Lord Nuffield scheme?'

'Well, I ain't no politician,' replied Bobby. 'If he's a bleeding lord, I ain't got no sodding time for him.'

The small jockey Tim went off into a cascade of hoarse cackles and Edward fell silent, while Dinny's silvery cool voice said lightly, 'Nearly there.'

Bobby looked down the road towards a low-lying modern bungalow and at the sleek horses in the paddock.

'This is Innaslee, our country home, Bobby,' said Edward. 'Like it? Got some fine blood stock in training here.'

Once more he was overwhelmed by the ease and comfort of

the place. He toured the stables with Edward, who suggested that he might like to ride with him in the morning.

'Sorry, guv'nor, I can't,' said Bobby.

'Well it's not difficult. I can find you a nice quiet mount.'

'No, no,' grinned Bobby. 'That horse, poor sod, ain't never gonner carry a big bloke like me.'

Once more Edward was very amused and they retired indoors to drink whiskey till nightfall. Because the house was quite small, various chalets had been built in the grounds to accommodate guests.

'Might have to bed down in one of those chalets. There isn't a lot of sleeping room inside the bungalow. I got those chalets put up especially for visitors and they're quite comfortable,' said Dinny in that same cold, indifferent manner.

Bobby was puzzled, but said nothing.

It was well after midnight when Dinny found him. She slipped very quietly inside his chalet, attired in a white silk robe.

'Blimey!' cried Bobby, 'I thought it was a bloody ghost.'

She sidled up, put her arms about his neck and pressed her body close.

'Crikey, Dinny!' he cried. 'You're taking a chance. What about the old man?'

'Oh, Edward is very drunk and has been put to bed,' she said, slipping off the robe. She stood there in a see through white nightie, the nipples in her well formed breasts visible, her body hot and anxious for love.

Bobby buried his head in her bare shoulder. 'Oh Dinny, I feel such a bastard.'

'Not to worry,' she whispered. 'Love me, Bobby. I've missed you so.'

What could a fellow do? She left just before dawn, neither of them having had much sleep, for it had been a night of almost continuous love.

'Edward might ask you to go with him to Dublin, Bobby. Make some excuse and stay here with me,' Dinny had said.

'Oh no, I won't do that. I like the fellow, I won't stick my neck out.'

'Oh, he is convinced you are a racing friend of my father. He has no idea about us.'

'All the same, he's treated me very well. I am not sure I can go on with this, Dinny. I'll go back home tomorrow.'

'Ah well,' she said sulkily. 'That is up to you.' And swept out, her white silk robe trailing on the floor.

So Bobby kept Edward company and went to Dublin to meet various influential people. Edward and he got on very well together and the days ticked by. Before he knew it he had been there nearly a week, and he began to think of going home.

At the weekend they drove back to Montenotte. Edward announced that they were taking a trip to the States. 'Come with us. That's good horse country, and racing dogs are the coming thing out there.'

'Thanks all the same; it's a nice thought, but I've too many commitments in England.'

Dinny shot Bobby a very sullen look.

That afternoon, when Edward had gone off to Cork on some business, Bobby sat in the cool patio that looked out over the harbour. Dinny came out to sit with him, dressed in a strapless sundress and a lovely powder blue handmade shawl draped over her white shoulders.

Bobby sat drinking, as he had most of the time since he reached Ireland. The small table was always filled up with bottles and glasses, replenished by the soft-footed servants. Bobby looked at Dinny. She fitted so perfectly into the surroundings, despite being East End born.

'I pull up stakes tomorrow,' he said to her.

She looked at him curiously, not always catching on at once to his cockney slang. 'Leave me, Bobby? Why? There is no reason for you not to travel with us to the States.'

'Now turn it up, Dinny. You know I've got a wife and family at home,' he replied tactlessly.

Dinny turned like a spitting cat. 'Oh go,' she cried, 'go back to that ugly old woman you're tied to.'

'Hey!' yelled Bobby. 'Don't you talk about Lizzie like that.'

'Oh dear,' sneered Dinny, 'we are getting fussy. Why, she looks like your mother.'

'Now, Dinny,' he said, 'I've warned you.' He got up a little unsteadily, the Irish whiskey taking a delayed effect.

'Why,' she cried, 'those children you support are not even your own! What responsibility have you got to them?'

This was too much for Bobby. He took a swing at her and missed, knocked over the small table full of expensive crystal glasses, and they crashed on to the marble floor. He stood looking down horrified.

Dinny swept haughtily out of the room, and he heard her icy voice just outside the door commanding the servant girl to clear up the mess.

Bobby sank back in the comfortable cane chair and swallowed another whiskey. Oh dear, it was just as well he'd missed her. He had certainly done it this time. He watched the fat-bottomed young servant girl as she swept up the broken glass and wanted to touch her. He grinned and gave way to his impulse.

'Oh soir,' she cried with a giggle as she scuttled out of the room.

Bobby got up and swaggered out. He went upstairs, packed his bag, walked to the harbour and booked his passage home. The next day he walked into the big kitchen crowded with kids and was greeted by the smell of wet washing strung across the room.

Lizzie got up from the table and looked at him with a kind of incredulity.

'Well, Lizzie, old gel, I'm back.'

'Oh Bobby, you did come home,' said Lizzie in a trance-like manner.

Bobby plonked down his suitcase. 'Where did all these bleeding kids come from?'

'Two of them are Sallie's boys,' she said timidly.

He threw his hat down onto the table. Lizzie picked it up, dusted it in a tender way, then hung it up behind the door.

'Don't tell me that fat, lazy cow, your sister, has dumped two more kids on you!' he yelled.

'They had nowhere to go,' said Lizzie very quietly. 'And that's not all. I let the two rooms upstairs to Sallie.'

'Oh Christ, Lizzie, you're a bigger mug than I thought,' he said. 'Come on, make us a cup of tea, I'm parched. All that bloody Irish whiskey has dried me out.'

'Uncle Bobby is home,' Lizzie called out of the window to the kids and gave a slow, gentle smile as she put the kettle on.

CHAPTER TEN

The Accident

On Saturday night Bobby was back at Clapton, catching up with old acquaintances, and the tic-tac boys signalled all around the track, 'Look out, Bobby is back.'

Bobby was exceedingly happy when his dog called Irish Mick romped home at ten to one. It was a nice home-coming present, a little packet of lolly to give to Lizzie. She seemed remote lately; he thought that perhaps he might try to get round her, boost her up a bit. She was strange, was his Lizzie, there was no comparison between her and the glamorous Dinny, but at least he was sure of Lizzie. She did belong to him.

He began to turn over in his mind the recent events in Ireland, the conversations late into the night with the often well-boozed but gentlemanly Edward O'Leary. Now, there was a bloke who had made it. How long had it taken him? Bobby wondered.

'I don't know much about racing dogs,' Edward had said in his clipped accent, 'I am essentially a horse man myself.'

Bobby replied, 'Well, it's a working man's sport; not for the likes of you.'

Edward had lost his cool for a second. 'What exactly do you mean, Bobby? "Not for the likes of me", I'm not sure I like being categorized.'

'Well, no offence, but I reckon you're the guv'nor, like in the army. You couldn't be mates with an officer no matter how you liked him. It's kind of a fence — and that I learned when I was just a kid and in trouble with the law. That's how it is with dogs and horses. We both make the lolly from the mugs of punters but mine are my own kind.'

'I see you are also a good judge of character,' Edward had smiled at him and, relaxing a little, added, 'You know I love a well-bred animal. I wouldn't give you sixpence for a mongrel dog no matter how pleasant its nature was. And strangely enough that's how I like my women, a bitch that strays I'd shoot sooner than keep her.' There was a kind of wariness in his tone.

Completely sober, Bobby did not miss the insinuation. He was quite sure that Edward had meant his wife, Dinny, and was thus giving Bobby a kind of warning.

'Yes,' said Bobby to himself, as he turned the matter over. 'Edward is not such an idiot as Dinny thinks he is.' As for himself, he might be a mongrel, but he was no bloody fool. He had sussed that one out, so perhaps it was just as well he had hopped it back home. But it had been a grand experience, and he would remember it all his life. For a while after this the scene in Mortimer Road was cosy and domestic. Bobby still objected to Sallie and would often holler, 'Keep that fat cow out of my sight.'

But Sallie had mended her ways, got herself a job at the sweet factory, and kept to her own quarters when Bobby was home. She came home at four o'clock and Lizzie minded the little boys all day. They were company for Carol, who in turn bossed them around and played games which they called muvvers and farvers. Carol would ape Lizzie and order the two little boys about, and they loved her and fought each other for her favours. Sallie brought them back sweets which she had quietly dropped in her bag on her way out of the factory, and the small kids would run to greet her.

'Oh well,' sighed Lizzie. 'It's an ill wind that blows everyone harm, and Carol is so much more content with Paul and Derick to play with.'

'It might be a bloody miracle,' said Bobby, 'but it wouldn't surprise me if she started again off to the pub or bingo.'

At the weekends Sallie helped Lizzie to clean the big house, something Lizzie never seemed able to get around to doing. Lizzie was always washing and ironing all the pretty things and titivating herself. She always cooked a good meal. But for dusting and cleaning she would never find enough energy. Luckily Sallie was full of it, and on Saturday mornings she would scrub and dust all down the stairs even to the front doorsteps, singing and humming to herself as if she thoroughly enjoyed it all.

Sallie was always nagging Lizzie about her thrifty ways.

'Why don't you get a vacuum cleaner? That old carpet sweeper has had it.'

'No, I could never stand all that noise,' Lizzie would reply.

'Don't understand you. When was the last time you got your hair done? And what about these bloody old-fashioned dresses? Why, Lizzie, he gives you good money, I've heard you say so.'

Lizzie smiled in her gentle way. 'I like to put some away for a rainy day, Sallie. I've had bad times which I can't forget. If I can make do I will, as long as the kids don't go short.'

'All I can say is that you are bloody mad, and that one day you'll be sorry. I've had more rainy days than dry ones and I don't worry. That bloody Bobby don't miss nothing,' she muttered.

Lizzie pretended not to listen. Often her miserly habits would annoy Bobby. She would hide money everywhere, and the Toby jug remained empty because that was too handy if Bobby ran short of ready cash. Bobby spent money like water, treated the kids to all they wanted, and took himself out to the gambling clubs up West on Saturday nights.

That year, when Carol was five, the legal adoption papers were signed and at last Lizzie had a child of her own. Bobby loved her, she was so pretty with her dark blue eyes and black curly hair. He would lift her high into the air and say to her, 'Say Daddy.'

'No, Uncle Bobby,' she invariably said, 'put me down.'

Bobby was not offended, he laughed uproariously. 'She's got a mind of her own,' he would say proudly. 'Come on, kids, let's all go over the fields.'

Robin was tall and very active and Maisie still plump and very precise in her manner, while Sallie's boys Paul and Derick were two terrors. They had lost their pale and spindly look and really filled out.

Lizzie would watch proudly as they all went with Bobby to the Highbury Fields, but she did not once offer to join them.

Bobby carried Carol on his back and galloped along like a horse on his strong, long legs, his hair blowing in the breeze.

'He's such a little boy at heart, my Bobby,' Lizzie said fondly.

Sallie replied suspiciously, 'He's a big boy everywhere else, or haven't you noticed?'

But Lizzie would not let her mind dwell on such things.

That year the three youngest children went to school. Lizzie would escort them all to the door, then give them all a kiss and go off to do her shopping. Once back home she would make rice pudding and suet pudding and have their lunch ready at twelve o'clock. Then she would bring them home at four o'clock, and in this way her days were very full.

Maisie would say, 'I'll take the kids, Aunt Lizzie. No need for you to trot up to the school.'

'No dear, I like going, and I'm afraid of the roads. You know what Paul and Derick are.'

Lizzie would trot along in a leisurely way with all the kids around her and she became a kind of landmark in the district.

Every Tuesday she stopped off at the Post Office on her way home, put Charlie boy's cheque in his account, bought savings certificates for the children and then posted Bobby's pools.

Lately Sallie had been going out at night. She had bought herself new dresses, long earrings and lots of make up.

'I've got to have a bloody break, Lizzie. It's all right for you. You seem to keep busy. I feel like going mad stuck up in that poky set of rooms all the evening.'

'Please yourself, Sallie; the boys are all right. I never leave the house after dark.'

The boys played their mother up. They tormented her, wreaked havoc with her beads and earrings, put lipstick on their faces and played cowboys and indians. She often chased them downstairs, screeching, 'Bloody little gits, wait till I get my hands on you.'

Lizzie would stand severely before her. 'Sallie, you don't put a hand on them children while you are in my house.'

'Oh get on with spoiling them, the little bleeders.' And Sallie would flounce back upstairs.

They were a couple of imps and badly needed to be chastised. A note was often sent home from school with them complaining about their fighting. They tore wildly around the house making more noise than any of the other children, but Lizzie, by some strong sort of instinct, was able to handle them, and they loved her.

Bobby was down on his luck once more. He had sold two of his greyhounds, had one in litter, and the only runner was a loser most nights, so Lizzie hid her money more carefully than ever and doled him out a few pounds at a time. Bobby was a trifle disheartened.

'It's only temporary, Lizzie. My luck will turn soon,' he said.

'I'm glad you think so,' she replied a little bitterly.

Then one night, at the Clapton dog track, someone handed him a note that had been left at the office for him. It was addressed in a nice neat hand and written on perfumed stationery. Who else could it be from but Dinny? 'Dear Bobby,' he read. 'How are you? We are now back from the States. It was a good trip. I wondered if you would be at Aintree in a few weeks time. Edward is taking a party over; you would be most welcome to join us. Love, Dinny.'

'Oh, the olive branch; she wants to make it up.' Bobby was jubilant. Even if his luck was out with the dogs, it seemed it was in with women. 'Oh well,' he thought, 'slow dogs and fast women. The story of my life.' He grinned to himself and immediately began to turn over in his mind plans for a trip to Liverpool. It was the Grand National. Must be up for that. The Irish came over in boatloads; it would be a good week.

'Might take a chance on the National, Lizzie,' he said that week. 'Can get a job as tic-tac man up there. I know a few people.'

Lizzie had grown used to him always popping off somewhere and had no idea where Aintree was. 'How long will you be gone?'

'About three days. Back on Sunday night,' he assured her,

and packed his travelling case with the expensive after shave and his silk pyjamas.

'Pooh!' said Robin, sniffing around as Bobby packed. 'Don't that stuff pong.'

'In my day,' said Lizzie, 'men smelled like men.'

Bobby was grim and silent, determined not to be discouraged from taking this trip. He kissed Lizzie on the cheek. 'Bye, duchess, got all you want? I won't be long.'

Lizzie's brown eyes had tears in them. Was her Bobby at it again? Still it was no use worrying about him; she had too much to do. She sat down and wrote a long letter to Charlie, telling him that they would all be welcoming him home. Then she went to get the kids from school, and posted her letter.

The next morning she was a little down-hearted, so she decided to start moving the two boys' things out of Charlie's bedroom, which they had occupied since they arrived. She decided that she would move them into the small room to share with Robin, for Maisie really must have her own bedroom now that she was growing up. With these thoughts in mind, she kept herself busy cleaning. She painted it, she washed the curtains and spent most of Thursday making the room look nice for Charlie to come home to.

On Friday morning she hit a snag. She had decided to move the big old-fashioned wardrobe which the last tenant had left behind, so as to make room for another bed for the small boys. She pushed and pulled the huge piece of furniture and slowly it moved towards the door. Sweat was on her brow, but she would not give in. She had just succeeded in getting there when it got wedged in the doorway, trapping her in the room. It was nearly half past eleven; she must get up to the school. Panic-stricken she pushed and pulled, then suddenly it gave and fell on top of her, jamming her arm in the lintel of the door. With a gasp of pain she fell down, her breathing getting shallower as she faded into unconsciousness.

At twelve o'clock Maisie came out of the girls' school. The young children were still playing in the playground, but Aunt Lizzie was not there.

Aunt Lizzie was never late, so when Robin arrived, Maisie

said, 'I am going to take you all home.' She marshalled the small fry in her most authoritative manner.

When they reached the house, everything was very quiet. Maisie pulled the string on the latch and went in. No lunch was on the table and the fire was nearly out. Where was Aunt Lizzie? They all trooped upstairs and saw poor Aunt Lizzie's arm sticking out from under the wardrobe. All the younger kids started to cry.

'Take them downstairs, Robin,' said Maisie. 'I'll run up to Mr Blew to get help.'

Mr Blew always had time for Maisie, and when she burst in, shouting, 'Our Aunt Lizzie's had an accident. She's under the wardrobe,' he acted at once.

'I'll come along, but first let me telephone for an ambulance.'

Mr Blew went round to the house and waited while the ambulance men took Lizzie away. He then stayed with the children until Sallie came home.

'Oh my God!' cried Sallie, on hearing the news. 'She's not dead is she?'

'Not as far as I know,' replied Mr Blew. 'I could see that her arm had been badly damaged and may be broken.' He turned to Maisie. 'Well, I hope you'll keep in touch, Maisie,' and he patted her cheek.

'Thank you very much, Mr Blew.'

But Sallie said, 'Come on, kids, we had better try to find out how she is. So Robin, you can stay at home and mind the children, and give them some tea.'

Sallie took Maisie up to the Grays Inn Road Hospital to see Lizzie, but the nurses were noncommittal.

'Your sister is in Intensive Care. It could easily have been fatal. Did you know your sister had a weak heart?'

'No,' wept Sallie, 'but our Mum used to say that Lizzie was not very strong.'

'Well, she's recovering. Except for a broken arm she had no other injuries, but we are concerned about her. Where is her husband? He should be contacted.'

'Ow!' wept Sallie very loudly, and Maisie stood looking up

wide-eyed with fear, 'I don't know where he is. Off racing somewhere, won't be back till Sunday.'

'I think I'll put out a police call for him,' said the doctor. 'Now go home and don't worry. She'll be all right.'

Poor Sallie could not stop crying all the way home on the bus, but Maisie sat very solemn and dry-eyed. 'I wonder if our Aunt Lizzie is in heaven now.'

'Ow!' cried Sallie. 'Shut up, you morbid little cow.'

So that Saturday afternoon, just before the pools forecast, an urgent message was put out. 'Will Bobby Erlock, believed to be travelling to the racing at Aintree, please return, as his wife is dangerously ill in the Grays Inn Road Hospital, London.'

Bobby had gone into Liverpool and headed for the hotel bar where he hoped to meet a few old acquaintances. In the bar were Edward and Dinny with a crowd of friends. His heart jumped, she looked so lovely in her grey suit. Her skin was deeply tanned and her hair now shone like burnished gold.

'Oh Bobby, fancy meeting you here. How nice.'

Her sweet tones overwhelmed him.

'Look, Edward, here's our friend Bobby. What a pleasant surprise.'

Edward shook Bobby warmly by the hand. 'Order him a drink.' Then he introduced him to his friends. Among them was the London-born actor whose horse Edward had been training for the National. The party was fairly lively and part of the stake, which Bobby had been carefully keeping to put on the race, soon disappeared in the huge rounds of fancy drinks.

'We're going to have dinner at the club. Come with us, Bobby,' suggested Dinny, and by the longing look in her eyes he knew she was still hot for him. It hadn't been a waste of time coming after all. Once again Bobby was entertained royally and sent back to his hotel in a cab very drunk, but still Dinny had not made her move. Tomorrow was Saturday when the big race would be run; after that there'd be no more opportunity. On Friday morning Dinny arrived, knocked on his hotel bedroom door, having told the receptionist that she was his sister, and asked how he was after his night of heavy drinking.

Bobby crawled out of bed and opened the door. Dinny was wearing slacks and a woolly jumper, a chiffon scarf covered her hair and a pair of big coloured specs hid her eyes.

He gave a wide grin and held the door open for her. 'What's all this? In disguise?' he jested.

'Oh Bobby,' she cried, 'I was desperate. I had to take a chance and said I was going to early Mass . . .'

'Well, darling, you can come and confess to me,' he said, pulling her towards him. His chin was rough and whiskery and his breath very bad after the previous night's booze up, but beautiful, refined Dinaper could not have cared less and almost fell into bed with him. Stepping quickly out of her slacks and her fancy knickers, she wound herself about him.

'Oh Bobby, my lovely, lovely Bobby, I've missed you so much.'

They indulged themselves in their usual round of passionate lovemaking.

Bobby sighed, 'Oh Dinny, and I thought I had got over you.'

By mid-morning she pulled herself together. 'I'll see you at the meeting tomorrow, Bobby. I might not be able to make it any more this trip, but I promise I'll come to London soon to visit Dad.'

The next day was the big race. The crowd was immense and Bobby could not seem to keep in touch with Dinny. She was here and there and everywhere, being made a fuss of by the old actor who owned the favourite. But in the end an outsider won, so Bobby lost his last few pounds, and was left with just his return ticket to London.

That evening he was sitting in the hotel bar having a lone drink when he decided to listen to the wireless in order to check his football pools. Dinny and Edward came in with a party of people. She was very high and looked nervous when she caught sight of Bobby. He got out his paper, put it on the bar and waited for the news. There was a small silence, then the announcer's voice said, 'I have just been handed a police message. Will Mr Bobby Erlock, travelling possibly to Liverpool, please contact the Grays Inn Road Hospital where his wife Elizabeth is dangerously ill.'

Bobby, poised with pencil in hand suddenly gasped, 'Gawd blimey! That's my Lizzie!' He dashed through the bar, practically knocking Dinny over, and before midnight was sitting beside Lizzie, holding her hands.

'Oh Lizzie, old gel,' he whispered hoarsely, 'what the bloody hell have you been up to?'

She gave him a wan smile. 'Back the winner, Bobby?' she whispered.

'No I bleeding well did not, but Lizzie I got such a shock, I heard it on the wireless.'

She squeezed his hand. 'I'm all right, don't worry, love.'

'Oh Lizzie, how did you do it? Where was that silly cow, Sallie?'

'Now, Bobby,' she admonished, 'don't fuss. Just get me out of here as quickly as you can. I've only broken my arm. I can look after myself at home.'

'No, Lizzie, you must stay here and rest,' he urged her. 'I'll come in every day.'

'Who's going to look after the kids?'

'I will,' he said, 'and I'll get that Sallie working.'

Lizzie smiled. 'I want to come home, Bobby.'

When Bobby saw the doctor he said, 'You know we were very lucky with your wife. Just got her on to the respirator in time. Did you know she had a heart attack?'

Bobby was stunned. 'No, not Lizzie. She's as fit as a fiddle.'

'I am afraid she was born with a heart murmur and has slowly deteriorated. She must take life very easy when she leaves here.'

'Oh my Gawd, I just can't believe it. My poor Lizzie.'

Then, after discussing it all with Sallie, Bobby decided not to let Lizzie know just what was really the matter with her, and every night he was at the hospital with flowers, grapes and boxes of chocolates.

After two weeks, Lizzie, with her arm in plaster and a bit tottery on her legs, was brought back home.

'It will be advisable for her not to climb the stairs for a while. We have given her some tablets and until her system adjusts itself to them it would be wise to take great care of her,' the doctor told Bobby. 'Oh, and by the way, no sex activity for a time if you don't mind.'

Bobby looked ruefully at him. He could not remember the last time he had had sex with Lizzie. She never wanted it. Still, she was not entirely to blame. He had been a bit of a bastard. Well, it had taught him a lesson. From now on he would take good care of her, he vowed to himself.

All the kids welcomed Lizzie home with greetings cards and flowers and Lizzie was thrilled to see them all. Bobby, in his ham-handed manner, caused much noise and confusion by having a royal row with Sallie, telling her to give up her job and look after her own kids.

'Oh yes,' cried Sallie saucily, 'and who is going to support me? Because it's obvious you can't.'

Bobby liked to feel he was a big man and this really riled him.

'No, please don't quarrel,' pleaded Lizzie. 'Bobby, bring one of the single beds down from the spare room, and I'll rest down here during the day — I'll still be able to give eye to the kids. Let Sallie keep her job.'

So Bobby carried Lizzie down in the mornings and back up again at night. He became very domesticated, spending part of the day at home and never staying out all night.

Slowly but surely Lizzie recovered and became once more her old cheerful self. The family life began to revolve again. Robin and Maisie got the small kids ready and took them to school. Then Maisie did the shopping, Robin made the tea and the little ones played happily with Aunt Lizzie, who spent most of her time in bed, but always found time to play Ludo with them and told them fairy stories.

Sometimes Uncle Bobby cooked the dinner, and on Saturdays Sallie busily cleaned up the house with a big bucket and broom. So they all managed to survive, and became a very much more united family. Bobby was a changed man: to think that he had been romping about in bed with that bitch Dinaper, when his

Lizzie had been drawing almost her last breath. Never again; he felt so guilty. He would never go off the rails again, he vowed to himself.

Bobby sat beside the fire and mentally flayed his conscience. He even contemplated getting himself a steady job, so as not to leave Lizzie alone so much. His memory slipped back to when he was a nipper. No one had ever showed him any real affection and inside he was hard. It had embarrassed him to be soft. But, from now on he would put his home first, to hell with that bitch Dinny, and to hell with the dogs if it came to that.

So Bobby became a family man, and bathed the kids in the big tin bath out in the scullery on Saturday nights instead of going to the dogs. He then flogged his last greyhound to get enough money to keep them going, and Lizzie looked at him with a worried expression. It was nice to have him around but he was not happy.

CHAPTER ELEVEN

A Rift in the Family

'Not going to the dogs, Bobby?' Lizzie inquired one Saturday night.

'No,' he replied, 'I've chucked it in. Going to sign on the bleeding dole with all the other layabouts.'

So Lizzie began to get very worried. She had to keep doling out her money to feed them all and it wasn't easy. Gradually she had regained her health but she was considerably slower, quite pale, and inclined to weariness. Her arm was now out of the plaster cast and she had begun to potter about the house doing little odd jobs. It was great to be back home with the children all around her, and to be able once more to see the huge old gnarled sycamore tree in the unkempt garden. It still held Robin's swing, now owned by Paul, Derick and Carol. So many, many sunny days had been spent out in that garden watching the children at play. The thought that she had almost left it all behind her, made this home and its memories more precious to her than ever before.

To see her big moody husband mooching about the house all day unshaven, clad in an old pair of flannels and a greasy pullover with holes in it, bothered her quite a lot. Keeping the peace between him and Sallie was also a great trial to her. The Toby jug on the dresser was now empty and she had begun to draw on her savings. Bobby still did his pools regularly, and made Lizzie fill in her own coupon, and fork out a five shilling stake each week.

It was Maisie now who had strict instructions to post the pools on her way to school on Monday mornings. Lizzie was not interested; she did not like games of chance, but to keep the peace and to give Bobby something to keep him occupied, she agreed to do it.

'Get a big win on the pools, Lizzie, and we'll be made for life,' Bobby declared.

Lizzie was very sceptical. 'I don't hold with throwing good money after bad. Someone will get rich, but it won't be us.'

Yet she hated to complain at Bobby who was doing his level best to be a good husband to her. He did not go dog racing but popped out to the pub to put a bet on every day. He spent the rest of the time in her company and was kind and considerate, but strangely cold. He did not kiss and fuss her, and he had made no attempt whatever to make love to her since she came out of hospital.

One day she said, 'I know I've always been a cold fish, Bobby, but I am still alive, you know.'

He grew very red and very angry. 'Turn it up, Liz,' he said, 'I'm here all the time like some bleeding wet nurse, what else do you want?'

Tears formed in her eyes, but bravely she replied, 'I think you ought to go out a bit more, Bobby. At least you did bring in a few pounds, this way no one is getting anywhere.'

He shot a look at her almost of hatred, then snarled, 'Please yer bloody self,' picked up his cloth cap and went out over to Clapton in time for the big race. In no time he had linked up with the tic-tac boys, with his old friends and the bookies. Once more Bobby Erlock was in circulation.

Sallie's boys had grown tremendously. At six and seven their cheeks were rosy and their thin stick-like limbs were now sturdy. But still they were a couple of terrors. Both were very attached to Carol, who seemed to grow prettier every day, but was extremely spoilt, domineering, and had also begun to ask some very embarrassing questions.

'If Aunt Sallie is my grandmother and you are my aunt, who is my Mother?' she demanded.

Lizzie cuddled her close. 'I am your Mother and Uncle Bobby is really your father. You should by rights call us Mum and Dad.'

But this Carol disputed. 'Why? You didn't have me. I never came from your tummy, did I?'

'No dear,' Lizzie tried to explain gently, 'we have adopted you so now we are your legal parents. Your own dear Mummy was killed in the blitz.'

Carol scrutinized Lizzie with bewilderment in her large dark blue eyes, then said, 'Well, why does Paul say that him and Derick and me are all bastards?'

Lizzie was startled and very shocked. Sharply she put Carol from her. 'Go and get Paul. I'll talk to him,' she said angrily.

Paul, who was never far away from Carol, had been listening at the door and now scampered away.

'So,' Lizzie remarked later to Bobby, 'I was really flummoxed, I didn't know what to say. Such things to come out of the mouths of babes.'

Bobby sat studying his racing page and did not seem unduly disturbed. 'They're not babies,' he said, 'but growing kids and they're getting to know it all. Leave them alone, they'll suss things out for themselves.'

'Well perhaps you are right,' sniffed Lizzie, 'but I wish Carol did think of me as Mummy.'

That weekend Charlie-boy came home. Lizzie was thrilled to see him again. He was so tall and so straight, with his fair curly hair cut very short and a small fair moustache cordoning his upper lip. It shone golden, contrasting with his deep suntan. Oh how different was this youth to the little urchin who used to hang about outside the tube during the blitz, with ragged arse and no shoes. She recalled how he used to chase after the passers-by calling out, 'Gor a ha'penny, guv'nor,' and when the Yanks came, how it had been, 'Gor any gum, chum?'

Now Charlie spoke slowly and precisely in a high-pitched cockney slang, but pruned each word carefully. That night they held a family party with lots of sweets, cakes and lemonade. No alcohol, for Lizzie did not like the stuff in the house, and Maisie thoroughly disapproved of strong drink.

Only Bobby was absent, for Charlie had been a bit distant towards him. 'What, no bloody booze?' Bobby had said. 'I'll pop out and have one,' and he did not return.

When Sallie wanted to kiss and fuss her eldest son, Charlie coldly retreated, so Sallie just sat very quiet and did not join in the conversation. Lizzie could see that she was really hurt.

When all the rest of the family had retired Lizzie said to him, 'Charlie-boy you must not bear a grudge. Life's too short; it's better to forget and forgive.'

'I am sorry, Aunt Lizzie. I love you and I'm sorry for Sallie, but I can't acknowledge her as my mother, and as for Uncle Bobby, I'll always have a certain amount of contempt for him because of the way he's treated you.'

Lizzie gave a deep sigh of resignation. Charlie had a mind of his own, no one would ever persuade or rule him because he had come up the hard way.

'When I get out of the army in two months' time,' he went on, 'I'd like to get married. She's a Russian born girl but has lived in Germany since the war. She was in a concentration camp and her name is Luber.'

'I'm very happy for you, dear.'

'Of course I'm not sure she'll have me yet,' he said, in his very serious way. 'I've got a good job to return to, but I'll need to work hard to catch up now. I hope to get on to the publication side of the paper. I've had good experience being in the army mess office.'

'Oh I am sure that you will succeed, dear,' Lizzie said fondly.

'You know, Aunt Lizzie, it might not be easy to get Luber over here. She is a displaced person and has no passport. It might take time and money, and that worries me.'

'Well, Charlie, you needn't worry too much. I never touched your pay cheque. It's all in the Post Office waiting for you.'

'Oh, Aunt Lizzie, I'm really disappointed. I wanted to help you support the kids so much.'

'Never mind. I managed,' she said optimistically. 'Now it's all yours.'

He kissed her. 'I always said you had a heart of gold.'

She smiled. 'Yes, but unfortunately it's a dodgy one.'

'Oh don't say that. What would I do if I lost you?' he put his arms around her.

'I do,' she smiled. 'You'll marry this girl of your dreams while I'm still fit enough to enjoy a wedding.'

So Charlie-boy returned to Germany to finish out his time and Aunt Lizzie's final words were, 'Now don't forget, Charlie. Luber has a home with me until you can provide one for her.'

Later that year the news came that Charlie had married his love. The house buzzed with the news.

'We won't like her,' declared the small boys. 'We bet that she's a Nazi and is coming here to spy on us.'

'The war has been over a long time, boys,' Lizzie informed them. 'Also she is Russian, and they were on our side.'

Maisie in her dark, melancholy manner said, 'Will she be a Communist then? Because that's much worse, they don't believe in our Lord Jesus Christ.'

Sallie joined in, 'What a shame, he's much too young. Why, those German girls only click on to our boys so they can come over here.'

Robin said, 'Some of those German birds are pretty nifty. Dunno about Russians. Never seen one.'

'Oh please, children,' cried Lizzie, 'we've never seen the poor girl, and now she is a member of our family. Let's all be very nice to her.'

Yet when Lizzie thought of Germans, her mind heard the crump and thump of the bombs and she was filled with a kind of dismay, wondering if she could like Luber. After all she must be almost German, having lived there since she was a child. But for Charlie-boy's sake she would do her utmost to make her welcome.

When the day came Lizzie was most surprised to find that Luber was quite unattractive. She was short, under five foot, had black frizzy hair, high cheek-bones and small, deep-set dark eyes. But her wide friendly smile and strong, even white teeth seemed to cancel out her other defects. The hug, combined with her affectionate and friendly smile, drew Lizzie to her, and they immediately became friends. Charlie-boy treated his petite bride as if she were made of precious porcelain. She did not speak many English words but because she had worked in the forces canteen, she understood most of the conversation going on around her. Her smiles and warm gestures made her very popular with the family.

Bobby picked her up by her elbows and said, 'Blimey, ain't you a little sprat!'

She giggled, but Charlie's expression was angry and disapproving.

Despite this it went off very nicely on the whole. All Lizzie's family were now together and that pleased her very much. The Mortimer Road house was full almost to overflowing, Charlie's room had been redecorated and a new bed provided for the newly weds.

Luber became a very useful member of the small community, and spent the day at home with Lizzie, once Charlie had returned to his old job. She was very neat, clean and a marvellous cook. She made light of the hardest chores, and was always up early, always busy.

Sallie began to get very jealous of Luber. 'I don't believe in all that spit and polish,' she would complain loudly, for Sallie's methods of cleaning the house were very slapdash by comparison.

Maisie was still inclined to be a little suspicious of Luber, and the small boys tormented her, but Luber took it all in good part and was very attached to them.

'Now coom, you rest, put up the feets, Aunt Leezie,' Luber would insist when the kids went back to school after lunch. 'I vill vashun de boedens.'

Lizzie would laugh and say, 'You mean you will wash the dishes.'

In this way Lizzie acquired a few German-cum-Russian expressions and Luber many English words.

Slowly Luber lost her shyness and would hold long conversations in her broken English, telling Lizzie of her youth, of the day when she had worked late in her father's fields, when the Germans came, threw her into a lorry and she was driven off to a concentration camp.

'You know, Aunt Leezie,' she would say, her deep-set eyes wet with tears, 'my parents I have never seen since that day. They completely disappeared.'

'Oh don't look back, dear,' cried Lizzie. 'We all had a bad time in that lousy war, this is a grand country to live in and you are married to a fine, affectionate, ambitious boy.'

'I know, Aunt Leezie,' said Luber, coming forward to kiss her cheek.

Occasionally Luber would exclaim very loudly, 'Oh Gawd blimey,' with a pseudo-cockney twang and everyone would laugh.

Soon she began to take the children to school, and sometimes went shopping with Maisie; they made quite a comical sight — tiny Luber and the tall lanky girl who talked of nothing else but Jesus Christ and Mr Blew the vicar.

Every Saturday evening before leaving for the dog track, Bobby checked his pools coupon with the aid of the relay wireless. This was a recent addition to the house. The programme was transmitted from a kind of sub-station in a shop in the Main Road. Just before the news the monotonous voice of the announcer would give out the football results: Arsenal one, Tottenham Hotspur two, and so on.

Having ordered the kids to keep very quiet, Bobby ticked off the results. The little boys sat still, suppressing their giggles, while Luber fussed over Carol, brushing her lovely hair till it shone like glass, for Carol loved this sort of attention.

This particular Saturday Robin was out at the pictures while Maisie was doing her charity work for the church, so Lizzie sat beside that big coal fire in her armchair. It was a nice cosy domestic scene, until suddenly Bobby leaped up and yelled, 'Oh Gawd Blimey, Lizzie, yer drawers have come 'orf.'

Lizzie in amazement looked down at her feet.

'No, you silly cow!' roared Bobby. 'You've won the bleeding pools!'

On the day it was officially established that Lizzie had indeed the right amount of "drawers", she was presented with a ten thousand pound cheque and had her picture in the local paper. But the strange thing was that everyone was excited about the win except Lizzie. She just could not help feeling very disturbed about it all. There were continual discussions in the house about how she should spend the money. Listening to them

Lizzie thought of vultures squabbling over a carcass. All her life she had been very thrifty and dreaded gambling. So when Bobby announced, 'For half that dough, duchess, I could buy a fair stake in the new dog track they are building out at Walthamstow,' Lizzie was appalled. She just stared at him very oddly and did not reply.

In the end she decided to ask Charlie's advice. 'It bothers me this money. If Bobby gets his hands on it, it'll disappear,' she said anxiously.

'Take my advice, Aunt Lizzie, and stop worrying. Put it in the bank, then you can draw out the interest if you need it and still keep the capital.'

So Lizzie paid that big cheque into the bank and forgot about it. Everyone hung on, waiting for Aunt Lizzie to have a big spend up, but they could not have known her as well as they thought they did. When Bobby was out late at night and she was ironing the children's clothes, Lizzie promised herself that she would never let him spoil the stability she had created in her adopted family.

Charlie was doing well at his job and saving up to buy a house in the suburbs.

'When I make a home for mine kinder,' Luber would say, 'it must be good, happy and permanent one.'

That was the kind of talk Lizzie appreciated. Now that Maisie was out working all day in the Stationery Office and Robin about to leave school, she saw less reason than ever to change their mode of living.

'Miserly old cow,' Sallie would mutter behind Lizzie's back.

Bobby was most indignant. 'Lizzie, old gel, you've got a lucky streak. Don't hoard it.'

'The money is safer where it is.'

'When Lady Luck is with you, play it back. That's my policy.'

'No, Bobby, I'll not gamble it. You know I hate gambling.'

'But Lizzie, you got the money through gambling. I don't see the point,' he protested.

'I'm determined. I won't let you squander all that money,' she replied huffily.

So for the first time in their married life, they quarrelled with their tempers very high and their voices raised. But Lizzie had no intention of giving in.

'It's ill-gotten gains,' declared Maisie. 'She should donate it to some much needed charity, like war relief or cancer research. "It is easier for a camel to get through the eye of a needle than a rich man to enter the Kingdom of Heaven".'

Normally Luber kept out of these affrays, but tonight she said sharply, 'I do not agree. If this is God's good world why does he let such misery survive?'

'Oh you would say that,' retorted Maisie. 'All your lot are Communists, they don't believe in God.'

Luber became very annoyed, 'I am not a Communist, Maisie. I was brought up a good Christian, but I have seen and heard such bad things that I have lost all faith.'

But Maisie continued to argue until she reduced Luber to tears, and Lizzie, listening to all of it, felt very sad.

Robin, when home, lazed about stuffing sweets and reading comics.

'My idea,' he said with his mouth full, 'would be to buy some of those new fruit machines. I know a bloke who is making a fortune out of them.'

Lizzie woke up from her doze in front of the fire. 'Where did you see those machines, Robin?'

'In the cafe. It's great if you get the jackpot, it pays a fiver.'

'Robin!' Lizzie cried sharply. 'Keep out of those low class cafes, and don't let me catch you gambling.'

Robin flushed scarlet. 'I'm fifteen and leave school soon, so if I want to play the one-armed bandits I will, and that's that.' With that he stalked indignantly from the room.

'Well, what on earth is a bandit with one arm got to do with it?' cried Lizzie and everyone laughed.

'That's what they call the fruit machines, silly old sausage,' said pert Carol.

'Oh dear.' She seemed to be upsetting everyone.

Lizzie sighed and went out to tuck the younger boys into bed, as she did every night. Slowly she climbed the stairs, pausing half way to catch her breath. Lately she had begun to feel very down.

Paul and Derick dived into bed as she entered, having been up to their own particular devilry. It consisted mostly of nailing pictures of their favourite film star or jazz musician to the bedroom wall.

'Are you rich, Aunt Lizzie?' asked Paul unexpectedly.

'Well I did win a lot of money,' she replied mildly.

'Will you buy us presents?'

'Yes, darling, what would you like?'

'Well I'd like some drums, and Derick wants a guitar.'

'All right, dear,' said Lizzie tucking in the blankets firmly, 'I'll ask Luber to see what they've got in Woolworths when she goes shopping.'

The boys burst into uproarious laughter.

'What's the joke?' asked Lizzie.

'Aunt Lizzie, they won't be in Woolworths. Why, my drums cost a hundred pounds, and Derick's guitar won't be cheap either.'

Lizzie gave a snort of annoyance. 'Well,' she said, 'that's too much money for two naughty boys. Get to sleep, I'm turning off the lights now.'

As she closed the door she heard Derick whisper to his brother, 'No luck, mean old cow.'

Lizzie was really hurt, she couldn't believe that those little boys, whom she had taken under her wing, had been so rude. It seemed that the money would only destroy the loving family that she had built up so painstakingly. That night she confided in Charlie once more.

'Am I doing right?' she asked.

'Aunt Lizzie, if you hang on you will never have to struggle again. That interest on the money will build up very quickly. Don't let them bother you.'

Bobby was still very disgruntled, got out his best suit and went off down the East End to his old haunts.

Sallie flatly refused to do her share of the housework. 'I ain't no bleeding skivvy,' she snapped. 'Let her pay for someone to clean the passage and stairs.' So saying, she dressed herself up and went off to the bingo on Saturday nights.

Lizzie began to feel very much alone. Only the tiny, warm-hearted Luber still clung close to her. Soon even she would be going to her own house that was being built out in Epping.

One day Lizzie mentioned to Bobby that Maisie was very moody now that Mr Blew had left the church. 'I wish she would do something to improve her mind. Go to evening classes, like Charlie did.'

Bobby just said shortly, 'Leave her alone, Lizzie. Don't try to brow-beat her. She won't be a child forever.'

Lizzie suddenly got very short-tempered. 'Oh,' she cried, 'you don't understand! All that you think about is dogs and gee-gees.'

'Well, seeing as you are so irritable, Lizzie,' he retorted, 'could be you've got a sore arse from sitting on all that lolly.'

Lizzie trembled with rage, but replied quietly, 'You're becoming very hard and bitter.' Her brown eyes stared steadily at him. 'I don't understand your attitude to me lately.'

He grabbed his cap and bellowed, 'Oh nuts!' then fled out of the front door, down to Pat's bar.

His old pal had died that year and Bobby truly missed him, but Pat's wife, Mary, still carried on with the running of the bar. Mary O'Keefe was dark and still attractive in a pleasant, plump way. She was quick and lively, and had a kind of dry Irish cockney humour. Bobby liked her company and always ran to Mary when out of favour with Lizzie.

'You look glum, Bobby,' Mary said, as she poured his pint for him.

'I'm right browned off,' complained Bobby. 'Haven't had a stroke of luck lately.'

'Well, you certainly don't seem to be the happy-go-lucky lad I used to know, and I've known you a long time, Bobby.'

'I've come to the end of my road,' said Bobby ruefully. 'Just got rid of my last dog. Couldn't afford to pay the kennel fees.'

'Well, you should be all right for money. Didn't Lizzie get a good win on the pools last year?'

'Well,' Bobby sighed, 'you know Lizzie. She's always been thrifty, but now she is positively tight.'

'Oh I see,' grinned Mary, 'so that's what is eating you. Why don't you buy the tenancy of a pub between you? It would be better than giving it to the bookies.'

'Lizzie isn't strong. The doctor told me her heart is weak. Don't think she could do all the work.'

'You can have this one cheap. I'm getting out soon. Going home to Ireland.'

Bobby looked interested.

Mary's eyes twinkled. 'No, Bobby. I'm not going to live with Dinaper. She left Edward, did you know?'

Bobby shook his head.

'She went off with that darned poofy English actor. You know, the one that Edward trained horses for. They live out in Hollywood now.'

'Well that don't surprise me,' Bobby said acidly.

'I shan't be sorry to go, now that Pat has passed on. The population's changing all the time and I get a lot of trouble here on Saturday nights. It's all these foreigners, blacks and Indians. Don't know where they all come from. Mind you, they are quiet enough, it's the locals that don't like them.' She sighed. 'Live and let live that's what I say, but I'll be glad to go back to the old country. Those were good old days, Bobby, when Pat had his pub down The Nile.'

Bobby stood silent, looking around the familiar bar at the picture of Pat in his wrestling regalia, and at photographs of the dogs they had owned. Marzipan and The Duchess and on the other side was Mick the Miller. That was a wizard dog. Yes, times had changed. It was no good to be small fry now; the big bookies had the monopoly with their tough minders and heavy odds. It was over for him, and well he knew it. He sighed and drank his beer up quickly. Now it was all in the past he felt very depressed. 'Goodnight, Mary,' he said, and went home.

Lizzie still sat with elbows on the table, chin cupped in her hands, looking very doleful.

Bobby, still sorry for himself, sat down and started to read the paper.

'What's the matter with you, Bobby?' she asked.

'Nothing's wrong with me,' he snarled with distinct animosity.

Lizzie began to cry. 'You can't even speak to me civil these days.'

'Oh don't cry,' he said, as her shoulders shook with sobs.

He went over and cuddled her. 'Lizzie, old gel, don't get upset. It won't do you any good.'

'It's all that money,' wept Lizzie. 'Take it, Bobby, I don't want it.'

'Don't cry, Lizzie. I wouldn't upset you for all the money in the world.'

'Get rid of it. Give it away as Maisie suggested,' she wept.

'No need to be as drastic as all that,' said Bobby. 'Just let's keep a happy medium about it.'

'I can't go on living if you leave me, Bobby,' she said. 'I am not the tough body I was when I married you.'

'Look, love, if you want me to give up the track and go into business, I'll bloody well do it, because I am fed up with all this squabbling.'

Lizzie smiled up at him. 'Do you mean it, Bobby?'

'Scouts' honour,' cried Bobby, imitating young Robin's scouts' salute. Lizzie smiled, then she giggled: 'You'll never grow up, Bobby, but I do love you so.

CHAPTER TWELVE

The Shop

By the time that the festive season had arrived Lizzie had overcome most of her scruples and was having a big spend-up. Money was no object; everyone had a handsome present, the house was warm and comfortable and the table was laden with food. Bobby, a very boozy but merry Father Christmas, distributed the presents from the big tree in the hallway.

After the traditional dinner they had a knees-up. The love-birds, Luber and Charlie were there, very happy because they had just put down a deposit on a new house in the suburbs. Sallie was attired in a short red dress and heavily made up, while long, lanky Maisie was dressed in a plain skirt and a plain white blouse, trying hard to remain very solemn, this being, she informed them all, the birthday of the Lord Jesus. The boys had got their drums and guitar and were driving everyone mad with a cacophony of thumping and singing. Bobby and Robin just got completely sloshed. Carol, dressed in a frilly blue dress, entertained them all as she sang in a high-pitched voice, 'My sweet little Alice blue gown'.

Lizzie, with her cheeks aglow and starry-eyed, was dressed in a new black bead-trimmed dress, and sat surveying her family with immense pleasure and satisfaction. At last she had achieved her dream; all her loved ones were together, celebrating Christmas. It gave her great happiness.

In January, there was terrific excitement in the family because Bobby's shop officially opened. He had kept his promise to Lizzie and had bought a small lock-up shop in the High Road. Because it had been empty since the war it was very run down, and Bobby had acquired it cheap from a 'fella he knew'.

For several weeks now they had all been very busy cleaning

and painting and giving the place a good redecoration, the younger boys working as hard as Bobby and Robin. Even Maisie and Sallie had come in with buckets and mops to help clean the floors.

Now the shiny red apples were polished and piled high, contrasting perfectly with the bright oranges laid in neat symmetrical rows on top of each other. Overhead swung bunches of purple grapes spaced alternately with bunches of bright yellow bananas. This artistic effort had been completed by Paul and Derick.

Robin stood outside to attract customers, and in his loud husky voice yelled, 'Spuds a tanner for two pounds, nice fresh greens.'

Bobby bought an old van in which he and Robin went out early in the mornings to the market to buy the wares for the shop. All the takings were given to Lizzie, who dished out the money for stock and paid them all wages as long as they earned it. She kept the money in a special box she had for that purpose. Lizzie loved counting it, she had an obsession for making money go round, and could not help planning and scheming.

Once he had left school, Robin had grown up very quickly. He had whiskers on his chin, a strong muscular body, and was almost as tall as Bobby, Although there was no blood relation, they were not unlike each other and could have easily passed for father and son. A very comfortable, mature relationship had grown up between them. Robin was not a gambler, but he was very fond of the birds, as he called the young girls who came from the factories at lunchtime to buy fruit from the shop. It took Bobby little or no time to get bored with the shop. 'Fed-up with dishing up those dirty spuds to a lot of complaining old gels,' he would say to Robin.

So he would sneak off every day to the pub across the road. It was called the Odd Fellows but it was shortened to Oddy's by the local folk.

'Off to Oddy's to put a bet on,' Bobby would inform Robin at twelve o'clock. Then he disappeared till about three o'clock, for Bobby truly missed the excitement of the race track. Over at Oddy's he would tell tales of his days as a tic-tac man, of the great winners like Mick the Miller and Millreef and he became a very popular figure.

Robin kept his mouth shut and told no one about Bobby. Besides he had certain goings on of his own. He liked the long-legged factory girls in their tight slacks and jumpers, with their heavy boobs. He would entice them into the back room of the shop for slap and tickle, and sometimes a bit more than that.

There was blonde Elsie who loved a bit of petting but that was as far as she would go, then came sweet silly Milly who went down with him onto the pile of potato sacks and forsook her virginity. After her was Sue, a real good-looker, but determined to hang onto Robin. She came regularly each day and they made passionate love in the lunch break before she went back to work.

All this while Bobby was over at the pub backing the gee-gees but the best laid plans of mice and men often gang awry, for Sue got pregnant. An irate cockney Mum descended on Bobby one Monday morning while he was suffering from a heavy hangover, and said she'd like to know what Robin was going to do about it.

So Robin was taken to task, and the family held a conference to see what was to be done.

'I don't know who the dirty little sod takes after,' cried Sallie.

'I do,' said Robin giving her a sly grin.

Lizzie said, 'Well, Robin, what are you going to do about it? You're too young to marry her.'

'Marry her,' scoffed Robin. 'Why, she was just a pushover.'

Bobby roared, 'Let the bloody little runt take the consequences.'

But Lizzie said gently, 'Surely you must love your little sweetheart, Robin?'

Robin looked a bit shamefaced, then said, 'I don't want her, Aunt Lizzie. She just came for a bit of the other, and I obliged her. That's all there was in it.'

'Oh dear, Robin,' cried Lizzie in dismay. 'That is really

awful. Bobby, you must negotiate with this girl's mother. Can't let the boy ruin his life by having a loveless marriage.'

Then she turned to Robin and asked him mildly, 'Where was Bobby when all this was going on?'

'Over at Oddy's. He goes there every day.'

Lizzie's lips tightened. 'Well it's his fault, I am quite sure of that.'

Later Sue's Mum settled for twenty pounds from Bobby, to see her daughter over her troubles.

Lizzie nagged Bobby, 'You're getting on for fifty. It's time you settled down.'

'I know, Liz,' he said ruefully. 'But I get involved in a good game of rummy. I don't mean to stay out so long.'

'But you do, and you're responsible for what's happened to those youngsters.'

'Give over, Liz, they would have done that anyway. Could've been in a dark doorway down the street, times ain't changed that much.'

'Now, don't be coarse, Bobby.'

'Well, Liz, I'm earning a bit over at Oddy's; I take their small threepenny bets and hedge them over the blower onto the big bookies. I've got quite a good clientele, I have.'

'Oh dear,' sighed Lizzie, 'gambling again. You'll never change, Bobby – not while you got a hole in your arse.'

He grinned. 'Now, coming from you Lizzie, that's not very nice.'

Nevertheless Bobby and Robin both went back to work, promising Lizzie that it wouldn't happen again.

Bobby still popped off to Oddy's and Robin still eyed the lunchtime girls but at least he went no further than an occasional wolf whistle as they went giggling, arm-in-arm, past the shop.

Then one day a girl walked by who was more attractive than all the rest put together. She was tall and willowy with short cropped chestnut hair, rather big features and a wide charming smile. Her clothes fitted like her own skin and she walked with her hips moving rhythmically. In front of her she wheeled a lovely little girl in a push chair.

Robin was stunned; he could hardly believe it when she stopped beside the shop.

'I'll have a banana for the baby,' she said in a high, clear voice. 'How much?' Her white hands and long polished fingernails slowly peeled the banana and handed it to the child.

'It's on the house,' said Robin, moving close to her.

'Thanks,' she said without any argument. 'Got to go. Taking her to the nursery; got a job up town.'

'Where's hubby?'

'There isn't one,' she said shortly, 'I am an unmarried mother.'

'You don't say.'

But abruptly she pushed the chair forward, said, 'So long,' and went on her way.

Robin watched the swing of those slim hips all the way as she walked up the road.

Bobby in the meantime was peeping out of the pub window signalling to Robin to behave himself, but Robin put up two fingers at him, then went inside the shop whistling ruefully. 'Blimey, what a bird,' he muttered. Her name was Bella and she came by regularly each morning. Sometimes she came quite early when Bobby was there, and he agreed with Robin that she certainly was some bird. He made a fuss of the little girl, gave her a banana, and Bella would hang around for a chat. She did not seem at all interested in Robin. But her clear hazel eyes looked steadily into Bobby's as she related her troubles, and told him about her inability to hold down a steady job because of the baby. Bobby was very intrigued, and Robin extremely jealous.

'Old enough to be her farver,' he would mutter.

'Well, could be you are too young and inexperienced, son,' Bobby replied.

No matter how hard Robin tried, he could not persuade Bella to date him.

'Can't,' she would say, 'got no one to mind the kid.'

But she always had a slow, charming smile for Bobby, and would halt outside the shop.

'Not sold all them spuds out yet, then?' Her words were well formed but still she had a kind of flat cockney intonation.

Robin would sidle up to her in his sexiest manner. 'Where you off to and who's the lucky guy?'

'It's not you,' she said haughtily, and cast a very amorous glance at Bobby.

When she had gone on her way Bobby chuckled loudly. 'You know, Robin, you're wasting your time. It's me she fancies.'

'Get away.' Robin became extremely annoyed.

Bobby still liked his Saturday night out at Clapton. Silence fell in the house while he checked his pools, then everyone got out of the way while he spruced himself up for his Saturday night out.

Lizzie calmly sat in her usual spot at the long table, sometimes sewing, sometimes preparing the vegetables for Sunday lunch.

Carol had become very vain. She was only thirteen but she used lipstick and nail varnish and had quite a lot to say for herself. This particular Saturday she sat at the end of the table plucking out her eyebrows with a pair of tweezers.

'For Christ's sake stop that,' demanded Bobby, 'it gives me the shivers.'

'What's it to you?' she replied cheekily. 'I don't interfere with your pleasures.'

Bobby guffawed very loudly. 'Well I'll be damned. If that's pleasure you ain't never had any.'

But Carol stared at him coldly. 'I suppose you are off to the dogs, leaving poor Aunt Lizzie all alone.'

'Why, you saucy monkey.' He made a dive at her, but she got up and dashed upstairs to where Paul and Derick were in their room practising the drums.

'It's coming to something when those bleeding kids tell me what I am to do,' Bobby complained, 'and those noisy sods upstairs, I'm glad to get out of the house.'

'Well,' said Lizzie mildly, 'not much ever kept you in on Saturday nights, Bobby.'

'You side in with them. One of these days I'll give them all a good thumping,' declared Bobby, as he put on his cap at a jaunty angle and made for the front door.

Lizzie, a little pale-faced and tired-looking just put her elbows on the table and gave her slow, sweet smile. There had been quite a lot of friction lately among the kids, fights at school and lots of japes and jokes played on the rest of the family by the boys, now aged thirteen and fourteen.

One day they came running in from school, Paul was leading Derick, who seemed to have his face covered with blood. 'Aunt Lizzie! Aunt Lizzie!' he yelled. 'Derick's got run over.'

Lizzie's face blanched; she dashed out to see what was wrong but her breath went, her legs crumpled under her, and she fell down the steps.

Carol ran to her, helped her up and then dashed at Derick. She snatched off the false clots of blood that he had stuck onto his face.

'You daft pair, you've upset Aunt Lizzie with your silly jokes,' she cried, delivering Paul a good punch on the nose.

Lizzie took her heart tablet and slowly recovered. That night Bobby went up and threatened them with his belt, so the japes ceased. But they certainly needed a lot of handling. Sallie did her best but they only laughed at her. Later they came into Lizzie's room to say how very sorry they were. 'Poor little boys,' she thought, and gave them money to go out to the pictures.

'It's a waste of time trying to discipline those sods,' said Bobby, 'because you've completely spoiled them, Lizzie.'

He marched off to Clapton dogs, deciding to forget them all for one good night out. He was late, having missed the first race and this annoyed him. He went into the bar to get a pint to steady his shattered nerves. A young woman was sitting at the bar, she wore a little black pill-box hat and a wide-skirted green taffeta dress. Bobby thought she looked very smart. When a familiar voice said, 'Hullo, Bobby, backing all the winners?' he saw that there, large as life, was the lovely Bella. Bobby looked around half expecting to see Robin lurking somewhere in the background.

'Hullo, what are you doing here?'

'I often come here,' she replied casually.

'All alone.' He was a little surprised; dog racing was still considered a man's sport.

'That's right,' she returned, looking at him with a challenge in her hazel eyes.

'Want a drink?' He looked appreciatively at the neckline of her emerald green dress and the little rows of black jet beads which decorated it.

'No,' she said, 'have one with me.' And she called him a drink with the kind of poise that Bobby had never seen before in a woman. In Bobby's generation women took a back seat. Then she leaned over to inspect the racecard which he was reading. The perfume of her permeated his nostrils and almost took his breath away. This must be the equality of women business that the papers were always raving about. It really intrigued him.

'What are you backing?' she asked.

'I think that I'll do the favourite. It's a grey dog, I always fancy a grey dog.'

She was an old and accomplished gambler and loved dog racing. Bobby felt he had known her all his life.

'I love a little flutter. My old man was a bookie, you know, so I get a baby minder Saturday and go to the different tracks. First time I've seen you, Bobby.'

'It won't be the last,' said Bobby. 'Let's go and have some supper.'

Supper was steak and chips with wine at a late night restaurant. Then she was sitting beside him in the old van and Bobby felt as if he was sixteen again, so sexually excited that he had a job to disguise his emotions.

She ran her hand along his leg. 'Got it bad, have you, Bobby?'

Bobby slammed on the brakes and kissed her, completely carried away by her kind of straightforwardness. 'In the back of the van,' he whispered hoarsely.

'No thanks, I've got my best dress on, and I know how mucky it is in there.'

Smoothly her hands calmed him. 'We'll have to take pot luck tonight, Bobby,' she said. 'I can't ask you in because my sister is babysitting for me, but here's to the next time.' She wound her slim legs around him. 'Bobby, I knew you would be mine. It was you I wanted, not Robin.'

'You're not kidding me?'

'No, lover, just looking forward to the next time. Good-night.'

Bobby drove home in a dream, but as the house came in sight he felt very guilty. He was getting mixed up with women again, was it worth it? Poor old Lizzie. He hated to let her down. But this Bella was some woman. It was going to be very hard to resist.

Lizzie was in bed and the house was quiet, so Bobby lay down on the couch in the kitchen. He couldn't face her tonight.

CHAPTER THIRTEEN

La Belle

When everyone else got up in the morning Bobby sloped off to bed.

The house was usually in an uproar on Sunday mornings. Robin went to play football, Maisie to the church, while Sallie caught up with her chores — sweeping, dusting and cleaning her room and chasing the boys out of the house.

Lizzie slowly and methodically prepared the Sunday lunch; there was always a roast with baked spuds and batter pudding. Charlie often came visiting by himself now, as Luber was expecting her first baby.

But it was Maisie who had really changed lately, she no longer had the melancholy hang-dog look she had worn since Mr Blew had left the local church. She seemed more human and often smiled secretly from behind the thick specs which she was now obliged to wear, her eyes twinkling as if at some hidden thought.

'Don't you go up to the local church now, Maisie?' Lizzie inquired.

'No, Aunt Lizzie. I go to a different one and I like it much better.' And that was all she would say.

It was Paul and Derick who brought Maisie's secret life out into the open.

That week had passed without incident. Bella came to the shop, chatted to Bobby and Robin, and gave Bobby a prodigious wink, although there was no hint of their relationship.

Robin said, 'I really go for her. Pity she is so cold. I don't think she likes the opposite sex.'

Bobby who was arranging the fruit, just muttered, 'Yes, Robin, you could be right.'

But on Saturday morning Bobby got Paul and Derick to help him clean up the old van. 'Sweep out the back,' he said, 'and put some clean sacks in there.'

'I wonder what he's up to,' whispered Derick.

'Going to pull a bird, I reckon,' said Paul. 'Never mind, we're going to get half a crown each, so why should we worry?'

Saturday afternoons there was always a lot of skylarking going on when everyone was at home. Maisie was taking her turn at cleaning the front steps and the terrors Paul and Derick sat on the stairs, sniggering, whispering and sometimes singing a song.

'Wash me in the water that you washed your dirty daughter and I'll be whiter than the whitewash on the wall.'

They then banged their hands together in a good imitation of a tambourine yelling in chorus, 'Whiter than the whitewash on the wall.'

Then Maisie suddenly got up, threw the bucket of dirty soapy water all over them and dashed inside, crying bitterly.

Bobby was shaving at the kitchen sink when she rushed in, yelling, and the boys were kicking up a shocking din, having got soaked in dirty, soapy water.

'For Christ's sake,' roared Bobby, 'what the hell is going on?'

'She threw water at us,' they cried.

Maisie sat at the table, her head down, crying bitterly.

'Come here,' cried Bobby grabbing each of the boys by the ear. 'What did you say to her?'

'Nuffink, we was only singing about the Sally Army,' said Paul.

'Well, she's in the Salvation Army and don't want no one to know,' explained Derick.

'Got a bonnet and everything,' cackled Paul.

'How come you're so well-informed?' asked Lizzie, who had been trying to comfort Maisie.

'We saw her when she came in the pub selling the *War Cry*,' the boys declared triumphantly.

'And what were you two devils doing in the pub,' demanded Bobby.

They both looked worried. 'Only go to hear the pop music,' they cried. 'We don't drink.'

'I should bloody well think not, you're still at school,' roared Bobby, giving them both a clout about the head. 'Upstairs and into bed and stop there, that's your lot for this weekend.'

The boys dashed out and ran upstairs to the den, as they called the little back room they shared.

'Now, Maisie, have a cup of tea,' said Lizzie, 'and don't get so upset. Why shouldn't you want us to know you are in the Salvation Army? Why! that's a great organization and it did wonderful work among the poor folk down The Nile when I was a girl.'

Maisie wiped her eyes, 'Thank you, Aunt Lizzie, but the youngsters are forever taking the mike out of the army. I like it because it's so warm, sincere and so interesting.'

Bobby patted her on the back. 'Well then, you get on with it, gel,' he said. 'Might do this house of sinners some bloody good having you to keep an eye on us.'

Then Bobby got ready, put on his best suit and went off to the dogs to meet the amorous Bella.

Lizzie was worried. Bobby had not worn that suit for several years, not since he went to Ireland. As he made to leave she smoothed the back down for him.

'Haven't put on an ounce of weight, have you, dear?' she said affectionately.

Bobby looked awkward. 'Might as well wear it out 'fore the moths get at it.'

Bella was in her usual spot, looking as sweet and pretty as ever. They settled immediately to studying the race cards as if they were both of one mind. Already there was a kind of mature relationship between them, even though it was only the second time they had been alone together.

It was a good night; Bobby got several winners, but Bella lost her money.

Bobby handed her a bunch of notes. 'For the baby,' he said.

She took them calmly and put them in her purse without comment or protest.

'We'll drive out to Epping and have a good drink,' he suggested. 'Is that all right with you?'

'It's fine with me,' she said, with that slow, charming smile.

After many drinks at the Roebuck they parked the van deep in the forest, than got into the back and lay close together. Bella took off her dress and her panties. 'Come on, lover, I am all yours,' she said, with not a hint of shyness, just swift, hot, passionate love.

'I could get very fond of you,' he said when they sat up to smoke a cigarette.

'I've noticed that.' She smiled ironically.

'What I mean, Bella, is that I am nearly twenty years older than you, also I am a married man, but I never ever felt for anyone as I do you.'

'Bobby,' she said, 'don't cross your bridges; I hate to be tied down, I chose my own way of life. Also I have a kid to support.'

'Where's her father?'

'In the nick, got ten years. We never married, but he was my man.'

'You know, I admire your courage and your straight talk. I don't mind what I give you, but I'd like to know if you'll stick with me.'

'Bobby! You have a wife.'

'Yes, but that's different. Lizzie and I understand each other. She's got a heart condition. I'd be terrified to have sex with her and she knows that.'

'Well,' declared Bella, 'if that's true then it is certainly a different proposition. I can't afford to get involved with some hot-headed fool who will give me another child and then hop off and leave me. I'm out to get all I can. That's why I pick on those with a bit of money.'

'I don't blame you, Bella, we've all got to survive. Tell you what, how would you like to work for me?'

'I just did.' She grinned.

'No, I mean be employed by me, money in hand, no tax, no questions asked.'

'What! Selling spuds?' she cried, very amused.

'No, I'm thinking of opening a betting shop. I've already got quite a few punters on my books and now betting has been made legal, there's no reason why we can't run a shop taking bets and so forth.'

'It's a damned good idea,' she replied, 'but will I be able to do it?'

'You're a gambling gel and know all the prices, odds and whatnot, down to your fingertips. I applied for the lease of that empty shop next door to Oddy's. I'll know if I've got it next week.'

'Well then, it's a deal,' she said.

'Good,' said Bobby. 'The night is young, let's have a little more love shall we?'

They rolled about in the old van like two teenagers, Lizzie and the family completely forgotten when he was in the arms of the lovely young Bella.

It was about this time that Sallie began to go out regularly on Saturday nights, she had taken up ballroom dancing with a fellow she met at work. He was the foreman at the Clarnico sweet factory where she worked, a small, thin, very meticulous man of about fifty. But because he had taken good care of himself, he looked much younger. He would call for Sallie in an old Morris car and wait outside. So far Sallie had not asked him in, because she was a little scared of Bobby. He wore a dress suit with a little black bow tie; his shoes shone like glass and there was plenty of Brylcream to keep his sandy hair in place.

Sallie would descend the stairs in a very queenly manner in all her glory, wearing a wide frilly dress and a beehive hair-do, adorned with beads and earrings and whatnot.

The two little terrors would hang over the banisters and shout, 'Slow slow, quick quick, slow.'

Lizzie would call out from her abode below stairs, which she seldom left these days. 'Have a good time, Sallie,' then, 'Come down, boys, we'll play draughts.'

'We was going out, Aunt Lizzie,' they argued.

'No, Uncle Bobby said you've to stay in.'

So they reluctantly came down into the kitchen where Carol sat sulkily arranging her hair in different styles.

'It's not fair. We ought to be allowed to go dancing,' she would protest. 'That fat old pudding Sallie is having all the fun.'

'Now Carol, don't be bitchy,' Lizzie would say. 'Surely you don't want to go out and leave your Aunt Lizzie all alone.'

'Can we go up to the pictures on Sunday night,' asked Paul.

'Yes, as long as you stay with Carol, I'll treat you.'

So they all settled down to a long-winded game of Ludo.

'Don't see why we can't have a television,' Carol would grumble. 'All my friends have got them.'

'My goodness, what's wrong with the wireless? I've heard of people going blind over those new fangled things.' Lizzie in her old-fashioned way was convinced that she was right to hold her young ones close. She had no pleasures other than being with them, but the sap was stirring in these teenagers, the last of her adopted family, and she often wondered how long she could hold onto them.

Meanwhile, Bobby went ahead with his plans to install Bella in his own betting shop. Not even mentioning Bella, he said casually to Lizzie, 'I've applied for a licence to run a betting shop. I think I'll get it. I've not been in trouble for a few years with the law and that's the only thing that would have stopped me.'

'I thought betting was against the law.'

'No, Liz, we move with the times now. After taking all those fines off us they've made it legal.'

'Well that does take a load off my mind,' she replied. 'What is it you want, a loan?'

'Well not much, a couple of hundred will see me over.'

'That's all right Bobby. As long as you put it to good use, I don't mind. I don't like the idea of gambling, but, if you say it's all right then I'll stop worrying.'

'Nothing to worry about, darling.' He gave her a big hug.

'Robin has agreed to take over the greengrocery and it's only over the road, so I'll be able to keep an eye on him.'

CHAPTER FOURTEEN

A Legal Bookie

Having decided to go ahead with his betting shop Bobby became extremely gracious to Lizzie, explaining to her in detail his plans for making a great fortune.

She smiled fondly at him as she wrote the cheque. 'You'll never change, Bobby, but let's hope you make a success of it this time.'

He gave her a swift peck, then grabbing his new felt hat, he put it on at a very jaunty angle and dashed off to meet Bella.

When he had gone she sighed and sat thinking. This betting shop was almost next door to Oddy's, the pub, but, as Bobby had said, 'Where the hell am I to get my punters from? Only got the boozer.'

Soon that old shop was cleaned, redecorated and a red and white sign informed everyone that The Bobby Erlock was now in business. Anyone fancying a little flutter on the dogs or gee-gees were to bring their bets to an honest, reliable and legal bookie.

Within a week Bella was installed behind the counter. In her cold callous way she was very successful. Winners or losers she stood no nonsense from them, just took their money and calmly counted the takings each evening, deducting her own percentage as Bobby had promised her she could.

Robin came over the road to chat up Bella. 'What a crafty sod you are, Bobby. What's the idea?'

Bobby rubbed his hands together apprehensively, a habit he had when disturbed. 'Well, Robin, the kid was on the rocks. She's got a baby to feed and clothe, and it gives me a lot more time to spend in Oddy's encouraging the punters.'

'Well, that's as good an excuse as any,' grinned Robin, 'but you lay orf, because I still fancy her.'

'Not interested, mate,' replied Bobby. 'Got past it, I have.' Then, becoming a little furtive, he said quietly, 'There's no need to let Lizzie know, she's happy in the home. What goes on in the outside world needn't worry her.'

Robin stared at him with slight suspicion then, in his generous way, said, 'It's OK by me. I won't let on.'

The shop proved to be an ideal arrangement and began to make a good profit. Bella proved to be a wizard at reckoning up the bets and also at handling the customers in a bright cool manner. Bobby sent home huge bouquets of flowers and baskets of delicious fruit with the excuse that he was working late or off to the dogs. And all the time he was becoming more and more involved with the lovely Bella, who was as cold as ice on the surface but had the burning heat of a volcano inside her beautiful body. Bobby was bewitched and bewildered and could not bear to let her out of his sight.

Lizzie, as always, had quite enough to keep her occupied and gave very little thought to Bobby. She had got used to his late nights through the years. At home there was plenty going on, for Sallie was courting very heartily with her small dancing partner, Phil Lester. She would go out with him on Saturday nights all dressed up in the height of fashion, while her boys waited in the hall to giggle and torment her. Sallie would hesitate on the stairs in her big beehive hair-do and wide frilly dress; she would get so annoyed that she would shout and scream at them.

Lizzie would come slowly from below stairs. 'Now boys, let Sallie go past. I've a nice bread pudding in the oven.'

The boys now went out on Saturday nights with Carol to the youth club at the local church hall down the street. They thumped their drums, played the guitar, and gave impromptu performances for the other teenagers to dance to while Carol sang on the mike.

Bobby would say, 'Why! They ain't never learned a note of music. How can they play in the band? And as for Carol, she screeches like a tom cat on the tiles. I don't call that singing.'

Lizzie would say to him, 'Don't be unkind, Bobby. The kids know what they like to do, and anyway this pop don't seem to be music.'

But the kids were happy and not far away, and then came home at ten o'clock, so Lizzie did not mind being alone and would catch up with her ironing.

Charlie, who was now a father, often visited her. 'Aunt Lizzie,' he said one day, 'why don't you go out Saturday night? Everyone else does.'

'I am all right, Charlie. I like to be quiet,' she replied.

'But Bobby's got a brand new car. He could bring you over to visit us on Sunday.'

Lizzie leapt to his defence immediately. 'You know I'd never ride in a car. Why, I'd be scared stiff.'

'Oh nonsense, you would soon get used to it. You're not an old lady. You've brought all us kids up, so now it's your turn to step out a bit. It's time to enjoy yourself.'

'But I do, Charlie,' she assured him sweetly. 'I've always enjoyed my life. I'm happy down here in my kitchen, and I find plenty to do.'

'Oh well,' said Charlie, 'please yourself.' He was angry because he had seen that the lovely Bella was well installed and obviously under Bobby's protection.

Robin seemed lately to have changed considerably; he had begun to drink heavily. He came home and fell into bed every night, having at last realized that Bella was Bobby's mistress.

The kids were having a great time; they talked and lived pop and pop singers. Their bedrooms were littered with posters of the current stars, they spent all their money on records and played these on the old cabinet gramophone far into the night. Carol had decided to be an actress and registered to attend a drama school. In this way each was wrapped up in his or her own hobby.

Lizzie was quite content. The money she had loaned Bobby for the betting shop had all been returned to her, which was unusual in itself.

One evening Sallie came in for a chat and a cup of tea and confided in Lizzie that Phil Lester wanted to marry her.

'He's got a nice little house. His first wife died a few years ago and he's fed up with being on his own.'

'I am so pleased for you, dear,' said Lizzie, and leaned forward to kiss her sister.

'You know, Lizzie,' said Sallie, 'I'll at last be able to give the boys a good home, something I've always wanted to do.'

Paul and Derick, as always, 'ear-wigged' from the top of the stairs, leaning over the banisters to see what was going on in the kitchen.

'Did you hear that?' exclaimed Paul. 'She's going to marry old creeping festers,' this was their nickname for the small, timid man who was escorting their mother.

'Yes, and we are supposed to go and live in his house,' declared Derick.

'No we ain't, not if I knows it.'

'What will we do?' asked his brother.

'We'll nobble him, make him a non-starter,' said Paul, who had picked up a lot of racing slang from Bobby.

On the next Saturday afternoon, a very happy Sallie, wearing a diamond engagement ring, hustled little Phil into the front door. He was neat and natty, with his highly polished shoes, his dress suit and his little bow tie. They went upstairs to tell the boys their news and found them both lounging at the top of the stairs with a sly grin on their faces. Phil suddenly seemed very wary of them.

'Hullo, boys,' he said nervously. 'I've come to ask you for your mother's hand in marriage.' This he thought was a nice jovial approach.

The boys, however, guffawed loudly. Phil put out his hand, Paul took it and twisted it backwards and poor Phil went head over heels down the stairs and lay at the bottom moaning and groaning.

Sallie started screaming hysterically, causing such a pandemonium that it roused Bobby from the bed where he lay recuperating from a hectic night out.

'Blimey! What's going on?' he yelled, as he staggered from the bedroom.

Bobby got Phil on to his feet but he could see the poor man's arms were hanging limp and broken.

'Oh dear, better take him up the hospital,' said Bobby. 'I'll kill them sods when I come back, and I'll never get to the track on time tonight.'

Nevertheless, four weeks later, Sallie married her small hero, a pathetic sight with his arms in plaster casts.

The boys did not attend at all, but stayed home with Lizzie. While the ceremony was on they installed themselves in Sallie's apartment, sticking up lurid pop posters all over the wall and announcing that this was now their den. Paul banged on his drums and Derick strummed his guitar, while Carol lay on the bed painting her nails.

'You didn't ought to have done that to old creeping festers.' Then on second thoughts she added, 'I never liked him either.'

Shortly after Sallie's wedding, Maisie announced that she would like to bring a young man home to tea.

So the family gathered, all but Carol and the boys, who had all been packed off to the pictures. This was Lizzie's idea because Maisie could not bear the sight of the boys.

Maisie was still a lanky sort of girl, dressed very badly in frowsy looking dark jumpers and shabby skirts. She wore her hair in a kind of knot dragged straight back from her high forehead which shone from much scrubbing with hard soap. But her eyes were nice and kind, a deep hazel obscured by thick lenses. She wore her army uniform with impunity, now that she had lost her shyness about it. Everyone was now very anxious to see her choice; Bobby had been convinced that she would end up an old maid.

Lizzie had prepared ham and salad followed by home-made cakes for the occasion. When Maisie arrived with her intended only one sentence passed almost silently between them all, and it was, 'Why, it's Mr Blew!'

This affable Salvationist was the image of Maisie's late friend from the old church, Mr Blew, the vicar. He had the same tip – tilted nose, skimpy fair hair and little steel-rimmed specs on the end of his nose. He was immediately popular with the family.

Lizzie's cheeks were flushed with excitement to see them all sitting around the big table and all getting on so well together.

So Maisie put up the banns and married her man in the Army church hall just down the road. It was a quiet wedding, the only excitement was when the young boys arrived, poshed up and complete with their new Teddy Boy outfits; black suits with wide shoulders, straight tight trousers and their hair long, waved and curled, white shirts and bow ties.

It was the first time that Lizzie had ever travelled in a taxi; the hall was not very far up the road but Carol had insisted on it. Lizzie had argued about the expense, but Carol got her way.

Then Charlie took her back home in his car. 'Now what's wrong with that?' he asked. 'Right to the front door; don't tell me you can't travel in a car any more, and see that bloody Bobby takes you out at weekends or I'll be down on him like a ton of bricks.'

She smiled. 'Don't be silly, Charlie. I can go out with Bobby if I want to.'

But in her heart she knew it was all pretence, for Bobby hardly knew she was there these days. He was completely obsessed with that girl in the betting shop, who was young and fresh with short chestnut curls. What chance did she stand against her? She had been through all this before; she must not let it defeat her. Bobby tired of his fancy women very easily and always came back to her. At least he always had, so why should it be different this time? Lizzie got Carol to walk with her back and forth along the high road to get a good look at this new paramour of Bobby's.

Carol said to her, 'You're cuckoo. If it was my husband I would go and beat her up.'

'Violence solves no problems.'

'Maybe, but I'd like to see the cow that could take me on,' returned Carol aggressively.

Lizzie surveyed Carol with her deep brown eyes and slowly smiled. This girl was so pretty, dark with white skin and very dark blue eyes. Her figure was perfect, but her mouth was small, tight and thinlipped. Lizzie thought that Carol could be a bitch with a very nasty temper and it was a pity because she was so lovely.

They went back home to have a cup of tea and Carol childishly scoffed up the cream cakes that they had brought back with them.

'Leave one each for Paul and Derick,' Lizzie said.

'I don't know why you worry so much about them, Aunt Lizzie. I am supposed to be your child and they are Sallie's.'

'Yes,' Lizzie smiled. 'You're all my babies.'

'I don't understand you,' complained Carol. 'Someone pinching your husband and you take it all in such good part. Just give us permission and me the boys will go up there and do her over.'

'Now Carol, stop this terrible talk. What a thing for a nice young girl to suggest.'

'Ow,' cried Carol getting up and leaving the room. 'You really give me the pip, you do, Aunt Lizzie.'

Lizzie sat wiping away a stray tear. She was trying to cope, but somehow each day it got a little harder, and each day Bobby grew more distant, often staying out two or three nights a week.

Robin grew more morbid and uncommunicative, he slouched around in his working clothes never bothering to change in the evening, just eating his dinner silently then off out to the pub, avoiding Bobby. His face had grown red and kind of weatherbeaten. He was a broad-shouldered, husky lad but he certainly was not a happy one.

When Lizzie was alone in the house one Saturday night a constable knocked loudly at the front door. Lizzie came out from the basement entrance and looked up at the big solid man in blue who stood there and a sudden fear possessed her. Memories of the days when they were always after her Bobby came flooding back. She gasped for breath, held on to the wall and beckoned him down.

'You all right, Ma?' he asked kindly, noticing her pallor.

'Just come in, I'll be all right once I sit down.'

So he guided her in and she sank down into her chair. 'Well,' she gasped, 'what's the trouble?'

'Not a lot,' he said going to the tap to get her a glass of water. 'Sorry I scared you.'

'It's not you, but my heart is weak. I have to take things easy.'

'Well Ma, it's those boys here. They're down at Southend and have been arrested for fighting. We need a parent to go and get them out. Where is your husband?'

Lizzie was not sure. 'Oh, he'll be home in the morning,' she said. 'I'll give you a telephone number and my nephew Charlie will go and get them.'

'It's nothing to worry about. Just some sort of affray; the kids do that on Saturday nights. Teddy Boys and Mods or some such nonsense; give them all the birch, I would. In my day we got the cat-o-nine tails and was all the better for it.'

'Thank you, constable,' said Lizzie. 'Charlie will get them.'

'You be all right?'

'Fine. My daughter will be in soon.'

'Right then, I'll see myself out,' he said, and as the door closed Lizzie collapsed weeping. For the first time in a long while she felt the need of Bobby and he was not there.

Charlie brought two very subdued Teddy Boys back home in the morning looking very battered.

'They have to appear before the magistrate tomorrow. Stupid sods, perhaps it will teach them a lesson. I've got to go, got a busy day myself.'

The boys crept upstairs without a word to say.

When Bobby arrived home at midday on Sunday looking very much the worse for wear and was informed of the escapade, he immediately took off his belt and dashed upstairs to set about the boys.

Carol got out of bed, stood in a frilly dressing gown looking alarmed, and Lizzie put her head on the table and her hands over her ears to keep out the noise. The shouting, yelling and thrashing went on for quite a time.

Then Bobby ran downstairs with his arms full of clothes, went straight out into the garden, took the smart Teddy boy suits, poured paraffin over them and set them alight.

'Rotten devil,' muttered Carol.

Lizzie said, 'They cost a lot of money, Bobby.'

'Well they won't wear them again nor get into bleeding trouble.'

On Monday the boys appeared before the court and were put on probation because they had done quite a bit of damage to plate glass windows and to several young Mods.

After it had all calmed down, Lizzie looked at herself in the mirror, at her tousled hair and white face, at those nice hands that were once so well cared for.

'Oh dear, I feel ten years older,' she said to her image. 'Look at me, what a wreck. Has it all been worth it, I wonder?'

CHAPTER FIFTEEN

New Relations

On Monday morning it was back to work. Carol was the first to leave; she was now in her last term at the grammar school. Bobby was usually next and then the boys, who worked at a local factory. But, so far this morning there had been no sounds from upstairs, no cheery whistling or feet stomping in time to the radio. Lizzie was puzzled, but decided they were sulking, so thought it was better to leave them alone.

At midday they crept very quietly out of the front door. Lizzie went to the window and noticed them struggling along with their precious musical instruments, and wondered what they were up to.

In the evening, when Carol had gone to her drama class, the boys came downstairs and stood solemnly in front of Lizzie. They looked very clean and tidy, they had on thick woollen jerseys and had packs on their backs.

'What's all this?' she asked. 'Supper will be ready soon. Don't go out yet.'

'We're sorry, Aunt Lizzie, but we've come to say goodbye.'

Lizzie looked in amazement at them. 'Why! Where are you off to?'

'We're leaving home. We've come to the conclusion that Uncle Bobby is not our father and we are not going to stay here and be ordered about by him.'

'Oh don't be silly, darlings; he lost his temper. He'll be sorry already, and you were naughty boys.'

'No, Aunt Lizzie. We're going on a hike. Probably end up abroad.'

She smiled, thinking that it was some kind of a jape. 'Shall I cut some sandwiches for you?'

'Well,' said Derick, who loved his tummy, 'they would come in handy.'

'Now take them bags off and have some soup, and I'll give you some sandwiches, then you can go to the camp, or whatever you are about to do.'

Obediently they sat down and scoffed up the hot soup and bread, then put the sandwiches in their pockets. Paul looked at his brother and said, 'Ready Derick?' Both rose very solemnly, kissed her and said, 'Goodbye, Aunt Lizzie. When we make our fortune we won't forget you.'

Lizzie, still thinking it was some game, said, 'Now, what about pocket money?'

'No, thank you, we've sold our drums; Paul is keeping his guitar and we'll sing and play to earn our own money.'

'Very nice,' said Lizzie clearing away the dishes.

The two long-legged lads left the house without a backward glance.

Feeling extremely puzzled, Lizzie kept turning it over in her mind. Surely it was some sort of practical joke; they were full of them.

When Carol came in at nine o'clock, Lizzie asked, 'Seen the boys?'

'Why should I see them? They've left home, haven't they?'

'Oh! They are playing some camping game,' said Lizzie. 'I'm not sure what they're up to.'

'Oh, wake up!' snapped Carol rudely. 'They've gone. They're not coming back, and I don't blame them after the way that Uncle Bobby treated them.'

Lizzie gasped with fright, 'Oh no! You knew. Why didn't you tell me? What am I going to do? They've been gone six hours.'

'Not my business,' said Carol brusquely.

'Oh Carol,' wept Lizzie, 'how can you be so hard. They're like your own brothers.'

'It's their business, not mine, and after all Paul is seventeen and Derick is nearly sixteen. They ought to know their own minds. I'm not being mixed up in this, I'm going to bed.'

So Lizzie sat half way through the night till early dawn

watching, waiting and listening for the sound of the boys returning or even the sound of Bobby coming home. Then she fell asleep with her head on the table.

At eight o'clock next morning Carol roused her; this time she was a little bit more sympathetic. 'Oh dear, you sat up all night. Come on get near the fire, I'll give you a cup of tea.'

Lizzie's white, tear-stained face told its own tale.

'All right,' said Carol, 'I'll ring Charlie. Poor old Charlie, he has to do all the dirty work. Can't find Uncle Bobby now, can we? Not since that bird took a posh flat.'

Lizzie's woebegone face stared at her. Another knife of hurt entered her heart, for Lizzie was quite unaware of this new move of Bobby's.

Bella had grown tired of the sky-rise flat, they now shared an apartment not far from the dog tracks, so Bobby spent less time than ever at home.

Charlie called at lunchtime, dressed in a lovely silver-grey suit, his fair hair cut to a nice new style.

'I've been to the police. They're on the lookout for the boys, but if I was you, Aunt Lizzie, I'd let them go. After all, they've always been a bloody nuisance.'

'Oh dear,' wept Lizzie, 'poor little boys.'

'Little boys!' yelled Charlie, losing patience. 'Blimey! I went out to work when I was not quite fourteen. One of those boys is seventeen and able by law to leave home. It's Uncle Bobby you should be chasing, not those two layabouts, unless, of course, you want to end up a lonely old woman.'

From Charlie this was a bit much. Lizzie broke down into heartbreaking sobs and Charlie cuddled her saying, 'Sorry, old gel,' almost in tears himself. 'I never meant it. You know I think the world of you, but it's a hard, tough place outside and we have to live in it. Come on, love, stop crying, I'll do what I can.'

Carol stood looking at them, dry-eyed. 'I told you how soft she was, didn't I?'

'You get off to school, you little bitch. You're as bad as anyone.'

She put her tongue out at him then disappeared.

Charlie held Lizzie's hands and comforted her. 'Leave this gloomy old house, come and live with me and Luber,' he said. 'She would love to have you with her.'

'No,' said Lizzie, 'I'll be all right. This is my home, I'll not leave it.'

When Charlie had gone back to the office, Lizzie got out her ironing board and smoothed over Bobby's shirts, dreaming of the days when they were young and happy together. Then suddenly into her mind flashed the realization that Robin had not been home all night.

She had no idea that in fact another drama had been enacted that day. Robin had also discovered about the posh new flat in Leyton, the cosy love nest, and he was full of vengeance.

Bobby had gone off to the Ally Pally, the Londoners' race track at the Alexandra Palace, leaving Bella to run the betting shop in her usual efficient way.

Robin, who was still drinking heavily, closed the green-grocers shop early, then watched while Bella locked up the betting shop and went off to collect her little girl from the nursery school. Furtively he followed them, watched her get the bus, and then he got on the one behind. They travelled through Hackney to Leyton and alighted at Leabridge Road where there was a street of very nice two-storey flats, red-brick buildings with lace curtains at every window, and small front gardens. It all had an air of respectability, which was exactly why Bella had chosen it: 'Somewhere nice and quiet, where no one knows our business,' she had told Bobby. She meant eventually to force Bobby to leave Lizzie. She had furnished the flat nicely and it had all the modern conveniences like a bathroom and an indoor loo.

Bobby was happy on the whole, although he did feel trapped when he couldn't hop off to the races whenever he wanted to. But the little girl was sweet and lovable. She reminded him of Carol when she was a baby, and he spent less and less time at home.

On this particular day, quite unaware that Robin had dogged her footsteps, Bella held her little girl by the hand, walked gracefully down that quiet suburban road and proudly put her key into the front door of her own nice flat. Once inside she put on a loose gown and started to prepare a meal for Bobby, who she knew would arrive later. Meanwhile Robin stood on the corner surveying the place, not having the courage to go any nearer.

At five thirty the pub was open, so Robin went into the local and sat drinking whiskey all alone, brooding on his troubles. That crafty sod Bobby had swiped that lovely girl from under his nose and here he was living it up, while poor Aunt Lizzie was sitting down in the basement kitchen, waiting for him to come home. Robin thought he would go in there and tell Bella what he thought of her, the little whore. He made to leave the pub and stared bleary-eyed and tipsily down the road. There was Bobby, turning into the road, so Robin darted back into the pub and consumed a few more whiskeys. Then at ten o'clock Robin lumbered drunkenly down the road and knocked at the nice brass door knocker, rat-tat-tat, just like the law, he thought in his fuzzy mind. Bella's head appeared at the window of the upstairs flat, then she popped her head in again quickly.

'Bobby,' she cried, 'it's that bloody Robin, and he is as drunk as hell.'

'Oh Christ!' cried Bobby. 'See if you can get rid of him.'

So Bella smiled charmingly out of the window. 'Hello, Robin, what do you want?'

'Send that bastard out, that bleeding Bobby,' called Robin drunkenly. 'I've got a score to settle with him.'

'Don't be silly. This is my flat, why should Bobby be here?'

'You lying little cow,' roared Robin loudly. 'We all know about your love nest.'

'He's not here, honestly, Robin,' she pleaded.

'Well come down and talk to me then.'

'Please, Robin, go away. All the neighbours will hear you,' she entreated tearfully.

'Not till you let me in,' roared Robin again.

So Bella closed the window and consulted a very frightened Bobby. He did not want to fight with his foster son over a woman, for he knew that if he did so this nice hideout would be blown, and Lizzie would know all. He put on his shoes.

'I'll sneak down the fire escape and over the back wall. Keep him talking at the front door, then you can show him that I am not in the flat, and I might get away with it.'

'Can't see the point,' she said. 'I feel a little sorry for Robin; you ought to face him.'

'Now do me a favour, duck, and don't argue,' said the wary Bobby, making for the fire escape.

Bella went down and opened the front door. She put her finger to her lips. 'Hush, Robin, don't wake the baby. Bobby is not here. You know I'd never allow it.'

Robin pushed his way in and held on to her, completely distraught. 'Oh Bella, I love you. I'm mad about you. Why couldn't it be me?'

She tried to push him off but he held tight. 'Let me come up, Bella, just a little kiss and cuddle, I won't ask for more. Let me be sure that he's not here.'

Bella heard the back door shut. 'All right,' she said, 'you can come in and have a cup of coffee to sober you up, otherwise you'll get arrested.'

So Robin edged his way up the stairs and looked around for some sign of Bobby's presence there. Drunkenly his eyes roved, seeing very little but the distressed Bella, her hair all over her eyes, and her loose flowing gown showing the tops of her white breasts. It was too much. He grabbed her tight, pulled her on to the settee, his drunken weight almost paralysing her. She tried to escape; they rolled onto the carpet.

'Oh Robin, don't,' she begged.

'Bella,' he cried, 'my lovely Bella, you are mine. Always have been.'

Repeatedly she fought him off but his hands held her tight. Her loose gown came off as they rolled about on the floor, then suddenly she stopped struggling.

'All right, you bastard,' she cried, 'take what you want and go.'

But Robin was past all thought. In his arms he held the naked body of his lovely Bella and that was all he cared.

Meanwhile, poor Bobby was walking along the main road dripping with mud and slime. He hailed a taxi and the driver said, 'No thanks, mate, you ain't getting in my cab in that state.' And the last bus was long gone.

In making his hasty retreat, Bobby had forgotten about the Dagenham Brook, the dirty slimy stretch of water that ran along the back gardens of the flats. He had jumped over the garden wall straight into it, wearing his best suit, and seven miles from home.

Lizzie was lying on the couch in the kitchen waiting for him. He came in at three o'clock and crept upstairs very slowly, silently grunting and shivering.

Taking some tea to him early in the morning, she noticed the pile of stinking clothes on the floor. Bobby had the bedclothes pulled right over his head and would not come out.

'Something must have happened to Uncle Bobby,' Lizzie said to Carol. 'It looks like he fell in the river.'

'Serve him right,' said Carol who always had a cob on early in the morning. Grabbing her school satchel, she said, 'He's more like a bloody kid than a man. Don't know how you've put up with him for so long.'

But Lizzie was worried about Bobby and reached in the larder for the Bovril jar. She would have a nice hot drink ready for him, in case he caught a cold.

At about the same time Robin lay asleep on the floor in Bella's flat. She pushed him with her foot. 'Get up and get out, if you don't mind. I've got to go to work and take my child to school.'

Robin sat up, looked at Bella in her blue suit with her hair neatly waved, and her long silk clad legs. Nothing was out of place; and there was not even a trace of last night's nightmare. He got to his feet put out his arm to her, 'I am sorry, Bella. I was drunk.'

'Makes no difference to me,' she said angrily. 'I've been raped before, but usually they paid me.'

He put his hand over his eyes. 'Oh Bella, don't be cruel. I love you. I want to marry you.'

'Robin, you got what you came for, now disappear. I'm

Bobby's woman; he keeps me, so at least I owe him some loyalty. If he ever got to know about this he'd kill you, so let's avoid a lot of trouble and you go on your way.'

He looked lost. 'Bella I love you, let me come again.'

'No, Robin. If you do, I'll tell Bobby.' She picked up his jacket, threw it at him and gave him a very disconcerting push towards the door. 'Get going,' she cried. 'You'll make me late for work.'

Robin, almost blubbering, walked down that long suburban street with his jacket over his arm, then got on the wrong bus and ended up in dockland where the pubs were open early, and he began another drinking session.

Lizzie, still hoping that the boys would return, whiled away the day until Bobby rose. He was like a bear with a sore head.

'The boys have run away from home,' she informed him tearfully.

'Bleeding good riddance,' said Bobby. 'I was getting so fed up with them, I was going to boot them out soon.'

Lizzie's face wrinkled in grief. 'Oh Bobby, those poor unwanted little boys.'

'Piss off,' cried Bobby crudely. 'You spoilt those little sods rotten. This isn't my home any more, what with you and that saucy bitch Carol and those rotters. They've ruined it for me; can't wonder I am always out.'

Lizzie's lips tightened. 'Bobby don't blame those children for your misdemeanours. I am quite aware of your affair with that redhead, but I've survived several others, and so far I haven't interfered.'

'Well,' snarled Bobby, 'you're not much good in bed, so what am I supposed to do?'

Lizzie's pride came to the fore. Her face flushed and that small frame seemed to grow a little. 'Bobby Erlock,' she said very precisely, 'it is entirely your own fault our married life has broken down, but I seem to recall that before my illness it was not very difficult for you to remain faithful to me.'

He stood gaping, lost for words, so Lizzie took up arms and declared that if he wanted to go and live with that Bella he was welcome to do so. She no longer needed a part-time husband

and was well able to cope by herself. 'And,' she cried indignantly, 'when you run out of cash don't come to me for a loan.' Then very slowly she walked out into the garden and sat on the old seat under the sycamore tree.

Bobby did not understand her defiant attitude, so he decided that he just could not quarrel with her, picked up his hat and left the house.

Lizzie sat very, very still. The autumn breeze whistled gently through the trees and the brown wrinkled leaves tumbled down about her. She looked at the house, at the grey brick walls towering up to the tiled roof with its little attic window where the boys had their den. It was all so still and eerie, just as if she were a stranger and the house was no longer the place of love and friendship that she had created. She had burned her boats by attacking Bobby; she had given him carte blanche to leave her. And she cared – oh God, how she cared. Perhaps it was the end of the road, her life might be over soon. A deep melancholy possessed her, but not for the past; she had received lots of love and happiness, she had no regrets. She sat so still that it began to get chilly. Eventually Maisie, in her army uniform, popped her head round the side door. She was paying one of her infrequent visits. Since her marriage, she had lived in the army hostel and was serenely happy and secure with Peter, her Salvation Army captain.

'What are you sitting out there all alone for?' she demanded. 'And where is everyone?'

'They have all left me,' said Lizzie in a most depressing tone.

'Oh my goodness, what doldrums,' cried Maisie helping her inside. 'I'll put the kettle on and you can tell me your troubles, Aunt Lizzie. I've burdened you often enough with mine.'

So Lizzie poured out her tale of woe.

Maisie said, 'Is that all? Bobby won't leave you, he knows which side his bread is buttered and it will do those little devils good to have to rough it. And as for Robin, I'll find him. He has taken to drink. I have often seen him, and my husband and I have prayed that he will be saved. It's that immoral woman in the betting shop that's the cause of all this trouble of yours,' declared Maisie. 'A serpent in the garden of Eden.'

Lizzie was amused, for when Maisie got astride her religious hobby horse she was like a fiend.

'Peter and I will find Robin,' she said, 'and rescue him from the depths of iniquity. We will tour the taverns of the devil to search for him.'

'I wouldn't have thought the pubs were quite your husband's cup of tea,' Lizzie said quietly.

'Well dear, that is where you are completely wrong. Why, my man has rescued sinners from all the dark places in the world.'

'Robin isn't a bad boy. He has changed just lately, but he was getting on so well with the shop. Do you think he and Bobby have quarrelled over that woman?'

'Yes, of course. Why, even Carol knows that, Aunt Lizzie, and you sit here in this gloomy kitchen, seldom seeing the light of the day let alone the light of the Lord. You must come to the meetings and make friends with those who will share your burden. Don't just sit and brood on it.'

Lizzie closed her eyes wearily. She found Maisie a trifle overpowering. 'Carol will be in soon. She's doing some sort of voluntary work at the old Royal in Stratford and is out most evenings.'

'Another house of the devil,' cried Maisie. 'No wonder those kids go wrong.'

'I'll have that cup of tea now, Maisie,' said Lizzie. 'I'll be all right now if you want to leave.'

'Oh well, I've got plenty to do, but don't worry, we'll find Robin and straighten him out.' She tied the long strings of her bonnet very neatly and pulled on her thick woollen gloves. Then she picked up the little suitcase she always carried, and giving her aunt a nice warm hug, said, 'Now, Aunt Lizzie, stop worrying. Leave the family to sort themselves out. With your heart as it is you can't afford to worry.' Then she trotted off and Lizzie was not sorry to see her go. She could not stand all that moralizing.

The next week Carol was home with her every day and

Bobby popped in and out of the house. It seemed as if the storm had blown over, although there was still no news from the boys, and she had little to say to Bobby, who still acted very sulkily. Lizzie did, however, tell him that the greengrocers shop was shut and the stock was rotting. It was time he did something about it, as it was money down the drain.

'All right,' he said, 'if that stupid sod isn't coming back I'll put someone in to keep it running, and then put it up for sale.'

'I don't care what you do about it as long as it doesn't go to pot. I hate waste.'

The weeks went by, then Charlie popped in to say that Robin was staying at his house. Maisie and her husband had taken him there one night in the most terrible condition. He had been drinking and sleeping rough and was completely broke.

'He won't come home,' said Charlie.

'Why not?' asked Lizzie.

'It's to do with that cow up at the betting shop,' said Charlie. 'Robin is nuts about her and it seems that she's had both Bobby and Robin on a piece of string.'

Lizzie's lips trembled. 'I'd have thought Bobby would have shown a bit more good sense.'

'Well, we all know Uncle Bobby,' said Charlie with irony. 'Still, Robin is all right with me. He's talking about going into the Merchant Navy when he's fit. Bloody awful condition he was in, kipping under the arches with all the down and outs, so Maisie's husband said.'

'Oh dear, the silly boy,' sighed Lizzie, her mind drifting to those other two vagabonds. God only knows where they were or what they were up to.

It was six weeks later when Robin sailed away on the briny and Carol left school. She had taken a part time job at the chemist's shop to make up her pocket money and not to interfere with her drama school classes.

The weather had become cold and Lizzie spent most of the time below stairs beside the coal fire. The big house was very quiet, no children larking about, no music playing. So she sat and dreamed of the good old days when the house was full and everyone needed her and loved her. It would soon be Christmas and it was going to be a very lonely one for her.

One day Carol came home from her part time job very excited. 'Guess what?' she said to Lizzie. 'That bird of Uncle Bobby's is pregnant.'

'How do you know?'

'Well, twice she came in for pills. They keep a certain kind under the counter. They're supposed to bring you on when you're overdue.'

'Well I never!' declared Lizzie.

'It's a new thing. You pay a fiver, bring a sample of your water and they send it to a special laboratory, then they can tell you very early on if you are pregnant.'

Lizzie was truly amazed. 'Well, what will they get up to next?' she cried.

'You're missing the point,' said Carol in her cheeky way. 'If she is pregnant she will get Bobby to divorce you. What about that?'

Lizzie looked very worried. 'Well let's not cross our bridges.'

'I'll find out. I'll take a peak at the report when it comes back and I'll tell you, Aunt Lizzie.'

'I am not sure that I'd be interested and I don't believe in these new-fangled ideas.'

'You wait and see,' declared Carol, thoroughly enjoying the situation.

Lizzie was dismayed and hurt. For all her married life she had been childless and had concentrated her love on other folk's children. Now, at forty-eight, Bobby was to be a father. Yes, she thought, but was he? That she must be sure of.

Several days later Carol came in jubilant. 'I was right, the rabbit died of pneumonia.'

'What are you talking about?'

'That's the medical term for being pregnant,' said Carol. 'That Bella has clicked. I read the report.'

Lizzie felt suddenly sad. Then, one lunchtime, after a term of reflection she said to Carol, 'Go up to the betting shop and tell that young woman I'd like a talk with her.'

'Well,' cried Carol, 'you are getting courageous. Suppose she won't come?'

Lizzie said, 'I'll give you a note for her, then you disappear. I don't want you listening.'

'I was going down the Royal anyway,' said Carol haughtily.

Lizzie wrote in her neat hand, 'It will be to your advantage, also mine, if we meet for a chat; no need for anyone else to know. Please come down to my house tomorrow afternoon. Lizzie Erlock.'

CHAPTER SIXTEEN

Love Finds a Way

It was a dull, rainy afternoon as Lizzie sat and waited for Bella to arrive. She was not even sure that Bella would come, for when Carol had handed the note to her, she had read it, then stared at Carol in a very supercilious manner before saying, 'I might if I find the time.'

'Who does she think she is? Stuck up cow,' declared Carol indignantly.

'Now dear, keep out of it. I'll be very clever. I can if I want to. You go down to the theatre and have a good time.'

Watching the raindrops trickle down the kitchen window, Lizzie sat quietly waiting for her rival, that dreaded other woman. On the dot of four she saw her come down the steps holding her child by the hand.

'I had to bring Gloria,' she said, 'I've got no one to look after her, once she comes out of the nursery school.'

From her five foot, Lizzie looked up at Bella, surprised that she was so tall, almost as tall as Bobby. She was smartly dressed but looked pale, tense and very nervous.

'Little Gloria will be no trouble,' said Lizzie, taking the little girl by the hand and sitting her by the fire. 'She's very pretty. Would you like a cake, dear?'

The child nodded and Lizzie placed a sweet pastry in her hand.

Bella said, 'I can't stay long. What did you want to speak to me about?'

'Oh, stay for a cup of tea,' said Lizzie sweetly, beginning to pour one out.

Bella relaxed and sat down opposite her.

'Now, dear,' said Lizzie, sipping her tea. 'Don't let you and

I fool each other, for I know you are a smart girl and my Bobby really appreciates the way you work so hard in the betting shop.

Bella flushed and raised her eyebrows disdainfully. 'Come on,' she said abruptly, 'you know the score. What is it you're after?'

Lizzie put down her cup. 'Yes, I know all about your affair with my husband. I also know Bobby, having been married to him for thirty years and surviving several mistresses. What I'd like to know is, do you love him or are you just using him?'

Bella shrugged. 'Well, in the beginning he had money to spend and I was very short of cash but he has been so good to Gloria and me that I'll try not to lose him, whatever you may say.'

'Well,' said Lizzie, 'that's a straightforward enough answer, but what about Robin?'

'I never had anything to do with Robin. He did hang around but I was after the lolly.'

'Am I supposed to believe that?'

Bella flushed. Surely Robin would not have told this faded woman what had happened that night. She looked down, her long lashes held tears.

'Well dear?' said Lizzie. 'Why don't you open up, something is on your mind, and I believe you are now probably pregnant.'

This brought Bella into action. 'Why! Bloody sauce! Who said so?'

'I know,' said Lizzie.

'But how can you?'

'Well, at my age there are certain signs that you notice.'

Strangely enough Bella believed her.

'I am getting an abortion,' she said. 'I have been left in the cart once and no one is going to do that to me again.'

'What does Bobby say about it?' asked Lizzie.

'I haven't told him yet.'

'He is nearly fifty. Never had a child myself, it's funny that he managed that with you.'

Bella began to get annoyed. 'What are you suggesting?' she cried.

'That there's someone else,' said Lizzie. 'If this child is Bobby's, I'll step down and wish you happiness, and I will love this baby as if it was my own. But I want the truth. Why are you so anxious for Bobby not to know? You know, love, he tires of his women very quickly. Bobby is a boy at heart and has never grown up. Think carefully before you mess up your life. Abortion is a dangerous thing.'

Tears started to leak out and black mascara ran over those fair cheeks.

'Lizzie,' she said suddenly, 'I don't know how you found out, but I think it was that bloody Robin. I'm always careful when I sleep with Bobby and use a preventative, but Robin forced his way into my flat and practically raped me.'

'Oh! So that's what it's all about,' said Lizzie.

'What can I do? Only get out of trouble the only way I know.'

Lizzie sat looking at her very thoughtfully, while Bella wiped her eyes. Then she said, 'Robin truly loves you, did you know that? Since you went to live with Bobby he has gone on the drink.'

'I am so sorry. He's a nice boy, but I didn't encourage him. only wanted Bobby because I was hard up for money and I'm ed up with young men.'

'Bella dear,' said Lizzie kindly, 'I feel sure that Robin will want to marry you. He is young and healthy; Bobby is a waster and past his prime. You're a sensible girl, why don't you think it over?'

Bella got up and went over and kissed Lizzie's cheek. 'You re an amazing woman, Lizzie. No wonder Bobby isn't keen o leave you. I promise not to tell him until I've decided what o do.'

'That's it, dear, no more tears. I know where to find Robin, e's coming home next week, so don't worry, it'll all come right.'

So Bella went on her way, promising to keep in touch, and izzie sat down and wrote a letter to Robin. 'Come and see me, obin. Better still, go and see Bella, for I am sure you both have something to discuss.' This she sent to Charlie's house for Robin to get as soon as he came ashore the following week.

Bobby, quite ignorant of the intrigue around him, still went his own merry way. But he was a little worried by the fact that Bella had suddenly gone very cold on him, insisting that she had to see a sick relation that weekend. She said he was not to come round, and managed to relieve him of his latch key, pretending that she had lost hers and wanted to get another one cut. Big, clever Bobby fell for it.

On Saturday morning Robin and Bella got married by special licence; Luber and Charlie were witnesses. Bella's little girl, Gloria, stayed with Carol, who also looked after Charlie's boy. Robin and Bella went back to the flat in Leyton for their honeymoon; Bella had found a family, and Robin his true love.

Bobby went off to Kempton Park on Friday afternoon, then to the dogs on Saturday, and on Sunday he lay in bed recuperating, while Lizzie walked about the house humming a little tune to herself.

'I'm getting married in the morning, so get me to the church on time,' she sang.

On Monday Bella did not come to work, so Bobby had to hold the fort. Then in the evening he went round to the flat to see what had happened to her. He knocked on the front door, yelling, 'Bella, come down, I've not got a key.' There was a slight movement inside and the door opened to disclose a jubilant Robin wearing Bobby's slippers.

'My wife is resting,' said Robin coolly. 'I'll give her a message from you.'

'What the hell is going on?' roared Bobby, trying to push his way in, but Robin pushed him out again.

'Go home, Bobby,' he said. 'You've had your time; cash in your chips, lad. Bella is mine now,' and he slammed the door in Bobby's face.

For a moment or two Bobby stood, dumbstruck, then he pounded on the door, crying, 'Bella! Bella! Come out, it's Bobby. I must talk to you.'

But Bella sat huddled in an armchair, weeping, and Bobby was left out in the cold.

At about midnight Bobby went home, staggered in and upstairs. Lizzie came to the door and watched him, then she heard the sound of dry sobs coming from his room, so she decided to leave him alone.

Early the next morning, she took his cup of tea up to him, sat beside him and whispered, 'What's the matter, Bobby, have you got a cold?'

He put an arm across his eyes to keep out the daylight. 'You know, Lizzie,' he said hoarsely. 'You all know. She married Robin; you all did the dirty on me, and that bitch, she just took me for all I had to give. I'm through with women.'

Lizzie stroked his forehead. 'Bobby dear, it's all for the best. Now drink your tea.'

Later that day he walked about the house, mouthing threats to all concerned and uttering a long string of swear words.

'I'll get that bitch, I'll have her out of that bloody flat. I paid the rent, I swear she won't get the laugh on me.'

Lizzie, listening to all this, said mildly, 'No you won't, Bobby. Leave them alone. By the way, I have given them the greengrocer's shop. They must have some means of making a living.'

'Well, for Christ's sake,' roared Bobby, 'what the hell am I here? You're all ganging up on me. What about me and the bleeding betting shop? Lost me quids, she has, not turning up on Monday.'

Lizzie give a gentle smile. 'Never mind, Bobby. You'll get by, you always do.'

CHAPTER SEVENTEEN

Prosperity

For a week or so Bobby mooched around from Oddy's to the betting shop, apparently unable to decide where to go from here.

The loss of Bella had really hurt him. Lizzie was very conscious of this and, despite everything, she felt sorry for him. So, in order to help him and keep him sweet-tempered, she prepared all his favourite things to eat, like stewed eels and cooked bread pudding.

'More stewed eels, and more bread pudding,' grumbled Carol. 'I'll have my dinner out. I'd sooner go to the Chinese restaurant.'

'Well, my dear, I'm not sure what the Chinese cook, but it will cost you. And eating at home with me is free,' said Lizzie a little sharply, for Carol's battery of complaints was getting on her nerves.

It flared up one day when Carol said, 'Why don't you just say you want me to give up the money which I earn in the shop?'

'It's not that, my dear, it's your pocket money, after all. But I do wish you'd stop complaining.'

'Well it's very little, not enough to buy makeup, but it's hell here with you and Bobby not on speaking terms. One day I'll run away like the boys did.'

'Please yourself,' replied Lizzie with a deep sigh.

Then one night Bobby brought in a big pile of bank notes. 'Put them in the dresser, dear,' he said, while putting an elastic band round them. 'That's the takings from the betting shop. I'm turning it in.'

'But, Bobby, what will you do?' Lizzie asked.

'Well I certainly won't join that bumptious sod over the road.'

He meant Robin, who was back at work, having cleaned up the greengrocer's and restocked it. Now he could be seen whistling merrily as he arranged his wares and calling out loud, 'Tanner a pound spuds, ripe bananas,' and such like. He was like a bantam cock, strutting and crowing before the battle, but Bella stayed out of sight.

One day Bobby rose early, brought out his suitcase and packed it with his silk pyjamas and best shirts. Then he took out the bundle of notes from the dresser, aimed them in, then snapped the case shut and said casually, 'I'm going to York for three days racing. Be all right, duchess?'

'I usually am,' retorted Lizzie dryly.

He looked contrite and kissed her cheek. 'Sorry about all this, Lizzie, old gel. I've got to get away for a while.'

'It's all right, Bobby, I understand,' she answered. 'Mind how you go.'

Then, with his smart case in one hand, Bobby put on his hat with the other and hurried out of the door. Lizzie wiped away a tear and went on with her chores. No good sitting down whining: she hadn't been able to hold him when she was young, so what could she do now?

Once Bobby had gone, the family came visiting. Charlie and Luber came with their son Luber once more happily pregnant. Charlie was belligerent.

'Now where has Bobby gone?'

'To the York races.'

'He gets my bloody goat. Why can't he do a proper day's work instead of wasting his time and gambling? I don't know how you stand it, Aunt Lizzie.'

Lizzie shrugged. 'Well, that's Bobby. He has always been that way.'

Robin came in with a subdued-looking Bella. Lizzie affectionately hugged them both and said, 'I hope you will be very happy.'

Robin cried, 'We are fine, Aunt Lizzie,' and turning to Bella, 'ain't we, Bella?'

Her hazel eyes smiled but her lips remained still.

'Thanks for letting me keep the shop, Aunt Lizzie,' said Robin. 'Bella thinks we should work up a good business, then sell it for a profit and go into something else.'

Lizzie nodded her approval. 'The rent is paid for a year, Robin, so it might be quite a good idea.'

Once they had all left the house was eerily still, there was no one upstairs, and no noise but the ticking of the clock in the hall. Lizzie sat dozing by the fire till Carol came in.

She was overcome with excitement because she had been offered a small part in the theatre workshop. 'A performance down at the Royal, picked me out of ten others in the audition,' she cried jubilantly. 'Miss Smallwood said she likes me.'

'That's nice for you, Carol.'

'It means that I shall be out every night of the week. Got to go to rehearsals. Will you be all right, Aunt Lizzie?'

'I'll be all right,' said Lizzie, but really she was dreading the long lonely evenings, wondering where Bobby was and how her wandering boys were faring.

That week seemed like a month to her. Then on Monday morning Bobby returned, wearing a grubby beer-stained shirt, and needing a shave. He looked very much the worse for wear.

'Right,' he said, throwing his hat on the chair. 'I'll have a nice big mug of tea and two rounds of hot toast made on the fire.' Just as if he had never been away.

Lizzie smiled and put the kettle on. She stirred up the fire and Bobby put his feet up on the fender. He had removed his shoes and his socks steamed in the heat, giving out a very strong smell!

'Lizzie, old gel,' he said after a while. 'I really believe that I've cracked it this time. I stand to make a million pounds one day.'

She smiled and reflected, oh dear, here we go again. Then she said, 'Is that so, do tell me.'

'Well, me old darling,' he said affectionately, 'if this works I'll load you up with all the jewels you can carry. Why, I'll even put a ring in your bloody silly nose!' Then he went into guffaws of laughter.

Lizzie sat next to him and stroked his knee. 'It's good to have you home, Bobby,' she said.

'Now listen,' he said, 'I'll tell you all about it. I went to York fed up to the neck, had a few hundred to speculate and, you know, I couldn't bloody lose. In three days I trebled my stake. What do you think about that, duchess?'

'Very nice,' said Lizzie doubtfully.

'Well, that's not all. I met a chap I used to know over at Clapton and went with him to have a game of cards. You know, Lizzie, it's all going on up there, just as many villains as there used to be in London before the war.

'Very nice,' muttered Lizzie, wondering what was coming next.

'Well, you would never believe it, I couldn't go wrong. I spent three nights at this club. This old bloke was a cockney trader from Stepney; he got evacuated up there and he is the big time boss now; believe me he's got his fingers in many nice pies. So, after three nights I had his IOU's for several hundred quid. Jesus! Bobby Erlock, I said to myself, they ain't goner let you out of here alive. But you'll never believe it, we made a deal. I got a cut in his business and I'm about to promote his stuff down here. So I chucked in my betting shop and a bit more cash and we are now partners.'

Lizzie stared, aghast. 'But, Bobby, didn't you say he was a villain?'

'Yes, I know, but they're all bleeding villains in that game. What's the bloody difference?'

Lizzie kept silent.

'He's got a place up west. It's a betting shop, bingo hall and pin table parlour all combined, brings in a bomb of readies and I am starting off up there. So, duchess, there's no need to worry any more. At last I got me a regular job.'

'Very nice, Bobby dear,' murmured Lizzie, but she was still unconvinced. It all sounded a bit dodgy somehow. The only thing to be said for it was that Bobby was his old happy-go-lucky self and easy to live with again. And that, after all, was what she wanted.

So Bobby entered into that world of crime which hid behind

bingo halls and fruit machines, and he found that the criminal fraternity of the sixties were a lot different from the shabby down-at-heel corner boys of the thirties. Since that time a whole generation of young men had gone down in the battlefields of Europe, in the North African deserts and the steamy jungles of the Far East. Those who survived were of a different mettle. They were hard, vicious types who made a living on the backs of others. Beside them, big, tough Bobby was like a babe in arms.

Flash gambling clubs had sprung up in Soho and in the big towns since gambling became legal. It was a good business with plenty of money to be made, but the young lads were entirely without scruples; honour among thieves did not exist any more. For a time Bobby bathed in the sunshine of his new-found property; he wore hand-tailored suits, smoked big cigars, was very generous to the family and quite amicable to everyone. He spent a lot of time away from home, grew fat on the free lunches and dinners and built up a big bank balance. In two years, he told them all, he had really cracked it.

As Bobby had promised, he loaded Lizzie with jewellery, more rings and heavy neck chains replaced those turquoise earrings that she could no longer wear. For Lizzie had lost one of her earrings in hospital, and wore the remaining one on a chain about her neck. Bobby bought her smart modern diamonds and turquoises that she would seldom wear, for Lizzie still clung to the old days, old jewellery and old associations. If she changed at all it was to become even paler and thinner as she watched Bobby's prosperity.   One day she received a picture postcard with a foreign stamp on it. The card read, 'Dear Aunt Lizzie, We are in Spain working in a hotel but by the time you get this we will have gone to Miami, going to work on the ships, Love Paul and Derick.'

'Oh dear,' cried Lizzie, 'where is that place?'

Carol said, 'It's in America. Wish I was with them.'

Bobby grinned and said, 'Why, those two sods really have made it! Well, good luck to them.'

Carol, now nineteen, attended classes at RADA and had

small parts in various fringe theatres and plays. She was happy at her work but was continually pestering Lizzie to move.

'How can I bring anyone home here to this?' she complained. 'Why, we ain't even got a decent bathroom, and it's like a bloody morgue with all those empty rooms upstairs.'

Bobby agreed with her. 'Look here, Liz, got to give the kid her due, she is trying. If you don't make her comfortable she'll get her own flat. The kids today, you should see them up west, four or five of them sharing a room.'

Lizzie said obstinately, 'I won't move.'

'All right, let's modernize this bloody place. You can have the money for it.'

'Oh, I can't stand a lot of workmen buzzing about in and out.'

Carol said, 'They have closed down the church and they are going to pull all this lot down, so you will have to go.'

'I don't believe it,' said Lizzie.

'Well, I know someone who is on the Council,' said Carol, 'so don't believe me, Aunt Lizzie, if you don't want to.'

Bobby said, 'That kid's no fool. I am going to find out for sure.'

Feeling very deflated, Lizzie declared, 'If I go anywhere it's back to The Nile where I belong.'

This really amused Bobby. 'Oh gor blimey, duchess, you kill me.' He roared with laughter. 'The bloody Nile has gone, it's disappeared. It's all big office blocks and skyscraper flats now.'

Lizzie looked desolate. 'I used to like the City,' she said, 'and walking in Bunhill Fields and seeing St Paul's dome from the upstairs bedroom window.'

'Now they got the Post Office Tower to look at,' said Bobby, 'and a bloody horrible sight that is.'

'Oh well, if it's true, I'll move. But I'll go nearer to Charlie and Luber.'

But Bobby did not reply. Both he and Carol had ideas of their own.

Robin and Bella had settled down very well also. Their small son was called Mark, he was a sturdy toddler with long legs like Bobby, a very loud voice and a big wide mouth.

Lizzie would look at the baby and wonder if it had been possible. Could Bobby have managed it? The babe certainly looked like him. Sometimes. Oh well, what was done was done, but she felt a kind of pull towards the mischievous child.

Robin and Bella had sold the greengrocer's and returned Lizzie her money. Now they had a smart restaurant and wine bar out at Greenwich.

Bobby still ignored them and did not like anyone even to mention their names, but little Mark kept Lizzie company through many dull afternoons. If Bella and Robin had a very busy day ahead of them, Robin would drop Mark off at Lizzie's in the morning and then collect him again in the evening.

Mark was such a live-wire that it was almost impossible to keep him out of trouble. He was not yet three, but Lizzie loved him. He could hold a long conversation with her and, to her dismay, had picked up a lot of swear words. They would play cards together, Mark and Aunt Lizzie, but snap was too dull for him. He liked to play brag and find the lady, they were his special games. With a terrific performance he would rub his tiny hands together, and imitate the real cockney patter: 'Someone now find the lady, for one half penny on a card, who is the lucky winner?' Lizzie would giggle and make sure she lost.

'He amazes me. Where does he learn it all? He's already a gambling man,' she would say to Bella.

Bella's lip curled. 'Could be in the family,' she said sardonically.

Then one day Bobby arrived home early. Mark was rummaging in the hall cupboard and Bobby fell straight over him. 'Who the bleeding hell is this?' he said, as he hauled him out.

But little Mark stood sturdily in front of him. 'Here, lay orf,' he hollered at Bobby, 'you ain't the bloody guv'nor.'

Bobby stared at him in amazement. 'Who's he?' he asked Lizzie.

'It's Mark. He's Robin and Bella's boy,' she answered timidly.

He scratched his head. 'Blimey!' he said. 'No wonder.' But

he made no attempt to make friends with Mark, who sat beside him, casting him dirty looks all the time, as he devoured his meal.

Bobby hid his head in his newspaper after dinner and Mark said in his high childish treble, 'Ain't got a lot to say for himself, has he, Aunt Lizzie?'

'Now Mark, here's your Daddy,' said Lizzie, as she hustled him towards the door.

That evening they both sat quietly beside the fire but avoided the subject of Bella's young boy.

On the whole Lizzie was much more content than she had ever been and lived more comfortably, although she still hoarded her money and spent very little on herself. When she did spend money it was usually on presents for Bella's children. Gloria now went to a private school, and she visited Lizzie on Saturday morning in her grey gym slip, with a little straw boater hat perched on her red-gold curls. Lizzie was wild about her.

Luber had disappointed her lately by turning her children over to a nanny, and travelling with Charlie on his business trips abroad. The nanny was a Philippino, a very nice clean, intelligent girl, but still Lizzie could not understand it.

'How can she go and leave those darling babies with a stranger, and a coloured one at that?'

Carol would scoff, 'Aunt Lizzie come down to earth. She's not letting Charlie do what he likes, and I don't blame her.'

'Charlie is a real nice boy, he wouldn't do anything like that.'

'Don't make me laugh,' said Carol. 'Aunt Lizzie, you don't live in the modern world.'

'Well, I would have taken care of the children for her.'

'Aunt Lizzie, you are getting on, and not in good health. No sensible mother would leave her children in your care.'

Lizzie was so hurt that she stared at Carol speechlessly with tears in her eyes.

'Oh, here we go,' said Carol, 'start weeping. All right, I never meant it, but sometimes, Aunt Lizzie, I think I grew up and you never did.'

'Well,' said Lizzie, 'I wonder how you would have grown up if I hadn't taken care of you.'

'OK,' snapped Carol, 'don't rub it in. I said I'm sorry.'

Bobby pulled strings until he discovered that there were firm plans to develop the whole area, in two years' time.

'Well, Lizzie, old gel, that's it, we have to make a move.'

'Oh Bobby!' she looked at him in dismay.

'I like it here too, you know. We made this home together after the war. Do you remember how we scrounged that table and those chairs from the other bombed places?'

She smiled. 'I know, and you put up Robin's swing, and how proud he was of it! I can see them all now, playing around that old tree.'

'Well, love, that's life; nearly over, let's face it. The bulldozers will show it no mercy, so duchess, it's time we moved on.'

She rubbed her chin on his shoulder and sat close to him. Lately Bobby was more his old affectionate self; she asked very little of him – only that he came home and acknowledged that she was there.

Was it possible that there were no women in his life now? He came home very late but did not often stay out all night and was more concerned with making money than in having a good time. Lizzie had no clear vision of the West End business, which now included blue films and strip joints.

'We will sell this place to the nig-nogs before anyone gets the wheeze that it is going to be pulled down.'

'Nig nogs?'

'The coons, wogs or whatever they call 'em. London is lousy with them, and they all want to buy their own house. It was a good move on your part to buy this as a sitting tenant. We should make a fair good profit.'

'But is that fair, Bobby? Those poor people will just be getting settled and then they will have to move again.'

'That's their bleeding worry,' declared Bobby. 'I'll go to the estate agents tomorrow.'

From then on a series of people came to view the house. Most of them were coloured immigrants, Jamaican, Asian and

Indians from the hordes who poured into London in the late sixties and seventies.

Lizzie was inclined to be nervous of them, but Bobby would talk them into buying the house by putting the price up and then reducing it just to impress them.

Once, when Bobby lay sprawled out on the couch asleep, a timid Chinaman knocked at the door.

He looked puzzled and pointed at Bobby.

'The boss,' he said, 'I like a word with him.' He sat down beside Bobby, who lay there with his mouth wide open. By now Lizzie was also perplexed, and stared at the polite little man who continually bowed and smiled at her.

She prodded Bobby and said, 'Wake up.'

Bobby woke slowly, muttering and complaining, then with a big four letter word, stared into the face of the little Chinaman sitting beside him. 'What the hell?' he roared.

But the little man got up bowing and scraping. 'You big boss sir. I come to put up banns for wedding.'

'Well, you ain't bleeding well marrying me,' said Bobby irritably.

Then suddenly the penny dropped with Lizzie. Two doors away was the old rectory that was attached to the church. The church was empty and being demolished, but the young vicar still resided there and had his living in another big church in the main road.

Lizzie ushered the Chinaman to the door. 'Sorry,' she said, 'wrong place, next door but one.'

Nodding and still smiling, he went out of the side door.

'Oh dear,' she cried, 'I thought he had come to look over the house.'

But Bobby was in stitches laughing. 'Blimey!' he cackled, 'it's the first time anyone ever mistook me for the vicar.'

Eventually a family of Jamaicans bought the house for a good price, and the time came to move.

'I'll leave the choice of another house to you and Carol,' said Lizzie. 'If I go I won't like whatever I see.'

So Carol and Bobby went house hunting in his nice big car, and eventually chose a house in Ilford, a smart, modern, double-fronted villa just off the main road. It had all the mod cons and was ideally situated for getting back into London. This had been their first consideration; they quite overlooked the fact that it was on top of a hill.

It was not easy to get Lizzie moving. Bobby wanted to leave most of the furniture behind, but Lizzie insisted in taking her own special treasures and was still rather sorry for the new owners.

'Let the nig nogs have all the rubbish. I've bought new stuff.'

'Oh, poor little woman, I hope she will be happy here.'

'Blimey, gel! They'll make a fortune out of this dump,' declared Bobby. 'They will fill every room up with bloody woolly heads and they'll charge them twenty quid a room.'

Lizzie sighed. Bobby was so unsentimental, and she was worried about the new home that she had not yet seen.

CHAPTER EIGHTEEN

A New Home and a First Night

With a very sad backward glance, Lizzie took a last look at the house she had lived in for twenty years. It was a cold winter's day and the windows were frosted up, the house bare and empty. She stared at the nice big kitchen stove that summer and winter had always held a blazing fire.

'Let's hope those poor devils can afford all those tons of coal,' she said quietly.

'Give over, Aunt Lizzie. They'll modernize it, have electric fires and a hot water system put in; you'd be surprised what these immigrants do to the houses they buy, they really appreciate having a large house that they own,' Carol informed her.

Bobby said, 'I don't care what they bleeding well do with it; I got a good price, now let's get on our way.'

It had been years since Lizzie had taken a long journey, not since she was evacuated during the blitz. She stared apprehensively out of the car windows at the big lorries tearing by, while Bobby and Carol discussed the possibility of buying a television.

The almost new terraced house, looked very nice. It had big bay windows and rose trees lined up like soldiers along the front path. The road ran up hill from the main road and her house was almost at the top.

'What do they call this? Hillford?' muttered Lizzie. 'I should think so; I'll never be able to climb that hill if I go out.'

'No, Aunt Lizzie, it's Ilford,' giggled Carol, 'and you are not one to go out much. Uncle Bobby is going to teach me to drive so that I can take you shopping, and I might get my own car later when I can afford it.'

But Bobby irritably puffed at his cigar and said, 'Come on, gels, unload. I've got an appointment in town.'

Once they were inside the front door he was off, calling out, 'I'll be seeing you later.'

As Carol took her arm Lizzie felt her knees becoming weak with apprehension. She looked at the bright ultra-modern wallpaper in the hall, at the wide stairs and the new carpets.

'Do you like them?' asked Carol. 'Uncle Bobby let me choose.'

But purple and yellow was not quite Lizzie's cup of tea. They went into the well-furnished sitting room and Lizzie looked furtively around for a small quiet spot to hide herself. The luxurious settee and the tremendous armchairs really frightened her.

'Sit down,' said Carol, 'I'll get the supper.' She switched on the new electric fire and a red glow warmed the room. 'See how easy it is,' she said, 'no dirty old cinders to clear up; you won't know what to do with yourself, Aunt Lizzie. 'It's time we lived according to our means.'

'Whose means?' thought Lizzie, knowing that Bobby had borrowed quite a big sum from her to pay for all this splendour, and with her thrifty ways it really worried her.

'Sit down then,' cried Carol impatiently, giving her a little shove towards the deep, upholstered armchair.

'No I won't,' said Lizzie. 'If I get down there I'll never get up again – at least not without a struggle.'

'Oh dear,' sighed Carol, 'I'll get a chair from the kitchen. You have got your own bedroom, you know, it's on the downstairs floor and there is a toilet down here. Please, Aunt Lizzie, say you like it.' Carol was also beginning to get depressed.

'Sorry dear,' said Lizzie a little contrite, 'I'll be all right. It's all so confusing. I know that you have both done your best and I'll soon settle down.'

'That's it,' said Carol. 'You won't know yourself, dear, and we are going to get someone to come in and do the housework. Now I'll cook eggs and bacon, then tuck you up in bed, because I've got to get to the theatre in time for the performance. It's nice and handy; I'll get a bus right into Stratford from here.'

Lizzie sighed, not really liking the prospect of being alone in this new and pretentious house. It had a hostile feeling about it; she felt like an interloper, and it was a feeling she was never to lose. Thank goodness they had let her keep her own bed and that nice oak dressing table. She was pleased about that, and lay down her head and tried to sleep.

Carol dashed up and down the stairs into the bathroom, then into her bedroom, and then out the front door calling, 'Won't be late, Aunt Lizzie.'

Lizzie closed her eyes and tears ran down her cheeks. Where was the nice, warm, friendly family that she had raised? Why, even Sallie never bothered about her these days. Everyone was so busy doing their own thing. Well, she supposed that was life, but she was not all that old, so why was it so hard for her to adapt herself to new things and new surroundings? She wished she knew the answers.

Bobby lumbered up the stairs at midnight well boozed, and she heard Carol arrive shortly after that in a taxi.

Oh well, she sighed, they were home again so now she could sleep.

Eventually Lizzie managed to settle down. It took a few weeks, but she began by putting out her ornaments and the photographs of the children, mostly in the little bedroom on the first floor.

So, she would sit during the afternoons, looking at the glossy magazines which Carol brought home and staring out of the window, down the hill to the main road. All that traffic rushing past terrified her. Never would she venture down there. Where were the shops, she wondered? Not one in sight. All the houses were much alike, wandering down the hill, but they must surely be empty, for she rarely saw another human being; it was all so quiet and secretive. Smooth-running cars crawled up the drives at a certain time each day, but who got in or out she could not see.

Soon she found things to do. She would go around that smart sitting room with a feather duster, wash and iron Carol's frillys and Bobby's best shirts, but she was not allowed to do anything else.

A huge girl came twice a week, took away the laundry and replaced it with clean, then went around with a very noisy vacuum cleaner which was plugged into the electricity. Lizzie would never have used it even if she had known how to, but it held no fears for Ruby, with her big red face and large bottom, who smoked all the time and went around the house like a member of the Trojan army.

'All right, Ma?' she would ask pleasantly, or say, 'Nice day.' But that was the limit of her conversation.

Lizzie slowly got used to this very quiet, very lazy life and sat manicuring her nails and cold-creaming her face as she used to do down the shelter. Her hair was now a very light silver; she would curl it and brush it and look at herself in the mirror, put on her jewellery and a nice dress, then parade about the new house, enjoying the luxury of the soft carpets and the warm atmosphere. She would bring flowers in from the garden and arrange them. Carol would say, 'You know, Aunt Lizzie, you've got very artistic ideas; the flowers look lovely,' and Lizzie would smile.

'Yes,' she would say, 'I always did like nice things.'

Bobby remarked jovially, 'Well gor blimey! I believe the old gel is settling down at last.'

To this Carol replied tartly, 'I don't know how you can say that. She isn't any older than you.'

'Well, you know what I mean,' Bobby would try to sneak out of any argument with Carol.

'No, I do not,' she'd say haughtily, 'but I do know that it's a woman who gets all the worry. It will be a long time before I get married.'

Lizzie amused herself in her new surroundings but made no friends. She never went out alone, only with Carol or Bobby to the shops. She still missed the old house. She would try to talk about the days before the war, and about her mother selling flowers outside the hospital. But neither Bobby nor Carol wanted to listen. They would sit engrossed in their new status symbol, the television. It confused Lizzie; she tried hard to listen, but found her mind wandering off in another direction, and eventually she would doze off.

Bobby still went on making more and more money. Lizzie had no notion how many blue films or strip clubs he was now involved in. He would bring in bundles of notes, telling her to keep them in a safe place. 'Can't put money in the bank these days, the bloody income tax man is after it.'

Dutifully Lizzie would hide the money in various places in her bedroom, sometimes with a very uneasy feeling inside her, wondering if it was honestly obtained.

Carol conned Bobby for lots of extras, like driving lessons and very modern clothes. At times Lizzie would sit watching Carol in amazement as she made up her face, usually with a mirror propped up on the coffee table so that she could still watch the evening television show. On went layers of make-up, long black lines under her eyes and two tones of shadow which made her lovely eyes look almost owl-like. Then the artificial eyelashes and very bright lipstick, to match her long, lacquered finger and toe nails.

Lizzie said one day, 'It's a pity to hide your nice creamy skin, Carol.'

'Oh, don't be silly,' she retorted. 'In my profession you have to make up.'

'Well, surely not off the stage?'

'Oh, do be quiet,' Carol rebuked her. 'You are so old-fashioned.'

Often now, on Sunday afternoons, the family came visiting, and in the summer they sat in the patio and had ice cream from the fridge and cool drinks. Sometimes it would be Robin and Bella and their two children, sometimes Charlie and Luber and sometimes Sallie with her small man. If they all came together Lizzie was especially happy.

Sallie said, 'Crikey, Liz, you've got the lot. What I'd give for a posh house like this.'

Lizzie replied sadly, 'It's all right, but I still miss my old home.'

'You must be mad. Living like a queen and still complaining. What's wrong with you, Lizzie?'

Lizzie sighed deeply but did not answer. Then the telephone would ring, that jangling thing, which had recently been installed in the hall and which made Lizzie nearly jump out of her skin, and it would be Bobby to say he had been delayed and might not be back tonight.

Lizzie did not know why he bothered. He had never worried about it before. Then Carol would ring to state that she was staying over night with some girlfriend and Lizzie would sit, hour after hour, worrying about her. She hated the telephone, and never used it herself except to answer the calls. Many were from Carol's boyfriends, and some from Bobby's gambling friends.

One night Carol brought home a boyfriend. Well, to Lizzie, staring curiously, he looked more like a girlfriend, with his long hair and plucked eyebrows, painted in long, thin pencilled lines. He was a good boy with very little to say, and when he did talk to her it was in a kind of slang that Lizzie did not understand. He and Carol spent long hours on the settee, making love, and Lizzie in her bedroom would quake with fear lest anything happen to Carol.

One day Lizzie said, 'I don't think Jerry should stay all night.'

'He can't get home, he lives up London.'

'Well, dear, I am so afraid for you,' said Lizzie.

'Why should you be afraid for me?'

'Well, you know. I worry in case you get into trouble.'

'Well, don't worry, because I won't,' said Carol. 'I'm not that daft.'

So Lizzie's mind was put at rest and she endured the languid Jerry, the loud pop records on the new record player, plus his dog ends all around the house, and the fact that he seldom went home at nights. Although Lizzie did not really approve of him she knew that he was good for Carol. He was a young, ambitious actor, and made Carol stick to her parts. Sometimes she would hear their voices raised and think that they were quarrelling. Carol would say, 'We were rehearsing; you are not to worry.'

Eventually the opening night for the play arrived, and

everyone had a ticket forced on them by Carol. It was put on and directed by the theatre workshop at the Royal in Stratford, East End of London, where a tiny but very dogmatic lady known as Miss Smallwood worked hard and, at her own expense, trained young players.

Carol had a fairly big part in a kind of cockney comedy which later became very popular and went to the West End, thus starting many of these ambitious youngsters on the road to fame.

This was a special night, because Lizzie was going out with Uncle Bobby, who made quite a joke of it. 'The last time we went out together was when we was bombed out,' he roared, and Carol said very severely, 'Why can't you behave yourself, Uncle Bobby?'

Lizzie looked very nice; Carol brushed her hair and piled it up on her head, and she wore a nice long black dress with lace trimming and all her nice jewellery.

'Gor blimey! Here comes the duchess,' cried Bobby when he saw her.

Lizzie stood still and looked soberly at him. 'There was a time, Bobby, when you always called me duchess,' she said.

He looked guilty, then said, 'Come on, duck, let's go and see our Carol in action.'

The old Royal was packed that night, you could not get near the bar. Carol had been very thorough in her sale of tickets. There were Bobby's racetrack friends and Carol's schoolfriends. The family all sat in the second row. All the red plush seats were full and high up in the gallery there were long lines of faces. There were even people in those seldom-used side boxes, for this was a new venture and all the talent scouts and news boys were there. The first night was for charity. The whole idea was to help promote the young folk and make the theatre more popular, for films had broken the theatre's back, and the war had taken its talent, but this young company had a lot to offer.

Lizzie felt like a queen, sitting there surrounded by family, with Bobby beside her.

When Robin and Bella came in late and got in at the end of the row Bobby turned his head in their direction. Bella's figure was tall and lithe; her light green chiffon dress revealed her white skin and the light shone on her burnished head. Lizzie sensed Bobby's emotion as he looked at her, then felt him get fidgety as they waited for the curtain to rise.

The play was good and Carol played her part of young sister to the star very well. The star was a husky young cockney who later found fame on the television shows. There are many stage folk who remember that night, and Lizzie had a memory to last her a lifetime.

During the interval Bobby disappeared and Charlie said, 'We're taking you home, Aunt Lizzie. Bobby hopped it; we thought he would.'

Lizzie felt a little tug at her heart but she knew he could not bear to see the lovely Bella so happy with Robin.

So after the show Charlie transported her home. Carol and Bobby stayed out all night, but Lizzie lay thinking of those bright lights and the funny parts in the play. Yes, it had been one of the best evenings of her life; she wondered why she did not do something like that more often.

CHAPTER NINETEEN

Wanderers Return

After this Lizzie tried hard to settle to her life in Ilford, but it was as if something was missing from her life. She often sat dreaming, savouring in her mind the old aromas of the market street. Rotten cabbages and that strange odour of oranges when the speckled ones were thrown into the street for the scavengers. The cries of the traders loading up their wares, the quarrels that often broke out among them; this was the atmosphere in which she had been bred; it held a kind of hungry nostalgia for her. She recalled her Bobby in a cloth cap and muffler hiding in the factory doorway to dodge the coppers. Sometimes in her lunch break, when no one was looking, they had had a kiss and a cuddle. Yes, but those times were long gone; love had faded as her Bobby had done.

She often looked at her tiny, shapeless figure, and saw that her legs were still slim, her hands nice, and that she was not brown and wrinkled as some old people were. Her hair was very light and her skin soft and white. Was she repulsive to Bobby? She hoped not, for to her he was still that big, strong, good-looking lad who had stolen her virginity. Her love life had finished even before she was thirty, and yet even when Bobby still slept with her there had been other women. A little frown creased her forehead. It was certainly a puzzle. Now just a friendly peck on the cheek was all she got from her fat, prosperous husband, before he dashed off on his highly secret business.

The lack of affection really dated from the time she had been in hospital. The doctor had told Bobby that her heart was weak and he had been terrified in case he hurt her. She had understood all that; Bobby was always a coward at heart. She had felt better these last years, now that she did not do any housework and had no one to cook for and plenty of time to rest. But she missed having no one to comfort in times of stress; now that all her family had gone their own ways, she was very lonely. She must not grumble. She looked around her; just look at the nice house, so warm and so splendid, and all that money which Bobby kept giving her, piling up in that old suitcase under the bed. Yes, she supposed she was lucky, but the road ahead seemed long and dreary. Often she wished she did not have to travel it alone. It was on one of these long afternoons as she sat dreaming, looking out of the window down the hill, past the line of front gardens, waiting for something to happen, that she saw a cab come along slowly up the hill. The driver was looking at the house numbers, then stopped suddenly outside. Her heart missed a beat; was it Bobby home so early? What was wrong?

Instead, two tall young men almost leapt out of the cab and began unloading suitcases and musical instruments. The boys had come home! Lizzie's feet would not get her quick enough to the door to greet them.

With deep, husky voices they called out, 'Hallo, Aunt Lizzie.'

'Oh, my boys, my fine boys, how did you find me?'

'We found Carol down at the Royal. She told us where you were.' They looked around at the house. 'Well, look at this. Here you are, Aunt Lizzie, living it up in this posh place. We've come to stay with you.'

'This is your home, darlings,' cried Lizzie. 'What shall we have? A nice cup of tea?'

'Great! Got any cakes? You know, the kinds we used to get from Allerdyne the bakers?'

'No, only biscuits. Can't get anything nice in this dreary hole.'

So they sat in the lounge around the new electric fire, something which Lizzie seldom did, and she listened to a long account of their adventures. They had joined a pop group and played their way around America, travelling from Spain as cabin boys in a rich man's yacht.

As they unpacked their bags, they loaded Lizzie with coral and beads. They gave her a feather from the bird of paradise for her to wear in her hair, and Derick produced a hula-hula skirt which he insisted she put on. When she refused, Paul wore it and Derick played, 'She wore red feathers and a hula-hula skirt,' on a small banjo, wiggling his hips in imitation of a hula dancer.

'Come on, Aunt Lizzie, you can dance sitting down. It's all the go, clap hands, come on now.'

Lizzie's eyes gleamed brightly; her cheeks glowed pink, and she clapped and wiggled and woggled delightedly to the music from her chair.

'She's great, ain't she, Paul?' cried Derick. 'We'll put her in our floor show.'

Oh! That afternoon remained in her memory for a long time. Lizzie even trooped into that modern kitchen and messed about with the switches until she understood how the intricate oven worked. Most nights Carol and Bobby had already eaten, so Aunt Lizzie's diet usually consisted of sandwiches and the fruit that she was so fond of.

'I'll bake a cake,' she said with a sweet smile on her face.

'You do that, Aunt Lizzie,' said the boys. 'But first of all cook us a steak, we're starving,' and from his pack Derick produced a huge parcel of rump steak.

'Well I never,' cried Aunt Lizzie, 'where did you get that?' She sniffed it cautiously.

'Now don't sniff it, Aunt Lizzie. Cook it,' they cried.

'Well, it seems fresh,' she said, trotting off to the kitchen. 'You was always very fond of your tummy, young Derick.'

They laughed uproariously. 'Still the same Aunt Lizzie! Always was good for a laugh.'

So Lizzie got cracking on the supper, as the boys had told her to, and soon, for the first time since they had lived there, the house smelled of savoury cooking. The usual cold smell which had pervaded the new house and which got on Lizzie's nerves slowly disappeared that night.

'It's that horrible disinfectant Ruby uses,' Lizzie had complained one day.

'No, Aunt Lizzie, it's just that you're not used to a smell of cleanliness,' Carol retorted rudely.

So tonight Lizzie wallowed in steam and cooking fat and sat down with the boys to a splendid meal: grilled steak, potatoes in their jackets and a big home-made cake full of currants and raisins and served hot, just how the boys liked it. Then they helped themselves to Bobby's booze and played Carol's records.

Lizzie sat by the fire with a sweet smile on her face and dozed off, feeling very happy and content once more. The dirty plates and the cooking utensils were still piled high beside that gleaming sink, but Lizzie was too tired to do anything else but doze.

When Carol came home, she sniffed the air, her dainty nose in the air. 'Cripes,' she cried, 'what a pong.'

The boys grinned. 'Not us, Carol, not guilty. Must be Aunt Lizzie.'

'Oh don't be vulgar,' she said, sweeping haughtily into the kitchen. 'Why! What a bloody mess! Who did it? Now get out there and wash up.' She pointed dramatically to the kitchen. Carol was an actress even off stage.

'OK! OK!' the boys cried. 'We'll clear up; don't lose your wig. But first let's carry Aunt Lizzie to her room; come on, old gel, handy chair.'

They linked hands under Lizzie's bottom and carried her off to bed. 'Let's wash up, the boss has come home.'

Carol had always ruled them even as a small child.

'Put me records away,' she demanded, 'and don't let Aunt Lizzie knock herself out waiting on you.'

'Yes mam, yes mam.' They touched their heads and bowed low.

'You can have Uncle Bobby's bed tonight,' she said, 'he won't be coming home tonight.'

'He won't come home and turf us out, will he?'

'No, he's gone to Liverpool for the big races, but I warn you he will be back at the weekend.'

'That's a nice way to treat your poor uncles, Carol,' joked Derick.

This really made Carol mad; she didn't like being reminded

that they were really her uncles — being her grandmother's children.

'Turn it up,' she yelled and ran to Paul, who cuddled her close while Derick kissed the back of her neck. 'It's all right, love, nothing to get niggly about, we're all back together again.'

Because there was a special kind of relationship between them, Carol wept, then cooled down and said, 'Blimey, I ain't arf missed you.'

'That's better,' said Paul, 'now let's all get some kip.'

Soon the house settled down to the peaceful stillness of the night; Lizzie and her young ones were together again.

Lizzie awoke in the night and, as she often did, started making plans for the next day. It was winter, not long before Christmas, and she had all sorts of plans, including a tree for the hall, just like in the old times in Highbury Grove.

The days passed very quickly now the boys were home, but she began to find the Saturday night parties a slight hazard, they went on so late and the music was so loud. There had been complaints from the quieter residents along the road.

'Didn't even know anyone lived there, so now they show themselves,' said Lizzie in disgust.

'Well, tell them sods to pack it up,' roared Bobby, 'otherwise we will get chucked out of here.'

But it was a waste of time. On Saturdays the young boys and girls still came, the music began and they wiggled and waggled, fetched the booze from the local and the parties went on till early morn.

'I thought they were supposed to be on the road,' said Bobby, who assiduously avoided all the noise by staying out all night on Saturdays.

'Well, at the moment they're having a rest,' said Lizzie a little timidly.

'I hope they are paying for their board and keep,' growled Bobby.

But Lizzie hung her head and said, 'Oh yes, Bobby. They're very good boys.' But the truth of the matter was that they did not pay for anything; in fact they borrowed money off her for fags and drinks.

'We're a bit skint at the moment, Aunt Lizzie,' they had informed her, 'but as soon as we get another job we'll reimburse you, don't worry.'

'But I thought you did very well in America?'

'Well, we did, but after the band broke up, we had a little holiday in Las Vegas.'

'What goes on there?'

'Gambling mostly, but we didn't gamble, did we, Paul?' asserted Derick.

'No, Aunt Lizzie, only birds and booze,' Paul grinned.

'Well, I never,' cried Lizzie once more. 'Who is it likes the booze and who the birds?'

'Well, it's Paul who likes the birds. With me it's the booze,' grinned Derick.

'You're both as bad as one another,' said Lizzie, eyeing them fondly. 'Still you must mend your ways now you're back at home.'

The weeks raced by and Carol, who was between jobs, came home to lounge around with the boys all day.

The noise often gave Lizzie a headache, and she began to feel a little tired, but she did not complain. Bobby shouted and growled, threatening to put them out, but these happy-go-lucky lads didn't give a damn.

They squared up to Bobby saying, 'O.K., go ahead, there are two of us and maybe you ain't the tough old guy you make out to be.'

It snowed heavily that Christmas and they all went out in the garden to have a big snowball fight, then returned indoors, treading snow into the fine carpet. Carol seemed to have stopped trying to keep the house so spick and span.

As the festive season approached, Lizzie made hoards of mince pies, and Christmas puddings old-style, 'like Mum used to make'.

On Christmas Eve she was finishing off the fine Christmas tree in the hall, with little pieces of tinsel, when suddenly she stopped and looked very odd.

It was as if a grey goose had walked over her grave. 'Carol,' she called, 'did Bobby come in last night?'

Carol was idling on the settee; the boys were sitting in the armchairs looking at the large television screen. 'Ain't been home for two nights. Still, what's odd about that, can't rely on Uncle Bobby, never did.'

But Lizzie was silent, she went to the window and looked out at the cold, still, silent street, at the white blanket of snow undisturbed by human feet. It gave her a frightened feeling that she could not explain. She must go and sit down. Perhaps she was going to have one of her attacks, must have been overdoing it a bit. She sat on the the little polished seat near that beastly thing the telephone, a kind of apprehensive feeling overwhelming her. Then almost as soon as she sat down the thing jangled, making her nearly jump out of her skin.

'Carol,' she cried, 'come and answer the phone.'

'You're out there, you do it,' cried Carol in her saucy manner.

'No, Carol, come here. I don't feel too good.'

Carol came bouncing impatiently out into the hall, grabbed the telephone, then said, 'It's for you, Aunt Lizzie, it's Uncle Bobby. I think he's drunk.'

In a bewildered manner Lizzie took hold of the phone, and a strange husky voice that was something like Bobby's said, 'That you, Liz? Get one of the boys to get my car out of the garage and come and pick me up. I'm in the phone kiosk behind the station; tell them to be quick.'

'Are you all right, Bobby?' she asked. He sounded very hoarse.

'Never mind, Liz, you do as I say,' he almost groaned.

The boys were beside her now. Carol had told them that something was wrong and Paul took the phone from Lizzie's hand. 'We're coming, Uncle Bobby. Where are the car keys?'

Then there was a scamper to get Bobby's car out of the garage. Usually when Bobby went away for a few days he went on the train and left his car at home.

Carol looked at Lizzie's frightened face. 'Now don't worry,

let's make some coffee. Got himself drunk and incapable, no doubt.'

It seemed an endless wait, although it was only twenty minutes before the car came back. The two boys helped Bobby inside along the snowy path. Behind him lay a trail of blood. The boys laid him on the settee and the blood leaked down onto the carpet, for Bobby's kneecap was shattered and a bullet hole was in his trousers. His face was bruised and battered, and a long knife slash ran across his cheek. Lizzie covered her face with her hands to shut out the sight.

'We will see to him. Get Aunt Lizzie out,' said Derick.

Carol took her into her room and sat with her. 'What has happened?' Lizzie asked.

'Dunno. Got run over, by the looks of him,' said Carol. 'Now don't you worry, the boys will get the doctor to him.'

But Bobby stoutly refused medical attention. 'Get a bandage and tie me leg up tight. Now put a plaster on me face. I've got to get going,' he said desperately.

'Why, Uncle Bobby? What's the trouble?'

'Plenty, lads,' gasped Bobby fighting the pain. 'These boys who are after me are real villains. Don't mess about; done up old Sims, they have, but I tried to get away, they did a nice razor job on me.' He held a towel to his bloody face. 'Then they took a shot at me. I dodged them because they don't know I live out here, but I've got to go because the bastards will find me.'

'Oh Christ, what will you do?' said Paul.

'You drive me to Harwich and I'll get aboard the cross-Channel ship tonight.'

'I'll do it, Uncle Bobby, but I'm scared you'll bleed to death.'

'I'll be all right. Tie that bandage very tight and put another one high up on me thigh. That's it, lad. It takes a lot of hurting, tie it tight.'

So Paul pulled the bandage very tight, pressed the wound on his face together and put a big plaster on it.

'They won't get me, and they didn't get the lolly. It's all there.' He pointed to his briefcase. 'But they'll come looking, so one of you stay with Aunt Lizzie and don't open the front door to anyone, and keep the back door barred. Just ring the coppers if those bastards come knocking.'

Bobby opened his briefcase, which was stuffed with bank notes, and took out about one third. 'Take that to Lizzie. She knows what to do with it and we'll get going, lad.'

So Lizzie took the money, and put it in the suitcase under the bed in her usual slow, quiet manner. Then she went out to see Bobby, who was now cleaned up. But he still looked shaken and had a ghastly pallor.

'Got to go, Liz. Sorry, old mate, but I'll let you know where I am later.'

She put her arms about him and laid her head on his blood-soaked chest. 'Don't leave, Bobby,' she cried. 'Stay with me.'

'It's only for a while, Lizzie, and it's better for all concerned that I blow. You got plenty of lolly, be careful with it. Give me a hand, boys.'

The boys pulled Bobby up and helped him out to the car. Carol brought rugs, a bottle of brandy and a flask of coffee, then kissed him. ' 'Bye, Dad,' she said, a word she had seldom used.

Lizzie stood in the hall, the light shining down on her small desolate figure with her silver hair and her old-fashioned black dress. Tears poured down her cheeks.

'Take care of yourself, Bobby dear,' she wept.

'Then you do the same, old darling,' grinned Bobby. 'I won't be long.'

Paul drove Bobby down to Harwich, while Derick bolted and barred the doors, took the phone off the hook then turned off most of the lights. 'Now come on, girls, off to bed. You had better sleep with Aunt Lizzie tonight, Carol. Just in case.'

'In case of what?' she asked.

'They might come here. Those guys that were after Uncle Bobby. I'll stand guard.'

'Is it as bad as all that?' whispered Carol.

'I think so,' he whispered back.

Carol tucked in beside Lizzie saying, 'Tell me a story like you used to.'

But Lizzie, in a choked voice, said, 'Not tonight, dear.'

Then Lizzie heard the Christmas bells pealing from the church up the road. Why, it was Christmas Day, she had really forgotten. What a pity, she had planned such a lovely family affair.

CHAPTER TWENTY

Goodbye Uncle Bobby

The snow fell in bucketsful that Christmas, right into the New Year. Outside all was frosty, white, still and silent. No one emerged from those quiet houses. Big Christmas trees lit up with coloured lights sat in the bay windows in all their splendour. Yet not a sound of festivity could be heard anywhere.

As Lizzie remarked, 'It's as if they were all blooming well dead.' In Highbury she had heard the noise from the local pub, and down in The Nile every house would be having a knees-up on Christmas night.

'Oh don't get depressed, Aunt Lizzie,' said Derick. 'This is a posh area. They don't go to town like we normally do.'

Carol complained that it was all very boring, and that her friends were probably having a right good time at the party in the Royal bar. 'It's all Uncle Bobby's fault,' she said, 'that we are stuck here with nothing to do.'

'Now Carol,' warned Lizzie, 'don't be unkind, it's not fair to condemn Uncle Bobby.' Then Lizzie glanced at the clock worriedly. 'I wonder why Paul hasn't returned? Shall we have dinner?'

'No thanks,' said Carol, 'not for me.'

Derick said very solemnly, 'I'd rather wait for Paul.'

So Lizzie went sorrowfully into the kitchen and turned off the heat in the oven where the turkey lay browned and basted to a turn, just waiting to be eaten. They all sat gloomily watching the television till midnight, then they went to bed.

The next morning Paul came home looking very cold, soaked through with icy wet snow. Lizzie cuddled him, then took his wet coat, pressing his cold face close to her own, 'Oh darling,' she cried, 'you look frozen.'

'Had to walk from the station,' said Paul, blue-lipped with the cold.

'How about Bobby?' whispered Lizzie.

'He went on the boat early this morning. There were no sailings on Christmas Day.'

'Did he get his leg attended to?' she inquired, once Paul was installed by the fire with a hot drink.

'Well, it's a long story and I am absolutely starving. Let's eat, shall we?'

This drove Lizzie straight into action. 'Now we will have our Christmas dinner.' She toddled off into the kitchen, put the turkey back into the oven to warm through, and then put on the baked spuds.

'Lay the table nicely, Carol,' she called. 'Don't forget the bonbons.'

'Oh, anything for a quiet life,' grumbled Carol, getting up to do as she was bid.

'I'll polish the glasses and open the wine,' volunteered Derick, very pleased to see his brother back again.

Soon the table was set and Lizzie was fussing with minor details, putting holly on the pudding and a little wine in the giblet gravy. Then they sat around that modern polished table with its lighted candles and flowers, while Paul told of his adventures.

Everyone was trying hard to be cheerful but something was missing. It was, of course, big, jovial Uncle Bobby, who had always made a point of eating Christmas dinner with the family. After the pudding came the pulling of the bonbons. Then they sat drinking brandy from the best crystal glasses while Paul told them how he and Uncle Bobby had managed. They had arrived very late in the strange, snow-covered town. All through the long journey Bobby had lain in the back seat drinking whisky straight from the bottle, moaning and groaning, until eventually he passed out. The roads were icy and really dangerous; they had stopped at a small rural inn and got themselves a room for the night, but Bobby was still bleeding profusely, shivering, moaning, and still drinking whisky while he was conscious. Very late on Christmas Eve, after chatting with some of the local lads in the bar, Paul had at last persuaded Bobby to go to the emergency hospital just along the road. There they had patched Bobby up, stitched his face, dressed his knee and had also given him an injection.

The doctor had asked to see Paul. 'I'd like to keep him in overnight,' he said. 'What was it, an accident?'

'Well, just a bad skid,' Paul answered warily. 'No one else was involved.'

'Nevertheless, he has been drinking heavily. Better let him stay, in case there is any reaction.'

'I don't think he will,' muttered Paul looking over at Bobby on the stretcher.

'By the way, I must report this to the police,' said the bossy nursing sister. 'I'll do it at once; it's hospital procedure.'

Paul wavered, but Bobby had one leg off the stretcher and in a flash had hobbled to the main door, with Paul dashing after him.

'I'll go and get him,' hollered Paul, as he ran past the astonished nurse. But both Paul and Bobby continued running till they got to the car, then Paul drove like mad down to the dockside. They parked in a dark lane; Paul covered Bobby with a rug, and he slept fairly peacefully till the morning. Trying to keep warm, Paul had huddled in the driving seat, and luckily no one had come by to disturb them. At daylight Bobby awoke with his usual grin and fished around for the briefcase that he had not allowed out of his sight.

'Go and get me a ticket on the next car ferry, then buzz off home, lad. I'll be all right now.'

'I'll come with you.'

'No you bloody well won't,' argued Bobby.

At five o'clock, just as the grey light of dawn came drifting over the North Sea, Paul watched Bobby drive carefully onto the car ferry, then he went to the station and waited for the train home.

'Well, that's the end of the story.'

Lizzie wiped away a tear, Carol got up and said, 'Come on, let's all have a good drink. Put some records on, Derick.'

Lizzie said, 'You are a good boy, Paul. I won't forget what

you have done for Uncle Bobby. But why he has to go on a ship to a foreign country beats me. He's been on the run before, several times, but he never left the country, just stayed out of sight until everything quietened down.'

'But this is different, Aunt Lizzie,' said Paul seriously. 'It's not the law he is running from, it's these villains, and he has pinched all the money.'

'Oh dear,' sighed Lizzie. 'That bloody Bobby, when is he going to settle down?'

On Sunday morning, the first newspaper came through the door. The snow had all gone, leaving just a slight trace of frost on the hedge.

Lizzie liked to read *The News of the World* on Sundays, but this morning Carol was out of bed first and picked the paper up off the mat, anxious as always to read her star forecast. She stood in the hall looking at the paper, then dashed off to the boys' room.

'Here, wake up,' she cried. 'Read this, the headlines. "West End Gang Murder. An old time bookmaker Jacob Simmons had been savagely beaten and stabbed to death in his office on Christmas Eve. His body was not discovered until after the holiday." '

'Look!' cried Carol, pale and very disturbed. 'That's Uncle Bobby's partner; perhaps he did it!'

'Crikey!' exclaimed Paul, as he sat up and read the account of that grisly gang murder. 'Are you sure, Carol?'

'Of course I am. I went up there when I was flogging the tickets for the first night of *The Sparrows*.'

'Oh blimey, did Bobby do it?' asked Derick sleepily.

'No chance,' said Paul. 'Someone tipped Bobby off, so he got away with the takings. They chased him, took a shot at him, slashed at him with a razor, but he got away, so I suppose they done the old guv'nor. But I bet they will come looking for Bobby.'

'Don't let Aunt Lizzie know. Better hide the paper.'

But Lizzie was out in the hall. 'Where is *The News of the World*? Who's got it?' she demanded. 'Carol, what are you doing in the boys' bedroom?'

Sheepishly Carol came out and went back to bed, saying the paper had not come.

Paul rammed the newspaper under his pillow. 'Haven't seen the paper yet, Aunt Lizzie. It will probably come late today,' he called out.

So Lizzie buzzed about in the kitchen, now quite used to all its gadgets. She made tea and toast for everyone, but they seemed very quiet and her own instincts told her that something was wrong. She thought of her Bobby in some strange, far-away country and prayed that he would be taken care of. Bobby was like a bad penny, he always turned up. She was quite convinced that he would soon come home again.

Early in the afternoon they all sat watching the Sunday film on the television. The news followed and announced the gory details of that Christmas murder. The police were anxious to contact the partner of this bookmaker who had been a victim of the gang war in the various gambling haunts. They were anxious to find anyone who had seen a Mr Bobby Erlock, six-foot-one, thinning brown hair and blue eyes. He had collected the takings from the various gambling places and areas of vice in the big city which had been controlled by Jacob Simmons, now deceased.

Paul jumped up and switched the television off, but Lizzie cried, 'They are looking for my Bobby.'

'No they're not,' said Carol. 'Why don't you make a cup of tea?'

But strong determination showed in Lizzie's face as she said, 'Now where is me bloody *News of the World*? I knew you were hiding something from me.'

They produced the crumpled newspaper and Derick read the case out to Lizzie.

'Bobby would never beat up an old man,' declared Lizzie very firmly when he had finished. 'He might take what was owed to him, but that's all.' She sighed. 'Oh well, the cops will be here soon.'

'No, Aunt Lizzie. Uncle Bobby told me. He never gave this address to anyone; he wanted to protect you,' answered Paul.

'Protect me! From what?' snapped Aunt Lizzie. 'I've been

through this all my life, so a visit from the law won't bother me.'

'But you mustn't tell them anything,' begged Paul. 'Uncle Bobby made me promise.'

'Well, let them come. I'll be ready for them,' threatened Lizzie. Then she said, 'Now all of us must tell the same story, that the last time we saw Bobby was when he went to work on the morning of Christmas Eve.'

All the kids nodded.

'It's not the cops that worries me, it's that mob,' confessed Paul.

'What mob?' cried Lizzie. 'Why, down The Nile I lived amongst the toughest boys in town. So this lot won't bother me.'

'Good old Aunt Lizzie,' cried the kids in unison.

Within two days the London and the local police arrived with blue lights flashing and sirens screaming; an unusual event in this quiet suburban cul-de-sac. The heavy rat-tat came at the door and Derick, very pale-faced, opened up the door to them.

'We're making enquiries regarding a certain Mr Bobby Erlock, who we believe resides here.'

'Come in,' said Derick pleasantly, holding the door open wide.

Two hefty men in plain clothes entered and the constables took up their positions all around the house.

Lizzie, in a plain, black dress, sat looking small and melancholy in her armchair by the fire. Carol stood behind her, alert and very cheeky.

'Sorry to bother you, Mum, but this is a murder inquiry. We have a warrant to search the house.'

'Go ahead,' said Lizzie brokenly, 'but that won't bring my Bobby back, will it?' She took out a dainty hanky and began to weep pathetically.

Carol, with a pretty blue comb in her dark shoulder-length hair, stared flirtatiously at the youngest copper. 'Do me a favour, don't pull the house about will you?' she exclaimed.

Paul said, 'We haven't seen Uncle Bobby since he went to work on Christmas Eve morning.'

The police ignored him and went all over the house, opening drawers, looking behind pictures and pulling up rugs.

'What the bleeding hell are you looking for?' asked Carol. 'You won't find him under there. Pigs!' she muttered, as Paul motioned to her to shut up.

Then they came back to Lizzie, who still covered her face with her handkerchief.

'You are sure that your husband did not return home?'

'Well, I should know. I've been sitting here all Christmas, waiting for him,' cried Lizzie very emotionally.

'Well, if you hear from him, ring us immediately. He is the most important witness in a murder case.'

'Ow! Ow!' howled Lizzie, as if it were all an unpleasant surprise to her. 'Where is he? What have they done to my Bobby?'

'Don't distress yourself, lady. We'll keep in touch. Come on, lads,' said the sergeant, and they all left. Just one police car was still parked at the end of the road.

'They haven't really gone, the crafty pigs,' said Carol watching from the window.

'Carol, you must really have more respect for the law,' said Lizzie.

'Not me. Seen how some of them behave when we was having a demonstration in town.' Then Carol started to giggle. 'Good, wasn't we? Couldn't have done it better at the Royal.'

Lizzie sighed and got slowly up from her chair. 'Oh dear, I'm glad they have gone. That was really hurting my bottom.' She raised the cushion of her chair and there, underneath, was the battered old suitcase. 'Put that back under my bed, will you, Paul?'

'Oh dear, Aunt Lizzie. Whatever have you got in there? The crown jewels?'

'Never you mind,' she said abruptly. 'None of those coppers was going to get a look at it.'

Later that evening Charlie arrived, and soon after him, Robin.

'What a show up,' said Charlie. 'I couldn't believe it when I read the papers.'

And Robin whispered, 'He's been done in, or I'll eat my hat.'

'Propping up the motorway by now poor sod,' replied Charlie.

'But he bloody well asked for trouble if anyone has.'

'I don't doubt it, but we've got to look after Aunt Lizzie.'

Lizzie accepted all their condolences with a kind of cool humour. 'He's not dead and buried, he'll turn up. I know Bobby, so don't look like you both have come to a funeral, because me and the kids have coped quite nicely, thank you.'

'You know where he is?' asked Charlie.

But Lizzie shot a warning glance at the kids. 'If I did I wouldn't be sitting here worrying, would I?'

'You ought to come and stay with us for a while till it all blows over. If his body turns up, the newspapers will drive you mad,' said Charlie.

'No, I am all right here with the kids.'

Robin shot a puzzled look at the boys. 'I suppose you pair of sods are still poncing on Aunt Lizzie,' he growled.

'Now Robin, that was an unnecessary remark,' cried Lizzie.

'We are not working, if that is what you mean,' replied Derick. 'But the last bloke who called me a ponce hit the deck very smartly.'

Paul stepped forward with clenched fists in defence of his brother, and Charlie got in between them, shouting, 'You know where to find us if you need us, Aunt Lizzie.'

'Oh dear,' sighed Lizzie. 'Give me a hand, boys. I'm tired and fed up. I'm going to bed.'

From January to February, the police visited Lizzie occasionally. The newspapers printed items on the mysterious disappearance of Bobby Erlock; two well-known underworld gangsters were charged with the murder of the old bookmaker, and efforts were made to clear up the gambling ring of vice that had been operating in the West End for a number of years.

Lizzie still lived in comparative seclusion, sitting looking out of the window during the day, watching the spring flowers coming up in her small front garden. Carol had returned to her drama classes and had a small part in a play at the Half Moon Theatre with one of the fringe companies that were now springing up all over London. Paul and Derick were working in the bar of a big hotel in town. Lizzie missed them, but knew they must earn their own pocket money.

Every day she waited for a letter from Bobby, but none ever came. Whenever the phone rang she was sure it was him, but to date no luck. It was as if Bobby had disappeared into space. Inside her was a kind of hurt feeling because she missed Bobby so much. He had never been very kind and he was always inconsiderate, but she missed him. She missed the noise he made, the muddle he created, his sense of humour and his big hearty laugh. She had never liked this house, but without Bobby it was a prison. Since that bit of trouble, Robin and Charlie had stayed away. She suspected that they were jealous of her fondness for the other two boys.

Sallie wrote to her, offering condolence, but never came to visit, saying that Phil would not approve of her getting mixed up in all that terrible business. Maisie, now living in Liverpool, wrote to say that she was shocked and very upset, but that Uncle Bobby had always been a sinner, so she prayed that God would take mercy on his soul.

Lizzie screwed up the letter impatiently. Oh dear, she thought, it was a strange little brood that she had brought up, and now she had lost her Bobby, the only person she had ever truly loved. But he would come home, she was sure of it, once the affair had died down. He was alive, that she knew, and it was going to be her secret and the kids', of course. They had been really great, she was proud of them.

Then one afternoon, as she sat dreaming, a stranger knocked at the door. Lizzie looked at him through the curtains of the window; he was stockily built, wore a long black overcoat and a black bowler hat and black leather gloves. He carried a black briefcase under his arm. She shivered, for she did not like the look of him. She stared at him through the window. He held up a paper to her; a salesman, she was not going to open the door.

'No thanks,' she said.

He gave her an oily sort of smile, then went off down the path and got into a car parked further down the road.

But it worried her, there had been something very evil about him. Maybe it was just her nerves, she would try to forget it. Then another day a car parked within sight of the house with three men in it, and stayed there nearly all day. Was it the police? They had been known to watch a house if they were suspicious of the occupants. Lizzie began to get really worried. They might decide to do another search, and she still had all that money that Bobby had given her the night he had left. Now what could she do, and who could she trust? Not the kids, they were too young to be involved. Not Charlie, he was too strait-laced. Not Robin, he was loyal but very big-headed. Then she thought of Bella, cool, slick, good-looking Bella, who ran that wine bar like the Ritz. She would write to Bella, asking her to come and visit her, but alone.

Bella came the next week, driving a smart little Mini, dressed impeccably in a blue suit, her hair like a shiny cap set close to her head and well-lacquered. Once they had been rivals for Bobby's affections, yet now they greeted each other like mother and daughter.

'I am sorry about Bobby,' said Bella. Tears came into those clear hazel eyes. 'But he always courted danger, so I am not surprised.'

'Bobby will be all right. He will turn up,' said Lizzie with confidence.

Bella stared at her curiously, but made no comment.

'I am going to ask a favour of you, Bella,' said Lizzie.

'Only too happy to oblige.'

'Well, I have papers here, and a bit of jewellery, and I am sure the coppers are still watching the house. I've seen them in plain clothes sitting in a car outside, down the street.'

'Well, it's possible,' said Bella.

'In case they come in again, I want you to mind my suitcase for me. Let it be a secret between you and me, don't tell Robin.'

Lizzie carefully produced the old battered suitcase covered

with old luggage and hotel labels, evidence of Bobby's trips to the various race tracks. Lizzie wrapped the suitcase in brown paper and tied it with string just like a parcel.

'There you are, love. I trust you to take care of it for me, so if those buggers come in again there's nothing for them to poke their noses into.'

Bella smiled with amusement at the old case so securely and well wrapped. 'It's all right, Aunt Lizzie, it will be safe with me,' she said. 'Sure you wouldn't like to come and stay with us for a while?'

'No thanks,' replied Lizzie. 'I've got the kids to think about.'

'That reminds me, I must be off. Got to get mine from school. So long, Aunt Lizzie. I'll look after this for you.'

Lizzie waved from the window as Bella went off in her smart little car. She was a fine girl and seemed so happy with Robin. Never had Lizzie regretted befriending her. 'Oh well, that's a worry off my mind,' she said out loud to the house as she sat herself down in her armchair. 'Kids will be home after ten.' She sighed; it was going to be a long lonely evening, one of many that she had spent lately.

A loud knock roused her from her reverie. She peeped through the window, careful not to be noticed, and saw that it was that horrible salesman again, with his black shiny gloves. She would pretend she was not in. It had just begun to get dark and she had not yet switched on any of the lights. With a sick feeling of apprehension she sat in the dark, waiting for him to go away. Then to her horror and amazement she heard his footsteps going down the side path to the back door; then the kitchen door rattled as if he was trying to get in.

'Oh God,' she gasped, 'a burglar.' What was that number that Carol had told her to ring in an emergency? She went towards the phone in the hall, but suddenly a black shiny-gloved hand came over her mouth and almost stopped her breath. A voice hissed in her ear, 'Don't scream. If you do, I'll strangle you.'

Lizzie's knees went weak, the front door burst open and two other men in navy blue raincoats appeared.

'Come in, lads,' called the gloved one. 'I've got the old girl. Get her into the sitting room while we turn the place over.'

The big, hefty lad grabbed Lizzie under her elbows, then carried her speechless with fright, and dumped her onto the settee.

'Now, Gran, hold yer noise or I'll croak yer,' he said in a sort of friendly tone.

'What do you want?' gasped Lizzie. 'I don't keep any money in the house.'

'Yer kidding. Didn't that bastard of an old man of yours make off with thirty thousand quid?'

Lizzie put her hands over her face. Oh, so this was the mob, the ones that were after her Bobby. What could she do? Then suddenly she sat upright, deciding to brazen it out.

'My old man? I never bloody well knew where he was. Never came home very often, now he's disappeared. I've not seen him since Christmas Eve morning, when he went to work, and I don't care either way.'

'That's it, Ma, you let off steam,' said the hefty one, going to the sideboard. Looking inside, he took out a bottle of sherry, tipped it up and took a good swig. From upstairs there came the sound of crashing and banging and the breaking of china as they wrecked the bedrooms and bathroom in their search for the lost money. Then they came down and all three stood staring at her, while the little frail lady, perched on the big settee, looked pathetically at them.

'I reckon she knows,' growled one.

'I know he came back, I was tailing him. Rough her up a bit,' suggested the man in the gloves.

The hefty young lad rubbed his nose with his finger and said worriedly, 'She ain't very big, I might kill her.'

'For Christ's sake get on with it,' roared the gloved one, starting to pull everything out of the cupboard.

So the young fellow reached over, grasped Lizzie by her hair, and jerked her head back sharply. She screamed, and he shoved a dirty hand over her mouth. 'Come on, Gran,' he said, 'open up, it ain't worth your while protecting him. Where did he go? Now quick, answer up.' He took his hand away from her mouth and gave her head another jerk with the other hand, which was still clutching her hair.

'I don't know,' sobbed Lizzie. 'I told you, I haven't seen him.'

'Oh dear,' said the lad, letting go of her hair. 'What do we do now?'

The hefty one in gloves rushed forward, his mouth working in anger. 'You know, you old bitch,' he cried, striking her across the mouth. Some of her teeth bounced out onto the carpet, and blood poured from her mouth, but she valiantly yelled out loud, 'Help! Help! Leave me alone, you bastards,' and with her last ounce of strength, got up and ran towards the phone.

But they were on her like a pack of wolves. Fists and boots went into action, till Lizzie lay just a crumpled, bloody mess on the floor. Afterwards they went mad; one put his boot through the television, another one jumped on the hi-fi, then the third one got his penis out and pissed over the walls of the room, until a car hooter sounded from outside, and they stopped their rampage of destruction.

'Come on, get going. That's Johnny's warning someone is around.'

'What about her?' asked one. 'Ain't done her in, have we?'

'Never mind, get going,' cried the gloved one, already on his way out of the back door. 'Waste of bleeding time, there's nothing here. That bastard got away with it.'

Carol and the boys all came home on the last bus together. They had gone to a late night disco after work, and now they came down the road, laughing and talking.

'Aunt Lizzie's waiting up,' said Carol. 'Told her not to.'

'The side door is open,' cried Derick. 'That's unusual.'

Then they all ran into the house and were confronted with a scene of horror, the wrecked room and Aunt Lizzie, lying unconscious in her own blood.

Carol started to scream hysterically, but Paul slapped her into silence. 'Shut up, they may still be here,' he whispered to her.

He picked Lizzie up, and laid her on the settee, wiping the blood from her face.

Carol threw herself down beside Lizzie, shivering with terror, afraid to look round the room at the terrible destruction. The beastly smell of urine that pervaded the air made her feel nauseated.

'They have pulled the wires out of the phone,' cried Derick. 'I'll run up to the phone box,' and he tore down the road as fast as his long legs could carry him.

Paul sat Lizzie up and poured a little brandy down her throat. 'She's still breathing. Oh thank God! Hurry up, Derick!'

Soon the police came and then an ambulance. Carol went with Lizzie, and the boys stayed behind to answer questions; afterwards they tried to make the house shipshape, weeping as they cleared up the mess. 'Poor Aunt Lizzie!'

Soon Charlie and Robin were alerted, and the whole crowd of them gathered at the hospital waiting for news.

'Oh, how can she survive? She already has a weak heart,' said Bella.

'She has got plenty of spirit, don't let's despair,' said Robin.

Their grief was terrible, for had not Aunt Lizzie meant everything to them? For once they did not argue with each other.

Charlie, with his organizing ability, talked to his local newspaper reporter and the police, while Robin took all the young ones home and gave them a meal. Then he went back to await news of Aunt Lizzie.

At five o'clock in the morning the nursing sister came to tell them that Lizzie had regained consciousness but was still in the intensive care unit. They were to go home and rest.

The kids all went home with Bella.

'Oh God, I can't face that house,' wept Carol. 'Our lovely house, what those horrible rotten gangsters did to it don't bear thinking of.'

CHAPTER TWENTY-ONE

Recovery

When Lizzie came back into the world on the second day after her terrible ordeal, she saw lovely flowers on the bedside locker. They were pink carnations, and the perfume of them was so breath-taking that she seemed to float on air, and could not move her limbs. 'Bobby,' she cried, 'where are you?'

The nurse came in, and with gentle hands soothed her brow. 'Oh good, you're still with us. Steady now, don't try to move, I'll get you a drink.'

Lizzie sipped the iced water, and quite suddenly the memories of that terrible night came back to her. The man in the black shiny gloves and the untidy looking hoodlum who had held so viciously onto her hair. Her lip trembled, and she started to weep.

'No crying now, all your big family are out in the foyer waiting to see you. I won't let anyone in if you don't behave,' threatened the nurse.

Lizzie smiled her gentle smile and nodded her head.

Charlie and Luber came in first, Luber tearful and Charlie pompous. 'Feeling better?' he asked. 'You're lucky to be alive.'

Luber kissed Lizzie's hands and face and wept. 'Oh, poor little liebchen, how could anyone do that to you?'

Lizzie viewed them as if from afar, thinking what a good-looking man Charlie was, and remembering him in ragged breeches and bare feet, darting in and out of the shelter.

'You are to come to live with us,' cried Luber, 'promise me.'

Charlie said, 'Quite right, we can't stay long. The others all want to come in.'

So off they went. In came Robin and Carol. Carol's eyes were puffed up with crying. She put her head down on the bed, crying. 'Oh darling.'

Robin looked very solemn and said in a choked voice, 'Bella had to mind the bar. She will come and see you tomorrow.'

Lizzie wanted to speak, but found it too difficult. She just clasped their two hands together in front of her. 'Take care of each other,' she whispered.

The last visitors to see her were the two boys, so alike but Paul the bigger and heftier of the two. He was the leader, and Derick the protector.

'You look like Rocky Marciano,' Paul told her.

Derick said, 'That's a beauty of a black eye you got there. Take care, Aunt Lizzie, and get well.'

And with more emotion than she ever thought they had in them, they gave her a kiss goodbye, saying, 'We are looking after the house.'

When all the family had gone, the nurse tucked her up for the night and said, 'Now wasn't that nice? How many children did you have, Lizzie?'

Lizzie shook her head, and those terrible bruised lips whispered sadly, 'None, they are all adopted.'

A few days later she was sitting up, and one by one they popped in to see her.

'What's wrong with me?' she asked the doctor.

'Well, you are extremely lucky to get off so lightly. But a broken hip will soon mend, as will four fractured ribs, and you are not so old. I was surprised to see that you are only just fifty.'

'Well, I suppose I get old quickly,' said Lizzie. 'I've never been very active. Not since the war, when I gave up work.'

'But you have a lovely big family, and they are all concerned about you, and so are the public. In fact you are quite a famous lady.'

'I can think of better ways of becoming famous.' Lizzie almost grinned.

'Now, now, you must forget about all that. Your sons tell me that you had a bad heart. So far I find no indication of it, but later, when you are well we will do a few tests. Can't understand how you survived that terrible beating if you had a heart condition. So we must find out, mustn't we?'

Lizzie lay there and thought about the past. It would be ironic if there was nothing wrong with her heart — when she thought how she had lived, not climbing stairs and being careful not to walk too far. Gran, that damned hoodlum had called her, and she knew she looked old with her small shrivelled shape, and her white hair. Bobby, her darling Bobby, that was why she had lost him. He had been terrified to have sex with her in case he hurt her. It was all so ridiculous, really; the thought of all those wasted years made her squirm. Now she would probably be an invalid, with a broken hip and her ribs fractured; even her little finger was broken. Oh dear, what a waste of her life.

She was sobbing silently, when the nurse came in, saying, 'Don't cry, dear, you will forget it all soon,' and then gave her a sedative to make her sleep.

Four weeks later she went home to Robin's flat above the wine bar in Greenwich. Robin and Charlie had argued about it, then agreed to take turns caring for her. She could not yet walk, and spent most of her day in a wheelchair.

'I'd sooner go home,' she protested.

'No way,' said Charlie. 'That house is going up for sale. We can't let you take the risk of living there; they never caught those villains. Bloody police, I don't know what's wrong with them.'

'Carol is still with us,' said Robin, 'so you might as well come home with me, until you make some permanent arrangement to sell the house and get a small flat nearer to the family.'

But Lizzie was choked up. Where was Bobby? Not a word in three months. 'I'll have to find out what Bobby wants to do,' she said timidly.

'Now, Aunt Lizzie,' cried Robin, 'don't keep dwelling on it. We all know that poor old Bobby's dead and gone.'

As Lizzie twisted her hands together nervously, Carol went into the fray, her mouth tight, her eyes hard. 'Leave her alone, Robin. She knows what she wants. OK, we will stay with you until we move, and Aunt Lizzie's on her feet, but don't keep bullying her.'

'I wasn't,' protested Robin. 'Just trying to get her to see reason.'

'Well, turn it up,' said Carol rudely. 'She knows what she wants to do.'

So the atmosphere was a little strained in Bella's flat, but she coped very well. Despite always being busy in the bar and restaurant, she found time for her invalid guest.

Mark, who was now five and still a very bright precocious child, with a shock of dark hair and long legs, always seemed to be dashing off somewhere. He was a great source of amusement to Lizzie. She had ousted him out of his room, and he now had to share with his sister Gloria, Gloria was quite a young lady now, and very interested in her dancing classes. Mark still kept most of his treasures in his bedroom, and would sneak in on the pretext of finding his school books, then, putting his finger to his lips, would close the door quietly.

'I'll keep you company,' he would say.

Then it was the same sort of conversation each time. 'Show me your broken finger, Aunt Lizzie.'

She wiggled the bent finger which was bound up in plaster.

'Those gangsters that bashed you up, what did they look like?'

'Well, I don't remember much, except that one wore black, shiny gloves.'

'I seen him!' Mark cried. 'Followed him up I did, was going to tell the cops, I was.'

It was obvious that Mark fancied himself as a detective. Lizzie, unable to suppress a grin of amusement, said, 'Now Mark, you must not speak to strangers.'

'If I catch him I'll put the cuffs on him,' said Mark with great satisfaction. 'Might get a reward.'

To change the subject Lizzie said, 'Not playing cards tonight, Mark?'

'We might as well have a game of banker,' he replied, getting a pack of cards from his trouser pocket.

Lizzie really enjoyed the company of young Mark, the one

bright spot in her long sojourn at Robin's flat. He reminded her so much of Bobby, and when he had gone to bed, she would lie idly dreaming.

If fate had been kind to her she might have had a son of her own, just like Mark. Still she must not complain, for if there was one thing she had never gone short of that was children. How many had she brought up? She would count them on her fingers: Charlie, Robin, Maisie, Carol, Derick, and Paul, not forgetting Rene whose lovely young body had been flattened and lifeless when they carried her from the bombed flat.

It was strange how many different homes she had occupied; the little house that had been her mother's in Market Street down The Nile, then those gloomy buildings, she had always hated them, and been pleased to get down into the warmth and safety of the tube. The house at Highbury had been a real home; she wished they had not made her move, never liked Ilford. It was cold and pretentious, she never wanted to see it again. Yet now, at her age, she was homeless once more. How strange it all was. Where did her destiny lie? Only with Bobby, and he was in some foreign land. He had probably got another woman, if she knew her Bobby Erlock, and she did only too well. Oh, it was all too heart-breaking, she wished she had died. Here she was, homeless and a cripple, it was too hard to bear.

It was Bella who found her weeping; kind, capable Bella, who often looked tired, and who worked very hard to make a good living for the family. Robin was inclined to be lazy and still liked a drink. He had his nights out at the dogs as Bobby had done. But Bella said very little, her face was still calm and unlined and she was always chic.

'Now Lizzie dear, don't get depressed. I know it's not easy to sit up here all alone, but the doctors say you will soon be on your feet again.'

'It's not that, Bella. I just keep wandering back over the past in my mind. I'd like a home of my own, I don't want to abuse your hospitality, and you know there is not a lot of room here. Also you have Carol to contend with, and I know she's no picnic.'

'Charlie is arranging to sell your house, so you can buy another. It's no problem, but we don't want you to be at risk. You know that they never caught those hoodlums, and Bobby's body has never turned up, so the danger to you still goes on.'

'Bobby will come back,' said Lizzie firmly. 'I am sure of that.'

'Well said! You know, Lizzie, I do believe you know where he is. I'm not probing, I don't want to know, but I'd be happier to know he is alive. I'm still quite fond of him, you know.'

Lizzie held her hand. 'Who but I would understand that? For in spite of the ups and downs I had with him, I still love him. No man ever took his place in my affection.'

A tear rolled down Bella's cheek. 'Bobby and I were very happy together. You know that, Lizzie.'

'Yes, darling, I know that, and nothing can replace him in my heart, either.'

They sat still and silent for quite a while, their minds revolving on past memories.

Then Bella said, 'If we could afford it I'd take a bigger place in the City with lots of rooms and a good luncheon trade. That's where the money is to be made.'

And Lizzie said, 'I'd like another little house like the one down The Nile, among the friendly people and the little shops. We only had an outside toilet, and a cold water tap, but that was really home to me.'

'Oh well, darling, we all have our dreams. Come on, let's help you undress, and I'll get back down to the bar.'

Because of the pain in her hip Lizzie spent many sleepless nights lying there thinking over her future. The hospital doctor had told her, 'Nothing wrong with your heart, Lizzie. You had a slight murmur when you were a child, but you have grown out of it. Probably caused by the rheumatic fever.'

'Why did I feel so poorly in the thirties and forties then?' she asked.

'You had anaemia, probably lack of nutrition or shock during the war years.'

'So I'm not an invalid. Well, I suppose I should be very

pleased,' she replied. 'I feel it was such a waste. I have achieved so very little.'

'Well, I should say you have achieved quite a lot, the way your family love you and are all so concerned for you.'

Lizzie lay there thinking this over. She might live till she was eighty, yet without Bobby it would hardly be worth it, thank you. She began to worry about the money he had left with her. Nobody, not even the kids knew about that. If he never came back to her what use was it to either of them?

Charlie told her he had been offered a good price for the house at Ilford. So now she supposed she ought to think about making another home for the young ones. Carol was acting a little strangely lately. She wasn't working, and had allowed her hair to hang very loose and untidy; her bare feet were thrust into sandals, and she wore no make up, which was unusual. She had arrived last week with a boy who looked very grubby, he had hair growing out of the sides of his cheeks and wore patched trousers.

Lizzie had been very shocked at her appearance, and Bella had sniffed disdainfully, and taken the young man in through the back entrance. Carol was apparently starving hungry and immediately started to hack lumps off a loaf of bread and search in the fridge for something to eat.

Lizzie, who was by now walking with the aid of two sticks, went to greet her, but she was disapproving. 'Carol! What are you doing? It's not nice to forage around for food in someone else's house. Bella will be serving lunch shortly. Why can't you wait?'

'Oh go on, start moaning,' cried Carol, handing her boyfriend a sandwich made from two thick lumps of bread and a large slice of ham.

This he took hold of with his grubby hands and began to devour, while Carol sat at the kitchen table, putting pickles on her sandwich before eating it wolfishly. Her wan face had a very disgruntled expression.

'Why haven't you been home for two nights?' demanded Lizzie.

'I'm not coming back. I'm in a squat. Don't call this home, do you?'

'In a what?'

'I'm squatting in a big house in Holborn with a lot of others.'

Lizzie looked puzzled. 'Well, whatever you are doing, come home to your own clean bed. You look positively dirty, and look at your feet. Whatever is wrong with you, dear?' Her voice softened, for Lizzie could never be angry with Carol for long.

'Nothing's wrong with me. It's stuffy people like you that need to change their ways,' Carol asserted aggressively. 'That's right, isn't it, Teddy?' she inquired of the youth, who by now had finished his big sandwich and stood there sheepishly with crumbs all around his mouth.

'Well?' queried Lizzie, giving him a shrewd, hard look.

'Well, lady, all these folk with money won't let the houses, leaves them empty so they don't have to pay rates on them. So we occupy them and live a bit rough, but we get by.'

'Well I never, take over someone else's property. Why, that's against the law. You will get arrested.'

'No, it's not illegal and we have some good blokes on our side, lawyers and MP's.'

'I don't believe you,' said Lizzie, getting very angry once more. 'You come back home tonight, Carol, or I'll send someone to bring you home. Paul and Derick will soon find you.'

Carol got up, starting her one act drama as it was known in the family, marching up and down waving her hands about. 'They don't care about me,' she cried tearfully, 'staying in the house, playing bleeding cops and robbers. They don't want me, they're pulling all the bloody birds in the district, having bloody parties every night.'

'Oh dear me,' gasped Lizzie. The situation was certainly getting out of hand.

'Anyway, I'm off. I'll call in next week. Might need some money, don't get much on the dole.' Then in a magnificent exit reminiscent of Sarah Siddons, Carol swept out, her thin boyfriend with shambling footsteps loping after her.

Lizzie sat down, sighed, and ran her fingers through her hair till it stood up on end.

Bella came bustling in. 'Lunch won't be long. Where's Carol?' Then looking at Lizzie, she cried, 'Why, the little bitch, she has upset you!' She knelt and put her arms around Lizzie, and as her tears fell, Bella continued, 'My goodness, look at the state of your hair.' She smoothed the untidy hair down gently. 'I'll have to take you to my hairdresser. Please don't let Carol worry you. You were just picking up nicely, too.'

'Oh dear me,' wept Lizzie. 'She is sleeping in some empty house, boys and girls together.'

'I thought she looked like a hippy,' said Bella, 'but it's only a phase. Lots of the kids get the craze; she'll get fed up with it.'

'Oh, how I wish my Bobby were here,' Lizzie continued to weep.

'Lot of bloody good he would be in circumstances like this. He'd only make them worse,' declared Bella. 'Now Lizzie, you got to live your own life. Women can, you know; they can be so much stronger than men. I've been alone and down on my beam end, so I should know.'

'Sorry, Bella,' said Lizzie, wiping her eyes. 'But I get a little confused lately. I'd like my own home again; it's nice here, but I feel that I'm a burden to you. I don't want to live with Charlie. He's a good boy, but a trifle overbearing, if you understand me.'

'Yes, I do understand, Lizzie, but it will all take time. First we must sell the old house and find you a flat or something you like.'

'If it's money you want I'm not short of that. Come to my bedroom with me, Bella, there is something I must show you.'

Bella took her arm and they went along the passage to Lizzie's room. Once in her bedroom Lizzie carefully closed the door then groped under the bed until she produced the old battered suitcase covered with a film of dust.

Bella assisted her and in her tidy way dusted the top of the case with her hanky. She was just putting it back in her apron pocket when Lizzie opened the suitcase, and there, stacked neatly on the top, were packets of crisp banknotes.

'Crikey!' ejaculated Bella. 'Where did you get all that money, Lizzie? Don't tell me you did a bank.'

'It's what Bobby gave me,' said Lizzie shyly.

Bella picked up a packet of notes and flicked them through her long fingers. 'Good God! There must be twenty thousand quid in there, Lizzie, and all in old notes.'

'I know,' said Lizzie. 'That night, before he left, he gave them to me. "Here you are, Liz, take care of this lot," he said, and he had more in his briefcase.'

'Oh! So you did see him?' said Bella. 'Well, that's amazing. You never let on to the cops.'

'I'm quite used to covering up for Bobby,' said Lizzie sharply. 'I've had a lifetime of experience.'

Bella smiled in her cool way.

'Well, Lizzie, and to think I was hiding all that lolly for you. I never dreamed it was money. Thought it was all your old treasures.'

'My jewellery is in there, too! I'll show you,' she said proudly, opening a little green evening bag and displaying those superb rings of hers, a gold watch and heavy gold chains, earrings and a bracelet full of gold charms.

'Why, Lizzie, they are lovely!' exclaimed Bella. 'Why on earth don't you wear them?'

'Bobby bought them for me. I used to wear them, but without Bobby I lost heart.' Lizzie was close to tears once more.

'Now, no more grizzling,' cried Bella. 'What are you going to do with this lot? It's too dangerous to leave under the bed. There might be a break in. I don't suppose any of the jewellery is insured? Knowing your Bobby, he probably bought it hot.'

'But he will be back, Bella, I know. How will he be able to find me, if the house is sold?'

Bella looked concerned. 'How long is it since you heard from him?'

'It's about ten months since I last saw him. It was Christmas Eve. He was in a terrible state, his face cut and his leg was damaged; Paul put him aboard a ship for somewhere, I'm not sure where.'

'Oh! So the kids know!' said Bella.

'Yes, but they will keep the secret, I am sure of that. Please, Bella, don't tell Robin, will you?'

'No, of course I won't. But Lizzie, if he's coming back you would have heard from him. You really ought to start living your own life. I feel awful when I think what I have done to a nice little body like you.' She sat on the edge of the bed and put her arms around Lizzie. 'Lizzie, you are only a middle-aged woman, there is still a lot you could do with your life and you've got all that lolly to do it with.'

'What is there for me, Bella? The kids have found their own life.'

'Never mind about the kids. Think of yourself, smarten up, travel, go places, find another man. That's just a few of the things that you can do.'

Lizzie's mouth twisted into a grin, showing a huge gap in her mouth, where her teeth had been knocked out by those terrible thugs. 'Who would fancy me? Look at me.'

'With all that dough it don't matter if you look like an ape,' replied Bella, 'once some guys get wind of it. You know, Lizzie, I could fix you up to look forty-five and feel like it. I'm quite a wizard at that sort of lark. Used to think I'd like to run a beauty salon, not a pub.'

'You can have what you want of this money if you still want it,' said Lizzie generously.

'No,' said Bella. 'We have got to be a bit careful about that money. Find a way of getting rid of it without drawing too much attention to you. Those bloody coppers never let go.'

'He stole that money from the gangsters. I heard them say so.'

'Oh well, bloody good job,' said Bella. 'That makes our task a bit easier. Put it all back under the bed until I think of something. It is worrying me silly knowing that it's there.' So saying, she snapped shut the case and pushed it back under the bed. 'Come on, Lizzie, let's go down to the bar and have a stiff drink. I think we need it.'

CHAPTER TWENTY-TWO

The New Image

In Bella's capable hands Lizzie emerged like a bright little butterfly from a cocoon.

'First, love, we get you set up with some good teeth. My dentist will build you some false ones, and it will restore the shape of your mouth. Then we'll get your hair cut and permed, with a nice rinse on it, and then to the dressmaker to get some decent suits made for you. You'll look nicer in a suit; those long flowing dresses only make you look weird. Lizzie, darling, you won't know yourself; like that we will get rid of some of the lolly and you will see the benefit of it.'

Lizzie obtained her new image in a matter of weeks. She endured long hours of beauty culture, skin treatment, saunas, massages, the lot. It was all very expensive, but as Bella said, 'It's not wasted if it helps to keep you young.'

Lizzie, who had seldom left her own home, now walked down the street to the small but stylish dressmaker, who was fitting her with two well-tailored suits to wear in the spring.

'When I was young,' Lizzie told Sadie, the tall, chic, Jewish girl, 'I used to try to look nice. In fact before the war, when I was forelady at a factory, I was the smartest lady there.'

Sadie grinned a toothy grin: to her the war was past history. 'Well, Lizzie, you are still young enough, so I am going to do a nice job on these suits. You'll look like Lady Docker by the time me and Bella are finished with you.'

There was a visit to the chiropodist to have her corns removed and then to a big store up west for four pairs of expensive shoes. Under Bella's tuition Lizzie threw caution to the winds and spent money like water.

'Now you really look nice,' Bella informed her, as Lizzie

happily showed off her neat black suit with a white straw bonnet, white gloves and a big expensive handbag to complete the outfit.

'Now walk down the town, go into Lyon's and have a cup of coffee. You must learn to mix with people.'

So Aunt Lizzie's new image progressed, and she learned to walk slowly and sedately, a slim little shape with a confident smile on her face.

Charlie passed her on the street and never recognized her, and Robin said, 'Blimey, I could fancy yer meself.'

Lizzie was fairly content and did not think about Bobby quite so often. The scars on her mind from the terrible beating had practically disappeared.

The only real worry was Carol, who arrived one day looking very much the worse for wear, and discovered Aunt Lizzie actually minding the bar. Lizzie sat on a stool with her hair a kind of pale gold colour and set in the latest fashion. She was wearing a pretty blue dress, her rings and diamond earrings sparkled in her ears.

'Oh my Gawd!' cried Carol. 'What have you done to yourself? You look like mutton done up as lamb. Look at the colour of your hair!' she shrieked.

Lizzie's bottom lip trembled, but Bella sprang immediately to her defence. 'Oh, why are you such a nasty little bitch? Lizzie looks fine, and it's time she started taking care of herself.'

'Oh hark who's talking,' jeered Carol. 'I think she looks like a tart, and so do you with your dyed hair and cheap jewellery.'

Bella paled in temper but kept her cool. 'Well, Lizzie has got no cheap jewellery, they are all genuine. It's time she got some wear out of them.'

Carol sniffed, surveyed Lizzie dramatically, then said, 'They're only what Bobby pinched.'

Now it was time for Lizzie to have her say. 'What a nasty person you are becoming, Carol. Bobby did not steal these. He paid good money for my jewellery.'

'Only to ease his conscience,' said Carol, determined to have the last word.

Bella gave Carol a terrible look, shrugged her shoulders and went out into the restaurant bar.

Lizzie looked at Carol and Carol stared back disconcertingly at her, then Lizzie put out her arms and Carol rushed into their warmth and safety, shedding tears of self pity.

'Now, my love, why are you behaving so badly?' asked Lizzie. 'It's not like you.'

'Oh I am so fed up. Can't get any work since I walked out of the Pavilion. That horrible stuck up choreographer has taken it up with Equity. I'm so fed up.'

'You can come home,' said Lizzie. 'Why let yourself go? You look like a tramp.'

'It's an image. I'm a hippy,' snivelled Carol. 'I'm thinking of going with Teddy to Amsterdam, but I don't think I like him.'

'Well, don't go, then,' said Lizzie, holding her tight and looking very puzzled. 'Charlie has sold the house, so come back here and we will look for another one.'

'No, not with her,' said Carol.

'Bella! Why, she is one of the best,' replied Lizzie.

'But she don't like me.'

'Darling, you don't give anyone much opportunity of liking you. You're always on the defensive.'

Carol did not comment, just snuggled close to Lizzie and wiped her eyes. 'Charlie sent a note to the squat. I've got to go and take all the things I need; he is going to put all the rest of our stuff in store.'

'Well, do that love, then put on your pretty dress, and get your hair cut. You'll find the boys there, I think.'

'They don't speak to me,' moaned Carol.

'Oh nonsense,' said Lizzie. 'Now, you do as I say. Have a nice bath and a meal, put your stockings on, and go and collect your things. Then come back here tonight. Promise.'

Carol dropped a petulant lip.

'Now give me a promise,' said Lizzie.

'All right,' said Carol. 'But don't you change, Aunt Lizzie, it upsets me. I like to see you how you were.'

'And I like to see you how you were,' said Lizzie. 'Come on, let's have something to eat, and I'll give you the money for a taxi, so you can collect your nice clothes and things.'

'Oh ta!' cried Carol. 'Well, Aunt Lizzie, you haven't changed really.'

So after lunch Carol went off in a cab to Ilford, clad in warm shoes and stockings, and wearing a raincoat borrowed from Bella over her shabby clothes. Lizzie had brushed and combed her hair, and tied it back so that it lay just in one dark shiny sausage curl on her shoulder.

But Carol was still deeply depressed. She had lost her loving, warm, understanding mother, the only one she had ever known, lost to that hard-faced bitch Bella. Bella, who had been Bobby's mistress, causing Lizzie so much heartbreak. Carol was furious, eaten up with spite and jealousy, sick of her own roaming existence and looking for a place to hide.

In the taxi she gnawed her thumb and closed her eyes to keep the tears from falling. When she alighted outside the old house, she called the taxi driver a swindling bastard because she considered he had over-charged her. Then with trembling hands and sinking heart she inserted the latch key in that once familiar door. This was the first time she had entered it since that horrifying night when the gangsters had wrecked the sitting room and injured Aunt Lizzie. Her mouth was dry with the taste of fear again. As she struggled with the lock the door suddenly opened from the inside, and she nearly dropped dead with fright as the tall shape of Paul loomed out of the dusk. Recognizing him, she rushed into his outstretched arms, crying wildly, 'Oh Paul, it's you!'

'Carol! My little Carol, what have you done to yourself?' he asked, while he guided her inside.

The room was still in disorder. Brown paper, string and packing cases littered the room, yet the electric fire shone bright, Paul had the sideboard open and was finishing up Bobby's brandy. He poured her a stiff drink and sat her by the fire.

'Cripes, Carol, you look a wreck. What have you been up to?'

'Nothing,' snivelled Carol, 'just squatting, that's all.'

'Blimey, those dead beats ain't going to get you anywhere. Why didn't you come down and stay here with us?'

'Didn't think that you wanted me,' grizzled Carol. 'According to Derick, who I met in London, you were both having a great time sleeping with the nurses from the local hospital.'

Paul looked embarrassed, and knelt down beside her, pushing her long hair away from her pale face. 'Oh, that was just a bit of fun. God knows I've missed you, darling. You were always the only pal for me.'

He held her close and Carol snuggled up to him, feeling suddenly warm and happy. They sat on the settee that had the stuffing coming out of it where the gangsters had ripped it with knives.

'Are you hungry?' he asked, pouring yet another brandy.

'No, thank you. I had a meal with Aunt Lizzie. Oh Paul,' she began to weep once more, but he held her tight. 'I can't believe it. Our Aunt Lizzie has been took over by that rotten old Bella. She's all made up and sitting in the bar like some old tart, I can't bear it.'

'Oh well, it's time some one brought Aunt Lizzie back into the world of the living. Don't cry, darling.' He kissed her lips, and she clung round his neck, rumpling his black curls.

'Oh Paul, what are we going to do without her?' she cried in anguish.

But Paul looked very seriously at her. 'The question is, what am I going to do without you, Carol? Derick and I have got a flat in London. Why don't you come with us?'

'Oh! Can I Paul? I'm so fed up with those bloody hippies. I was going to Amsterdam with them.'

Paul looked angry. 'Carol darling, I love you, I always have. No girl ever took your place in my heart, so you come with us, and that's final.'

Carol looked at him very strangely. She sat down, and he pulled her on to his lap. She could feel the heat of his body as they kissed passionately. This was no brotherly affection, and they were both aware of it. She released herself from his embrace. 'Better go up and pack my gear,' she said.

'I'll help you,' he replied, looking strangely at her. She

glanced down at the floor; this emotional feeling was embarrassing to them both.

Her own bedroom looked the same. The wardrobe was open and all her pretty dresses were still hanging there. On the dressing table were her perfumes and make-up; big tears trickled down her cheeks.

'Oh Paul, we were so happy here. I can't believe that it's all happened to me; it's like a nightmare.'

She got the big suitcase and they began to fold up the things she needed. They sat on the case to close it, then they sat on the bed and lit a cigarette.

'You will come with us, won't you, Carol?' he urged.

'Oh, I want to, but Aunt Lizzie might not let me.'

'Why, for God's sake?' He put an arm about her. 'I love you, darling, it has always been you. Ask Derick, he knows.'

She snuggled closer to him. 'Paul, I'm so happy with you, but we have been brought up almost as brother and sister.'

'But we're not, we're uncle and niece.' He grinned. 'But what's the bloody difference? Neither of us knew our fathers, so how can we be that closely related? And what the hell? I don't care, if you don't.'

Her big blue eyes looked so sorrowfully at him. 'Oh Paul, I feel that you're all I've got left in the world.'

He closed her tight to his breast. 'Yes, darling. That's how I feel.'

They lay close together on the bed. 'You know, Paul, some of them rotten sods at the squat would try to get me, but they made me feel sick.'

'You belong to me, darling, and always have.' He pressed his body close to hers.

'Oh darling,' said Carol, throwing her arms about his neck. 'I love you and I need you so. Who cares? Turn out the light, we will stay here till the morning.'

And the darkness of the night wrapped the two illicit lovers in a silent blanket of love, each caring for the other, careless of the consequences.

The next day the moving van was at the door very early; all the rest of the furniture was going into storage.

The two lovers leapt out of bed and peered out of the window. 'Oh, it's Charlie with them,' Carol whispered in terror.

Paul looked out. 'Now love, get cracking. We'll let them in, then make it to the bus stop.'

Ten minutes later they ran down the road hand in hand, Paul carrying the suitcase, his long legs shortening the distance, and their healthy laughter echoing as they boarded the bus to start a new life together. No regrets, no guilty conscience, just that wonderful feeling that they belonged together.

The next day Lizzie was worried. 'Carol didn't come back.'

'Oh, stop worrying over her,' cried Bella, a trifle irritably. 'She's probably gone off with those horrible hippies, and there is little you can do about it.

Lizzie looked sad. Bella was rather overbearing at times.

'It might not hurt Carol to rough it a bit.'

Lizzie continued with her new image. She never sloshed about any more in her nightie and dressing gown as she used to. She took a shower, set her hair, put on a smart dress and went off for a walk, sometimes with Mark to his school. They would walk through the park. He was growing up very sturdy and would look at Lizzie and say, 'I am nearly as tall as you. Why are you so short?'

'I guess it was how I was born,' replied Lizzie. 'I must say you look a lot taller than you used to.'

Mark gave her a look of great scrutiny. 'Yes, you are walking upright now. Before you used to creep around with a walking stick and lean forward like those monkeys at the zoo.'

'Well, I do declare!' exclaimed Lizzie. 'Now that's very uncomplimentary.'

'Well it's true, but I don't love you any the less. In fact, I'm very fond of you,' he said in his most grown up manner.

'Well, that pleases me,' replied Lizzie with a gentle smile.

'Also, you've got a lot of money, so I heard. Don't spend it all, because you are bound to die before me, and you can leave me some in your will.'

'Well I never,' cried Lizzie again, but even more amazed.

'Ta,' called Mark as he bounced into school.

Then Lizzie went to the bus stop and rode down into town, getting immense satisfaction from the ride, for it was something she had never done till she came to stay with Bella. It was strange how different she felt. That timid approach to life seemed to have entirely disappeared. She pulled on her nice kid gloves and put her handbag on her arm. She wandered around the big main store because it was warm in there and there were so many nice things to look at, but she seldom bought anything unless Bella had particularly asked her to make some purchases. The thriftiness of a lifetime was still with her. She just could not conquer it, unless Bella was with her, taking charge.

'Come on, Lizzie. Get a nice nightie and a slip, always handy.'

On the whole Lizzie was a more relaxed person and looked twenty years younger. After a stroll around the big store she would go to the ABC and have a buttered bun and a coffee. She had just learned to manage the complicated self-service system, when a very pleasant elderly gentleman had offered to carry her tray for her. Now he sat in the same spot every morning his eye on the door, waiting for Lizzie. He always had egg on toast, and Lizzie her coffee and buttered bun, but the conversation, as they ate this simple meal, was quite stimulating, for they regaled each other with little episodes of their past lives. So far names had not been mentioned, but Lizzie knew that he had been a ship's purser and, although now retired, that he did a part-time job at the Maritime Museum.

He, on the other hand, knew that her nephew owned the wine bar called the Cherry Tree at the bottom of the hill, that her husband was travelling abroad, and that she was the guest of her nephew until she found a satisfactory residence. For almost an hour each day they sat and chatted about world affairs and their own personal problems. Then Lizzie would squeeze her hands into her natty gloves, wish him good day, and set off to help Bella with the lunches.

Robin would invariably say when she got back, 'How's yer boyfriend?'

Lizzie blushed. 'He's just an acquaintance, and we like to talk, that is all.'

Bella whispered, 'Now don't spook her, Robin, she is just getting her confidence back.'

With a huge grin, Robin replied, 'Don't know what for. If Bobby comes back he'll bash his head in.'

Bella left in a huff; she hated any mention of Bobby.

So Lizzie really enjoyed herself for the rest of that summer in Greenwich, and began to like it so much that she even considered buying a house there.

Her gentleman friend in the tea shop had said, 'Property is getting a bit expensive, but there are some very nice old Georgian houses down at the bottom of the hill. I own one which is really far too big for me, now that I am alone, even though I let to the naval college students. Would you like to come and have tea with me, and view the house?'

Lizzie blushed and declined, not yet having gained sufficient confidence to go visiting, although, as she told Bella later, he *was* a very nice clean-looking man.

But Bella with her quick mind had other ideas for Lizzie, and did not want some intruder taking over. 'That's right, Lizzie. Can't be too careful, love. Never trust men; might get you in there and murder you.'

'Oh don't say such things, Bella,' Lizzie cried, still having hazy memories of the hoodlums who had beaten her up. After that Lizzie was not so friendly to her seafaring man and eventually he stopped coming to the ABC, but the experience had boosted her ego, and taught her that someone outside the family could be interested in her.

Then one day Bella said, 'Lizzie how would you like to own half of a pub?'

Lizzie looked at her with surprise. 'I never thought about it Bella.'

'Well, Robin and I are a bit fed-up. The trade in this place is kind of static. We'd like to branch out and buy a big place in the city with a fast lunchtime trade.'

'Now, that is up to you and Robin.'

'Well, love, if we sell this place, the way property is rising we won't have enough to get the kind of place we're looking for.'

'Do you want a loan, Bella? You are quite welcome.'

'No, we won't go into debt, that's not our way of doing things. But we are suggesting that you become a partner and own half the place with us. We still do the work, and you can have a nice apartment and still be earning. What do you think of that, Lizzie?'

'Well, I definitely will have to think of getting a house soon, Bella, because of the children. I can't desert them.'

Bella heaved a deep sigh. 'But Lizzie, they have deserted you. When did you last hear from them?'

'Two months, maybe three. They're working at a club, playing in the band, and according to Charlie, Carol is there with them.'

'Well, they've found their niche in life, so leave them alone. Think seriously of coming in with Robin and me, like that we can lose the money you are hoarding. We'll find a big old-fashioned pub and spend money on modernizing it. You can always fiddle a bit on the bills with the builders and what not, and no one will know.'

Bella had been good to her, but that was Bobby's money. Suppose he came back broke, as he always had done in the past? She thought for a while, then said, 'I'd like to live in the city, and if it isn't far from The Nile, it would be nice to go some again. Look around, Bella, I'll be easier in my mind when the rest of the money is out of that suitcase.'

Bella gave her a big hug. 'Good. Now Lizzie, I swear to you, you will not regret it. I'll make you a fortune once we get started and a legitimate one with nothing to hide.'

So Lizzie contented herself with Mark and her trips to the beauty parlour, getting her hair set in different styles and her nails manicured. Her nails grew long like Bella's and she had them painted different colours to match her various outfits; she was becoming very chic, and heard the customers say to Bella, 'Is that your mother-in-law, Bella? Smart little body, isn't she?'

Bella would grin, remembering the old Aunt Lizzie who had been her rival.

Then one day Lizzie got a visit from her three younger children, Derick, Paul and Carol. They came bringing gifts and overwhelming everyone with their good humour; flowers for Lizzie, chocolates for Bella. They looked very fit and wore natty light-coloured suits and Carol looked beautiful in a blue dress and a shady hat, with shoes and stockings on.

Lizzie was so pleased. 'Oh darlings,' she cried, 'you all look so nice. Where have you been?'

'Never mind about us, look at you!' cried Derick. 'Looks like a film star, don't she Paul?'

Paul looked down at Lizzie very seriously. 'You are looking a lot younger, darling, and that's good,' he said.

'Well, are you going to tell her?' asked Carol.

Lizzie looked at them. There was something different about Carol and Paul. What was it? Carol was jubilant, more happy than she had ever seen her.

'We're all going to America, Aunt Lizzie. Got in with a group and two other blokes. One used to work with the Beatles.'

'Who are the Beatles?' asked Aunt Lizzie.

They all began to laugh.

'Oh, Aunt Lizzie, everyone knows who the Beatles are. They are a famous pop group. They're making millions, they are.'

'So will we when we get to the States,' cried Derick.

But Lizzie was not convinced. 'Why can't you play in a band here?' she asked. 'Going all that way out there.' Tears came into her eyes.

'Now, don't start,' cried Carol. 'Tell her the rest of it, Paul.' Her mouth formed a hard line.

Paul looked alarmed and tried to stall.

'You know that Paul and I live together now, don't you Aunt Lizzie?'

'Oh, so that is where you were. I thought you had gone with the hippies.'

Carol sneered. 'Not that way, Aunt Lizzie. We live together as man and wife, and we are extremely happy. I'm determined before I go to America, to make you understand.'

Lizzie's mouth dropped open as it used to and her face went pale. 'Oh Carol, what are you saying? Tell me it's not true Paul.'

Rather abashed and without uttering a word, Paul nodded his head.

'But you can't. It's against the law. You can't be married.'

'Who wants to get married?' shouted Carol.

'Oh, but Carol, suppose you have a child?'

'No fear of that, I am on the pill.'

'Oh, I don't understand. You were brought up as brother and sister. It isn't right.'

'Listen to her,' said Carol. 'You didn't worry about us, so we are looking after each other, and doing well.'

Derick said, 'Don't get upset, Aunt Lizzie. Paul only ever wanted Carol. It happened and they are very happy together.'

'Oh my God! What can I do?' wailed Lizzie.

'Nothing, darling,' said Paul. 'I will love and cherish her all my life. She was all I ever wanted. Goodbye, Aunt Lizzie, we love you and we'll write to you.'

They kissed her very affectionately, and with a hasty goodbye to Bella and Robin, they went on their merry way.

Lizzie wept quietly. 'Did you know, Bella?'

'Yes, everyone knew, but even Charlie could not part them. It's just one of those things, and anyway they are not so closely related, are they?'

Robin said, 'No one knew their fathers, and Sallie is Carol's grandmother. Can't see any problems myself; just another skeleton in the cupboard.'

Bella said, 'Stop worrying, Lizzie. Let it remain a family secret and see how they get on.'

Robin said, 'They're a smashing little group, I've heard them play. Carol's got a fine voice, so they might make it out in the States. Lots of money in that pop business.'

CHAPTER TWENTY-THREE

The Changing World

In the sixties, millions of youngsters shouted and screamed, twisted and gyrated. The music got louder and the pace faster, as rock bands like the Rolling Stones became fashionable. Every schoolboy wanted to play a guitar, to strum his way to the top of the pop scene. They banded together all over the place in small groups, and agents, slick fellows who knew the drill, took over. Derick, Paul and Carol made up one such group, and were now playing regularly every night of the week. Gone were the hard days of one night stands. Paul strummed his electric guitar and Derick wielded the drumsticks, while Carol hung on to the microphone and sung her heart out, her slim body twisting and writhing to the rhythm of the music. They had been joined by a thin, fair boy who played the piano. His name was Archie, and he had previously played church organs and attended the Royal Academy of Music. But he had never made the grade, so had turned successfully to pop music. Then there was Dave, a Yorkshire lad, who played the base fiddle. He was very fat, and during the performances the perspiration would pour out of him. He had lots of good humour, and had kept them going when times were bad. The group were now known as The Dropouts, which was a name suggested by their manager, Izzy. Izzy was a real tough East Ender and knew the score, having played around the jazz cellars since he was a lad playing truant from school.

There had been six months of full bookings in London, and now they had made it good enough to sail away to America. They arrived in New York almost broke, but they had given several impromptu performances aboard ship, and had made many contacts.

America took these youngsters to their hearts; they paid them well and swept them off into the fast rising tide of pop music. Because they were very good artists and worked hard they made good, living it up in the big hotels with posh parties. The dreary pub where they had entertained in London was practically forgotten as they toured the big American cities. They sent an occasional postcard to Aunt Lizzie, but seldom seemed to have the time to write a letter. Aunt Lizzie, on the other hand, did not forget them. She always had the photographs on hand, collected all the newspaper cuttings of them and stuck them in a book. Bella would get irritated on the days when Lizzie sat weeping, either over the memory of Bobby, or over her wandering kids.

'Sometimes I lose patience with you, Lizzie. Get on with life, don't look back.'

'I suppose I'm not built that way,' said Lizzie mournfully. 'I miss them terribly, and I'm worried about them. This business of Carol and Paul is unnatural. I just can't bear the thought of it.'

'Well they seem happy enough. Who are we to judge?' said Bella.

The project for the new pub was still going ahead but as yet Bella and Robin had not found premises that suited them.

Charlie was a news editor in *The Daily News* and now that he had achieved his ambitions, lived in the stock-broker country down in Guildford, while his children received a private education. He was still the happy-go-lucky boy he used to be, in fact he seemed more cockney than ever in his middle age. He liked to put on his East End act to impress the big shots, but he was very popular and had even appeared on a television chat show.

Every week Lizzie inserted an advertisement in the personal column of his newspaper. It read, 'Bobby please come home, Lizzie needs you.' But no response ever came. Bobby was as silent as the grave. In some ways Lizzie was still unsettled. She had grown used to her nice new image and the glory was wearing off. She still kept herself nice, well corseted and neatly dressed, but inside her heart was heavy; she missed the love and warmth of the family.life.

Then one day Bella said, 'Put on your glamour, Lizzie. We're taking you out.'

Lizzie brightened up. 'Where to?'

'Well, we think we have found the ideal spot for our new business. We're taking you to see it. Robin knows something, but not all. In fact he thinks you're investing the money you got from the sale of the house, so use your head, Lizzie.'

Lizzie admired Bella's astuteness and trusted her completely. She often wished that she could make quick decisions like Bella did, for she was the brains of that marriage.

Soon Lizzie was in the car, a big saloon. Robin liked big cars, but was not too good a driver, and Lizzie clung to the edge of her seat with apprehension.

'Don't go so fast, Robin,' she implored.

'What! We got a bloody back seat driver, then?' grinned Robin.

Then Lizzie began to recognize places. 'That bridge we just crossed, that's the Regent's Canal. We used to call it the Cut,' she said. 'And look, over there, that used to be the film studios. I remember the night it got burned down,' she cried excitedly.

'So,' said Bella. 'You know where we are, then, Lizzie?'

'Yes,' she smiled, 'near Nile Street where I was born.' She craned her neck for a glimpse of the old market street, but all around were tall office blocks and high rise flats, there was no sign of that long winding slum street market she had known so well.

They parked the car in a side street. Huge wooden hoardings hid the remains of a small house still in the process of being demolished. Lizzie stood looking around, her small shape lost amid the tall buildings, as she searched for a familiar landmark. There was just one: the old gates of the hospital, where her Mum had sat with her basket of flowers for sale. But only that old gate was recognizable. The rest was lost. One huge building had been painted and renovated but still retained its old shape and was dated, est. 1873. But it was nothing like the old grey workhouse that used to be on that spot.

'That's where Mum sat,' she said, very pleased with herself.

Bella was not listening. She had crossed the road and was staring up at an old derelict public house that stood on the corner.

'Look at that, Lizzie. What do you think of it?'

'Why! It's Pat O'Keefe's old pub. I remember the night it was blitzed.'

'And it's called The William,' said Robin.

Lizzie went forward and touched the old green, painted door. 'No, it's Pat O'Keefe's. Why, my Bobby spent most of his young life in there.'

'Oh,' sighed Bella, 'back to Bobby again.'

'She could be right,' said Robin, 'because this is where Nile Street came out into City Road.'

'Oh well, let's get going. It's going to need a lot done to it, but it's an ideal spot, what with the big hospital and all these offices and factories.'

They escorted Lizzie into that place of memories. The smell of beer and sawdust was still there, but it had been modernized at some point. The old walls were bare, stripped of those grand old prints of famous racehorses and greyhounds. Gone were the silver shields and the trophies that Pat had won in his wrestling heyday, but here and there were patches of the flat emerald green paint that Pat used for everything. With a dainty, gloved hand Lizzie touched the spot where Bobby used to stand, shouting and drinking and having such a good time.

'It's Pat O'Keefe's,' she whispered in wonder, and looked down at the broken floorboards. Vivid memories flooded back. 'Poor old Gladys was buried down there.'

'Shut up, you give us the bloody creeps,' cried Bella irritably.

But Robin's laughter rang out loud just as Bobby's had done. 'Well, Lizzie, it's a good buy, and we are to get a lot of help from the brewers. It is an old landmark, and they want it preserved. What about it?'

'Yes, yes,' said Lizzie absentmindedly, as she sat on an old chair in that same corner where she used to sit on Saturday nights, recalling poor Gladys, and the night she had ordered a Pimms Number One. 'I'll sit here. You go over it,' she said. 'I'll wait here.'

So Bella, notepad in hand, conducted Robin all over the old ruin, describing to him how it would look when she had finished with it.

'Going to cost a lot of dough,' said Robin. 'Can we manage it?'

'Not to worry,' said Bella. 'We'll make a lot of money when we get going. Right then, are we all agreed?' she asked, as they returned to find Lizzie still dreaming.

'Yes, it's all right with me, Bella. And Bobby will know where to find me when he comes home,' she murmured.

Bella gave a shrug. 'Oh well, that's settled. Let's go and see the agent.'

Lizzie sat quietly and contentedly on the way home.

Robin said, 'You must be kidding, Lizzie. Is that really Bobby's old local?'

'Yes,' said Lizzie, 'we was both born just round the corner to the pub. There used to be a lot of little streets of two storey houses, but a landmine wiped them out. Our little house in Brady Street went that night.'

Bella sat calculating and writing in her notebook. 'You won't recognize this when it is finished, and we will have a fine apartment built up on the roof for you, Lizzie. Central heating, double glazing, the lot.'

'You can see St Paul's from up there,' said Lizzie dreamily. 'Used to look at it from the playground of the school. That's gone, didn't see the school.'

'No, Lizzie, it's probably part of the hospital now,' said Bella. 'It's not been empty all that long. The war damage commission repaired it and it's had three tenants since. They couldn't make it pay, so that's why they are selling it, lock stock and barrel. I think it's a bargain, but will take more than six months to get it into shape.'

'You know it's all right by me,' said Robin, 'because whatever you do is always a success. Whether it's luck or brains I am not sure, but you are certainly always ahead of me, darling.'

Through that long winter Lizzie played cards with Mark, also Monopoly, which he had been given for Christmas. He bought and sold property in the game with the greatest gusto, cheating Lizzie most of the time.

Bella's girl, Gloria, was now boarding at an academy for young ladies, so Mark monopolized Aunt Lizzie and kept her company. In fact she wondered what she would have done without him. Bella and Robin were always busy; all the plans had now been finalized for the new pub, and Bella went around dreaming up colour schemes. Often she did not even hear when Lizzie spoke to her. The builders had taken over and Lizzie had parted with half the money in the suitcase, telling herself that if Bobby came back he would be most pleased to find himself back in Pat O'Keefe's old boozer.

On Saturday night she would put on all her jewellery and her nicest new dress, and sit behind the bar, looking, as Robin said, like the Queen of Sheba. Anyone who observed her would have said she was a very pretty prosperous little lady, but her heart was heavy each time she thought of Carol, the boys and of Bobby wandering the world. Maisie still wrote regularly from the remote island somewhere off the coast of Africa where she and her husband were missionaries. Her letters were long and very pious, mostly concerned with the good work that they were doing amongst the natives.

Charlie rang punctually every week, and Luber was now expecting her third child. So Lizzie's family was growing larger and spreading out across the world. Yet Lizzie's heart was breaking for her big, rough husband, Bobby. 'If only I knew whether he was alive or dead, I'd face it,' she would say.

'Oh, no news is good news,' Bella would reply tersely. 'He'll turn up one day, like the proverbial bad penny, if I know Bobby.'

Lizzie supposed she would have been very happy, but for her empty heart and arms that longed to hold Bobby close to her. That some younger woman had taken her place Lizzie had no doubts, for if Bobby were alive he would not be able to live alone. It made her restless and unhappy just thinking about him.

Then one day a long letter came from Derick, telling them that they were doing very nicely, had an apartment in New York, and that if Lizzie would now like to visit them she would be in time for Carol's wedding in early spring.

Lizzie's reaction to this news was very strange. She burst out crying.

'Can't see what you are grizzling about,' announced Bella. 'Why, they seem to have settled down very well, and if they want to marry it's up to them.'

'I won't have it!' cried Lizzie.

'But why should you care?'

'Oh, but I do care,' wailed Lizzie. 'They will never be able to have children.'

'Can't see what is so terrible about that,' replied Bella. 'I only wish the pill had been invented in my day. I'd have had a bloody good time and no worries.'

'Oh Bella, I can't let it happen. I am, after all, her adopted mother, and I cannot condone it.'

'Please yourself, Lizzie, but I haven't got the time at the moment to go with you, and you can't make a long journey like that on your own.'

'Who says I can't?' cried Lizzie defiantly.

'That's up to you. You got the money and the time, that's more than we have with this new project on our hands.'

'I'll go,' said Lizzie getting up. 'And I'll go by myself, and I shall call out to the preacher when he asks if any one knows any impediment or reason why they should not be wed.'

'Oh, don't be so bloody dramatic,' said Bella. 'They probably do it differently out there anyway, but if you want a trip to the States I'll get it organized for you. It will get you out of the way while we are moving into the new place.'

'Thank you, Bella,' said Lizzie quietly. 'I knew you would see my point of view in the end.'

So Bella began to ring around for sailing dates and Lizzie started to get her wardrobe ready. She must go looking nice, can't let the kids down. They had made the grade, but she would not let them break the law.

CHAPTER TWENTY-FOUR

The American Trip

There were a few days of indecision while the family argued as to where, how, and when Aunt Lizzie should make her trip to America.

Astute Bella said to Robin, 'Let her go, it will be good for her. But that she is going to affect the affairs of Carol in any way, I very much doubt.'

'She's a game old gel. I wouldn't like anything to happen to her,' said Robin in his rather gruff way.

Charlie and Luber were really and truly shocked. 'Surely,' insisted Luber, 'one of us can find the time and the money to travel with her. I know how she will feel, all alone in a strange country.'

'Well, it's obvious that you can't go,' grinned Robin, staring at Luber's extended tummy. Being so short, Luber always looked very heavy when she was pregnant.

This remark of Robin's annoyed Charlie. 'I have too many commitments just now, so it won't be me. In any case, it is always I who do the dirty work for this family. It's time I considered myself and my own family.'

'Now! Now!' declared Bella. 'No squabbling. Lizzie is determined to go, so let her, and I will arrange it so that she travels in comfort.'

So eventually they all agreed.

As Bella remarked coolly to Robin after they all had left, 'Let's face it, we might get a good buyer for this place, then we can move into the new place and take pot luck. I know it's in a mess, but without Lizzie we can just make a part of it liveable.'

'Well, it's up to you,' replied Robin placidly.

'With Lizzie out of the way,' continued Bella, 'and Gloria away at school, Mark is no trouble. He will sleep anywhere. Yes, I think it's a great idea. Also I can keep my eye on the builders and make sure they don't fiddle me.'

'Just as you say, Bella.' Robin always admired his wife's quick decisions.

'Yes,' said Bella, rubbing her hands exultantly, 'at least it will all be done my way.'

Meanwhile Lizzie wallowed in a hot perfumed bath. She enjoyed a hot soak before retiring at night, and had got quite used to it now. Bella had insisted on it. 'A quick shower in the mornings, Lizzie, and a hot bath before bedtime will keep you healthy and as fresh as a daisy.'

Often Lizzie would lie there thinking of the big tin bath they had all used. The water was heated in the old wash copper and then poured by the bucketful into the tin bath in front of the fire. It had been hard work, and when eventually you did get your bath, you had really earned it. Then she would dreamily recall Bobby's bare white back, and how she used to sponge it down for him, usually on Saturday afternoons when he was getting ready to go out on the spree.

She then began to dwell on the American trip. She was beginning to lose heart, she was quite willing to confess that her old timidity was returning. It all seemed such a great upheaval, and even if she did find the courage to part Carol and Paul, they would never forgive her. Perhaps she had better dismiss the whole idea. She felt lazy and comfortable living with Bella, and soon they would all be going back to The Nile. Lizzie revelled in this thought; at the back of her mind was still the obsession that, if Bobby did return, he would know just where to find her. So, by the end of the week, Lizzie had wavered and was ready to tell the family that she had changed her mind.

However, Bella had ideas of her own. 'Lizzie,' she said, 'this will be the holiday of a lifetime. It doesn't take long in these new jet planes and you shall travel first class. Why! You will love it, I am sure.'

'Oh no!' cried Lizzie, 'you will never get me up in the air, that I can assure you.'

'Lizzie, it would be very foolish for you to go by boat. It takes twice as long and the crossing is bound to upset you.'

'I've changed my mind,' said Lizzie. 'I'll write today and tell them.'

'I've already cabled them that you are coming,' cried Bella angrily.

Lizzie remained silent, knowing that Bella had a quick temper when aroused, and did not want to provoke her, so in spite of her protests arrangements went ahead for the journey.

'We'll sort out your wardrobe,' suggested Bella, 'make sure you take the right things with you. Must have you looking nice. You will be travelling with all the nobs, you know.'

'I am still of two minds,' said Lizzie mildly.

'No, Lizzie,' declared Bella. 'Did I ever put you wrong? It's something you need to do, and, who knows, you might even find a rich husband out there.'

'Oh shut up!' cried Lizzie, blushing madly.

They packed her nice underwear and those smart suits, then went out to buy a good evening dress for special occasions. It was black and nicely fitting, with a sequin trim and a little coatee that covered the bare look of the shoulder straps.

'Now, look at that,' exclaimed Bella when Lizzie tried it on. 'Why! They will think that the duchess of London has arrived.'

'My Bobby always called me his duchess,' said Lizzie, admiring herself in the long mirror.

'Oh dear, are we back to Bobby again?' cried Bella. 'Try to forget about him, if only for a short while.'

It was arranged that Lizzie would travel at the beginning of May, thus giving her time to spare before the wedding, early in June.

'Now, Lizzie, I've insured all your jewellery, so you can take it to wear without too much worry. I've bought you a little jewel case that locks up,' Bella said. 'Also I had better take the rest of the money and put it in a separate account. Is that all right with you?'

'If you say so, Bella,' replied Lizzie mildly, then a gentle smile lit up her face as she realized that she sounded just like Robin.

So Bella took the rest of the money from the old suitcase, and, in her methodical way, put it in a large envelope and sealed it up. She gave Lizzie the little lizard-skin box with her precious jewellery in it. The battered old suitcase was nearly empty now, except for some of Bobby's special papers which Bella threw on the bed. Then grabbing the old suitcase, she prepared to leave the room.

'Where are you going with that case, Bella?' asked Lizzie abruptly.

'Throw it in the rubbish. What else can I do with it?'

There was slight tension in the room for a moment, then Lizzie said, 'Give it back to me, I'd like to keep it.'

Bella handed it back to her. 'All right, Lizzie, but for Christ's sake don't put it back under the bed to harbour dust, and you certainly can't take it to America with you.'

Lizzie did not answer, but just returned to the case those old papers of Bobby's.

So Bella gave a nonchalant shrug, and a brief coldness developed between them, but it was soon erased, for Bella's sunny nature never allowed her to bear grudges. Preparations for Lizzie's trip were well under way and soon she began to look forward to it, her arms longing to hold Carol once more and to see those lovely boys who had meant so much to her. Within a month a smart little woman stood waiting at Heathrow to board the plane for New York. You might well have cast an extra glance at her had you been travelling on that particular day. She wore a nicely tailored wine-coloured coat and a tall felt hat of the same shade. Bella had said it was a colour which suited her, that the hat made her look taller, and of course Lizzie always accepted Bella's advice.

Robin grinned at her and, as they stood waiting, he jibed, 'My Gawd, you look like some eccentric actress.'

Lizzie's humour had returned, even though she was extremely nervous of getting on the huge plane sitting out there near the runway. 'Well Robin,' she replied brightly, 'in my day they used to say, red hat no drawers, but that is not the case. I have a dozen very fancy ones packed, and a warm pair for travelling as Bella has insisted.'

Immediately there was laughter all around her. Even the sober Charlie showed his teeth in a white grin. This made her happy; she might never get back to them once she got up there above the clouds, so at least it was lovely to leave them all laughing.

Eventually the last goodbyes were said, everyone telling her this and that. Even the unemotional Bella had a hint of tears in her hazel eyes, and little Mark howled like a banshee. All that week he had been demanding that Lizzie take him with her. 'I'll look after you, Aunt Lizzie, you know I will,' he protested between howls.

'No, darling, you are too young, and I don't think your Mummy would like to be without you.'

Bella had smacked him and told him to hold his noise. She had no intention of letting her son out of her sight; he got into enough trouble with them all guarding him.

The long walk to the plane seemed endless, a very nice-looking young lady in a smart uniform welcomed her aboard. 'First time for you? Oh, you will love it, and I'll look after you.' She chatted as she escorted Lizzie to her seat.

It was very nice sitting there in the big comfortable seat. If she hadn't known she was in a plane, she might have thought is was one of those posh seats in that new cinema she had been to recently. She felt a sense of freedom now that the family were out of sight. 'I'll sit with my fingers crossed,' she decided, 'that might help.'

The hostess came and fastened her seat belt with a big buckle. Lizzie did not like this. Suppose they crashed. She could do little to save herself all tied up like this. 'I'd sooner not be fastened in ' she whispered to the hostess.

The lovely face broke into a smile. 'It is only while we are taking off, dear. I'll come and unbuckle you as soon as we are in the air.'

A lot of passengers had got on this plane, but where were they. She looked around, only about eight couples as far as she could determine, and the seat next to her was empty. But not for long. A little man bustled in at the last moment, muttering, grumbling and gasping for breath, and blowing his nose very loudly. With a little smile he settled in the seat next to her. Lizzie eased herself in her seat so as to observe this man. She did not even notice that they were already up in the air. She had closed her eyes for a while and her fingers ached from keeping them crossed. She opened them to see the latecomer peering at her.

'Relax,' he said, 'we are on our way. How about a drink? Nothing like it to give you a bit of Dutch courage. I do this twice a year and each time I am terrified. I hang about until the last minute trying to make myself change my mind.'

'Can we drink?' asked Lizzie.

'Of course we can, my old darling,' he said with great familiarity, 'and the first one is on me. I always have a large brandy and soda. All right with you?'

'Yes, if you don't mind,' replied Lizzie very sweetly, feeling at ease with this funny man. His skin was very wrinkled, but his eyes seemed bright and very young. He was obviously of Jewish extraction, she recognized immediately the twang in his voice, the cockney dialect of the Jewish trader. She recalled the stallholders down in The Nile. Yes, he was a working class Jew who had made it, and was able to travel first class. All the same he was very nice and friendly; so far no other passenger had even looked in her direction. They were all hidden behind newspapers and magazines. Once the brandies had arrived she took several slow sips and it certainly had the desired effect. Gathering courage, she took a quick look out of the window and saw before her a brilliant blue sky and a sea of fluffy white clouds down below.

'It all looks rather pretty,' she remarked.

'Yes, if that's what you like,' he answered. 'Personally I look forward to getting my feet on the solid ground again. Now, that does excite me. Come on, love, drink up, we'll have another.'

So they drank together and began to chat.

'I thought I saw a lot of people getting on this plane,' announced Lizzie.

'You did,' he replied, 'but they are most of them travelling in the rear. Not as lucky as you and me, able to travel first class.'

'Oh! Is that the reason?' Lizzie looked a trifle amazed.

He gave her a kind but critical stare, saying, 'You haven't travelled far. Is this the first time you've flown?'

Lizzie nodded her head and said quietly, 'I'm scared.'

'That makes two of us,' he cried with a chuckle. 'Drink up.'

Sammy Cohen was excellent company. He told her that he had lived in America for ten years and had just been home to England. 'To bury me Momma,' he said. 'Do you know she was almost ninety. She died in a Whitechapel Nursing Home. She would not budge from the East End. The times I've tried to make her come over to the States, but, no, she even gave the money I sent her to Jewish charities and went on living in the same old house we was all born in.' He shrugged. 'Now it's all over, and I can do no more.'

'I'm very sorry,' murmured Lizzie, looking up at him in that sincere way she had.

'Never mind,' he said, 'we'll have another drink. Anyway, what are you doing travelling all alone, a nice little body like you? I can tell you are my own kind, born within the sound of Bow Bells.'

'Well, in North London,' returned Lizzie, 'a place called The Nile.'

'I know,' he cried out loud. 'Used to play around there when I was a lad. I was born in Ludgate, you know, the old Whitechapel Road.'

'Well, to tell you the truth, I seldom left my own district when I was young.'

'Making up for it now,' said Sammy, handing her another brandy.

Lizzie sipped it appreciatively. She would never have admitted that this was the first time she had tasted brandy.

'Do you mind me asking your name?' said Sammy, looking closely at her.

'It's Elizabeth Erlock, but I'm usually called Lizzie.'

'Ahr! A grand old name,' cried Sammy, raising his glass. 'And here's to you, Lizzie.'

'Here's to you, Sam,' she returned, raising her glass in the same manner. She had really begun to enjoy herself.

They began to discuss the old, pre-war London that they both knew so well, that city of memories which had now disappeared.

'Do you remember, Lizzie, how we all played out in the streets till it was dark, and no one interfered with us?'

'Yes, and how the old ladies sat outdoors on summer nights, and often dozed off, and they would then be carried inside, chair and all, and no one robbed them.'

'Yes, Lizzie, times were certainly very different,' agreed Sam. 'And it's not any different in New York either; it's a very wicked city.'

'I wasn't sure that I wanted to make this trip. If I could have got out of it I would,' she confessed.

'Why are you going then?'

'To my daughter's wedding,' said Lizzie rather sadly.

'Great!' declared Sammy. 'What's better than a wedding in New York? They really lay it on over there; I've been married three times. I never forgot the first one; she died in London after the war. She never got over the Blitz, got bad health, what with those bloody shelters and the lousy food, I never had a bean in those days, had a stall in Whitechapel market. Used to sell sheet music and gramophone records. The war done that in, so I ended up in a munitions factory, as I wasn't fit enough for the army. Had flat feet and asthma, and Lord knows what, when I was young. Now look at me.' He grinned.

'Well, I'd say you were a fine figure of a man,' smiled Lizzie.

With that Sammy laughed out loud. 'Let's have another drink, Lizzie.'

But Lizzie declined. She had a strange floating feeling; she must be getting tipsy. She had forgotten that they were up in the air, flying above the speed of sound.

'I also have bad memories of the Blitz,' she told him in a rather maudlin manner.

'Oh, let's cheer up, Lizzie,' cried Sammy. 'Here, do you

remember this song,' and in a very loud voice he began to sing. 'When we were kids on the corner of the street, we were rough and ready guys, and boy how we could harmonize.'

The other passengers fidgeted restlessly, unaccustomed to such goings on when travelling first class. But because it was Bobby's favourite song, Lizzie joined in, and they went on singing cockney numbers till Lizzie dozed off and Sam ran out of steam.

Lizzie slept on Sammy's shoulder until the hostess roused them with the menu for dinner. Lizzie walked precariously along to the toilet and bathed her face and hands. When she returned, the little table was laid for dinner and she joined Sammy for a nice meal of soup, followed by chicken salad, with plenty more to drink.

Sammy told more lurid stories of his life and of how he had gone to America after the war, leaving his two sons with his mother. He had very little money but he did have a recommendation to a famous music publisher. Sammy had a rare gift; he composed the words of popular songs, so after a minor success in England he had gone to try his luck in America.

'I walked Tin Pan Alley dead broke, selling my numbers for just enough money to buy something to eat, then at last it changed. I got a good break, and with all those little pop groups springing up looking for material I never had to worry any more. Am I a happy man?' he cried, gesticulating wildly. 'What a question! Who's happy in this world? Get it one way and lose it another.'

Listening sympathetically, Lizzie began to like Sammy and the carefree way in which he approached life. He did not pretend; in some ways he was like Bobby, but not so handsome to look at.

'Have you a husband, Lizzie?' inquired Sammy.

'I've lost him.'

He squeezed her hand.

'My children are in the music business, got a small band,' she told him. 'They call themselves The Dropouts.'

'I know 'em,' yelled Sammy excitedly once more. 'Good

kids, seen 'em perform. When we get there, Lizzie, let's not lose touch. I'll come and take you out to dinner.'

Lizzie, feeling very full of food and drink and exceedingly mellow, agreed.

After dinner Sammy said, 'Better get our heads down, otherwise we will be fit for nothing when we get to New York.'

Lizzie settled down, closed her eyes and slept peacefully, waking eventually to find a misty dawn outside the windows, and the Captain's voice telling them they would be landing soon, and to fasten their seat belts.

So the great plane came in very slowly to land. Lizzie was a thousand miles from home in a strange new country, and she did not seem to care, she had a kind of nice feeling, as if she had really enjoyed her first flight.

Sammy was a little irritable, fussing and grumbling, but he gave Lizzie his card saying, 'Look me up, Lizzie, we will meet for dinner.' And off he went, still fidgeting and muttering, on his way.

The nice hostess took charge of Lizzie. 'Had a good trip, I noticed,' she said with a sweet smile.

'I never noticed I was in the air,' said Lizzie. 'Think I was sloshed most of the time.'

'Don't worry about your luggage, I'll see it's taken care of. Now, go straight to the arrivals hall, and your daughter will be waiting for you.'

Holding the handbag which contained her jewellery, Lizzie stood looking for Carol. Everyone was rushing past her; it was all a little confusing, and it seemed such a large place. Then she saw a familiar face in the crowd as Derick came dashing towards her. He hugged her affectionately.

'Oh Aunt Lizzie, you look wonderful,' he cried.

'Where are Paul and Carol?' she asked him.

'Oh they're all right. I'll tell you all the news in a minute; sit here and have a coffee while I get your luggage through the customs.'

He looked very fit; he had grown a little and filled out a bit. His skin was tanned and he wore a lightweight suit. His hair was long, black and curly, and almost reached his shoulders.

Lizzie did not approve of that and decided to tell him so later on.

Derick was soon back. 'Come on, darling, let's get you home. I've put your luggage in the car; we'll pick up Carol on the way.'

Lizzie, now feeling a little harassed and very tired, sat in the open car. The bright sun poured down onto her head, and the streets seemed to teem with people. The buildings rose up to a tremendous height on each side of her. As Derick drove through the heavy traffic Lizzie sat silent and a little glum, wondering if she would have the courage to do what she had come over for.

Derick said, 'You will like it out here, Aunt Lizzie. It's lively, like the old London you used to know.'

'How is Carol?' murmured Lizzie.

'On top of the world. She's out now in the big stores, getting her trousseau together. In five minutes we will be there, don't worry, love. Did you enjoy the flight?'

'Oh yes,' said Lizzie, 'very much. Made friends with a very nice man; he was a Londoner but he's lived over here twenty years. I drank three double brandies.'

'Well, Aunt Lizzie, you are really living it up. Here comes Carol.'

They had slowed down in a kind of square amid the big stores and Carol came tripping across the road to greet them, carrying a load of parcels.

Lizzie was surprised to see that she had cut her lovely hair off and that it was now short and curly. She wore tight blue trousers and a white silk top that showed up her young firm breasts.

Carol threw her parcels into the front of the car and almost leapt in on top of Lizzie, hugging and kissing her. 'Oh darling, darling, it's lovely to see you,' she cried.

Carol looked radiant and so happy that Lizzie could not believe her own eyes. Gone was the sulky moody teenager, this was the finished woman, and a very lovely one.

'Just done some shopping,' said Carol, once she had calmed

down. 'It's surprising what you need. I am having a big posh wedding, Aunt Lizzie.'

Lizzie's heart gave a lurch and she felt a kind of qualm. How pleased would Carol be to see her if she knew why she had travelled all those miles?

'I'll take you out once you are rested, and buy you the best outfit in town. Got to look the best, since you are going to be the bride's mother.'

Lizzie felt a twinge of pride, for Carol had always addressed her as Aunt Lizzie, never acknowledging the fact that Lizzie was her legally adopted mother.

'I brought a nice suit with me,' said Lizzie timidly.

'Oh yes, something that Bella got for you,' said Carol, more like her old self. 'And I don't like that hat.' She snatched if off Lizzie's head. Then she stroked Lizzie's hair softly, saying, 'But your hair is pretty, and a lovely colour.'

Lizzie's eyes filled with tears. How she loved this little one, and she was the one who was going to be hurt.

'Aren't you well, darling?' asked Carol, seeing Lizzie so quiet.

'Got a touch of jet lag, I expect,' said Derick from the driver's seat.

'Oh silly me, of course, darling, you must rest when we get home.' Carol cuddled close to her, and Lizzie sat wondering what jet lag was. Some unknown bug that she might have caught? It was all so very depressing.

Soon they arrived at the apartment. It was in a seedy street lined with lots of high, old-fashioned dwellings. All the houses had steps up to the front door, and reminded Lizzie of the house in Highbury. Some folks sat on the steps, and some idled on the corners. It was a bit noisy and Carol's apartment was on the third floor. A great, big, untidy room with magazines, records and clothes littering the chairs and the worn sofa, but it was warm, and an aroma of cooking filled the air. Lizzie looked around; Carol was just as untidy as ever, she had not changed.

'Make some hot coffee, Derick. I am going to put Aunt Lizzie to bed,' announced Carol.

'But it's the middle of the day, I don't want to go to bed,' protested Lizzie.

'No, darling, you've got jet lag. That's a kind of fatigue, because of the time difference between London and New York.'

'Oh, so that is what jet lag is,' said Lizzie. 'I thought it was some kind of flu.'

Carol giggled. 'Now come on, you haven't changed a bit, Aunt Lizzie. You still get the wrong meanings for things. I'll tuck you up and bring you a hot drink. You sleep till this evening, and tonight I'll introduce you to my future husband.'

Lizzie felt a little confused. 'I thought Paul was away with the band?'

'Yep! That's right, he's in Miami, but he will be here for the wedding.'

Carol helped Lizzie to undress, then tucked her up in bed. It was a nice little bedroom, all pink, frilly and surprisingly tidy. Lizzie closed her eyes, feeling very disturbed. Carol looked so happy, positively blooming. Oh dear, what should she do? With her finger and thumb she held onto the little turquoise earring which she wore on a gold chain around her neck. When distressed she would hold on to that little earring with finger and thumb, just like a rosary bead. 'Oh Mum,' she wept, 'what can I do?' Then she went off into a dreamless sleep.

When she woke she felt much happier and very refreshed. Carol came in, attired in a loose gown and a shower cap. She brought her a tray of tea which they shared.

'Have a biscuit,' Carol said, 'they call them cookies out here. Con will probably take us out to dinner. Oh, he is wonderful and also rich, darling. I didn't know that I could be so happy, and I'm so glad that you came, because seeing I'm not twenty-one yet and we are marrying in his church, you might have to give your permission. Oh, isn't it great, I've got my own mother to see me wed!'

To Lizzie the almost impossible had happened. Carol wasn't going to marry Paul. She was going to marry respectably in a church and to someone who could take good care of her. 'I can't wait to see him,' Lizzie declared, 'and by the way, how is Paul now?'

'Oh, he's coming to the wedding,' said Carol nonchalantly, beginning to take out her rollers. 'I think he is courting a girl steady from out West. That groupie kid got fed up in the end, but Paul is such a good musician that all he cares about is the band.'

'Why is Derick here? They are usually together.'

'Well, that's another long story. Derick got sick while they were touring, so that is why he is staying here with me. He shares an apartment with a guy downstairs; Paul is good and sends him plenty of money.'

'Oh well,' sighed Lizzie, 'I'm certainly pleased you are all looking after each other. I brought you all up very close.'

'I know you did, darling,' said Carol kissing her. 'I'm sorry that Paul and I worried you, but it was just one of those things. It's all over now.'

CHAPTER TWENTY-FIVE

New York Wedding

With a great sense of relief in her mind Lizzie settled down to enjoy her American holiday. Her relationship with Carol was better than it had been since Carol was a child. She had been such a lovely baby, but was a very wilful and headstrong teenager. Now, almost twenty-one years old, she was a mature and very beautiful woman, entering matrimony with all the hopes and dreams of a woman in love. Last week had been very invigorating, not that Lizzie had seen many sights of the big city, but she had certainly got to know its young folk. The big house teemed with young people. It was a kind of tenement all let off into one or two bedroom flats. There was always someone clattering up or down the uncarpeted stairs; sometimes they would stand in groups chatting on the landings and always one or the other of them threw a party at the weekends.

Carol's flat was like Waterloo station in the rush hour; people tripped in and out examining her trousseau, leaving little presents, and often a little souvenir for Lizzie. They were all poor but very generous. Lizzie revelled in this warmth and hospitality; it reminded her of her own youth in those poverty-stricken back streets of The Nile. They would arrive with bags of ready-cooked food, hot dogs, pizzas, apple strudel and pickled cucumbers. They would leave all the paper bags and cardboard plates behind them, and they jawed all the time they ate, while Lizzie served them coffee from the big pot which was always hot on the stove. Those young people lolled around and talked so fast that most of their conversation was quite unintelligible to Lizzie; nevertheless she enjoyed their company.

Carol floated in and out like a princess, buying new things

and making final arrangements for her wedding. Every afternoon she disappeared, off to what was called the health club
and came back looking very fit and very tanned, her eyes and
skin glowing.

Lizzie's happiness increased even more when she met Carol's
future husband. He was very tall, six foot at least, with a head
like a Greek god. His hair, which was very fair and close
cropped, emphasized his well-formed features. Together they
made a very attractive couple. He was quiet and soft-spoken as
big chaps often are. His voice had an unusual soft, slow drawl,
so different to those quick gabble, gabble New Yorkers.

'I am so delighted to meet you, Mother,' he said.

Lizzie felt a quick thrill of pleasure again at the sound of the
word mother. He had taken them out to dinner — a smart
restaurant — then on to a late night club. Lizzie sat watching
them dance together, so close and compatible; Carol had never
looked so happy.

'You will meet my folks at the wedding,' Con told Lizzie.
'They will love you. My mother is of English descent, and my
father Irish. In fact it was my grandfather, a penniless Irish
immigrant, who trekked out West and discovered an oil field.'

Lizzie listened politely, but it did not mean much to her.
She had never taken a lot of interest in anything outside her
own little world. But that he was affectionate, charming and
gracious she was quite sure, and so good for little Carol whose
father was unknown and whose mother was a war casualty. It
was indeed a fairy story.

Derick was always around, and took them for long, tedious
shopping trips in his little sports car. Carol insisted on buying
Lizzie a new outfit for the wedding. At dinner the previous
night she had worn the good black evening dress that Bella had
chosen.

'Oh it's not so bad,' Carol had exclaimed, 'but, Mother, I
want you to look like the rest of them, even better. Con has
given me a good allowance with which to buy these things.'

So Lizzie was provided with a silver grey outfit, a jacket
trimmed with mink and a dress of glowing silk with pink

accessories. And to finish it all off, a lovely grey hat with a pink rose on the brim.

'Now you really look like the bride's mother,' Carol exclaimed.

All this flattery and these loving expressions entered into Lizzie's very soul. It was just as she always dreamed Carol's wedding should be.

Carol's wedding dress, which had been hired from some theatrical costumier, arrived that day and Lizzie hung it up with care and love, admiring its wide white crinoline, the crackling petticoats, the soft lace frills and the silver embroidery. It was indeed a dress fit for a princess. Carol told her that it had been worn by Jennie Lee in the Churchill film. 'Isn't it lovely?'

'Yes,' said Lizzie weeping quietly. If only Bobby were here to see it; Carol had always been his favourite. He would have really loved all this.

'Don't grizzle,' commanded Carol, 'or your nose will be bright red tomorrow, and that is the big day.'

In the evening Paul arrived. He was bigger and brawnier than ever; he seemed to have left the slim Derick completely behind, although he still had that same old charm. He embarrassed Lizzie with his whole-hearted affection, but did not kiss Carol. They seemed to be cool and distant towards each other. Carol put on her 'look at me' act, but Paul just stared quietly at her and did not smile.

The arrival of Derick cleared the atmosphere, and they started to lark about in the way they had always done. Lizzie felt a sense of relief; it was really over, thank God. Derick lived in the same house and shared an apartment with another boy, a strange boy who wore very bright clothes and had a nervous sort of twitch and a funny voice which was audible above all others. When Lizzie had remarked that he was an odd boy, Carol said quickly, 'Derick has been ill, he is just settling down, please don't interfere with his life.'

'Oh, I had no intention,' replied Lizzie, a little offended.

Still Lizzie fussed about Derick, how thin he was, never

seemed to eat enough. So to Paul she said, 'I don't like that boy Derick lives with.'

'Aunt Lizzie,' said Paul, very seriously, 'leave him alone. He has grown up; we all have, and none of us care to look back down the road.'

So Lizzie wisely accepted this message, knowing it would do her no good to pry into these young lives; she was no longer responsible for them.

On the morning of the wedding the flat was in an uproar. There had been a late night party and everyone seemed to have a hangover; all, that is, except Carol, the bride, who rose as fresh as a daisy and started to get ready for her wedding with a kind of cool poise. No pre-wedding nerves, just a kind of overbearing calm as she organized everyone.

Lizzie thought it must be her stage training, and remembered her own wedding, when she had been a bag of nerves. A young girl came to dress their hair, another to help them dress. Flowers arrived, telegrams and congratulatory postcards. The flat had an overpowering aroma of perfume and stale booze, yet the finished project was a wonder to behold. The young girls who were Carol's bridesmaids were both the same height, one dark and one fair, both wore white wide-skirted dresses, trimmed with pink and blue rose buds. On their heads were quaint Victorian bonnets trimmed with more rosebuds, and they carried little posies with trailing ribbons.

Lizzie felt a little bit anxious, wondering if she was a trifle overdressed. She allowed herself to be poked and prodded into position by several affectionate young ladies.

Then came the moment when Carol appeared, drinks were handed around and they all ceased work to congratulate the lovely bride.

Derick was best man, and Paul was to escort Lizzie. This he did very gallantly, and all through the service Lizzie sat wishing Sallie could see her granddaughter with her lovely, serious face. She looked more like poor little Irene, her mother, than Lizzie had ever seen her. Carol had many friends on her side of the church, most of them very young. Only Derick, Paul and Lizzie were related to her.

On the other side were a formidable host of very smart people all belonging to the bridegroom, who had eight brothers and sisters, some of them married. This meant that there were lots of small children, uncles, aunts and in-laws. Con's father was tall like his son, and his mum was as short as Lizzie. The Roman Catholic ceremony was long for a mixed marriage.

While they all prayed piously Lizzie sat thinking, 'Well, at least Carol will not be lonely in a big family like that. At least she will be well protected.' Then the tears sprang into her eyes, for she knew that she had lost her, and that thousands of miles of ocean would be between them. Lizzie did not enjoy the reception in the big luxurious hotel. A buffet lunch was laid out with all sorts of strange things to eat, and champagne was served. Everyone seemed to be talking at the same time. Lizzie clung to Paul persistently, while the bridegroom's parents spent their time circulating among their guests and appearing to enjoy it all.

Lizzie sat, a little bewildered, in a quiet spot in this grand hotel, until Carol and her new husband went off in a cloud of rice and confetti. Then she whispered to Paul that she would like to be taken to her home, if he did not mind.

'It's OK, Aunt Lizzie. I've had enough too. It doesn't appeal to me either.'

Back in the apartment he made her a cup of tea and put her feet up on the sofa.

Lizzie said, 'I might start for home tomorrow.'

'Oh no,' cried Paul, 'that would upset Carol. She has given instructions that we are to hold on to you till she comes back in two weeks time.'

Lizzie sighed. So Carol was still the boss. 'But she is going to live in another place out West,' she said.

'I know,' said Paul, 'but she is reckoning on taking you with her.'

'Oh no, I am not!' declared Lizzie tartly. 'I am going home.'

'OK, there's no reason why you can't take a prolonged holiday just the same,' pleaded Paul. 'No one is waiting for you back home.'

'Robin and Bella are, and little Mark,' argued Lizzie. She

was very homesick for England and for the places and people she knew.

Paul looked worried and said, 'I have to get back to the group, but Derick will look after you. Why don't you try to enjoy yourself Aunt Lizzie, make it a nice long holiday?'

'All right, I'll stay until she comes back from her honeymoon. I'd like to say goodbye to her, so don't worry about me, Paul. Go back to your band.'

He smiled at her. 'I was hoping you would still be around for my wedding,' he joked.

'When's that to be?' asked Lizzie eagerly.

'God only knows,' said Paul. 'I change my mind too often, Aunt Lizzie.'

She sensed a hidden heartbreak, but made no comment.

In the morning Paul left, so Lizzie busied herself tidying up the apartment. Derick came home at midday, looking very seedy. She made him hot coffee, nagging him most of the time, as she did so. 'You drink too much, don't eat enough, and it's time you took better care of yourself.'

But Derick had dozed off on the old-fashioned sofa and did not hear her. He had placed a newspaper over his head to keep the sounds out.

So Lizzie sat looking out of the window down on the teeming population of this noisy town, and wishing she was back at home walking in the green park with Mark on his way to school. It did not remain peaceful for very long; the kids who worked with Carol at the theatre came in to chat about the wedding, bringing with them cakes and candy. Lizzie presided over the huge coffee pot, and felt wanted once more. They came attired in all sorts of odd garments, some in their nighties, others in short pants and their hair in pony tails, fresh from the morning rehearsals. They were very lively and interested in London, and pestered Lizzie about the Royal Family. They giggled when she said that she had never seen them, and was not sure if she wanted to, 'They've got their lives, and I've got mine,' she said.

'Don't you approve of them, Aunt Lizzie?' they probed.

'Yes, I do,' said Lizzie, 'it's nice to have a responsible

figurehead, but as for running around looking at them, well, I never had the time.'

Lizzie went down well with these modern youngsters. 'We will have a Cockney party for you, Lizzie,' they told her.

Lizzie enjoyed all this petting and fussing, and even looked forward to the party which was to be given in her honour. It was held in the first floor apartment which had a piano in it, a great room but still shabbily furnished.

When Lizzie remarked on the shabbiness of the room, Derick said, 'Well, the kids move on. Most of them are in the profession, and don't stay long enough to worry about furniture.

Lizzie was given a seat of honour in this room, which was getting more and more crowded every minute, and the old piano was being repeatedly pounded by a long-haired youth, who, every time he looked at Lizzie would play her signature tune: 'Maybe it's because I'm a Londoner'.

Everyone sang, danced and drank like nobody's business. That was what Lizzie liked and was used to. These shouting, yelling, twisting and turning teenagers reminded her of the teenage parties they had in Ilford. Here they were all dressed for the part. They wore checked caps and chokers, the girls had plaid shawls and Edwardian hairdos. They sang songs from the all-Cockney shows like, 'Fings ain't what they used to be', and, 'Any old iron', and 'Get orf me barrer'. The party went on most of the night, but Lizzie retired at midnight. She got no sleep because of the racket going on down stairs, but she would not have missed it for all the world.

In the middle of that week Derick came in to say, 'Aunt Lizzie, what have you been up to? There's a man asking to speak to you on the phone.'

The phone was a communal one out in the hall, and it was always busy. 'You're sure it's me he asked for,' queried Lizzie very timidly.

'Yes. Mrs Erlock. That's you, isn't it?'

Lizzie's heart missed a beat. Could it be Bobby? No, he could not possibly know she was here. She approached the phone cautiously, knowing that a few young folk were watching.

Then she heard the hoarse voice of Sammy Cohen as he yelled, 'Is that you, Lizzie, old gel?'

'Oh yes,' she said, 'but how did you find me?'

'Ah! I've got me methods,' cackled Sammy. 'I was calling to take you out tonight, okay? Then be ready eight thirty, so long.' And Sammy had gone again.

Lizzie was flabbergasted. 'That's the man I got friendly with on the plane. Do you think I should go to dinner with him?' she asked Derick.

'Well, I'm not too sure. What is he like? Who is he?'

So Lizzie rummaged in her handbag for Sammy's card. Derick held it up to the light and squinted at it for so long that Lizzie thought he must need spectacles. But she couldn't deny that she felt a bit harassed; she had never expected to hear from Sammy Cohen again.

'Blimey, Aunt Lizzie!' cried Derick. 'It's Sammy Cohen, the song writer. How did you get in with him?'

'On the plane, like I told you,' she said. 'Do you know him?'

'Everyone in New York knows him. He writes lyrics for those Cockney shows that have become so popular.'

'Well, he did mention it,' she said. 'Do you think, then, that I shouldn't go out to dinner with him?' Lizzie asked.

'No, I think you should go,' cried Derick. 'Get yourself togged up, Aunt Lizzie, you have made a conquest. Wait till I tell the rest of the gang.'

So Derick went off, waving Sammy's visiting card.

Lizzie looked at herself in the mirror, wondering what she should wear for this, her first date. She felt a little afraid; she had never been out with a strange man before. In fact she had not often been out with her own man. How should she dress? What would he expect of her? All these niggling little worries depressed her; suddenly she decided she would not go, she would pretend to be ill and go to bed. All sorts of ideas on how to avoid Sammy dashed through her mind.

But Derick returned and the two nice girls from downstairs came up. 'We hear you've got a date, Lizzie? Come on, we'll help you get ready.'

They curled her hair with the heated rollers they had brought

with them, then held a debate as to what she should wear,
which dress?

'Not the one she wore to the wedding. No, it must be
something different. We must make her look different.'

They sorted through the wardrobe and chose the black
evening dress which she had brought with her.

'Looks nice, got that London look.'

So they painted Lizzie's nails and made up her eyes. Lizzie
tried to protest, for so far she had never allowed Bella to put
make-up on her eyes, but there was no stopping these young
ones.

'Milly's a make-up girl, she knows just how to make you
look younger,' they told her.

So Lizzie gave in, and when they had finished she was afraid
to look in the mirror.

'Come on, little lady, look at yourself,' they cried.

Lizzie was very surprised. Her eyes looked big, her hair nice
and fluffy, and the black dress did suit her quite well.

They squirted perfumed lacquer on her hair, giggling all the
time and watched by Derick, then they gave her a drink,
saying, 'Now relax, you got ten minutes. We'll scamper.'

Derick said, 'Why don't you wear Carol's white fox fur stole?
She gave it to me to take care of.'

So saying, he dashed off, bringing it back with him.

CHAPTER TWENTY-SIX

Wining and Dining

When Derick draped that white fox fur stole over Lizzie's shoulders, she looked at herself in the long mirror and said quietly, 'Oh! Bobby would have loved to see me all dressed up like this.'

'Must say, you do look a topper,' said Derick. 'I wonder if Uncle Bobby is still alive?'

Tears came into Lizzie's eyes. 'I hope so, Derick. I'm sure that I'd have known if anything serious had happened to him.'

Derick looked thoughtful. 'It's strange the way he disregarded you, yet you both remained kind of close.'

'Oh well,' said Lizzie, 'I took my marriage vows very seriously. Not like to-day, chopping and changing every couple of years.'

'Well, have a good time, Aunt Lizzie.' Derick kissed her gently on the cheek. 'He's down in the hall, I can hear him. I'll make my exit as soon as he comes in, but cultivate his friendship, he might come in useful.'

'In what way?' demanded Lizzie, a trifle suspicious.

'Well, you know I couldn't take the hard grind of being on the road with the group and all those one night stands, so I am out of a job and would like to take up music seriously. But I'll have to get a job first.'

'Well you should, you always had a flair for those drums. Used to make a dreadful racket.'

Derick grinned. He was very fond of his Aunt Lizzie, but she always said the wrong things. He went to the door, opened it, and in came Sammy Cohen, bouncy as ever and shouting out loud, 'Well here we are, how are you, Lizzie, old gel?'

She looked at him shrewdly. He'd had a few, but was fairly

sober and he was certainly dressed very nicely, with a carnation in his buttonhole.

'Well, well!' he said. 'What's all this? You look grand. About twenty years younger.'

Lizzie flushed and patted her curls.

Derick asked, 'Would you like a drink?'

'No thanks,' said Sammy. 'Let's get going, Lizzie. We got a lot to do. I promised to introduce you to a lot of influential people.'

'I'm not a bloody film star,' grumbled Lizzie.

'No, but she looks like one, don't she?' cried Sam.

So off they went, and a smart uniformed chauffeur held open the car door for them.

'I've hired a car so that we can have a good drink,' said Sammy as they climbed into the immaculate car.

Lizzie had an overpowering desire to turn around and go home as Sammy fussed and fidgeted beside her. He smelled of a very highly scented aftershave, and was so nervous that he shouted louder than ever. Lizzie gazed out into the night. It was early July and a hot summer's night. There was a humidity in the air and those tall skyscrapers with a hundred twinkling lights seemed lost in a hazy mist that hung over them. Other cars sped past them, hooters were blaring and in the distance sirens screamed. It was a strange, unreal world. Her heart beat with a sort of hidden fear combined with excitement; this was the first time she had ever dated and now, at her age, she was going to be wined and dined by this nice generous man. She prayed she would not let herself or him down.

'You're looking very glum, Lizzie. Have you changed your mind?' inquired Sammy.

'Oh no, indeed not,' replied Lizzie. 'I'm very grateful to you, Sam. I was getting a little lonely and afraid to go out on my own.'

He patted her hand. 'Not to worry, love. We're going to have a good nosh up. It's a nice Kosher restaurant, you'll like it. I met plenty of people I know there.'

They alighted in front of a tall skyscraper and went up in the fast lift.

'I thought I could smell the sea,' said Lizzie.

'Well, you can, love, but we call it the river. It comes in from the Atlantic.'

When they got out of the lift, he said, 'Look, out there you can see the old lady herself. If it wasn't for the mist, I'd take you to see her in the daylight.'

'What old lady?'

Sammy began to chuckle. 'Why, the Statue of Liberty! Never saw it when we were coming in, both of us had too much to drink.'

Lizzie looked out at all the thousands of lights, reds, blues and greens. Neons flashed off and on, the silver strip of river reflected many, many more lights. It was all a little frightening; suddenly she longed for the safety of England, for the murky old Thames and things that were familiar.

The restaurant was crowded and very noisy, but beautifully decorated with huge paintings and lots of plants. There was gleaming silver on the tables and soft-footed waiters wheeled around huge silver tureens so that the food could be served at the tables. To Lizzie this was unique. She watched with interest as they lifted the huge cover, but she shivered at the sight of the red, bloody lump of beef. The waiter sliced large lumps off onto her plate.

Sammy said, 'Nice grub here, Lizzie. Salt beef, just like old Isaac's served down in Whitechapel, but here the price is very different.'

Lizzie ate very little but drank plenty of wine. Her face got flushed and she felt stifled by the heat. But Sammy tucked in heartily.

'I eat a lot before a night out. Booze don't effect you so much then,' he told her. 'You look hot, Lizzie. Have a nice lemon ice, do a good one here.' He was doing his best to please her and the white lemon ice cream refreshed her.

'It's always like this in New York at this time of year,' said Sammy. 'It has a very humid atmosphere. That's why I always get out. I'm going to the Canadian lakes end of July. Want to come, Lizzie?'

'Oh no, I am going home next week, when Carol comes back from her honeymoon.'

'What for?' shouted Sammy, who by now had consumed his third brandy. 'Don't yer like it here?'

'Yes, it's a nice change, but there's no place like home,' replied Lizzie.

'You could be right. Well, this is my home now. Lost me Momma and so I won't go back no more. Don't see why you can't settle down here, Lizzie.'

'Oh, no way, Sam,' said Lizzie. 'It's too noisy and sort of unreal to me.'

'Well, so it's hot and noisy in New York, but it's summertime. This is a great city even in the winter, once you get to know it. Besides, America is a very big place. You can live where you please. Go out West with your daughter; she's married into a big oil family, so someone told me.'

'No, Sam,' said Lizzie firmly. 'I have to go back home in case my husband arrives home.'

'I thought he was dead?' hollered Sammy in surprise.

Lizzie flushed angrily and looked around to see who was listening, but no one else seemed even aware of them. They all talked loudly, laughed and ate as if this was the last night of the end of the world.

'No, he's not dead, just away travelling.'

'Don't say?' said Sammy. 'Where's he gone?'

'I'd sooner not say,' replied Lizzie haughtily.

'Oh, I see, that's the way the cookie crumbles,' cried Sam. 'He inside? Oh well, Lizzie, you might just as well stay here and have a good time.'

She choked up with tears, wishing she had never mentioned Bobby.

'Oh come on, Lizzie,' cried Sammy. 'Don't get huffy. Let's go, I'm taking you to a party.'

She tried to cheer up. She did not want to be a wet blanket, after all it was nice of Sammy to entertain her.

In the car he planted a wet kiss on her cheek and caressed her bare shoulder familiarly.

'Something about you reminds me of Isabel, my first wife.

She always had a cob on about something or other, but I loved her. She was all the world to me, and I needed a firm hand on the reins then, you know.'

Lizzie smiled. 'Forgive me, Sam, if I am spoiling your evening. It's all a little new to me, you know.'

'It's OK, darling. Here we are, I'm going to introduce you to some of me Tin Pan Alley pals. Most of them came over the Atlantic.'

It was a great house with people everywhere, walking in the garden, dancing on the lawn and diving into the pool. It was an odd mixture of well-dressed and half-dressed people; soft carpets and flowers were everywhere. When Lizzie went to the powder room, she found quite elderly women, much older than herself, plastering make up on their eyes, and squirting expensive perfume on their naked shoulders. Everyone seemed to be smoking; the cigarette smoke and the perfume polluted the air, and they talked so quickly that Lizzie could hardly get the gist of their conversation.

Sammy greeted his friends, loudly. 'This is my little cockney pal,' he hollered, 'just over for a visit.'

They all fussed over her, handing her plates of food and glasses of champagne. Everyone told their own experience of their visits to London.

'I remember,' said one very smart, dark lady, 'we went down to the dock and outside the pub was a place that sold cackles; they were delicious.'

Lizzie supposed that she meant cockles but made no comment.

Several hours later Lizzie's legs were aching and the rich food was beginning to have an effect on her. Sammy had disappeared and the champagne had made her dizzy, so she sat down in a secluded corner to watch the antics of the crowd.

Some of the guests lolled on the couches making love, or sat on the floor crossed-legged and argued. The rest danced wildly in the middle of the ballroom. Lizzie felt strangely detached from it all. One drunken fellow slid down the banister and struck his head; his friends frogmarched him out.

'He'll have a bloody big headache in the morning,' muttered

Lizzie rather aggressively, then suddenly realized she was talking to herself.

The charming dark lady who liked cackles found her. 'Sam's having a game of cards. He won't be long, Lizzie. Care for a coffee?'

She took Lizzie to a small sitting room and prepared coffee for them both. 'You must think we are a very wild lot, Lizzie.'

'No, I've really enjoyed myself,' lied Lizzie.

'It's not always like this, it depends on the young ones. You must come over and have dinner with us one evening while you are here, just a quiet informal affair. You'll like that.'

'Thank you,' said Lizzie, 'but I am going home next week.'

This lady's husband now indicated from the doorway that Sam was in his car, so they both escorted her outside, and there was Sam, sprawled out drunkenly in the back of the car.

'You will see that she gets home all right?' they said to the chauffeur. 'Good night, Lizzie, hope we'll meet again.'

Lizzie stared at Sam, who was snoring and grunting. She was very glad when she reached home and Derick came to meet her.

'Had a good time, Aunt Lizzie?'

'Well, I suppose so,' she said, 'if that's what having a good time is all about.'

He took off her stole, helped her out of her dress, and fetched her dressing gown. 'How was Sam?'

'Drunk as a bloody fiddler's bitch,' complained Lizzie.

Derick laughed. 'Oh dear, don't seem to have a lot of luck with men, do you, Aunt Lizzie?'

'No, Derick. Between you and me, I don't like them much either. How I ever put up with Bobby beats me. I don't think I could ever go through all that again.'

'Good night, darling,' said Derick. 'It's all in a lifetime.'

CHAPTER TWENTY-SEVEN

Grass Roots

That year, at the end of July, New York had a heat wave. Temperatures were away above anything they ever had in London. In Greenwich there had been shady parks, cool and green to stroll in but out here the pavements were white hot and those very high buildings seemed to hem one in.

So Lizzie spent most of her time in the cramped apartment with the shades drawn and one small electric fan to cool the air. Lizzie felt very lonely, for Derick seemed to be out all night and in bed all day. It was a muddled kind of existence and one she was completely unused to. Her chief occupation was lying on the couch in her dressing gown and eating huge ice creams from the drugstore down in the street.

'I'll go home as soon as Carol returns,' she told herself every day. Yet the honeymoon seemed to go on longer than it was intended.

Lizzie had been in New York more than a month and was desperately homesick, when a letter arrived from home. She opened it eagerly. It was in Bella's clear broad hand, wishing Lizzie well, sending the family's love to her, and explaining that they had moved from Greenwich to the new pub down the Nile Street. The address was at the top of the page. Bella explained that it would be a little inconvenient if Lizzie returned just at that moment as they were living in a very higgledy-piggledy manner. Please would she give them another month. Then, with luck, Bella would be settled in, and she would have Lizzie's rooms ready for her. So why not have a nice long holiday? It would do her the world of good.

Big tears dropped down on to the paper as Lizzie read it, she was already feeling down, and this was the final blow.

'She doesn't want me back,' wept Lizzie to Derick when he rose at six in the evening.

'Who don't want who back?' Derick was stretching and yawning; he looked extremely washed out.

Lizzie looked at him in disgust. 'Oh, pull yourself together,' she cried impatiently. 'Bella! She's left that place in Greenwich. She says she is in a muddle and don't want me back yet.'

'Well, that's not so bad,' replied Derick. 'You're all right here, and Carol will be back soon. She might have plans for you.'

'I don't want no one to make plans for me,' cried Lizzie in great irritation. 'I want to go home to England where I belong.'

'All right, don't get shirty, Aunt Lizzie. If you're lonely I'll stay home from work and take you out.'

'Work!' shouted Lizzie in a real temper. 'What kind of work is it that keeps you out all night?'

'I have an all night job in a bar. I have to earn my own pocket money. Carol is good to me, but I don't expect her to support me entirely.' Derick was hurt.

'Oh dear,' sighed Lizzie, 'I am sorry, love. I never think about anyone but myself. If you need any money I've plenty of dollars left that I never spent.'

'I don't want to sponge on you, Aunt Lizzie. I've done too much of that when I was young. Please settle down, Carol will be here on Friday. In the meantime you ought to go out a bit more. No good staying cooped up here.'

'Derick!' cried Lizzie vehemently, 'I hate this place. It really frightens me.'

He grinned. 'Well, it's only a big town like London. It's not so bad once you get to know it. What about Sammy? Don't he call you now?'

'Well, he has,' agreed Lizzie. 'But I've always been a bit short with him. You know he's a proper old soak. Always sounds half boozed to me.'

'Well, I have heard he hits the bottle,' said Derick. 'But then he can afford it. It often happens when a guy is famous and getting on a bit.'

'Well, he can stay away from me,' declared Lizzie.

'Now, Aunt Lizzie,' begged Derick, 'if he does call again, try to cultivate him, will you?'

'I don't know what you mean, young Derick.'

'All I meant was that a guy like that could come in very useful if I ever study real music. You know, Aunt Lizzie, that I only play by ear. It would be nice to get some knowledge of the real thing and Sammy knows everyone that matters. He's been knocking about New York's Tin Pan Alley for more than twenty years.'

'Oh well, if that's what you want I'll remain friends with him, but that's all,' said Lizzie.

So, when Sammy telephoned a few days later, 'Just to say goodbye', he said he was off to the lakes and would she like to come out for a meal.

'No thanks,' returned Lizzie a trifle off hand. Then, feeling guilty, she added, 'Well, if you want to say goodbye, come over to the apartment.'

'Right,' replied Sammy, 'I'll come this evening.'

Derick on hearing the news said, 'That's the stuff, Aunt Lizzie. No need to be lonely in this town.'

'Well, you had better stop at home. I don't like the idea of being shut in here all alone with him.'

'Oh, Aunt Lizzie, surely you don't need a chaperone at your age.'

'As a matter of fact I do,' replied Lizzie. 'It might surprise you to know, young Derick, that even at my age I know very little of the seamy side of life. I've only ever had one man in my life, and that was my Bobby, and he was quite enough for me.'

'Well, Aunt Lizzie, all I can say is that it is time you learned. If you want me to stay, I will, but downstairs in my own apartment. I'll not play gooseberry.'

So Lizzie took a bath, put on her best lace blouse and pleated skirt and set her hair.

Soon Sammy arrived. He was perfectly sober and bearing wine and flowers. 'Oh, you look great, Lizzie, old gel,' he cried with his usual exuberance. 'Come and sit beside me.' He plonked himself down on the couch.

But Lizzie ignored his offer. She just took the flowers and put them in a vase.

'How are you enjoying this wicked city?' asked Sammy.

'I haven't been out a lot,' she replied. 'It's been too hot.'

'Well that's a pity,' said Sammy, 'You could have gone out to Long Island. There's a nice beach out there.'

'I'm only waiting for Carol, then I'll go home,' said Lizzie rather severely.

'Now cheer up. What's happened to me old cockney pal?' said Sammy. 'I've brought a couple of bottles of wine. Let's have a drink. Got any ice?'

He got up and bustled about, finding the glasses and pouring the wine. Lizzie thought that he was very forward but did go to the fridge and got some ice cubes.

'Sure you don't want to go out for something to eat, Lizzie?' he inquired as they sat sipping the wine.

'No, Sam, but I'll cook something for you if you are hungry.'

'Well now, that would be nice.'

'I'm not sure what's in the larder. Wait a moment, I'll have a look. Eggs and potatoes and tinned beans, that's all,' cried Lizzie in dismay.

'You can forget the beans, leave them for the cowboys. I'll tell you what, I'll have the good old English standby, egg and chips.'

Lizzie started to giggle. In fact right away she felt immensely cheered up.

'I'll peel the spuds,' said Sammy taking off his jacket. He chatted all the time. 'You know, Lizzie, when we was kids in the East End and there was no such thing as school lunches, we used to run home from school every day at twelve o'clock. Momma would have this big pot of soup on the boil, she would ladle it out and we would have a bit of black bread with it. We would all scoff it up greedily like, and then chase off back to school, but it got very monotonous. There was one special day, the day before shobias (that was Friday), then we got egg and chips and that was the day we really looked forward to. Dipping the crispy chips into the egg yokes, it was scrumptious, I can taste it to this very day.'

Lizzie smiled the gentle smile that made her brown eyes light up and betrayed her hidden beauty.

'Well, Sammy,' she said, 'that's one thing I know I can cook, because that was one of our chief diets too.'

When the chips were sliced and in the pan, they sat chatting.

Lizzie said, 'To think I would be lying here perspiring and absolutely sold out with the heat if I was on my own. Now I am cooking and thoroughly enjoying it.'

Sammy held her small white hand. 'It's the need to fill the unforgiving minute,' he said. 'You've been a worker all your life, Lizzie. It's not easy to become a drone.'

She smiled, not really understanding.

'You've got very nice hands, Lizzie, and such lovely rings.'

'Well, I always took very good care of my hands,' she told him, rising to put the golden fried chips on a serving dish. Then she began to break the eggs into the pan with careful precision; not one yoke did she break.

Sammy watched those small hands that hovered like butterflies over her task.

'You can lay the table, Sammy,' she called, 'we'll eat in here if that's all right with you.'

With a wry grin he found the tablecloth and set the knives and forks. Lizzie, very jubilant, served the eggs and chips. Her face was flushed and there were little beads of perspiration around her mouth.

'Well, sit down, let's tuck in while it's nice and hot.'

When they had finished she said, 'Now, wasn't that better than that stuffy old resturant?'

'It was much cheaper,' cackled Sammy dryly.

'Well, money isn't everything,' said Lizzie. 'It's not important because it don't bring good health or happiness.'

'Oh, you could be right there, Lizzie,' Sammy sighed and got up to pour some wine.

'Never mind the wine, Sammy, we'll finish up with a nice pot of tea. I brought a packet of Brooke Bond over with me. Someone told me that they only drank coffee over here, and I couldn't do without a cup of tea.

'That's fine by me.' Sammy had a twinkle in his eye. This little woman whose grass roots were so strong, how she reminded him of his first wife. It was incredible how English she made him feel. He had not felt like that for years.

'Why don't you change your mind and come with me to Canada?'

She put her chin on her hands, her elbows on the table, and stared at him intensely. 'What are you suggesting? That I live with you?'

'No, no Lizzie!' He gesticulated wildly. 'Just as a holiday companion. I've got a wife somewhere and she's trying to divorce me.'

'Well, you are not exactly free, are you?'

'I must confess that after three wives I'm still very unsettled. The last two were twenty years younger than me. They were after the lolly. But I still think about my first wife and you remind me so much of her. It's the way you Londoners have. There would be no strings attached, and you'd probably keep me off the booze. No one has been able to do that in years.'

Those brown eyes of Lizzie's looked softly and sympathetically at him. 'Now, Sammy,' she said, 'don't forget I still have a husband.'

'When's he due out?'

'He's not in prison, Sammy. You're jumping to the wrong conclusions.'

'Well, where is he?'

'I don't know,' she answered.

'You must be joking, Lizzie. How long has he been gone?'

'Two years. But I'm still convinced that he will come back, and I intend to be where I know he can find me.'

'Well, I must say Lizzie, you amaze me. I never dreamt you had such a strong character. How can you remain loyal to some geezer who went off and left you for two years? Does he correspond with you?'

'No,' replied Lizzie, 'I've no idea where he is. But one thing I do know and that is that as soon as he is able, he will find me.'

'Well, I'll be jiggered,' cried Sammy, 'it's just like some romantic novel. It's unbelievable.'

'Oh well,' said Lizzie a little huffily. 'You don't impress me with all your big words. All I know is I've only ever had one man, and even if he never comes back I'll not bed with another.'

Slowly Sammy dug the story out of her. Of Bobby who was continuously in trouble with the law, of her days of extreme poverty and of the big family she had brought up although none of them her own. Then, when things were looking up and they lived fairly comfortably, how Bobby had disappeared – and only God or the devil knew where he was.

'Well, Lizzie, it's certainly a fascinating story. Ever thought of writing your memoirs?'

'There's no need for poor jokes, Sammy,' said Lizzie dolefully.

'Sorry, love, but you seem to have been some sort of doormat for everyone. I reckon it is high time you started to live your own life.'

'That might be your opinion,' she retorted tartly, 'but I intend to return home to wait for him, because when he does find me he's going to find his true love.'

Sammy held on to both her small white hands very gently. 'Good luck to you, Lizzie. I hope you both get back together, and I hope this time he bloody well looks after you, because you deserve it.'

'Oh! I am not that helpless. I can still take care of myself,' returned Lizzie haughtily.

Sammy planted a wet kiss on her cheek. 'I'm sure you can, love,' he said, 'but let's be pals, and I'll always remember our brief encounter. I'll even give you my address in case you ever need me.'

'You can always contact me through the kids,' she said. 'You can believe me when I say I'll always be pleased I met you. You are the only friend I've made in this city.'

So they parted, and Sammy went out once more into what Lizzie called that wicked city; she supposed he had gone to lose his sad inner self in a bottle. Lizzie felt a little sad too, but it had been nice to make a conquest. At her age it was a definite morale boost.

Derick came dashing up the stairs. 'Cripes, Aunt Lizzie! What have you been cooking?'

'Eggs and chips,' declared Lizzie jubilantly.

'The smell of it was so appetizing it's made me feel starving hungry,' he said.

'There's plenty of chips left. I'll put on some eggs for you.'

Derick sat at the table. 'It reminds me of when we used to come home from school at lunchtimes. One day a week we had eggs and chips with rice pudding for afters. Do you remember that nice house in Highbury, Aunt Lizzie?'

'Yes, I do, those were the days. Here you are, two sunny side up.' She put the plate with the fried eggs in front of him. 'That's what you used to say when you were a schoolboy. Paul liked his eggs turned, but you always liked them sunny side up.'

He heaped the chips onto his plate.

Lizzie said, 'I suppose you wouldn't consider coming back home with me, Derick?'

'I'm OK here. I wouldn't go home unless I was due for a call-up.'

'What do you mean?' she asked sharply. 'Go into the army?'

'Well, there is talk of a call up, but I don't think I'd pass the medical. America is at war you know. I think I'll be all right, unless it spreads.'

'War!' cried Lizzie, extremely shocked. 'Well, now I know I'm going home.'

'It's out in the Far East, it hardly affects New York. Don't get so alarmed, Aunt Lizzie. There won't be no air raids or anything like that.'

'Should think not!' cried Lizzie, really disturbed. 'Now I know why I never liked this place. I never felt safe here.'

Derick was looking worried; he had really spooked Aunt Lizzie. Carol would be furious; she had told him to hang onto her because she had plans for getting Lizzie to make her home with them.

But Lizzie was determinedly taking off her apron and

muttering to herself, 'I'm not staying out here to be bombed.' Then she went in to the bedroom to start her packing.

On Friday, Carol returned. She swept in all sun-tanned, and glowing with good health and vitality. 'Oh darling, darling.' She grabbed Lizzie exuberantly. 'I'm so glad you're still here. I was worried in case you'd left me.'

'It's nice to see you looking so happy,' said Lizzie gently, surveying her with true affection.

'Con's over at the hotel. You see, dear, we've taken another apartment, more up town. So I thought it would be nice for you to stay here until we move to Texas. I'm going to have a nice big house and lots of kids. Being a granny is really going to suit you.'

Lizzie looked very solemn. 'Carol, dear, I'm going home as soon as it is possible. I can't stand this country, I feel so isolated.'

'But, darling, I'm back now. I'll take you out every day shopping and to the shows. You'll soon settle down.'

Lizzie was not going to let Carol charm her. 'Oh no, no, my Bobby might come back and he would never know where to find me.' Big tears began to fall.

Carol cuddled her. 'What is it, darling?' she coaxed. 'Who has upset you?'

This was a different kind of Carol, soft, gentle and considerate. Lizzie was a little amazed, but she had no intention of being cajoled into staying. 'There's a bloody war on,' snivelled Lizzie. 'I'm not staying here to be bombed. Had enough of the Blitz in London.'

'Oh dear,' sighed Carol. 'Who did that? You, Derick?'

White-faced Derick nodded his head.

'Well, of all the silly sods,' yelled Carol, back to normal. 'What did you do that for? You know what she's like.'

'I'm sorry, Carol,' stuttered Derick. 'I never meant to.'

'Well, you've certainly been and gorn and done it,' Carol cried, reverting to real cockney.

For almost a week they worked on Lizzie, coaxing and cajoling her to stay, but it was of no avail.

'Stay a while,' begged Carol. 'Bella don't really want you, and she's a bitch, you know that.'

'Bella has to have me,' replied Lizzie obstinately. 'I've made my home with her.'

So far Lizzie had never divulged the fact that Bobby's money had gone into Bella's business venture. That was still her own secret.

In a glossy magazine Lizzie had seen dreadful pictures of the Vietnam war, blood-stained soldiers, bodies of women and children all mutilated lying in a naked heap. She was horrified.

'It's a long way away,' Derick insisted.

But to Lizzie it was too near home, and she did not like it.

Con said, 'Carol, don't hang on to her. She's a fine lady, but your life is with me now. You don't really need her.'

So at last they gave in and booked Lizzie's plane ticket home.

Lizzie, very pale, said goodbye to her children. Paul had come specially to see her off. As the plane took off Carol wept on the shoulder of her fine strong husband. Then Lizzie was away, over the Atlantic, back to the safety of her homeland.

In the plane Lizzie sat turning over in her mind all the things that had happened during her two months in New York. She had seen nothing at all of that city, nor of the rest of America, but she had no regrets. As a matter of fact, she thought, she had seen very little of her own London in her lifetime there. She had never been to Piccadilly or to Oxford Street, both places that the Americans seemed to rave about. She recalled how funny Sammy had thought it was to be so near and yet so far from those tourist sights.

'Lizzie,' he had said, 'it's typical of your generation. My old lady only went up West just once, and that was when she was feeling ill. We went to a women's hospital for a second opinion. I'll never forget that day. It was early spring and a beautiful day, and we came out of the hospital. We walked through Regent's Park hand in hand; she was feeling very down and I so guilty, because I had often neglected her. We had a cup of tea sitting outside the cafe and she was really enjoying herself. Then we walked around the lake and threw crumbs to the ducks. There were hundreds of them, all baby ones milling about on the path, scrambling for the titbits. I can see them now – little fluffy brown ones, white and yellow ones, their mums floating around keeping a watchful eye on them. Oh, those tiny babies made us laugh so much and it was good to see my old lady smile again. "Look at the buggers," I said, "it's marvellous how they all survive.' "Yes," she said, "they will, Sammy, but I won't." "Don't be silly old gel," I said,' and here Sammy's voice had broken down before he went on in a choked voice, 'you know, Lizzie, she was right. She never ever saw another spring.'

High up in the clouds Lizzie recalled this conversation. Sammy had been a very nice man. She was certainly glad that she had met him, but she was still anxious to get home, to see her own familiar landmarks, St Paul's dome and the Post Office Tower, landmarks that one had only ever seen from afar.

Now she was going to live near the city once more she might go and see these spots, after all they were in her own home town.

She could take Mark with her on school holidays. She visualized Mark's saucy face, and wondered if Bella would let him have the Indian belt with dagger attached that she had bought for him.

Slowly she closed her eyes, and did not open them again till they came down at London airport.

CHAPTER TWENTY-EIGHT

Home Again

Both suave Charlie and stout, ruddy-faced Robin were waiting at the airport to greet her. This was a bit of a surprise to Lizzie because they had been very often at cross purposes in the past. They hugged her affectionately, both seeming very pleased to see her again.

Robin drove his big car and Charlie sat beside her in the back seat. She felt a little strange, overtaken by weariness of body and mind. When she mentioned this, Charlie said:

'Nothing to worry over, it's jet lag. You've been flying into a different time zone, it will pass when you have rested a while. How would you like to come home and stay with me and Luber? Be able to see the new baby boy.'

Charlie was very proud of his family and his prolific little wife. Through Lizzie's mind went the thought that this was why Charlie was there. To persuade her to go home with him.

'Not today, Charlie,' she replied. 'I'd like to go home and rest first.'

'Bella is still in a muddle. The builders are in the throes of rebuilding the pub, so we thought you would like a bit of comfort till we are ready for you,' said Robin.

'No way.' She wanted to get back to The Nile as soon as possible and that was exactly what she was going to do. She told them so in her most determined manner.

'OK, you can drop me off at the office,' said Charlie. 'Don't say I didn't try.'

'I'm not worried about the condition of the place,' said Lizzie. 'I live with you, Robin, and it's there that I expect to be made welcome.'

'Now don't get annoyed, Aunt Lizzie,' pleaded Robin. 'No

one could be more pleased than I to see you come back. But you know Bella, she will have her own way.'

'So will I,' muttered Lizzie defiantly.

Soon, as they travelled along, Lizzie began to recognize old landmarks. They had just passed the old nick where Bobby was often held as an overnight guest. It looked very spruce now, with its white façade, its blue lamp over those grim official portals, and a uniformed copper standing casually on guard. A real London bluebottle, never to be seen in the United States.

They came to a halt slowly outside the new public house. It was almost completely obscured by scaffolding and the workmen who were perched there, scraping and hammering.

'You know Bella,' said Robin almost apologetically. 'A job has to be done thoroughly to please her.'

They entered through a kind of hole in the wall, stumbling over loose bricks and a floor covered in cement dust. Then into the back kitchen which was fairly habitable. Bella was there, wearing a blue nylon overall and a dust cap, her lovely hair pushed out of sight, her big features looking oddly out of place, and spotted with dust.

'Oh, so you made it then.' She greeted Lizzie a little abruptly. 'I'll make us some tea. Mark will soon be in from school.'

Lizzie sank wearily into the familiar old wooden armchair beside the fire. This chair had travelled from Highbury to Greenwich; now it reposed beside the fire once more. She sighed and sipped the hot tea, thinking she should have gone home with Charlie and given Bella time to get herself settled.

'Had a good time?' inquired Bella. 'It's been bloody awful here, but we seem to be winning now, I hope.'

Lizzie said, 'Now don't worry over me, Bella. I can stand a muddle, and I might be able to give you some help.'

That wide charming smile flashed across Bella's grubby face. 'Oh, I am sorry, Lizzie. I didn't mean to be so crotchety. I know you will help me but don't expect too much. You see, one half of this place is being pulled down and rebuilt so we're living in a very cramped style.'

'I lived down in the tube during the Blitz, so it won't worry me,' declared Lizzie.

Bella leant forward and kissed her. 'All right, dear,' she said, 'we'll make the best of what we've got.'

So Lizzie sat looking at all the familiar things in the big old-fashioned kitchen. Her bedroom, she discovered later, was a little square room on the first floor. It had not been redecorated for years, and the faded roses of the old wallpaper reminded her acutely of the past. There was a kind of musty smell about the room but Lizzie did not mind. She wondered if poor old Gladys, the barmaid had slept here. In the room was her own old bed and the oak dressing table that she had transferred from Highbury. She wiped the cement dust from the mirror with her hands. It felt warm and comforting; she knew that she had come home.

It seemed that Mark had been using this bedroom, for his toys were piled up in the corner, and his books were strewn about the floor. A small camp bed had been erected for him, because he was to continue to share with her. This pleased Lizzie very much, even though he chatted till well past midnight, demanding to know all about America, and complaining loudly because Bella had allowed him to keep the Indian belt but not the dagger. She took no chances with her boisterous Mark.

'All the boys at school have got knives,' he grumbled.

'Mum is right. I should never have bought it for you,' said Lizzie.

It was nice lying there in the dark, listening to the child's comforting chatter. Lizzie felt very relaxed. At last she had returned, she was back down The Nile. And if Pat O'Keefe's spirit walked in his old pub she would be pleased to see him. The noises from the Main Road came drifting in as the traffic went rumbling past. Yet Lizzie was far happier than she had been for a long time; she slept very peacefully, then got up early to help Mark get ready for school. She tied his tie, brushed his hair, and he enjoyed all the attention.

'Will you meet me from school like you used to?' he asked

'I'll try,' promised Lizzie.

'I hate this rotten school,' he complained, 'all posh blokes and lots of coloured ones.'

'What, down The Nile?' cried Lizzie in quizzical amazement.

'Where's The Nile?' giggled Mark. 'This ain't Africa, Aunt Lizzie. It's down the City Road, that soppy school.'

'Never mind,' said Lizzie. 'Pop off now, or you will be late.'

'Ta ta, Aunt Lizzie,' yelled Mark as he dashed off on his sturdy legs.

Lizzie sat thinking about what a fine friendly boy he was and how like Bobby. She began to recall Bobby when he was about Mark's age. He used to sit in the donkey cart outside this very bar, waiting for his father, old Tom the Totter, while Lizzie had been playing hop-scotch not far away, just down the street. It was strange how quickly life passed one by. This was the third generation now growing up. Soon she would be fifty-three and Bobby, if he still lived, was already fifty-six, there seemed very little to look forward to. If Mark had been their son, how different life might have been. 'Oh well,' she sighed. 'No good sitting dreaming, I'll go down and give Bella some help.'

Bella was up and about, looking more like her old self without her overall. Her hair had been well set, a wide pleasant smile lit her face, and her long fingernails were beautifully polished again.

'No need to have got up, Lizzie,' she said, 'but the coffee is on and have some cornflakes. I'll cook a meal later on.'

So Bella bustled away to get the small bar, that was still open for business, ready for its regular customers at eleven o'clock.

'We've divided the building in half,' Bella explained, 'keeping the old part going so as not to lose the trade. The front half is being completely remodernized. You won't know it when it is finished.'

'I didn't doubt that you'd make a good job of it,' said Lizzie. 'I always had complete confidence in you, Bella.'

'Without your financial help I might not have managed.'

Lizzie smiled. 'Well, let's say Bobby's help.'

Bella looked very solemnly at her, she seemed to hate even

the mention of his name. Lizzie wondered what heartache lay behind that shiny surface and decided she had better use more tact in future, if this was to be her home.

After performing a few chores for Bella, like cutting sandwiches and washing dishes, she went out along the road to meet Mark from school.

'Don't go too far,' warned Bella. 'Stick to the main road and wait for him to get off the bus. Mind the traffic; it's pretty busy out there at this time of the day.'

Lizzie was most anxious to find some familiar old spots and went strolling up the long winding street, which used to be her own youthful playground. All the children from those slum houses played out in the street because there was no room to play inside. But there were no small streets with two storey houses to be seen anywhere. She was hemmed in by tall office blocks, and vast, heavily loaded lorries edged their way down the narrow road. She tried to peer through the huge wooden hoardings which had the few old houses not yet demolished, and spied broken windows, piles of rubbish, old mattresses, and old furniture that had been dumped.

'Well, that surprises me, it's worse than it was then,' she said to herself. 'At least people used their dustbins in those days. She took a quick look at the factory where she used to work, it stood empty and neglected. A big FOR SALE notice was on the door, it was all very depressing. She wondered if she could find her way to the tube station now. She recalled how they all used to amble along this street towards the underground station as soon as it started to get dark during the Blitz. She could see in her mind's eye the long stream of people carrying bags and bundles, pushing prams full of blankets, old folk being helped along, young children in arms, toddlers clinging to the skirts of their elders. It was long past, the war was over, but it had taken most of the old places she had known and there was no way she could find her way out to the new tube station. So she waited placidly at the bus stop in the main road for Mark to come out of school. At this spot there was a seat and a small flowering tree, also a pleasant little patch of green grass. Well, it wasn't so bad sitting here in the sun. In the old days there had certainly never been any patches of green grass or trees, even backyards had been paved, and nothing ever grew in them. She watched the city workers going home, the buses full of travellers. Oh well, this was still her home town and she was going to make the best of it, come what may. Soon Mark came boisterously off the bus after scuffling on the stairs with the other boys, his blazer over his shoulder, his school cap on the back of his head.

'Hello, Aunt Lizzie,' he cried when he spotted her. 'Come on, I'll show you where the ice cream shop is.'

Lizzie put an arm about his young shoulders. She would never be lonely while this lively lad was around.

As the new pub slowly took shape the relationship between Mark and Aunt Lizzie prospered. He still slept in her room and chattered till late at night all about his pals at school. There was this fellow whom he had duffed up personally because he had snitched on him.

'Well, that's not very nice,' protested Lizzie.

'He told the teacher I was smoking in the loo.'

'Well, were you?'

'Yes, you bet your life I was,' retorted Mark.

Lizzie smiled gently in the dark. 'Go to sleep now dear.'

Well, at least he was not a liar. In fact, a very straightforward lad was Mark. Often they would play cards until it was quite late and Lizzie learned to master banker and pontoon. They would gamble for halfpennies until eventually she would allow him to win and he would scoop up the kitty with the air of a born gambler.

'Oh dear,' Lizzie would sigh to herself, 'another gambling man.'

On Saturday they would go to White Cross market and sometimes Chapel Street. She would treat him to ice cream, cakes and always bought him a small present.

Bella announced, 'You're spoiling him, Lizzie. He can twist you round his little finger.'

Inwardly this remark made Lizzie very pleased, for Mark was replacing that spot in her heart left empty by Carol and the boys.

Often Mark would measure himself against her, his head now well past her shoulders.

'I'm taller than you already,' he declared.

'Oh well, you start going down into the ground again at my age,' she jested.

'Oh, you don't say,' he stared at her in great concern, as if expecting her to disappear any minute.

Accompanied by Mark she finally went to see the tube station at Old Street. It looked very different, and she refused Mark's invitation to ride up and down the escalator.

'Moving stairs,' she cried. 'What will they think of next?'

So they strolled through the city to see St Paul's and onto London Bridge to look down at the broad, slow moving Thames and to admire the Monument. For a young lad Mark seemed to know his way around London very well.

When Lizzie remarked on this he said slyly, 'Well, sometimes I do play truant from school. I like to go down the different markets. Smithfields and Covent Garden.'

'Oh, what a naughty boy!' cried Lizzie.

He grinned and hung onto her arm. 'You won't tell Mum, will you, Aunt Lizzie?'

'No, I suppose not,' sighed Lizzie.

Yet he was a most considerate escort, the best in fact that Lizzie had ever had.

'Where is Uncle Bobby?' he asked one day. 'And why ain't I never seen him?'

'He's travelling abroad at the moment. And you did see him. When you were little.'

'Well, where is he? Why don't he send you a postcard?'

But Lizzie would close up like an oyster at this, leaving Mark's curiosity unsatisfied.

The summer wore on and a cold autumn was upon them, with a cold mist in the mornings turning to a dank London fog on some days. The holidays were over and Mark and his sister Gloria were now back at school. They had squabbled over Aunt Lizzie for most of the summer holidays, for Gloria, Bella's first child, was now a sedate young lady with long slim legs and lovely red gold hair. She really fancied herself as a dancer and would demonstrate her steps for Aunt Lizzie, making Mark extremely jealous.

Mark liked pop records and would turn up the sound very loud to distract Lizzie's attention from Gloria, but Lizzie coped with them very placidly and her dry sense of humour helped her to keep the peace.

Bella had begun to look very drawn and was working like a Trojan to make the bar a fine work of art. The outside scaffolding was now dismantled and there was less dust about. The interior decorators were at work, and painters were all over the place. Bella was making the velvet drapes for the windows and Lizzie was helping her to line them in beige silk.

'I know exactly how I want them to look,' said Bella, 'and the best and most cheapest way to do that is to do it yourself.'

So they sat late at night and early in the morning, stitching these curtains. It seemed a never-ending task. The huge lounge bar had at last begun to take shape; it had scarlet and gold walls, expensive embossed wallpaper, every corner lit by a red-shaded light and lots of old fashioned brassware to set off the bar which blazed with lights and shining glass. Once the red carpet was laid and the velvet drapes had been put up, it looked, as Lizzie described, 'Very, very posh.'

'Oh, I am so excited,' exclaimed Bella. 'It's something I always dreamed of.' Her busy hands put the finishing touches to the bar. She wafted about leaving an aroma of expensive perfume behind her, as she placed brass ash trays on the little polished tables.

'We've decided to have a grand opening night to launch the new bar good and proper. We might call it Aunt Lizzie's bar. Would you like that?'

Lizzie argued, she could not really see the point of getting so het up about the surroundings you drank in. She liked it as it had been in Pat O'Keefe's time, flat emerald green paint, old-fashioned beer pumps and old Gladys's tousled head just appearing over the bar. Still, she supposed one must give way to progress. It must have cost them the earth, she reflected. Probably not much of Bobby's money left. But she was not going to let that worry her; she had a home of her own once more, and the workmen were now up on the roof building her what Robin called a penthouse. The idea was to build a complete modern flat on the roof for Lizzie. It all sounded very nice, but she was content enough to share the little bedroom with Mark. One did not want all that much room as one got older.

Mark was now nearly eight, a very bright lad and he confided all his secrets to his Aunt Lizzie.

'It's a very nice view from up there,' he informed her on the day that he had panicked everyone by climbing up the scaffolding.

Bella had boxed his ears. Still holding his ear, and bravely holding back the tears, he said, 'There's a grand view from up there. You can just see the dome of St Paul's and the sun setting behind it.

Lizzie stared fondly at him. This boy seemed to understand her attachment to London so well.

'I hope when it's all finished they will let me come up there to live with you,' he said.

'Yes, darling,' said Lizzie cuddling him very close. 'You will.'

The date for launching the new bar was all set for February. Christmas had been a nice and quiet one for Lizzie had been completely absorbed with Bella and her family. The damp cold weather had not bothered her one bit. It was still cold and very draughty in the new pub because the heating system had not yet been properly fixed. Mark got a bad chest cold from running around the draughty passages, so Lizzie was in her element, taking care of him, reading to him, or playing endless games of chance.

At Christmas she had dressed herself nicely and gone to help Bella and Robin in the old small bar. The locals came there for their regular drink. An old man played the ancient, out-of-tune piano and the OAP's, as Bella called them, sang their heads off.

One very old lady in a kind of home-made woolly hat stared bleary-eyed at Lizzie, who had been to the hairdresser, had her hair tinted and set, and was wearing all her jewellery. The beady eyes of the old lady stared evilly at her and then the hoarse voice croaked, 'Blimey! Is that you, Lizzie Erlock? To think I knew you when you didn't have a pot to piss in.'

Lizzie smiled sweetly. 'I remember you, Polly Finigan,' she replied. 'You used to live in Brady Street, next door to us. Have a drink on me.'

That someone had recognized her from the old days was as good as a tonic to Lizzie, someone who had known her Bobby and who had been a friend of her late mother. She must be well turned eighty and was still hale and hearty. Although her words were crude, they gave Lizzie a magnificent boost. She was back where she belonged.

CHAPTER TWENTY-NINE

Lizzie's Penthouse Flat

Eventually the penthouse took shape. No expense had been spared. Bella had really gone to town, so to speak, on making this flat a comfortable place for Lizzie. There was a nice modern kitchen with lots of gadgets, a cosy sitting room and two bedrooms. It was all carpeted and nicely furnished with built-in shelves and cupboards. The few old-fashioned bits of furniture that Lizzie still clung to looked a little out of place.

'Better get some nice new modern furniture, Lizzie,' said Bella, 'but make do for now. A lot of work and a great deal of expense has gone into the flat, so I hope you'll be happy here.'

'Oh, don't worry so much, Bella,' declared Lizzie. 'I'm all right. I don't need a lot. I'm so happy to be back here where I belong and your children give me great contentment.'

Bella gave her a strange look. There was an envious sort of expression on her smooth and usually inscrutable face.

'Well, Lizzie,' she said, 'I did my best for you, and all I have to do now is get a good business going. In a couple of years at the most I'll be able to repay the money I owe you.'

Lizzie looked amazed. 'Bella, I don't want you to return any money to me. I would never have spent it anyway. It worried me. Now I feel free and it's helping my family, so that's all I care about.'

'Oh for Christ's sake, Lizzie, be a little practical,' snapped Bella. 'If I had borrowed it from the bank I'd have had to pay heavy interest. It would have been like an axe over my head if I hadn't been able to make a success of the business.'

Lizzie looked hurt. 'Please, Bella,' she pleaded, 'don't spoil things. I'm quite happy as things are, let the situation stay just as it is.'

'Oh Lizzie,' cried Bella emotionally, 'is there anyone else like you in all the world? You really get under my skin because you always want to give.' She stepped forward and hugged Lizzie. 'But I love you,' she said, 'how can I help myself?'

So Lizzie smiled a little enigmatic smile. 'I'll move in tonight,' she said. 'Can Mark come up there with me?'

'You don't have to ask. He's already moving his rubbish up there, little sod,' replied Bella.

'Well, I'll see he gets up for school,' murmured Lizzie, 'just in case you oversleep. You don't get to bed very early now, do you?'

Bella gave a quick grin. 'All right, darling,' she said, 'but don't let him pester you.'

So Lizzie settled down into her nest like a broody hen. She was very house-proud and went around with a feather duster, skimming the white painted walls for every speck of dust. She arranged all her photographs of the children – from Carol, Paul and Derick, to the younger generation – Charlie's boys, Gloria and Mark. She was so very proud of what she called her art gallery. She mastered the electric stove quite well and loved the pop up toaster. She and Mark made tasty snacks like scrambled eggs on toast, and sat together every evening in the big airy lounge. Mark with his comics and Lizzie with her romantic magazines. Often as the sun went down they would stand close together at the window, Lizzie with her arm about his sturdy waist, for he was by now taller than she, and they would look across the forest of chimney pots and tall church spires towards London. Mark would point out the various landmarks and on a clear day their favourite occupation was to try to spot the dome of St Paul's hovering in the misty distance. This was her London, her home town, and it was peacetime. No German bombers came to knock it all down and this gave her tremendous satisfaction.

In this way the years passed, while Bella slogged to make her new place a big success, Lizzie did very little, but lazed the days away, taking walks to meet Mark from school and go over to the park with him at weekends. Downstairs, in the bar,

Bella now employed smart slick young barmaids, so Lizzie seldom ventured there these days.

Lately she had heard a lot of arguing going on between Bella and Robin. This was unusual, for Robin was a very mild-tempered man and usually gave in to Bella's quick demanding ways.

Still Lizzie could hear their voices raised in anger, but she kept well out of the way. Bella's face had begun to look very drawn and Lizzie thought she was probably pushing herself too hard. She was also puzzled by Robin, who always was such a steady man. Lately he had been dashing off to the dogs at least twice a week just as Bobby used to do.

'What is wrong with your Dad, Mark?' she asked the boy one day.

'Dunno,' said Mark, 'but she don't 'arf keep on nagging him. No wonder he goes down the dogs and loses all his money.'

Oh, so that was it. Robin was gambling heavily; that wouldn't suit Bella. She was too keen to get this business going.

Mark said, 'When I grow up I'll be a bookie, so that I can take the money, not lose it.'

'Indeed you won't,' cried Lizzie. 'Your Uncle Bobby squandered all his money on dogs and gee-gees. He would be here today if he had lived a more regular sort of life.'

'Well, where is he then?' demanded Mark very cheekily.

'Ask no questions and you will hear no lies,' was Lizzie's severe reply.

The next day she went down to the kitchen to find Bella with her head in her hands, weeping convulsively.

'Oh my dear, whatever is wrong?'

Bella sighed. 'Oh well, you might as well know. I expect you've heard us squabbling. I'm two months pregnant.'

'Well!' cried Lizzie, 'what's wrong with that?'

Bella got up and surged about the room like a demented woman. 'Lizzie!' she cried, 'I have put my heart into this business. I've worked myself to a standstill, and we are just getting on our feet, when this has to happen.'

'Oh Bella, it's not the end of the world.'

'To me it is, and no matter what Robin says or does, I will not go through with it.'

'Oh, so Robin does not mind! Whatever are you making such a fuss about?'

'Oh Lizzie, how can I make you understand?' stormed Bella, her face flushed scarlet, her eyes flashing. 'This bar was my brainchild not Robin's. All my life I've had to struggle to live comfortably. Now I can see my way clear to run this big city bar and maybe a restaurant. I'm expected to hide myself with a big fat belly and let those bloody young barmaids fiddle me out of my hard-earned cash.'

'Come on now, Bella, it's not as bad as all that.' Lizzie tried to console her.

'Oh yes, it is!' Bella yelled. 'Because Robin don't care. He's no different to Bobby. Dogs and horses is all he cares about, so I didn't gain much, did I?'

Lizzie was alarmed. She had never heard Bella refer to her affair with Bobby before. She must be losing control.

'Now sit down, darling. Let's talk it over quietly,' she begged.

Bella sat down with her elbows on the table, and Lizzie suddenly recalled Highbury, and the old table where she had sat so many nights, wondering what bed her Bobby was in.

'I know exactly what I am going to do,' announced Bella once she had become a little calmer. 'I'm going to have an abortion.'

'Oh now, dear,' cried Lizzie, 'don't take your own life in your hands. Think of the children if anything goes wrong.'

'It's not the same now, Lizzie. They don't have back street abortions. You go to a clinic up West and pay privately, and it's all done cleanly and clinically. There is no danger.'

'Are you sure, Bella, because my mother took me to some old hag in the next street when I was only seventeen, and I am sure that's why I never had a child of my own.'

'Oh, don't you worry about it, love,' said Bella. 'I know you will take care of my kids and I'll only be gone two days. Robin can go to hell, if he leaves me! Let him! I'm quite capable of going on, on my own.'

Lizzie felt a kind of admiration for her. She was no doormat for any man, not like the women of her own generation had been.

'I'll talk to Robin if you wish,' volunteered Lizzie.

'No! Leave him alone. He is like a bear with a sore arse, but he has got to get over it, for my mind is made up.'

Two weeks after this traumatic scene Mark came up to the flat one day to say, 'Mother's gone to have her tonsils out. She'll be staying in the hospital.' He went over to the mirror, opened his mouth wide, and stared down his throat. 'I wish I could have my tonsils out,' he said, 'then I wouldn't have to go to school.'

'Come and have your breakfast, then get off to school, there's a good boy,' cajoled Lizzie. 'And when you go out, ask Dad if he needs me to help him?'

When Mark had left for school a sheepish-looking Robin arrived for a cup of tea. He was unshaven and bleary-eyed.

'So you know, Aunt Lizzie?' was his first comment.

Lizzie slowly poured the tea and nodded assent.

'It's broken my heart,' cried Robin. 'Oh! Whatever will I do if anything happens to her?'

'These are modern times, Robin, don't worry.'

'It always seems so wicked to me, I hate the thought of it.'

'I can understand you not wanting to take a life. In some ways I agree with you, but Bella would never forgive you if she had to let go of the reins now.'

'I know that all right, Lizzie. That's why I gave in to her,' said Robin dolefully.

He was just like a little boy again, and her mind skipped to the days when he sat on top of the pile of blankets in that big old-fashioned pram, sucking a big red dummy as she pushed him towards the Old Street tube and the shelter. How quickly life had sped on. To avoid him noticing the tears in her own eyes she said quickly, 'Another cuppa, Robin?'

'Yes, please, Aunt Lizzie. And I'll have some of that special toast that Mark keeps on about.'

Then, having demolished several slices of scrambled eggs on toast, Robin was once more his own amiable self and went off, whistling away down to the cellar to do the morning chores. 'Might get her a nice bunch of flowers,' he said.

When he had gone, Lizzie sat thinking of past days and of that little brood of children she had brought up. Charlie was now a big man living in the stockbroker belt in Surrey and Luber his wife was as fat as a butter ball, very domesticated and proud of her new baby daughter, who had been named Helga.

'Isn't that a German name?' Lizzie had asked, scrutinizing the beautiful blonde baby.

'Yes, Lizzie,' said Luber a little huffily, 'because most of my good friends are Germans.'

'No offence,' Lizzie had said. But still, in her heart, she could not forgive the Germans and it upset her that they had given this lovely little girl such a name. Luber's sons were very smart and well-behaved. They were dressed in their school uniforms, both attended prep schools and they came to visit Lizzie during school holidays, Mark fought with them all the time so that Lizzie was relieved when they went home.

Yes, it was good to think about this family expanding all the time like a great oak spreading out its branches. Carol wrote long newsy letters about the great social life she had in the small Texas town, but no family yet. Maisie was out in some foreign place teaching the black children religion, and had no time for any of her own. It would have been nice if Bella had decided to have this baby. Lizzie visualised herself pushing the pram around the park.

'Oh well,' she sighed, 'one can't have everything in life.'

Bella came home the next day and stayed in bed for a few days to rest. Lizzie was in her element, looking after her, making egg custards that Bella loathed, and sitting beside her persuading her to eat. Soon Bella was up and about and had been to the beauty parlour to get the pain lines removed from her face. Her skin was smooth and white once more and with her hair newly styled and tinted a brighter shade of red, Bella was her old self once again.

The cold winter came and it was warm and cosy in that

centrally heated flat. Lizzie knitted long scarves for Mark to wear and kept indoors out of the cold. Often her mind dwelt on Bobby, wondering if he still lived, whether he was cold or hungry, he would be sixty years old now and she was fifty-seven. Their lives were practically over; would they ever meet again?

Some folk were sure that there was another world where everyone met and continued their lives together. She hoped it was true, but deep in her heart she did not believe it. Yet she still had an uncanny feeling that Bobby was not dead, that he would turn up eventually just like the bad penny he had always been.

One cold winter's morning after it had been snowing heavily, there came a sudden thaw and the streets were full of muddy slush and a bitter, biting wind howled around the roof tops. Lizzie sat knitting beside the radiator, thinking of the big kitchen range in the Highbury house where they had burned everything, coals, wood and even old boots when they were hard up.

Bella was busy downstairs preparing for her lunchtime customers to whom she served a nice hot, home-cooked meal, when into that posh lounge bar wandered a very derelict old man. It might have been the savoury smell of cooking that drew him in, or it could have been nostalgia from the past. He was tall and walked with a limp, propelling himself along with the aid of a walking stick. His clothes were old and crumped as if he had slept rough. His face was hollow-cheeked and his bewhiskered chin badly needed a shave. He wore a flat cap and a grubby-looking choker round his neck. He came slowly towards the bar looking about him as if he were not sure that he was in the right place. Then in a gruff tone he ordered a pint of bitter, fumbling in his pocket with his left hand for loose change. The right had limply held the walking stick and seemed practically useless.

The young barmaids looked very alarmed for this was the smart bar, and the lunchtime customers were due to arrive at twelve thirty. After a little hesitation they served him a pint of bitter. He limped away into the corner to sit by the artificial fire, his trembling hands grasped the big pint glass and he sipped the frothy liquid without looking in any direction.

'Quick get the missus,' gasped one young barmaid to the other. 'She'll get him out before we get busy.'

So Bella swept out from the inner regions, immaculate in her smart black dress and choker necklace, and cast a stern glance at where this old man was sitting.

'Oh Christ,' she said, 'that's all we need. A tramp at lunchtime. What the hell did you serve him for?' she accused the barmaid, then marching out into the bar with a duster in her hand, she moved the brass ashtray, polished it and placed it back on the table staring all the time, hard-faced, at this poor old man, who sat with head down, looking as if he was going to doze off. The old man scoffed his pint of beer, so Bella grabbed the empty glass and made a great performance of wiping the table. Suddenly, she stopped, her breath came swiftly and with an almost panicky movement, she turned her back on him. All without saying a word.

He just sat with his head bent, one hand on the table the other hand clutching the walking stick, but that thin claw-like hand on the table was wearing a ring. It was a black onyx signet ring with two B's entwined in gold in the centre.

It was the ring that startled Bella; it had almost winked in her face and paralysed her with shock, but she pulled herself together quickly and walked slowly and calmly back behind the bar.

'Ain't you going to chuck him out?' demanded the barmaid.

'No,' gasped Bella, 'run upstairs and get Lizzie. On second thoughts no, I'll go.'

The old man, meanwhile, made as if to stretch and yawn, then slowly dragged himself to his feet.

'Looks all in, poor devil,' said the girl behind the bar as he made his way slowly towards the door.

Bella was back, accompanied by Mark, for she had burst in on Lizzie and Mark's game of cards crying, 'Don't get too shocked, Lizzie, but I'm almost sure it's Bobby down in the bar.'

Lizzie got up and took one look at Bella's white face. 'Don't let him get away. Quick, Mark, stop him, I'll be right down.'

Mark dashed off and the tall man was feebly trying to pull open the door when a sturdy little chap looked up at him and said, 'Wait a minute, guv'nor, someone wants yer.'

Bobby's dim eyes looked down into that cheeky face. He turned around, and there was Lizzie, who just grabbed his arm.

'Why, Bobby Erlock! Where do you think you are going?' she cried.

A kind of grin crossed his harassed face. 'Cor blimey! It's the duchess,' he said.

'Now come on, sit down. What have you been up to?' Lizzie nagged in her inimitable manner. 'Look at you, you always was a bloody nuisance.' Yet big tears fell from her eyes and dry sobs racked her throat.

His hoarse voice replied, 'What are you doing here, Lizzie, old gel? I've walked all over London looking for you.'

'Come on, Mark,' said Lizzie. 'It's not the time for conversation. Take the other arm and we'll help Uncle Bobby up the stairs.'

Bella stood like a statue, just staring, as the three of them slowly progressed up the stairs. Then she put her hand over her face and began to cry. The shock of seeing that big, smart, cheery, rogue Bobby in such a low state was more than she could bear.

Lizzie and Mark eased Bobby down into the armchair. Lizzie took off his worn shoes, exposing socks with big holes in them.

'Put on the kettle, Mark,' she said. 'I'll make him a nice hot bovril, he looks like he needs it.'

'I thought this was Pat O'Keefe's old pub,' said Bobby. 'I just popped in. Thought I might see someone I knew. Just can't believe my luck, I've looked everywhere for you.'

'Now drink this,' insisted Lizzie, 'and have a rest. We can talk later on.'

Bobby sipped the hot drink, and his eyes almost twinkled as he smilingly watched Mark trying to walk with his stick. 'Who's that?' he asked.

'That's Bella's son,' said Lizzie very shirtily. 'Now you go downstairs, Mark. You can come up later on.' She turned to Bobby. 'I'll run you a nice hot bath and then, while you have a good sleep, I'll cook you dinner. I've still got those silk pyjamas you bought to go to Ireland.'

Bobby put his hand to his forehead. 'Oh Lizzie,' he said, 'I feel as if I must be dreaming.'

'No, Bobby,' she answered. 'I'm here in the flesh and a good few years older. Now come on, let me help you into the bath. You look very dirty.'

As Bobby relaxed in the bath, she poured hot water over his shrivelled limbs.

'Oh my dear, what have you done to yourself?'

Her fine muscular Bobby was so thin and so helpless that she could not believe her eyes.

'I've been in hospital a long time,' he said. 'Had a car accident out in the States and never really got over it. Never had a penny when I got home. You have to pay for medical treatment out there, and it cleaned me out. When I got back I couldn't find anyone. I've been sleeping rough and living in doss houses this past three months.'

'Oh Bobby,' she protested, 'why did you stay away from me all this time? Surely you could have written to me?'

'Oh don't nag, Lizzie,' said Bobby with a bit of his old charm. 'Help me get out of the bath, then I'll have a kip and I'll be fine in the morning.'

'I bloody well hope so,' grumbled Lizzie, putting a big warm bath towel around him.

'This side of me is a bit dodgy. Had a kind of stroke, but I'll be all right, love. Don't want to be a bother to you. You seem to be settled very nicely here. Who's place is this?'

'It belongs to Bella and Robin.'

'Oh, so it was Bella I saw in the bar,' muttered Bobby.

'This flat up here is mine, and I'm very pleased with it.' She helped him into his old dressing gown. It was so big and baggy that they both started laughing.

'Just like you to hold onto all my old clothes,' he said. 'Never threw anything away, did you, Lizzie?'

'No, Bobby,' she said, 'I'm still very thrifty.'

He looked down at her with great affection. 'There's something different about you. I can't place it but you have certainly not aged much. In fact I believe you look younger.'

'Well,' she replied coyly, 'I do take better care of myself.'

He put an arm around her and hugged her. 'It's great to see you again, old gel, but don't let me interfere with your life. I was never any good to you and now I am an old crock. So give me a few days to rest and I'll be on my way.'

Lizzie's face flamed scarlet. 'You'll do no such thing, Bobby Erlock,' she cried, giving him such a violent push that he fell back into the armchair.

His loud roar of laughter peeled out. This was what she had missed, the good humour of her Bobby.

'Fine way to treat a bloody invalid,' he yelled.

'Oh Bobby,' she whispered and knelt down beside him. As those tears, pent up for so long, began to fall, he stroked her hair.

'Now stop crying, because that's all I need to start me off. Get up and cook some grub, there's a good gel.'

She got up and wiped her eyes. 'Bobby, don't you ever leave me again. I've only been half alive these past years and I don't think I could take it if you were ever to go away again.'

He looked a little forlorn, then said, 'Get cracking with something to eat or I'll give you a good thumping.'

'You and who's army,' giggled Lizzie, who had picked up this cheeky repartee from Mark. Bobby smacked her on the bottom, Lizzie trotted off to cook a meal, and Bobby dozed by the fire.

CHAPTER THIRTY

A Prodigal's Return

Bobby's return could well be compared with that of the prodigal son. Lizzie fussed over him, brought in the local doctor to examine him and spent her days cossetting her lovable rascal.

Mark was a trifle jealous at first, then, discovering that Bobby loved a game of whist, he very soon changed his attitude. He spent many hours playing cards with Bobby, discovering that he was a wizard with the card deck and played Find the Lady like a professional.

Mark was thrilled; he would speculate two pennies at a time, and Bobby always beat him. Mark would put on a brave face when he lost his money, and Bobby would laugh heartily saying, 'Ah! Cleaned you out, didn't I, mate?'

Lizzie would disapprove. 'I don't think you should teach Mark all those card tricks.'

'He's a born gambling man,' replied Bobby. 'He really love it. That's why I won't let him win; he's got to learn how to lo with good grace. That's the first lesson.'

'Tut! Tut!' Lizzie clucked like an angry hen and forced th physic, which the doctor had prescribed, down Bobby's throat. 'Well, your gambling days are over and that's for sure,' she said.

'I suppose you got rid of all that hot lolly, Lizzie?'

'Yes I did!' was her terse reply. 'I spent it on building this flat. Why? What's bothering you?'

'I was just thinking and wondering, did you keep that old suitcase? You know, the one I used to take to the races?'

'You know I did,' she retorted. 'It's not like me to throw things away.'

'Good! Well, where is it?'

'What do you want it for?' She eyed him suspiciously.

'There were some papers inside it. Have you still got them?'

'You know I have,' grumbled Lizzie. 'And don't you start any big schemes, Bobby, because you are not well enough.'

'Go and get the case, Lizzie,' he almost pleaded. 'I only want a shuffti at those old papers.'

So Lizzie produced the battered old suitcase and put it in his lap. 'They're all there. I never bothered to read them, wouldn't have understood them if I had.'

Bobby sat browsing very quietly all morning over the papers in the suitcase. Then he gave the case back to her. 'Here you are, Lizzie, put it in a safe place. They're insurance policies and they won't pay them out till we are dead and gone. But this one will be useful.' He waved a sheaf of documents which he had retrieved from the suitcase.

Lizzie lost interest and was beginning to serve lunch. 'Come on now, Bobby, get ready for your lunch. I'll call Mark to keep you company while I go shopping this afternoon.'

So they sat together, enjoying the tasty lunch and the papers were forgotten.

Since Bobby had come home Bella and Robin kept very much to themselves. They seemed much happier and took their nights off together. They would go up West to shop or to attend a show. They never came up to meet Bobby; it was just as if they were waiting for something to happen.

On one particular afternoon Lizzie went off to get her hair set, leaving Mark in charge of Bobby. When she returned Mark was very flushed and excited, waving a bundle of papers crying, 'Look, I won these off Uncle Bobby, square and honest.'

Lizzie cast a shrewd glance in Bobby's direction. 'Well, what is all this?' she asked.

'Piece of a dog track,' burst out Mark. 'I am to give the papers to me Mum to give to a solicitor, and, when I am old enough to run it, it's mine.'

Bobby lay back in his chair, that carefree grin on his face once more. He was still thin and his face very lined, but lately he had looked more like his old incorrigible self.

'Now, Mark,' warned Lizzie. 'Don't let Uncle Bobby josh you. I know what he is like.'

'But it's true, it's true!' yelled Mark, dancing up and down excitedly.

'All right, go down stairs, and after tea you can come back up here again.'

She sighed, for sometimes Mark was a little too exuberant for her. Then her brown eyes looked at Bobby for some sort of explanation. 'Come and sit on my lap, duchess, and I'll tell you all about it,' he said.

Lizzie went to him rather reluctantly. She was still inclined to be off-hand with him.

He stroked her blonde, well-set, shining hair saying, 'You look tops, Liz. You're better looking in your old age than you were as a young girl.'

'Well,' she demanded, 'what's all this about young Mark?'

'I gave that to Mark because we don't need it. You seem to be happy and settled here. You have a little money in the bank, so you tell me, and I don't want to spoil our happiness by starting to gamble again.'

This seemed to be the moment of truth. She stared at him with disbelief. 'Well, what was it you gave Mark?' she demanded.

'It's the title deeds to a third share of a new dog track out in Essex. It was bought between Pat O'Keefe, his son-in-law and myself. I was never around to draw my share when it got started, and Pat passed on, leaving his share to his grandson. It's all on the up and up, Lizzie, so it won't be difficult to negotiate. I read only yesterday what a going concern they have made of it. Big bars and even a restaurant, and they say it's the most popular track for the Londoners who have moved out of town.'

'Oh! So that's what it was all about,' declared Lizzie, losing interest. 'Let me get up, I'll make some tea.'

'Just like old Lizzie. Never did get excited about anything.' The fact that he had given away a large fortune seemed nothing at all to her, she was not even disturbed.

'You don't mind then?' he asked.

'Why should I mind?' she replied. 'Mark's my favourite boy too.' She came back and held his hand for one brief moment, and said quietly, 'We both know why, don't we, Bobby?'

He squeezed her hand. 'Yes, duchess. Well, I think so.'

When later on a rather shamed-faced Bella and Robin arrived, they brought the papers back and they stood in the middle of the room, looking extremely awkward.

'We have brought back your property, Bobby,' said Bella coolly, yet not allowing herself to look Bobby in the eye. 'Mark has told us some cock and bull story about winning them from you.'

Bobby looked wistfully at the magnificent Bella. Her face was perfectly made up, her bright red hair was well-kept, and she was wearing her favourite emerald green dress. 'It's quite all right, Bella,' he answered slowly. 'Mark did win those papers from me honestly.'

'But they're very valuable. Do you know what they are?' she demanded in her fiery way.

Robin just stood silent and solid beside her.

'Yes, I do know what the papers are, and if you will be good enough to sort it out with a solicitor I feel sure it will be arranged as satisfactorily as Mary O'Keefe, who is still living, promised me.'

This was quite a long speech from Bobby, who for once looked very serious.

Bella's lips trembled. 'Bobby,' she pleaded, 'you can't do this to us.'

Suddenly little Lizzie came in like a whippet, snapping and snarling and very angry. 'Who says Bobby can't give away what is his own?' she challenged them. 'He has chosen to give it to Mark and I approve, so, Bella, you should be grateful, instead of standing there arguing the toss.'

There was a moment of stony silence, then Lizzie said, 'Sit down, for Christ's sake. Why are you standing in the middle of the room? I'll pour out a cup of tea.'

Zombie-like, Robin and Bella moved cautiously over to the settee and sat down very stiffly side by side.

Bobby started to roar loudly with laughter. Lizzie almost

flew at him. 'Now, Bobby Erlock' she yelled, 'shut up! Don make matters worse. Let us all sit down and talk this busines over as a family, because that is what we are.'

All three sat looking slightly embarrassed as Lizzie trotte off. Soon she came back with the tea trolley, laden with th teapot, cups and saucers and some plates of fancy cakes.

'Well,' she said in her most chatty manner. 'It's really nic to see you both up here having a cup of tea with us.'

Then Bella smiled and Robin grunted apologetically. Th ice was broken and they began talking about the old days. O the trips with Robin to the Arsenal football matches and o taking Bella to Clapton dog races.

Lizzie sat listening to them, her diminutive shape all screwed up in the large armchair, a smile on her small face. This was her family circle and now that her Bobby was back home, what more could she wish for?

So we leave Lizzie, at the peak of her life, warm and comfortable within the loving circle of her family. She had come back to her grass roots, to that small slum area between the borders of the city and old father Thames. This was her town, the one she was born in and the one in which she wished to die.

The future was bright for her new gambling man. For Mark took over his heritage when he was eighteen and, make no mistake, he became a millionaire tycoon of the dog tracks. Thus, as Lizzie would have put it: from little acorns big oak trees grow.